THE RESURRECTIONISTS

Also by Michael Collins

The Meat Eaters (stories)
The Life and Times of a Teaboy
The Feminists Go Swimming (stories)
Emerald Underground
The Keepers of the Truth

THE RESURRECTIONISTS

Michael Collins

Michael Collins (signature)

Weidenfeld & Nicolson
London

A PHOENIX HOUSE BOOK

First published in Great Britain in 2002
A Phoenix House Book

Copyright © 2002 Michael Collins

Second impression 2002

The right of Michael Collins to be identified as the
author of this work has been asserted by him in accordance
with the Copyright, Designs and Patents Act of 1988.

A CIP catalogue record for this book
is available from the British Library.

ISBN 1 86159195 0

Typeset in Minion by Deltatype Ltd,
Birkenhead, Merseyside

Printed by Clays Ltd, St Ives plc

Phoenix House
Weidenfeld and Nicolson
The Orion Publishing Group Ltd
Orion House
5 Upper Saint Martin's Lane
London, WC2H 9EA

Dedicated to my parents, wife, and daughter

Special thanks for advice and support to:
My editors
Dan & Judith Wesley
Peter & Lori Friedman
Mark Crawford
Steve Bamesberger
Tom Parker
Rich and Teri Frantz
Richard Napora

And for the cats who have haunted my office over the years,
Spike, Wicklow, Jasper, Esau and Maggie

Chapter 1

I couldn't quite get us back without incident for the burial of my father. We ran into a little trouble along the way. It took us two stolen cars along the Interstate to get us home. It's not exactly easy to go to a funeral halfway across the country when you're up to your ass in debt, when you don't have the money for an airline ticket, and you have a car with a shot gasket. You hear about bereavement fares, but have you actually ever met anybody who flew for free to bury a loved one? It's all part of some benevolent myth. Like everything else in life, there are stories within stories.

The us I am speaking of is me, my wife and our kids, the principal characters who sustained me, if not by love, then by the sheer extent of their need for me as provider. I'd taken on the cross of parenthood with an undue sense of heroism. My wife Honey diagnosed it as TAS, Terminal Asshole Syndrome. She says it is a terrible syndrome, since it usually kills those around the victim, not the victim. That sort of summed up how things were at the time we hit the road to bury my father.

I say our kids went back with us, but the eldest, Robert Lee, is not mine, in the sense that I didn't beget him, as they say in the Bible. I call Robert Lee 'Exhibit A' in a long line of grievances against my wife, Honey Wainscot, who still uses her ex-husband's name for the sake of Robert Lee, to give him stability, to give him a history, to help his transition into manhood, and, I also suspect, in no small measure because her ex-husband, Ken, an abject soul on Death Row in Georgia, is the true love of her life.

But I digress. I was reading a newspaper before my midday shift at Big Boy when in the back pages I saw this headline, *Farmer Murdered by Mystery Man*, and there, lo and behold, was a small photograph of my father staring back at me with that hard impenetrable Lutheran stare of his. The gist of the story was simple, if somewhat bizarre:

> Copper, Michigan – The tranquility of a sleepy backwater town was shattered when a 56 year-old man was found dead at his home. Police said the victim's son discovered the body in the family house about 1 p.m. The victim, Ward Cassidy died as a result of a single gunshot to the head.
>
> Reportedly, the victim's son heard noises from the upper part of the house, fled the scene, and the police were called.
>
> Upon arrival, authorities found a man sitting in a back bedroom and made an arrest without incident. Initial reports indicated there was no sign of forced entry, and nothing had been stolen.
>
> The suspect, described as in his early to mid-fifties, is currently being held without bond at the Copper County Detention Center. Nobody in the close-knit community has been able to identify the suspect.

I called my brother Norman collect from work, and shit, he didn't sound like a guy who'd found his father's head blown to bits. Right off he said, 'How did you hear about this, Frank?' I heard his sanctimonious wife, Martha, say my name and then say, 'Oh sweet Jesus!'

I said, 'Thanks for goddamn calling me, Norman!'

'You've moved so many times we didn't have an address.'

2

I said, 'If I won the goddamn lottery, I bet you'd have found me!'

I could hear Martha talking in the background, asking what I wanted. She said, 'This is none of his business, tell him!'

And in a way she was right and wrong at the same time. You see, in the convoluted nature of real life, things weren't so simple. My so-called father was, in fact, my uncle. When I was five years old, my parents died in a house fire, and my uncle took me in and raised me. But let's just say the arrangement was no bed of roses. And so when I announced, 'I'm thinking about coming back and paying my respects,' you can imagine the jaw-drop reaction I got. I said it in a contrite way, because the truth of the matter was I needed a loan to get back to Michigan. I said, 'Norman, you think you could see it in your heart to fly me home?'

Norman didn't exactly say no. What he said was, 'The price of hogs has bottomed out, Frank. Honest to God. I can't.' Norman had a way of talking, a thick clotted accent that made you think he was something like fifty years old, when he was only twenty-five. He was your typical rural yokel, all brute strength but dumb as shit.

I heard Norman's wife say, 'Ask him what's his agenda? Ask him! No, in fact, give me the phone, Norman, let me handle this! I want to have a few choice words with him myself!'

I put on the air of the truly hurt. I said, 'Is regret an agenda, Martha?' I said, 'I just want to pay my respects.'

Martha spelled out the word 'N-O.' She shouted, 'Things aren't settled here. There's an investigation going on right now. We don't know exactly what's happening. Things are hectic, it's a nightmare up here. You don't need this, Frank, not with your condition . . .'

She was, of course, referring to my history of depression, but I said, '*My condition*. Jesus, are you a licensed medical practitioner, Martha?'

3

My manager, Louis Schwartz, scowled and pointed at his watch.

Norman took the phone from Martha and tried to gloss things over. 'I'm telling you, honest, Ward doesn't stand looking at. It's going to be closed casket. It has to be with what happened, with how he was . . . how he was killed.'

It was maybe the first moment I actually thought of Ward as a corpse, but before I could say anything, Martha said real loud, 'Hang up on him right now. This is a collect call, Norman!'

Norman said, 'I'm sorry, Frank . . . I'm sorry, but you're not welcome up here.'

I said, 'Norman, where there's a will, there's a relative!'

I heard Martha shout in the background, 'Will . . . Sweet Jesus, there is no will! He cannot come up here!' and I just hung up, because the lunch hour was starting, and my manager was pointing at his cheap-assed watch.

That pretty much ended my career in New Jersey. Whatever opportunity there might have been for working things out amicably with my brother, it had passed, gone in that single conversation. Norman was really my cousin, but we had always called ourselves brothers.

I don't think leaving New Jersey was a legitimate option when I got on the phone, but now it was my only choice if I was going to get my share of the farm.

I had the conviction to finish what was on the grill, to serve up what I had started, since we shared the tips after lunch. I browned six meat patties, toasted some buns and stuck all of it in a plastic bag. Hunger loomed in the near future, out on the road. But I didn't escape work without one final indignity that underscored my decision to get the fuck out of there. The assistant manager, this fat shit, waddled over to me and said, 'Table four wanted their steak rare.' I got docked for that kind of screw-up.

4

I walked out of Big Boy and shouted at my manager, 'Come on, it's not a bad case of herpes. I swear these sores aren't even contagious!' It unnerved the shit out of the customers.

Driving over to Honey, it dawned on me that I'd not had a day off in two years.

When I arrived, I said simply, 'My father's dead.'

Honey Wainscot, my betrothed, was up in her glass case at the dispatch office, in her exalted position as Dispatch Agent, a voice to the dispossessed guiding truckers through the night. A sign above her glass door said, 'Mr Credit is on vacation. Until further notice please deal with Mr Cash.'

Honey shifted in her turret. She had a rope of hair that went beyond the crack of her ass, her one abiding link to youth and innocence. I said to myself, looking at her, 'Rapunzel! Life beyond the fairytale,' a castaway in a grim place fairytales dared not tread. I still remember her first words to me, or maybe not exactly her first words, but thereabouts anyway, 'I lost my virginity, but I still have the box it came in.'

Honey saw the look on my face, and the cogs in her head began turning. 'You think you might actually get something?' It was the usual tone she used with me, approximating indignation. A cigarette smoldered in the center of her face. I beckoned Honey down from her turret. She was not a woman to be fucked with. On more than one occasion, she had sat on top of me in bed and brought me to the point of suffocation. Honey was dangerous, in a physical sense.

She assumed her usual position of worldly defiance, arms apart like a beleaguered Christ at some second crucifixion, a Diet Pepsi in one hand and a cigarette in the other, a body language that said simply, 'Your problem is not necessarily my problem.' Honey slurped the Diet Pepsi, pulled on the cigarette, and then released a tendril of smoke out the corner of her mouth while I spoke.

I said, 'I figure I have a hell of a lot coming to me off that farm.'

'How's that?'

'Well.' I hesitated for a moment. 'I might have neglected to tell you a few things about my past. Not that I was hiding anything, it just didn't seem important.'

Honey raised her voice, 'Frank?'

'Okay. For starters, the man you always heard me call my father wasn't my father, really.'

'Who the hell was he?'

It was something I didn't really want to go into right then, but if I was going to get her to leave, she had to know the truth, so I gave her the low-down on the fire and how I'd come to live with my uncle and just shrugged my shoulders when I was finished.

Honey looked at me. 'And it never crossed your mind to tell me something like that?'

I didn't answer her.

'So, what's your point now?'

'Well, the way I see it, now that my uncle's dead, I figure that farm might just belong to me, right? Or at least I should be entitled to a shit-load of money when I make Norman either sell the farm, or buy me out of my inheritance.'

Honey just shook her head. 'I don't like this, Frank . . . not one bit.'

I talked right over her. 'Come on! I don't see how the courts could legally lock me out of what would have been mine if my father had lived. I bet you dollars for donuts that there was nothing legally signed giving my uncle ownership, and if I started proceedings right now, I'd get the farm . . .'

'Don't play curbside lawyer. This is all something a real lawyer should handle. I don't exactly feel comfortable taking a gamble on "What if?" As far as I'm concerned this is something that could all be done from right here. We don't have to go there.'

Before I could say anything more, Leonard, the Dispatch Controller, came by and eyed me. He walked with a bounce. I knew what he was going to say: one of two things, either 'Who left the bird cage open?' or 'Shit, here comes trouble,' and it ended up being, in fact, 'Shit, here comes trouble.'

If we had been dogs, we would have torn into each other, but we were of a higher species, so I said simply, 'Leonard,' stressing the L.

Leonard was already ignoring me. 'We got a truck haulin' frozen chicken in a collision outside Charlotte. Refrigerator unit is busted on the rig. We got to get that chicken on ice quick. You want to take care of that, Honey?'

'Sure thing, Leonard.'

Leonard just stood there. 'Well?'

'I'm on it, Leonard. Honest. Two minutes.'

I waited out the moment. I stared at Leonard. He was wearing an industrial grey shirt that had his name embroidered in red letters, *Leonard*. In fact, we all had our names embroidered onto our work shirts. That's simply where we were in life. Mine said, *Frank – Service with a smile!*

Leonard just turned and walked away. I watched him. He was thin, like a cricket, and had two perpetual spreading sweat stains emanating from his armpits that looked for all the world like two folded wings.

Honey said, 'I got to take care of this right now.'

I said, 'You are coming with me, right?'

'Jesus, Frank, you really want to up and leave just like that? Why not use a lawyer? You still haven't answered me.'

I said, 'Lawyers charge by the goddamn word – the word, Honey. Who's got that sort of money?'

'And just up and leaving like this isn't going to cost a fortune?'

'Jesus, I'm talking a windfall of cash, something that can get us set straight.' I looked around me. 'You know what this is here, Honey? A prison without bars!'

Honey said, 'It's always a production with you, isn't it?'

I said, 'This is a once in a lifetime opportunity!'

'You sound like a car salesman selling beaters on a lot.'

Leonard stuck his head out of a doorway and stared down at me, then his head disappeared in silence, and so did Honey.

I thought it was going to end right then and there, an unceremonious end to a meaningless union between two losers. I figured I might just snag my youngest kid, Ernie, from Immaculate Conception Pre-school, and make a break for Michigan.

But then Honey came back and said, 'You still here?' which was her way of saying, 'Stay.' Honey gave me that bewildered look, like she didn't know what to do. She said, 'In the break room, if you hit the coffee machine just when you put in a dime, you get the dime back, and you still get the coffee. It works on the candy machine, too.'

I said, 'This is the chance of a lifetime . . .' I said, 'This is your lucky day, that's what this is, salvation! It's like finding a lottery ticket . . .'

Honey said, 'I'm thinking . . . okay?'

I waited in the break room. It was cold, like a freezer. I got the dime coffee for free. It worked just like Honey said, but not the candy machine. The coffee machine dispensed a cup with a picture of a joker from a deck of cards on it. I sat away from the air conditioning unit with my hands cradled around the coffee. It felt good, the heat stinging my hands.

It was the first time I had sat still all day since I'd read about my uncle. Like I said, I can't say there was ever a relationship between my uncle and me. There were things between us that had haunted me all my life, what they called suppressed memories about the night my parents died. Shit, even saying *suppressed memories*, giving it a clinical name, made me wince. If I'd heard this from anybody else, I'd have said, 'How about we kick the shit out of you, and maybe that'll jog your memory!' But the simple reality was that something terrible had happened to me.

In the aftermath of the fire my uncle and I ended up giving conflicting stories about what happened the night of the fire. Shit, I was just five when my parents died, and who was ever going to believe anything I said against my uncle's account? The lines were drawn between us right from the start, the goddamn fear and eventual hatred that came to characterize our lives as I lived with him over the years. Just sitting there, looking back on things, I thought that maybe I'd been running from what had happened on that farm, maybe not consciously, but down deep all this time. It was something that took me halfway across the country, and I mean that literally. I got my ass out of Michigan the day after I graduated high school and headed for Chicago. It was something that got me institution-alized in Chicago for a time.

If it hadn't been for the goddamn sense that I was going to get something out of that will up there, if my own sense of indignation wasn't so strong, if I didn't have a vendetta against my uncle, I might even have heeded Norman and his wife. I might have had the decency to not drag them down with me. In fact, I wanted to shore things up with Norman. All I wanted was my share. Norman was a clod, but I always remember this one time when he stood up for me. I was seven years older than him, and I guess he was about ten when one day he just grabbed Ward's arm after I'd got the leather belt from Ward. Norman said simply, 'No,' and, though he was still only ten, he was on his way to becoming the giant he would become. I remember Ward being sort of stunned. Ward was holding the belt and he took one measured swing and hit Norman across the shoulder and chest, and Norman just flinched. It was just that solitary hit, but that single act of defiance made life bearable the last year or so I lived with Ward. I wanted to repeat that story to Norman right then, to get us back on track, but I didn't call him. In a way it was better that Martha had interfered, it made it easier to do what had to be done.

I think somewhere along the line I'd arrived at that point in life where the opinions of others didn't matter, where the humanity, if you can call it that, had been drained from me. And maybe deep down I was going back for other reasons as well. When I read that headline, *Farmer Murdered by Mystery Man*, I said to myself, 'I have to see this mystery man with my own two eyes.' A cold hand of justice had finally pulled the trigger like an act of divine retribution.

CB static hissed against the grey of the corridor. Leonard showed himself in the hallway, smoking a cigarette. He had his pants cinched high with a belt above his navel. He said straight, 'I'll make you an offer you can't refuse for that woman.'

'It's not me you've got to convince, Leonard.'

Leonard shook his head, 'Women.' He despised me. I could tell that. He just sneered and then disappeared.

The longer I waited for Honey, the more I knew I was doing the right thing. I don't know how we had lasted, really. In my head, I was trying for the right words to say to Honey when she came back to get her to leave. It shouldn't have taken any effort, not with what had gone on with us in New Jersey, but you get used to everything in the end. I mean, I'd give you the basic set of facts, and you'd say, 'I don't believe that. I don't believe you stayed. Nobody in their right mind would live like that,' but we did.

Take, for instance, the year we moved into the apartment. Honey was attacked in the elevator coming up to our apartment. Two guys got hold of her. One guy had a knife to her throat, and the other had pruning shears. The guy with the pruning shears said, 'You get that ring off your finger, or I'm going to cut it off. You hear me, bitch?' Honey broke her own finger getting the ring off. She heard her wedding finger snap, but she felt no pain, not then anyway. That much adrenaline was pumping through her. It was a hell of a thing to happen to a woman who had once won the State Typing Contest in Macon, Georgia. She talked about the contest the night she was attacked, after I picked her up from the Emergency Room. I felt the fingers of her good hand on my back, the rapid movement of an expert typist. She told me back then that the secret to typing was not to try and understand what you were typing, but just to let your fingers work on automatic, to process nothing. I didn't say anything, but I think that is how we live our lives, mostly, processing nothing. And of course, we stayed. There was never any suggestion of us leaving.

Honey was talking again in the background in the dispatch office. Things were heating up. I tuned in slowly to what was going on, listened to her and Leonard arguing with the guy who was holding out on them down there on the highway. He wanted more money to take on the thawing chicken. I listened despite myself. The frozen chicken disaster had its own sense of unfolding drama. Life had a way of sucking you into even the most mundane of things and making the most horrific normal. It was some leveling principle, I suppose, some rippling effect, a seismic tremor moving outward, away from the center of things. It was hard to pinpoint the genesis of what made us what we were, to circumscribe the events which defined us.

I still remember that night Honey was attacked, touching her face in bed, taking her finger in its splint and kissing it. We could hear Robert Lee sobbing in the next room. Honey knocked against the wall and said in a hushed voice, 'Don't make me go in there and have to hush you, Robert Lee. Quit it, you hear me?' She wanted to hit out at something. I could feel that tension inside her. She needed retribution. Robert Lee was it that night, I just knew it. I said softly, 'Remember when

11

Robert Lee had that fever, and we put him in the tub to bring his fever down, and I went screaming through the apartment block shouting I needed ice? I was screaming, "Robert Lee is burning up with a fever. Help me!" And everybody got out of bed and got ice from their iceboxes and came rushing up, and we got the tub filled.' I touched her face. I whispered, 'Honey, you've got to set that good against what happened.' I had her nightdress pushed up around her breasts. My eyes were closed.

But all she did was get up out of bed. I saw the paleness of her rump like a huge moon, and then the nightdress fell around her. Robert Lee was still sobbing. I heard her hit him hard. I felt the impact of his body against the wall. She was saying such horrible things, in a controlled whisper, maybe just like those guys did to her in the elevator. I stared at the wall. When she hit Robert Lee like that, there was a procedure. He buried his face in the pillow. This was something she brought into the marriage, something that went on between her and Robert Lee, long before I came into her life, all during the time she lived out of motels, after her ex-husband Ken had killed two people. There was nothing I could do. Then Honey got back into bed beside me and pulled her nightdress up around her breasts. Her thighs were damp and warm. I could feel her heart pounding under the loose weight of her breasts. I could still hear Robert Lee crying into his pillow. I heard our youngest kid, Ernie saying something to Robert Lee. I felt Honey press her back against my belly. 'He's out of control, Frank, way out of control.' I had my face against her damp back, and I listened to the soft suctioning sound of our intimacy, like a child suckling in the dark.

Honey came out into the grey dark of the hallway. She said, 'This day has been a total waste of makeup.'

I took her crooked ring finger that still didn't have a ring on it and felt her flinch.

Honey lowered her eyes. 'Please . . .'

I said, 'You came up out of Georgia, and what did you have?'

'I was younger then. It was a different time in my life.'

I said, 'You're still young!'

'You really think so?'

I nodded. 'Have you ever thought of living out west, in California, sunshine, the ocean? If I get that money from the farm, we have a shot at something better.'

'Oh, come on, Frank, how much you think that farm is going to fetch?' But before I could answer, Honey said, 'Look, maybe you should just go up and see what you can do without us tagging along.'

I got this sudden jolt of fear that maybe there was something going on with her and Leonard. I said, 'No, we do this together, all of us, or we cut our losses right now. You go your way, and I'll go mine . . .'

Honey stared at me. 'Don't give me ultimatums, Frank, just don't. This is not just about me and you. I don't think I can do this right now . . .'

I said, 'Goddamn it! This is about Ken, isn't it?' Ken was in the last stage of legal wrangling, and dates had come and gone for his execution, but it was something that inevitably loomed.

Honey didn't look at me. 'It's going to be soon. I got to consider Robert Lee. He might want to go back to see Ken when the time comes, and if we're off in Michigan . . .'

I interrupted her, 'If we get money, you and he can fly down to Georgia. When the time comes, maybe you'll want to go down there, and where the hell are we going to get the money if it comes to that, if you want to go down there and we have no money?'

Honey looked at me and said, 'Jesus Christ, why does everything come all at once?'

I said again, 'This is like winning the lottery, Honey. We got a chance to start over.'

13

Leonard appeared and said nothing but looked at his watch and then at Honey and then back to his watch again, and then he was gone.

Honey looked at me. 'I don't get paid for this week if we leave now. Leonard has a strict policy. Without a two week notice, you get nothing that is coming to you.'

'You two are friends, Honey. Make him see it your way. Shit, tell him you're coming back. You don't have to tell him it's for ever.'

Honey looked at me. 'He's going to see through whatever I say. He knows already. I know by the way he's acting.'

I heard Leonard shouting at Honey as I hit the brilliant light of the outside world. I heard him call me 'Asshole'. A smell of diesel perfumed the cool air.

I followed a brand new 78 black Cadillac in my rusting Pinto, watched the gleaming car in the late afternoon light and decided the requiem of my uncle's death would begin in this black Cadillac.

It was strange to engage in someone else's life for a brief time, to follow a person. We got some gas, and then went to a pharmacy in a mini-mall, then on to the dry cleaner, where the woman left the car running. It was then that I took possession of the vehicle, with the forthright knowledge that the owner was insured, that there was no real crime being committed here. The cost of this single act had been reckoned in the account books of insurance ledgers. They had anticipated my actions. I was a pre-ordained statistical probability.

Driving out of the lot, I was thinking about Ken. Unlike Honey's ex-husband, Ken, I had not killed anybody or given in to the chaos that envelops us. As ignoble loser, I had played my part in our great society, lived within the laws of the land, for the most part. A lesser man, like Ken, might have sought the victim's purse into the bargain and ended up killing them. I imagined the struggle, the strangulation, the frantic kicking as life ended for some innocent, all for the sake of a few measly bucks.

For the past year, and in large part due to the approaching demise of Ken at the hands of the State of Georgia's Correctional Facility, I have spent maybe too much time trying to prove God doesn't exist. Most of the people I've seen commit evil have been caught, but I don't think that accounts for the presence of God, or Justice, as much as it does for the general desperation of people who have nothing. Theirs is a world without irony, with the sole conviction of wanting to survive. Stupidity and desperation do not equate to evil, as some would have you believe.

I arrived home to find Honey packed and the two boys sitting before the television. Honey had given Ernie a haircut.

Robert Lee had his Richard Nixon Pez dispenser on the table beside him. He had a strange obsession with Richard Nixon that began before I entered the equation. Honey said he'd listened to the Watergate proceedings in a motel the year Ken was arrested.

And there was Ernie sitting with a plastic dinosaur in his hands. I think it was Tyrannosaurus Rex. Ernie had a hell of a lot of dinosaurs. He knew all their names – Brontosaurus, Triceratops, Pterodactyl. It was like some form of autism, this fixation with dinosaurs, some sublimation of the pain he felt, a pain so deep it could only be expressed through the gigantism of prehistoric creatures. It scares the shit out of me, what kids intuit, how the madness of our lives seeps into their souls. I always wanted to ask Ernie, 'Is that what it sounds like when Mommy and Daddy fight?'

Honey looked at me and winked. 'Ernie says he's staying here, Frank.'

I nodded and said, 'Sure thing. We got that extra key cut. You show him how to use the electric can-opener and he's all set. He doesn't mind taking care of Juniper? Fill the water dish and clean the litter box twice a day. That about do it, Honey?'

Ernie looked bewildered for a moment.

Robert Lee said, 'Ernie, stay. You got it made here.'

Honey said, 'Quit it, Robert Lee, you hear?'

I ignored Robert Lee. I went to shake Ernie's hand in a magnanimous gesture of imminent, but amiable, departure. I said, 'Honey, think of the college tuition we're saving.'

Ernie's lower lip got wet and started to tremble, like he was going to cry, but Honey said, 'He's not said for sure he isn't going.' She looked at Ernie. 'So, have you decided, Ernie?'

Ernie said simply, 'I'm going, Frank.' He was holding one of his dinosaurs in his small hands.

Robert Lee scoffed, 'Sellout!'

We ate the burgers I had taken from the restaurant at the small kitchen table, and I got out a map and planned our escape with the conviction of a field marshal surveying a battlefield. The strategy was to arrive on the periphery of big cities along the motel strips in early evening and steal a different car. I picked out Cleveland as our potential first destination.

I checked the back of the atlas, looking at the table grid that showed the distance between major cities across America, and we played a sort of game. I gave two cities and you had to guess the distance. You won if you got within fifty miles.

Of course, Robert Lee didn't play, and Honey seemed to have no real sense that places like Helena, Montana existed. I said, 'Jesus, Helena is the state capital of Montana, Honey.' I tried to show her, but all she said was, 'You want a trim for the road? No point showing for a funeral looking like you do.'

I smelt vodka on her breath, but she wasn't drunk. I let her snip away. I had a towel around my shoulders. She had a small bowl of water and used her fingers to dampen my hair. Then, when she was finished, she massaged my temples and squeezed the back of my neck. I could feel the tension leaving my body. I said, 'You lost weight recently, Honey?'

'I don't know, you think I have?'

'I think you have. I really think so.'

Honey turned her head and blew a smoke ring. That's when I saw the hickeys on her neck, three of them. She saw me looking at her. I felt my guts tighten. I said, 'I wish I was a long ways away from here right now. China, maybe.'

Honey said, 'Just don't start, Frank, don't!'

There was inevitably one final episode with Robert Lee, but we got him to the car eventually. He took sole ownership of the front seat of the Cadillac with the announcement that he would turn us in to the cops if it were otherwise.

Ernie looked at me when we got to the car like he understood this wasn't ours. I don't think he wanted to get in.

I said, 'I won this in a card game, right Honey?'

She said, 'Yeah, Frank won it in a card game, Ernie.'

Ernie had that kid look, like he wasn't convinced, but he got in anyway, scrambling into the back, bouncing on the seat.

Robert Lee played with the seat-control unit.

I said, 'That pressure in your lower back is lumbar support.'

Robert Lee said, 'I know, dumb shit. I know what goddamn lumbar support is. Lumbar is the lower region of the spine.'

I said, 'Jesus H. Christ. You hear that, Honey? Lumbar is the lower region of the spine. We got a doctor in the house.'

Robert Lee looked at me. 'You're never going to be my goddamn father, so stop trying, Frank.'

Honey said, 'Robert Lee, you watch with that chair that you don't squish Juniper, you hear?' She made a puss-puss sound, and the cat meowed somewhere in the nether regions under the seat. I knew in my heart of hearts it was only a matter of time before it lost its tail.

Outside I could see the electrical stanchions stretching off toward the factories and the wire mesh of industrial chain-link fencing along the highway. It felt good to be leaving this caged existence, and the Cadillac was something else, plush with a fragrant scent of cherry spray. It didn't feel stolen, but something rightfully mine in some peculiar sense. True, I had forgotten to change the license plate, which weighed on me somewhat, but I wasn't going to stop now. From a cop's perspective, we just looked like a normal family heading somewhere respectable in a new car. That was the idea, when it came to stealing things, to stave off the paranoia that you were being watched. The great truth was that we were not the center of things, or others' lives, but only so in our own mind's eye. We were all obscure nobodies at our essence.

I felt self-assured as we arrived at the tollbooth. Robert Lee was still working the seat controls. I said, 'Dr Strangelove, you want to give it a rest?'

New York City twinkled in my rear view mirror, a distant galaxy receding. I sank slowly into the brakes, and the car slowed as we approached the tollbooth. A faceless man obscured in the bright light took my money. We were shadows inside the car. There was something prophetic about all of it, like beginning a journey across the river Styx to the land of the dead, a journey back to the center of things, to secrets I had not let myself think about in years.

Chapter 2

The sky flashed like an X-ray all through Pennsylvania exposing the skeletal outlines of trees. The headlights shone a wedge of light in the silver scratches of falling rain. I cracked my window, and the cold wet whispered in my ear. The AM radio cracked and hissed. The weather service predicted storms to continue through the night.

Robert Lee kept sentinel against the dark for the first two hundred miles, as we drove through the low Pennsylvania hills.

At a gas station I did some jumping jacks beside the car. Ernie's sleepy moon face smiled and stared out the back window. He held one of his dinosaurs in his hands.

Back out on the highway, it was deep night. A loose rain hit the window as if someone was throwing a fistful of gravel. Points of light floated in the distance against the silken dark, the night's haul of goods.

Honey had probably talked over the CB at her job to some of these men. Many lived exclusively out of their trucks, making their cabs small grottoes with Christmas lights and photographs of loved ones left behind. Sometimes it was a husband and wife pair working in tandem, perpetual motion, precariously maneuvering a change of drivers without stopping, the truck barreling down the road at seventy-five miles an hour. And at the back of their minds, they shared some vague notions of eventual escape, dreams of a home along the Carolina coast or raising horses down in Kentucky. I wondered right then what it would physically look like if you actually piled up all the shit that one of these truckers had hauled over a lifetime, I mean, just stare at the quantitative mass spread out in some field, and say, 'That is the extent of your life's work!'

I could feel the bone in my hip socket from the goddamn jumping jacks. I saw a mile marker and got hooked, my eyes waiting in anticipation for the next marker to light up out of the dark. The mile markers were in descending order going west. Counting backward in the dark of the car reminded me of years back, when I was a kid, memories of lying down in this dark room and counting back from one hundred with a psychologist in those dark weeks after my parents' death, when things sort of went haywire, when I began to contradict what my uncle had said about the fire.

I felt the car pull slightly, as if it had got away from me for a moment. Robert Lee must have felt it. His eyes opened. 'What the hell are you doing, Frank, you ass, trying to kill us?'

In the rear view mirror, Ernie was huddled against Honey, who was snoring.

To the south, the hills showed in the silver afterglow of lightning, revealing a vast world beyond the precinct of the dark enveloping the car.

I felt my past open against the dark of the highway, things I had left behind coming closer with each passing mile. I was retracing a journey, converging on the past. I had this vertigo, almost tumbling through the windshield, feeling myself propelled into the oncoming dark. The open road did that to you, especially night driving, a silent interrogation. I should have stopped, but I didn't, pushing through the dark.

The notion of my uncle as now dead sifted through layers of denial and anger, before settling somewhere deep in the murk of guilt and regret. The bravado of how I'd talked to Norman, that bullshit joke about if there was a will, there was a relative, died out there on that first night. Something more flatly sad, something more profound, got me into the car. I saw the house in my mind, the small grey parlor with mission-style furniture, cold, austere, merely functional, and there was my uncle, the dark shape of him sitting in his coat and boots as always, a grim caricature of what hardship and the land could do to the human spirit. It was hard to think of him as ceasing to exist, that when I got home he would not be there, that the interwoven drama of our lives had come undone, that the guarded secrets we kept from one another meant nothing, that our struggle had been eclipsed by mortality and time, and that there would be no reconciliation and understanding. At a certain level I wanted to see him laid out, to face the simple fact that the man who knew the truth of what happened the night my parents died would never speak again, that it was well and truly over.

More lightning filled the sky, then a sudden downpour of hail popped against the car. Through the crack in the window, the air smelt clean and refreshing. It was the smell of autumn, cold and invigorating, with a hint of fermentation.

Honey's eyes opened. 'You okay up there, Frank?'

The cat meowed and curled around my leg. I heard Honey crumple a bag, then the smell of cheese balls filled the car.

'Pass me back a cigarette, Frank.'

Robert Lee pressed in the lighter. He was still awake.

'Cigarettes are in my bag, Robert Lee.' She said it in a whisper so as not to wake Ernie.

Robert Lee got the pack and took off the plastic wrap. He tapped the pack with the flat of his palm. He set the cigarette in his mouth, then lit it. His face glowed orange. He turned and passed the cigarette back to Honey, then turned and exhaled in a long breath into my ear. He said, 'What you thinking about, Frank?'

'Nothing.'

'You're lying. I can see you're thinking about something.'

Honey's face showed and disappeared as she smoked. 'You should smoke.' She passed the cigarette to me. She put her feet in between the seats. 'Right there, Robert Lee. Rub right there.' Honey had collapsed arches. She said, 'I lost my feet when I was a waitress. I told you that, right, Frank?'

Robert Lee worked against the hard skin of Honey's underfoot until Honey started to snore. And then Robert Lee leaned into the passenger door and slept.

I flicked the last of the butt out the window and watched it flare and fall away in a comet of ash.

Back in the fifties there was the presumption that the brain stored everything – sight, sound, smell, all of it. But there were times when the brain saw things that were best left unseen, and, in those cases, the brain had a way of hiding things from the conscious mind. What was seen in these extreme moments bypassed the circuitry of consciousness and went deep into the subconscious. They called it 'repression' in psychiatric circles, or 'selective amnesia'. War veterans suffered a similar syndrome. It could take months, or even years, before there was some slippage, before the brain found a way of confronting what it had seen. But in some cases of repression, there were outward manifestations that something had passed into the subconscious, signs that something terrible was lurking in the folds of the brain.

I shook my head. My eyes watered. A mile marker smeared across my consciousness. Jesus, just thinking back to those times made me squirm, the austerity and disease, the fear that permeated our lives. I felt my mind bombarded with the sullen images of so many terrible things. It was around the time my parents died that my uncle Charlie came back from Chicago to the local sanitarium, a victim of polio. His wife abandoned him when he got sick, and he came back to the only place he'd known. I remembered going with Ward and seeing Charlie in this iron lung at the old sanitarium. Charlie was kept in a long

22

hallway that looked like an atomic bomb assembly line with its rows of iron lungs. I'd seen pictures of the bomb in *Life* magazine, like a giant, squat metal football.

I took a deep breath, and yawned. I felt that slippage, the old memories that I had staved off for so many years.

In my case, the repression of my parents' death manifest as nail biting. I was known as Nailbiter. In fact, that is the name that stayed with me right up until I left Upper Michigan. Nailbiter. At school, they were all concerned about the nail biting, not least that it was a disgusting habit. If you were going to have a vice, let it not be nail biting. They tried some god-awful powder that tasted like shit, but still the urge overcame the taste. I think, if it had been any neurosis other than nail biting, I might have been left alone, but the elementary educational system was not so much about actually learning something as it was about socializing you as a herd animal. They put gloves on my hands at one stage.

And then one afternoon, months after the fire, I got up from my desk in elementary school and got my hat and coat and went outside. A teacher described me as a zombie, like a sleepwalker. She asked me where I was going, and I said something to the effect that I was going home to my parents. That single admission, that single delusion changed my world for ever.

When I was asked the following day by a county psychiatrist to tell him where my parents were, I would look around the room or behind me. I couldn't exactly tell the psychologist where my parents were, but I never said they were dead or mentioned the fire. I just bit at my nails.

Sometimes I wondered if psychiatry had given any thought to why evolution endowed the human mind with this gift of forgetting.

In hindsight I consider myself a victim of historical circum-stance, that what happened to me was bound up in the general paranoia of the age, that the County Educational Board felt obliged to take me like some specimen and examine me.

At that particular time in our history, in the early fifties, we weren't many years shy of having incinerated two Japanese cities. The horrors of nuclear war were all too apparent. We'd seen the shadows of people burned into the sides of buildings in Hiroshima, and the Cold War policy of mutual and total annihilation made the bomb a last resort. There had to be more sublime ways of defeating Communism. The suggestibility of the mind was a potential back door to shaping consciousness. There were variety shows about Russian defectors who could bend spoons with their minds, or read the thoughts of somebody who had picked a card from a deck of cards. Indian holy men lay on beds of nails, walked on burning coals, without apparent physical distress or injury.

As a child I absorbed all this, became inculcated in the fear and paranoia of the age projected through the TV out to our farm. And in school, they made us do drills where we went under our desks and covered our heads. We understood the basics of nuclear war. *Duck and Cover* was the song we learned. I can't remember if we learned that first, or if it was the Pledge of Allegiance. Either way, they were the first two things I learned in school. We were under imminent attack. Down in the school gymnasium, there was a yellow door that said 'Fallout Shelter'. If there was ever a nuclear war, we were to go down there in pairs, like animals into Noah's Ark before the flood.

And we as kids had our own devices, our secret ways of communicating, of evading the enemy, with our decoder rings where messages were sent over the radio by Captain Midnight.

And so you can see how my repression of my parents' death became an object of considerable note. How had I turned off the mechanism of memory, how had I *brainwashed* myself? I was the sort of case study on which a fledgling post-doctoral candidate could write a major dissertation. And what might just have been some academic thesis became a police issue by the time the psychiatrist working with me got me under hypnosis and I started talking.

I was taken after school down to the State College's Outreach Agricultural Facility (OAF), a makeshift modular labyrinth of connecting rooms stuffed with such things as leaflets about how to apply modern chemical farming techniques to increase yield. Pictures of shiny green John Deere threshers and tractors hung on all the walls. Down the hall, away from the leaflets, I went through a doorway back into another section of the facility. I would pass a room with a long window for observing what was inside, not unlike what I saw later in life at a hospital where newborn babies are kept. But inside this room were not babies, but stalks of corn and beans. There was classical music playing low in the room. I didn't know it then, but there was a general theory floating around back then that plants had emotions. Behind the plant room, the administrative office had no windows and was conducive to achieving altered states of consciousness. That's where I did my sessions after school.

One afternoon, my uncle was taken off his tractor by the local sheriff for a series of psychological tests at the Outreach Agricultural Facility. Seeing my uncle there like that, I understood something was wrong, even if I did not understand what was going on. My uncle was in his overalls, sitting in this white room I passed on the way back to the administration office. I heard him talking. I stopped and said his name, and he turned and just stared blankly at me. He didn't say anything. I think he was scared. He was sitting in a small chair in his overalls, his big legs bent so his knees came up almost to his chest. For all the world, he looked like some dumb shit who'd not gotten out of the third grade. He'd been staring down at something which I figured was an inkblot, because Miss Potts was in there with him, and she was always making me tell her what I saw in inkblots.

25

I went on down the hallway and into the administrative office, and got hypnotized in the dark, but the things I said were lost to my conscious memory. It felt simply like sleep. When I came out, my uncle was gone. I only saw my uncle there that one time, and he never said anything about it back out on the farm, but it changed things between us forever.

In retrospect, I think they set up that so-called chance meeting there in the Outreach Agricultural Facility like you rig an experiment, like putting prey and predator in a cage. What it did was scare the shit out of my uncle. He knew that what they'd said about me was true, that I was talking into some tape recorder in the dark of the administration office, that I was telling secrets.

Chapter 3

I don't know if you've ever been held hostage by your own kid, I mean in a literal sense, where your son decides that it's time to hold you hostage at a rest stop, and you can't do anything but sit and wait it out. That's pretty much the situation in which we found ourselves at an oasis along the Ohio Turnpike.

The night had ended. The morning emerged zinc grey, damp with the night's rain. The sky seemed to have fallen perceptibly toward the earth, making things claustrophobic.

We were all worn out and cold. The temperature had dropped since New Jersey, and the wind had picked up and blew in gusts.

Honey said, 'I got a balloon for a bladder.' She winced when she got out of the car.

We ate at a McDonald's situated right over the highway. If you looked down, you got a nauseous feeling. I watched trucks roaring down the highway, closing my eyes just as they passed right underneath the bridge. I felt what it must be like the instant before the impact of death. It made me shudder. I had this rawness after a night without sleep, feeling disembodied from things around me.

I drank my coffee black, staring out past the highway, across the morning dew in fields that stretched for miles.

In my head, I was running through things. The day should see us through Indiana and north into Michigan. I figured we'd get a cheap motel late in the afternoon, then wait it out until about eight, steal another car, and get ourselves well north under cover of dark. The weather bothered me. It was already cold, so I figured it would be freezing up north, maybe twenty degrees colder once you factored in the wind chill. Sometimes winter just poured out of the north. You went up a few hundred miles, and the snow started, especially along the Great Lakes where we were going. It had its own climate, with lake effect snows and freezing Canadian Arctic air.

Honey had gorged herself on pancakes drowned in maple syrup. A cigarette smoldered in an ashtray beside her. Robert Lee was eating an Egg McMuffin and orange juice. Honey was talking to him. I stood far enough away from them so they could talk the way they did when I wasn't around. I heard Honey say, 'A man can forget how to work, Robert Lee. It just happens that way. Something happens in a town, and things just close down. It can end like that for people. It isn't that those people are bad, it's just how things happen, is all.' Honey sighed for a moment with her usual fated silence that punctuated her discussions with Robert Lee. She said, 'Maybe when you're older, you'll understand.'

They were discussing their favorite subject in the world, *The Trials and Tribulations of Ken Wainscot*, so I tuned them out.

An old man sat alone at another table with one of those reptilian faces that has seen too much sun, the wattle of his throat like something on a lizard. He was one of those retirees destined to die on the road, dressed in a polyester shirt and shit-brown pants and beige vinyl shoes. He had his own food in a brown bag and a thermos of coffee, which told you he was union all the way back. He was talking across two tables to a young couple who were holding hands. The girl was maybe sixteen and in the family way, dressed in a hand-me-down skirt that had been let out at the seams. I could tell she was considering alternatives, simply because she was out here in the middle of nowhere holding hands like that in the early morning. She had been crying.

The old man said, 'Everybody has done everything twice at my age. First you do things all wrong, then you spend the rest of your life trying to undo everything to make it right.'

The girl said, not in a bad way, but with the defiance of love on her side, 'We're planning on doing it all right the first time, thank you very much. Isn't that right, Donny?'

Donny was wearing a baseball cap that was well worn, the bill pulled down over his forehead. He stared down at the ground in a way that was universal amongst farmers. 'I guess,' is all he said.

'Donny! You got a firecracker is what you got there. You understand that?' the old man said.

I watched the girl curl her greasy hair behind her ear. She had her other hand on Donny's broad back.

The old man stood up, and his body creaked. He came over and smiled at the girl.

The girl looked up into his eyes.

Donny sort of coughed as if he was uncomfortable. He took his baseball cap off his head and ran his hand through his damp hair. The rim left a perfect red scar running across his forehead and temples. He looked as if he'd had a brain operation or something, as if his head had been cut in two. Then he set the cap back on his head.

'I'm going to give some life advice, if you don't mind, because that's what old men like me do.'

The girl looked blankly up into the old man's face.

'There are three things a woman should never admit she knows how to do.' The old man put out his hand and counted off on his crooked fingers, 'Make coffee, clean fish, and start a lawnmower...'

I could see the smile break across the girl's face. Even Donny shook his head and looked up at the old man. He said to his girl, 'I guess you went wrong startin' that lawnmower.'

The girl mock-punched Donny on the arm.

The old man winked, his eye disappearing into a nest of wrinkles. 'Remember, it's not what happens, it's what you do with what happens.' With that he started walking away, as the girl said, 'You got a name, Mister?'

The old man turned. 'Walter. Walter Ames.'

The girl looked at him. 'I was wondering is all.' She said his name again, 'Walter. I kind of like that.'

'I reckon it got me by.'

The old man stared at me as he passed and tipped his head, and I did likewise. I thought right then maybe Walter Ames had been put on this Earth for this one act.

Ernie kept getting up from his breakfast to watch the trucks speeding by underneath. I said to him, 'If you close your eyes, it sounds like a bullet whizzing by your head.' Ernie stood before the glass. He closed his eyes and his face got all serious. Then he opened his eyes and half smiled at me. I could see the child inside him just then. He leaned toward me, and I put my hand on his head. I needed that like a drug right then, just having him there with me.

When I finally turned from looking out at the highway, the young couple was gone. I looked over and saw Honey. She had tears in her eyes, and Robert Lee was nowhere in sight. Honey had been staring at me. She squeezed the tears in her eyes and sniffled. 'I hope this is all worth it.'

I ordered a hot apple pie and ate it. Honey recovered enough to say, 'Do you think I've aged well, Frank?' She hesitated and said, 'Considering everything, that is.' She was looking into a small vanity mirror she had taken from her purse.

I said, 'You look good.'

Honey looked at me. Her face wrinkled and her eyes watered, 'Oh God . . . I just don't know if we're doing the right thing for Robert Lee . . . He told me he wants to . . . wants to slash my throat.'

Outside, the car didn't turn over. I flooded the engine. I smelt the sweet odor of gasoline filling the car. I felt my heart jumping around in my chest. I said out loud to myself, 'Let it just sit a moment. This is a goddamn Cadillac. It's going to start. Cadillacs don't do this sort of shit. Chevy Novas do this sort of shit, but not Cadillacs!' But it didn't start. I could see the cat on the back window looking out at the world. Its tail flitted back and forth. The nail biting started just like that, before I knew what the hell I was doing. I saw myself gnawing at my nails in the rear view mirror. I pulled my hands away from my mouth and spat the bits of nail out. I sat on my goddamn hands. I mean, that was the sort of urge that came over me. I felt my hands burn with an irresistible need to be eaten at.

I got out of the car. I was talking to the Cadillac. And then, behind me, I heard laughing.

Robert Lee said, 'Car trouble, Frank?'

'You son-of-a-bitch! What the hell did you do?'

Robert Lee smiled and held up the distributor cap. 'I bet you don't even know what this is, do you, ass?'

I felt a strange sense of relief, knowing that the Cadillac wasn't really dead. I looked at him calmly. I put my hand out like there was no real reason to be mad. I said, 'I don't know what your exact problem is, but I bet it's hard to pronounce.' I let a smile break on my face. 'You win, champ.' I held up my hands. 'I bow to your mechanical genius!' I made a fake bow like some religious nut.

Robert Lee took a step away from me as I came around toward his side of the car bowing.

'Frank! You don't want to engage me in hand-to-hand.' He made the motions of a karate expert. 'You don't even want to try it. I could have you eating beans on a tin plate tonight. All I got to say is you kidnapped us. That's all I got to say.' He snapped his fingers. 'Just like that. Taking a stolen car over state lines is also a federal offense, just in case you hadn't realized.'

Robert Lee waved the tentacles of the distributor cap in my face. I kept coming toward him slowly, and he kept stepping toward people filling up their cars with gas. I saw people begin to stare at us, so I stopped.

'Come on, Frank! Here it is.' He waved the distributor cap in my face again. I could have grabbed it, but I didn't. What I did was look around me, surveyed the cars coming off the ramps, the cars parked around us, and shook my head. I said, 'You know, you might think this is bullshit, but I thought by this time in history we'd all be driving flying cars. That was something everybody of my generation believed.' I shook my head like this was some sort of revelation that had just dawned on me. 'How the hell did we get that one so wrong?'

Robert Lee had this look of stupefaction on his face. He started shouting at the top of his voice, 'Frank, shut the fuck up! I mean it. Jesus Christ, you are so fucked up! I mean it! Goddamn it, leave me alone! Fuck you, Frank!'

A man pumping gas said, 'You got a problem over there?'

I said, 'You got anything for a love-sick adolescent?'

'God, don't I wish.'

'Hey, mister, he's not my father. He's a child molester.'

I said out loud so people could hear, 'You want to call your girlfriend, be my guest.'

The man pumping gas winked at me. 'You think boys are bad.' He mouthed the word 'Girls'.

By now the crisis had passed.

I watched Robert Lee walk off toward a small picket fence off on an embankment where the dog walk area was situated. He stopped and looked back at me and gave me the finger. I could see a miniature golf course in the background. It was done in the motif of Snow White and the Seven Dwarfs. Snow

White was sitting on a toadstool, holding a sign that said 'Closed for the Season'. In life, you take in so much shit. It all pours into the depths of your head. In psychology these days, it wasn't so much about remembering anymore, but about forgetting. They had a procedure for that, electroconvulsive therapy.

I went back in, and Honey was talking to a trucker in a studded rhinestone shirt that glittered when he moved. Honey looked up and said, 'You know Skylab is falling out of the sky? That's what Earl here was just telling me.'

I said, 'What the hell do you want me to do? Duck?'

The trucker said, 'Duck. I like that.' He made like he was ducking and just slid out of the seat across from Honey and walked off, still pretending he was trying to avoid getting hit. 'Duck! Shit, that's funny.'

I saw Ernie over by the window with his dinosaurs, looking out the glass onto the highway.

Honey looked me straight in the face. 'We all set?'

I said, 'That asshole pulled the distributor cap out of the car.'

Honey put her hands to her temples as if she was going to have one of her migraines. 'Jesus Christ. Maybe this is a mistake, all of it! I should never have come out here, never.'

I said, 'You know, I sometimes wonder what it is we have that makes us even want to stay together, because I sure as hell can't think of what it is right now . . .'

Honey hit me hard across the face. 'Goddamn you! Don't start into me like this, you hear me, not out here on a goddamn highway, not after you dragged me out here!'

Two more hours drifted by. I slept with my head on the table and used my arms as a pillow. My face throbbed. Sometimes I woke and felt like I was dreaming, but I wasn't. I wanted to will myself back to New Jersey. I still had my head on the table, but my eyes were open.

I said, 'Ernie, you stay near me now, you hear me, kid?'

He looked at me and said, 'Okay, Frank.' He was feeding his dinosaurs French fries and ketchup.

It was one of those moments when being called Frank by my kid hurt somehow.

I said, 'You want chocolate milk or anything, Ernie?'

Ernie smiled.

I went out to the vending areas and tried the trick on the vending machine, but it didn't work, and it ate my quarter into the bargain. I hit the machine again, but nothing happened. 'Goddamn it!' There was a sign on the side of the machine that said DO NOT TILT and a picture of a perplexed stickman with a vending machine falling on him. I hit the machine with a force that would have knocked down a grown man. I got a sudden sense that this was what we, as humans, would be reduced to, attacking inanimate objects in a world where there would be no recourse or mercy or pleading.

We went out into the parking lot and saw Honey and Robert Lee sitting in the car, the two heads like puppets. The cat was still staring out the back window, the eternal hostage. I thought the best thing that could happen in all the world now was for them to drive off and leave Ernie and me. I could see Honey with some guy like the one in the rhinestone shirt. She was an operator. I wished so much for her to leave that I focused on the car and put my hands to my head like those old Russian telepathists, and I said, 'Honey, drive away. Honey, drive away now. Leave Frank, Honey! Leave now!' Shit, it was worth a try. And for a moment it seemed like she might. But she didn't. I just saw her big head moving in the window.

I closed my eyes once more and said, 'Calling Honey Wainscot. Come in, Honey Wainscot! Leave Frank. Leave now.'

Nothing.

Ernie put his hands to his head and said, 'Calling Honey Wainscot . . . Leave now,' and that offset the tension in me for a bit, and Ernie and I went back in and ordered a Happy Meal, like happiness could come in a small box, but it did, for a kid like him, and I was grateful for that.

A man at the next table was telling a story about the guy who had founded McDonald's. The man said the golden arches were inspired by the founder's wife's breasts. The founder was sitting at home one night when he just looked over at his wife, and, bingo, he saw the 'M' of her tits, and the rest was history. I heard the man say, 'Cross my heart and hope to die, that is a true story.'

This other man said, 'It makes sense to me.'

I'd heard that story a thousand times. I got a feeling there were only so many stories to tell in life, like all the words had been used up. I found it hard to say anything that conveyed what I was feeling anymore. I suppose it's that other dimension those B-movies were always hinting at, the telepathy of pure communication, without ambiguity. I guess that is what we all want in the end, to be unequivocally understood.

The man who had listened to the story about McDonald's said, 'When the McDonald's sign says, "Millions served" on the sign outside, do they mean people, or burgers?'

I took a long, deep breath. I felt tired already, and the journey wasn't half over, and the notion of having to steal another car sent a wave of regret through me. I should have done like Honey said and flown home. I knew that now. But of course, like most of the things I've learned in life, it came too late.

Ernie had finished his Happy Meal and was working on a small kid's book that came as a prize.

I said, 'You okay, Ernie?'

'Look, Frank, look at this.'

It was one of those blank page books where you rubbed with a magic pencil and a picture materialized. Ernie rubbed back and forth, and Ronald McDonald emerged, waving out at him.

I said, 'I got to make a phone call, Ernie. Stay right here.' He nodded.

I called Norman collect again. It took some time before he accepted the charges. I said, 'Listen, Norman, we got off on the wrong foot...' I hadn't finished before he said, 'Where are you, Frank?'

'I'm ... I don't know exactly ... Nowhere ... Norman listen to me. I'm out on the Ohio Turnpike with my family. We have a problem with our car.'

'Oh God, you're not really coming up here, Frank? I hope to God you aren't ... Frank, I want you to listen to me good, you hear?'

I spoke over him. 'I quit my goddamn job, Norman! Don't stonewall me, Norman! I want us to come to some agreement right now.' Whatever sense of reconciliation I wanted was gone again.

A man passed with his wife and looked at me like I was deranged. They looked back at me when they got some distance away.

Norman started speaking to Martha, and I could hear her shouting, 'He can't come up here now! You hang up, Norman. This is a collect call he's making again. We don't have that kind of money. Just hang up!'

I said loudly, 'Norman, listen to me you dumb shit! You either do this amicably, or I'm going to take you on, so help me, Norman. I'm going to use every goddamn legal challenge to get your ass off that farm! You hear me?'

Norman started moaning, 'I never did anything to you! I don't know why you're out to get me. Why are you out to get me?'

I said, 'Listen to me, I'm at a goddamn rest stop along the

Ohio Turnpike, and I've run into some car trouble. I need you to wire me some money, Norman, you hear me? If you goddamn treat me like a civilized human being, then I'll act like one, but if you push me, Norman, so help me Jesus, I'm getting you off that farm, just like your goddamn father got me off it!'

Norman hesitated. 'Frank, the price of hogs has bottomed out, honest to God. I told you that when all this started, that we got nothing, same as you . . . Listen, if you want something, maybe we can send it back to New Jersey, but right now Frank, I got . . .' Norman just stopped speaking, and it was like he had burst out crying or something. I heard Martha say, 'Jesus, you're having a fit. Sit down . . . sit down . . .' Norman was roaring like a bear. It scared the shit out of me. I had a sudden realization that this was, after all, Norman's father who was dead.

I just waited. I didn't much like myself right then, but I was stuck. Martha finally picked up the phone. 'You're sick, sick like I always knew you were . . . You leave us alone, you hear? Get AAA or something to get you towed, get them to get you back to New Jersey!'

I mean, she let me have it. I had to take the phone away from my ear. The voice sounded like the gibberish you get on cartoons when somebody starts shouting down a phone. I put the phone to my ear again and said, 'I can't make out what the hell you are saying, you hear me?'

Martha lowered her tone and started again. 'There never was anything between you and Ward, you hear me? He did what he could for you when he was alive, and it seems it was never good enough for you. You ruined him, is what you did, what with what you did years ago, and what he did for you, took you in like a son, and you never showed him anything but contempt, Frank, so why make a pretense now? If there's anything in a will for you, and I doubt there is, you'll hear, by and by, since lawyers are obliged to make contact, and that is all I got to say on the matter! You are not coming up here bringing harlots that are the wives of men on death row. Just thinking about it makes me sick, SICK. I won't have you here, Frank! I won't! That's all I got to say.'

I lowered my voice. 'Listen, I'm sorry ... Every time I've called I've just wanted to talk civilized ...'

Martha seemed to ease for a moment. She took a long breath. 'Listen, this is not a good time. If you want to know the truth, I'll tell you. All hell has broken loose up here.'

'What do you mean, *all hell*?'

'God, I don't know where to start ... Ward's murderer was down in his cell late last night, and he hung himself. He's in a coma right now. They don't know if he's going to make it.'

I said, 'So why's that a problem?'

'Listen, when they got him into custody, they found a tattoo on his arm with the name, C Green, and underneath it the word, Korea.'

I felt a sudden shock. 'Chester Green? That ...' I hesitated for a moment. 'You mean Sam Green's kid?' I was shaking my head. The sudden impact hit me. The Greens lived in the next farm but the thing was that Chester Green had died close on thirty years ago in an influenza outbreak.

Martha raised her voice despite my silence. 'Frank, you listen to me. Stay out of this. Just stay out. All I know is it's got people talking. The police have been out here. They've dragged us over the coals. They aren't satisfied that we don't know what's going on. They think we do. They interrogated Norman for hours. I mean he is at the end of his wits here.' Martha shouted, 'We can't take any more. You listen good. I don't want you coming near us, not now. Just get yourself towed back to New Jersey.'

I felt numb inside.

'Frank, you hear me? Get yourself towed!'

I said more to myself than her, 'Chester Green is dead ...' Then I came around because Martha was repeating the same stuff about me getting myself towed. I sighed down the phone. I was lost at that moment, leaning into the phone booth. I said, 'Listen, I would, but the thing is, the car's not exactly mine.'

'What?' Then the light went on in Martha's head. 'You didn't ... you didn't steal a car, did you?'

There was this eruption of shouting in the background. It was Norman. I heard Martha cover the mouthpiece so I couldn't hear what was going on, then I heard her breathing again, deeply in a sigh. 'Frank, you're going to drive Norman to suicide, that's what you're going to do.'

Right then, I knew I never should have left New Jersey.

Norman got back on the line. His voice was shaky. 'I think it's all been said. I don't think there's anything else to say ... If you want, I can spare maybe something like five hundred dollars, to get you back home. Give me a town, and we'll wire you the money.'

I heard Martha say to Norman, 'His life has gone to hell in a hand basket.'

I was looking up into the sky right then. I wondered what was the statistical probability of actually being hit by Skylab, being flattened like a pancake right there and then. I said, 'You keep the money, Norman.' I hung up on him.

I felt detached from ordinary life, lost. It took a moment to calm down. The reference to Chester Green sent a chill through me. Honey had told me I'd shouted Chester Green's name in my sleep from time to time over the years. I had a history of recurring nightmares about the fire, and somehow Chester Green was a prominent feature of those dreams. I'd always put my association with Chester's name down to the fact that, when Chester was dying, Sam Green had come running onto our property screaming that his son was on fire – his son was burning up with fever. He'd come because we had a phone, and he didn't. He kept screaming that same thing into our phone. He scared me in a way no other man had scared me before. I wasn't used to strangers out on the farm.

And somehow, in the aftermath of my parents' deaths, I'd interwoven Chester Green into my own nightmares about the fire. As a kid, I imagined a young man on a bed covered in flames.

I went and stood on the bridge, put my face up against the glass and felt the whoosh of trucks speeding beneath me. The future right then was nothing more than a stretch of miles along a highway. I needed to get away from here. You couldn't technically be more marooned in all of America than in a stolen car at a rest stop on the turnpike.

I looked over at Ernie. He was sitting with some kids whose parents had stopped to eat. Ernie had his dinosaurs lined up along the table. He was talking in that earnest way he had. You could tell he was intelligent, not in the way you hear parents go on about their kids. No, he was unique, he was special.

I went over and sat with Ernie, and the other kids got up and moved to another table. I guess I looked scary. I hadn't shaved in two days.

'Those dinosaurs eat enough meat, Ernie?'

He looked at me and pointed at one dinosaur and said, 'He's an *herbivore*, Frank.'

'What's that mean?'

Ernie cocked his head to the side and said, 'That means he only eats plants, Frank.'

I said, 'Oh ... What if he eats both vegetables and meat, what's that called?'

Ernie looked at me and twisted his mouth and then shrugged his shoulders, 'I don't know, Frank.'

I said, 'An "omnivore" is what it's called, Ernie.'

He repeated the word, 'Omnivore.'

I said, 'You got it, "Omnivore". And here's something I bet you didn't know. Lots of words in the language we speak,

English, come from a really old language that was called Latin, and in that language the word for "everything" was "omni", and the word "vore" meant "eat". You see how that works, Ernie? Part of that Latin language is used in English. Our language is made up of what they call a dead language.'

I could see Ernie's brain making sense of that, the way it stored new things, creating the greater world beyond what we merely see and feel, how our human brains create history and meaning. Ernie looked from his dinosaurs to me to the kids who were starting to eat. He went over to the kids and told them what he'd just learned, and even the parents seemed impressed, or shocked, given Ernie was with me.

I was still lost. I didn't know if I had it in me to go back home. I mean I'd well and truly left that shithole behind. It had nearly ruined me, all of it, the fire and the relationship with Ward. Shit, it got me institutionalized for a time.

I decided to say nothing to Honey right then. I got Ernie, and we went out to the car. I knocked on the Cadillac and said, 'License and registration, please,' in the stern voice state troopers use, then I burst out laughing just because I was feeling good right then about Ernie.

Honey said, 'You are a card, a real card.' Honey was holding the distributor cap, and she was smiling, like she had accomplished something, which she had. Our escape.

I opened the backdoor for Ernie, then I got into the front. I said, 'There's a Holiday Inn not far from here. I got a coupon from the back of that Atlas we bought. It's fifty percent off weekdays. I think we all need an open-faced sandwich and a good night's sleep.'

Robert Lee cut in and said, 'They got a pool there?' I could see the dark orb of his head in the shadows.

'Holiday Inns always have pools.'

Robert Lee said, 'Damn it, I got no swim trunks.'

I said, 'We'll buy swim trunks.'

Honey said, 'You sure we got money to waste on a hotel?'

I lied and said, 'My brother Norman has offered to wire us some money,' but in the back of my head I was thinking how to get money, and, the problem was, there was no way, not legally anyway, and in that single moment, I saw a far more sinister future on the immediate horizon.

The sky faded fast toward night off to the east. I said softly, for lack of anything really to say, 'They got this weird deal for kids, Honey.'

'How do you mean?'

'Well it says right on the back of that coupon in the Atlas that kids' meals are based on a kid's weight. They got a scale, and you pay a cent for each pound you weigh.'

Honey said, 'There is no way in hell they are weighing me. No way.'

Ernie was sitting back. He leaned forward and said simply, 'It's just for kids, Honey.'

Honey said, 'Why are you so sweet, my sugar pie?'

I saw Ernie come and hug Honey and close his eyes.

Honey said, 'He is my sugar pie, my best boy.' Ernie had a dinosaur pointed at my face. It smelt of ketchup.

I felt my hands tighten on the wheel. I said, 'That's right, kiddo, it's just for kids, Honey. There are certain things only for kids in this world.'

Robert Lee worked on putting the distributor cap back on. It seemed like a complicated job. I could hear him cursing. I said, 'So what's his problem anyway?'

'Frank, leave it. He thinks nobody cares about him.'

'Oh really? I got a cure for that. If you think nobody cares about you, try missing a couple of car payments.'

'Frank, stop, please . . . He knows that Ken . . . that Ken's going to die soon . . .'

It was cold waiting in the car. We should have waited inside.

Something like twenty minutes passed. We watched Robert Lee under the hood. Finally, I opened the door and said, 'How long more?' and Robert Lee said, 'Fuck you.'

Honey glared at me. 'Frank, just leave him alone. You want to get out of here, right?' She kept looking at me. 'So what about the funeral? How are we really going to stay at a Holiday Inn with the funeral on tomorrow?'

I said, 'The funeral is on hold.'

'On hold?'

I raised my voice a notch. 'On hold. The body is evidence.'

Honey said, 'Evidence! I don't even want to ask, do I?' Then she said, 'What the hell is going on up there?'

I told Honey about the tattoo with the name of Chester Green. I told her the murderer was in a coma.

It took Honey a moment and then a look came over her face. 'Chester Green, that's the name you say in your sleep sometimes, you hear me?'

I said, 'I know.'

Honey squeezed my arm. 'What the hell is going on? Jesus, look at me! Do you know this Chester Green?'

I said, 'Chester Green has been dead twenty-seven years.' I waited a moment and said, 'Anyway, the tattoo said C Green, not Chester Green. Maybe it's just one of those coincidences, that's all . . .'

'Coincidence? What else aren't you telling me? I don't like this at all. There's something not right here. You hear me, Frank? There's something you're not telling me. I can see it in your eyes! Why are you really going back?'

I said, 'For the money. Isn't that why we do most things in life, for the goddamn money?'

'Don't you raise your voice like that to me, Frank!'

We stopped talking, though Honey muttered to herself.

I stared at people detached from any reality, faces I would never see again, or maybe there was a reality at this oasis on a highway. Maybe I was really dead, and this was some secular limbo where the good citizens with money got to drive in, and fill up, and then move on to the promised land of cities, but where the damned, like me, lived on fried food and black coffee, with our cars that were never ever going to start. You got to thinking in parables at a certain point in life, the parable of the good life, the parable of the bad life.

In the back of my mind, I was thinking this might be my last day of freedom. We were basically broke. I was going through how you rob somebody. I was scanning the rest area, looking for traveling salesmen, for the elderly in mobile homes, maybe a guy like Walter Ames: lock a guy like that up in his trunk, or bind and gag a businessman in his hotel room. I could feel my heart racing in my chest. If I had been married to anybody else, I might have been able to explain what had happened on the phone, that there was no money coming, but I just knew how Honey would have reacted, so I went about alternative plans.

I looked out at the cars in the rest area, looked at the lives of ordinary people doing ordinary things. A giant American flag fluttered on a massive flagpole. Something had always separated me from that life, something had kept me a scavenger at the edge of normal existence. I guess I never thought about it until that moment, but it was at a rest stop like this that Ken had slit the throats of that elderly couple, when the madness had finally erupted. At some gut level I sympathized with Ken. Honey should have been admitted into evidence as an extenuating circumstance.

Robert Lee broke the silence. 'Try her now, Frank. Pump three times, but don't gas her.'

I did, and nothing happened. I could hear Robert Lee cursing. His face materialized for a moment. 'Lay off the goddamn gas.' He looked at Honey. 'I might as well have a monkey here turning the ignition. I say, "Don't gas her", and what does he do? Gas her!' Robert Lee walked away. I heard him saying, 'My mother has hooked up with a damn retard!'

I felt a thrill of tiredness run through me. There was no real fight left in me. Life was all body blows, just insistent and relentless, no real uppercuts or jabs, just blows that got you so you breathed shallow and uneasy and you struggled to stand upright. I don't know if I would ever be able to say in the end what eventually would put me over the edge. I guess it wouldn't be one single thing. I'd have no real defense, well, not one that could be expressed in words anyway.

'Turn her again.' I did, and the car started right up that time. And then we were off, just like that, hostage crisis over.

I got us up to seventy-five miles an hour. I was thinking of the Holiday Inn like some promised land, of the plush carpet, the smell of the chlorine pool, the game room, all of it running through my mind, and maybe, most of all, about the king-sized bed and the smell of hotel sheets and HBO.

In the rear view mirror, I saw Robert Lee and Ernie already had their eyes closed. They hadn't properly slept during the night. Even Honey drifted off.

And in that silence, despite my best intention I was aware I was thinking about what was happening with Norman and the murder up at the farm. I said half under my breath that it had nothing to do with me, that I had my own problems, that by night's end I was going to have to make some critical choices about my own existence, but somehow I felt the aura of the murder insinuating itself into my head, simply because I was considering my own desperate options.

I kept driving, but eased off the gas. Somehow the murder and the appearance of Ward's murderer bearing that tattoo with the name of Chester Green had a parochial strangeness, as if some old secret was playing itself out in the murder of my uncle. It was weird thinking of Ward's killer just waiting in the house after killing my uncle, just waiting for retribution to be exacted upon him, and then finding himself unable to face the consequences, and opting for death . . .

45

I began passing a car. Its bumper sticker read, 'I've found Jesus. He's in my trunk.'

The guy driving turned his head toward me, and I swear he looked like Jesus Christ. He had long stringy hair and a beard. He looked like he could see right into my life, and this was Judgment Day.

Chapter 4

Robert Lee and Ernie were in the swimming pool which formed the centerpiece of the Holiday Inn. All the rooms faced the pool, with nothing but glass and curtains to hide you from people walking by outside. There was a glass roof over the pool as well. It had that echoing sound, and the smell of chlorine filled the air with a sharp chemical freshness. I said to Honey right when I saw it, 'If there was ever a hotel made for mermaids, this is it.'

'Frank, it's what dreams are made of. Let them be.'

Our moods had eased.

I said, 'I'm not complaining. I just want to know how to recapture that feeling is all.'

I was lying on my back with Honey curled against me, in the afterheat of what married couples are obliged to do from time to time, relenting to the same physical need.

The lights were out in the room, but light from the pool seeped in around the edge of the curtains, and the television was on, the sound barely audible. Two rollaway beds you might have for the wounded in some war were set out near a small table that served as the eating area.

I felt myself float on the waterbed.

Honey said, 'I remember that first night meeting you at that bar. Who would have thought we'd be heading to Michigan?'

I didn't say anything.

'God, I had that rusted-out Cutlass Supreme, you remember that car?'

I said, 'I do.' I remembered it all, her sitting alone, the eye-shadowed half-moons of her eyelids painted on like tribal suffering. It was the month Ken got sentenced to death, the month she filed for divorce, the month she finally understood that Ken had killed that elderly couple, that he had cut their throats. She told me she realized, right there at his sentencing, there were two choices in life: get over it, or die with it on your mind.

She got drunk and told me how Ken got busted, buying six pairs of snakeskin cowboy boots at a truck stop. They were all living in a motel, and that's what he did with the money he had stolen. When I heard that about the boots, I said to Honey, 'What was this ex-husband of yours, a goddamn centipede?' Maybe it was levity she needed, or the mutual distraction that we offered each other. I won't even bring love into the equation. On that first evening together, Honey wanted to know about electricity, about currents, the mechanical details of how a man goes about dying in the Chair . . .

I didn't want to get up from the bed. I said, 'I wish I could make things better for all of us. You know what it feels like to be out here in the middle of nowhere in a stolen car?'

'We're starting fresh, right? You said this was like winning the lottery, right? Your brother is wiring you money, so maybe he'll just settle things squarely.'

It was hard to get the courage to say anything, to stop the inevitable trajectory of what I knew I was going out to do.

I turned and faced Honey in the dim light.

'What is it?'

I whispered, 'I can't even begin to tell you about things that went on back when my parents burned to death . . . I mean, it screwed me all to hell.'

'How?'

I said, 'Jesus, don't you see that the potential in me and what I am is way out of whack? Don't you see that? I'm not saying that like you hear people say when they're down on

48

their luck, because deep down you know that what they are is what they really are. But it's different with me.'

'Frank, don't beat yourself up . . .'

I stopped her. 'Listen, I'll just tell you everything, okay, what you don't know about me and my life, then you decide!'

Honey shifted. 'Frank, shoo, we're safe for now. We can go down and eat. I'll let them weigh me if you like.'

'Just let me get this off my chest, okay?'

Honey nodded. 'Sure, Frank.'

I told her about the fire and the nail biting and about the hypnosis, all of it. 'They screwed me up real bad. I said things against my uncle, and, I swear to you, Honey, I don't know what the hell was the truth in any of it. I was a goddamn kid is what I was, and when they got me under hypnosis, I said things about my uncle. I mean it was all inaccessible to me when I woke up.'

Honey leaned and touched my forearm. 'You had to remember something, right?'

'I didn't. It's the honest truth, Honey, so help me God. I tried for years to see into myself, but I never got there. Shit, it took years before I could really understand the full conse- quence of my parents' death, years before I consciously tried to remember. And even then I was only trying to remember to fight against what my uncle said I did . . .'

'What did he say?'

'He said that I'd set the fire by accident, that I knocked over a candle, and, when I saw the blaze, I panicked and ran out of the house. He said when he found me, I was hiding in the barn, shaking. He said I told him what had happened, that I'd knocked over the candle, but that I was sorry, that I wanted him to make things okay between my parents and me. And so, in the end, I was blamed for the fire. Of course, back then, I was too young even to know that story about me knocking over a candle was going around. It was something circulating in the adult world, but I felt this weirdness around people, like

49

they didn't trust me or something. I know this all means squat, Honey, but it's been inside me all these years. You get so you can't stop thinking about things. When I got into high school I suffered the worst of it, that is when I tried to look back, but it was so long ago. I could never get back to that time.' I looked Honey in the face. 'You think I'm crazy, right? You don't believe me. I can see it in your eyes. You think that I killed my parents. Is that it?'

Honey said, 'No . . . You were a kid. You're not responsible for . . .'

I interrupted her. 'You see, even the way I tell it now, you think I set the fire, don't you? I got something in my voice that tells you I did, right?' I stared into her eyes.

Honey touched my face. 'Come on, now. I'm on your side. I'm just listening to what you got to say is all.'

I just started talking again. 'Just coping with the trouble at home with Ward, I got mean as hell. I became the resident psycho at the high school. Kids who hated their parents said things like, "I should have done what you did, man. I should have just wasted my parents." And of course, I played along with their bullshit.

'I smoked a hell of lot of pot back then. It numbed me somehow, just hanging out in the burnout area out back of the dumpsters. I used to pretend I could hypnotize girls. I had it all down pat, the way of making them count backwards. Shit, I loved a goddamn audience. I used to scare the shit out of people, but that draws others to you. I used to take girls out to the Driver's Ed cars and fuck them, long before things like that were done in those parts. The general consensus was that I was a time bomb.

'I used to call myself "The Specimen", because that's what I pretty much was, a piece of emotional wreckage on which members of the medical community were building a career. Some put me under hypnosis during high school, and I consented. "You better not take advantage of me, you hear?" I used to say things like that to the good-looking women doctoral candidates in search of a thesis. There are goddamn chapters in dissertations about me. I checked one out at the Michigan State library once when I was traveling through East Lansing. That's the God's honest truth, Honey. Now, you see what you didn't know about me? I'm a text-book reference, Honey, in the medical literature of selective amnesia.'

'Frank, you're too hard on yourself.'

I said, 'Maybe so, but since I'm just about finished, I might as well finish it out now that you got me talking. I ended up in all the retard classes, mostly because of the pot, but also because I never did the goddamn homework. I got some good scores in Honors Math my Freshman year, in algebra, but to get credit, you had to show on paper all the steps you did to get the answer. And so the answer wasn't really worth shit. It was proving how you got the answer that got most of the credit, and that pretty much pissed me off. I used to figure things in my head and come up with the answer. I mean, right is goddamn right, but that didn't sit in math class, so I got bumped into retard math, because I was obstinate. Okay, to tell the truth, I hit the goddamn teacher, if the truth be known.'

'Jesus, Frank.'

'Let me just finish this out . . . I was in Honors English, too, but survived that, because this teacher said I had a vague sense of tragedy. Being a screw-up was a prerequisite for Honors English. This teacher I had, Mrs Deluca, said all literature centered on tragedy, whatever the hell that meant, but I had what it took. We read a lot of shit about depressed assholes who neither loved nor believed in anything. They were called Nihilists. In four years of Honors English, I read it all, Honey. I'm probably the most educated asshole that ever flipped a burger. I read it all, the great works, *The Scarlet Letter*, *The Great Gatsby*, and some Hemingway, *The Old Man and the Sea*, which was supposed to be all about the "resilience of human life", or that's what it said on the book jacket anyway, and so I wrote a paper called, "Let's Just Catch the Goddamn

Fish", and, this kills me, Mrs Deluca wrote on my paper that I was "a pragmatist in a godless world". I still remember those words. I'd been hoping to get my ass kicked out of Honors English, but I lasted all four years.

'So you can pretty much see the sort of bullshit that trapped me, right? I can't say that I didn't see this shit coming to a dead end, that there were no life lessons being learned. I put down on a vocational career handout late Sophomore year, "Hotel Management", which got me into home economics, which is where the chicks were. It was like letting a fox into a henhouse, but thank God for that, because a skilled trade was the only real thing I ever took from high school.'

Honey smiled. 'I'd like to have seen you in high school. I bet you were real cute. Did you get to wear an apron in home economics?'

'Sure I did, Honey. If that's what you want to believe, go ahead. I walked around the goddamn school in an apron with a mixing bowl and a wooden spoon.'

'Jesus, you must have been a sight.'

I was laughing despite myself. Honey had that way of deflating a situation when she wanted, and I let it go. I don't think I got what I wanted to say said right. I said, 'We should do this more often, Honey.'

'You mean steal cars and hang out at hotels?'

'Sure, whatever it takes to keep a marriage alive.' We held each other like teenagers. Somehow the embers of what had originally brought us together had flamed again, out here on the road away from all the bullshit. I felt Honey's big leg on my waist. She trailed her fingers across my cheek.

I let the silence settle for a time between us. Then I said, 'Jesus H. Christ, when I think of the years I wasted.' I was silent for a few moments. 'That's all of it, Honey, end of story. What all that did for me was put me in dead end jobs, mostly, but it did get me out of dying in Vietnam, because of the mental condition I had, which was something I'm grateful for, really. I suppose any sort of living is preferable to dying when it comes right down to it.'

'Hey, at least you had an excuse. What can I say for myself.' She was half-smiling at me. 'It's over, right?' She kept smiling and touching my face. 'I ever tell you I was all-state in bowling?'

I whispered, 'No.'

'Yeah, I had to give up the bowling on account of typing.' Honey could see that look in my eyes, so she cut it short. 'Maybe I'll save that story. It's getting kind of late. Let's get them in out of the pool and eat.' Honey kissed me on the forehead. 'I know you're good inside, Frank.' She had eased somehow from New Jersey, even in this short time.

I said, 'I know this is a long way to go about figuring if that farm is mine, but things like wills go missing from lawyers' offices, and the best thing you can do is do things yourself, right? Snoop around and check the court records and such. There's no way in hell that I can just be left out in the cold. That's not the way the law works. I just want you to know that if I didn't think we were getting something, I wouldn't have dragged us way the hell up here. You understand that, Honey?'

Honey pushed herself close to me. 'I know it was no life back there in New Jersey. I'm no fool. You think I wanted our kids to grow up like they were? Frank, you may think you dragged me away, but I got a mind of my own. I saw the handwriting on the wall, just like you did.' Honey moved the long rope of her hair to the side of her head, and said, 'The life was literally being sucked out of me.'

Honey drew me up on her big body once again, and, beyond the membrane of glass and curtain that hid us, the world screamed with the voices of children waiting at the edge of destiny to come into being. Or maybe it was just those kids in the pool.

Chapter 5

We went down to the Holiday Inn lounge. Robert Lee and Ernie stayed in their swim trunks and wore tee-shirts. It was a dry heat in the hotel. The carpet was that high shag, industrial orange. Robert Lee dragged his feet along the carpet, then touched Honey and shocked her, and she jumped from his touch, then Ernie did the same to me. It was like a game, all of us playing tag, shocking each other.

The restaurant was like a crimson cave, like something I'd seen in that movie, *Looking for Mr Goodbar*. Honey even let herself be weighed. Inside they served complimentary warm peanuts in their shells that you were supposed to just throw on the floor when you were finished. Refills on beverages were complimentary, too, and there was an all-you-can-eat salad bar, along with an ice cream bar where you could create your own sundae.

A guy playing guitar took requests, and Honey and I danced, and Robert Lee heckled us and shouted, 'Shit, Frank, you got two left feet.'

At night's end I left Honey and said I was going to pick up a wire from a Western Union and ditch the car. I said, 'I figure I might be able to get us a car with the money I get, and we might just stay another night. I mean, they're not going to be burying Ward any time soon.'

'I could live like this for ever,' Honey whispered. 'I feel like I was made to lie on my back and make babies. I know that might not be the thing women are supposed to want these

54

days, but it's what I feel inside me. It's what I was put on this earth to do.' Her breath smelt of fried chicken and Diet Pepsi.

Outside, life moved on the conveyor belt of the highway as I shimmied a wire hanger through a window on a station wagon filled with luggage and kids' coloring books. There was no smell of animals, namely a dog, so I went and got Juniper out of the Cadillac and set him in the station wagon. I got his litter box and food and his mouse toy and set them in with him. I wrote in sloppy kid writing – *This is Juniper. My Daddy has no money. He likes milk.* Juniper was giving me that suspicious cat look.

I said, 'Come on, now, Juniper, this family is going to take a hell of a lot better care of you than we ever could. You're going to be thanking me in years to come. You mightn't believe that now, but you will. You don't know the first thing about family values, that's your problem, but once you do, you're going to thank me for this. This is a good career move for you, Juniper.'

Juniper licked my hand with his coarse tongue. I messed with his mouse and then threw it among the suitcases, and that got his back turned. It's hard to walk away from somebody who's staring at you, even a cat.

Walking away, I was thinking, what if you could put your kid into someone else's car, I mean, find some luxurious car, and just put your kid in it with a note? If you knew the kid was going to have a better life, would you do it?

I drove the Cadillac into a pond off on a side road, down by a rutted field of blackened corn stalks. I could see a town in the near distance. My breath smoked in the coldness of the night. I headed for the town, toward its shivering halo of light.

Main Street was like all those sets of B-movies in near-deserted small towns where the aqua lights of small retail stores glow against the unsettling quiet, where everything looks flat and two-dimensional.

But at the end of the town, a neon cherry flashed on a martini glass that tipped back and forth on the sign outside a bar called The Well. 'Happy Hour All Night Long' is what it said on the door, but nobody looked happy inside. The bar glowed a hazy crimson and smelled of insomnia and bitter-sweet love. It was half crowded with couples locked in those life conversations bars seem to elicit. The rest were mainly men bellied up to the counter, drinking, though there were some women by themselves smoking at tables. A poker machine flickered in the dark along a corridor leading to the toilets.

I took a shot of whiskey and chased it with an Old Milwaukee. My insides were warm. A guy down the bar from me said to the bartender, 'I just want to know how come we choose from just two people for President and fifty for Miss America?'

I followed with the same order again, and then the same yet again. My money was pushed forward on the counter, two piles, the tip and my change.

The bar had been festooned with small flags from a beer company. A plastic sign gave the illusion of a stream pearling down a waterfall, and a string of Christmas lights flashed in an alcove of hard liquor. A sign above the cash register read, 'If you are drinking to forget, please pay in advance.' Another sign read, 'Life is sexually transmitted.'

Three guys stood over a pool table in the stark aura of a hanging light, looking like sinister doctors about to make an incision on an unseen patient. I closed my eyes and listened to the click of balls, heard the rumbling thunder of pocketed balls traveling the dark gutter of the table.

It was hot and smoky. The alcohol made my face shine. I could feel my heart inside my shirt. I watched a guy in his early fifties drinking alone. The part of his hair was like a scar running along the right side of his head. His tongue showed after each drink. He coughed into his closed fist, and his eyes filled with watery tears which he wiped with the palms of his hands.

The bartender said, 'Same again, Melvin?'

He nodded, 'Yeah.'

I watched him take his wallet out and lay down a damp, dirty twenty, what they called farm money.

I drifted over to where the guys playing pool were talking earnestly, using their pool cues like extensions of their bodies, like antennae pointing at this and that shot. A drunk woman hung like a cheap coat off the shoulder of a guy called Lawrence who was eyeing up a shot. She passed her cigarette from her lips to his.

Another guy sat close with his girlfriend at a small table crowded with empties. They were arguing. The guy said real loud, 'Yeah, women may be able to fake orgasms, but men can fake whole relationships.' That got a cheer from a shadowy crowd of men lining the walls.

The woman went to slap the guy's face, but he caught her hand.

I felt outside my body, disembodied from everything. I guess I was preparing for something terrible.

I sat with a woman called Lonnie who was loaded. She shook my hand like a slot machine. She wanted me to buy her a shot of schnapps because it was her birthday, or so she said anyway. It looked like she'd had a long line of birthdays. She was watching the fight over in the corner. She said to me, 'No husband has ever been shot while doing the dishes, that's a fact.' She smiled when she said that, and touched the back of my hands with her long nails. I looked for a ring on her finger, but there was none. There was a story there somewhere, I figured.

We wove our arms together and drank from one another's glass. She thought that made a party, doing it like that. Up close, her eyelashes looked like long spider legs. I whispered, 'You see that guy there at the bar? Do you know him, Lonnie?'

She went like she was going to get up to look at him, but I took her by the arm, and she stayed and nodded. I said, 'I think I know him from someplace, but I don't want to make a fool of myself if it's not him.' I smiled when I said that. Lonnie leaned toward me with drunk familiarity and cupped her hand over her mouth, and whispered, 'Melvin Johnson is his name. Lives out on Deer Creek Road by himself. Got cancer in his lungs.' She seemed like she was thinking of something else to say, and I said, 'That could be him all right. He got a wife?' Lonnie looked at me strange. 'Carol Ann Hackshaw, but she died on him five years back or so with breast cancer.'

Lonnie seemed like she got suspicious for a moment, but then just raked her hand through her hair and suddenly smiled and said, 'In case you miss my birthday next year, you want to buy me another one?' I ordered two more drinks.

I wanted to know if Melvin had kids, but there was no way to ask that question. Lonnie got to telling me about this lost love of her life, some guy who was already married but who loved her, but also loved his kids dearly. He had a big heart is what his problem was. He just couldn't bring himself to hurt people. 'He loves too much. I can't hate a man for that, can I?'

Right after that I bought her a birthday drink for the year after next. The whole time I sat there with Lonnie I was watching Melvin.

I went to leave her, but she got huffy. I sat again only because I didn't want trouble. We wove our arms together again and drank from one another's schnapps. I left her shortly after that.

Outside, the sweat on my body cooled instantly. A moon glowed against passing clouds. In the back parking lot, I put my fingers down my throat and made myself vomit.

And then there he was, Melvin, a slouching figure in overalls and a flannel jacket. I watched him brace against the cold. His cough was deep and troubled. He spat into the night and moved toward his car. And when he had the key out and in the lock, I came out from the shadows, and suddenly everything centered in my index finger. I pressed it deep into his back and took him by the arm with my other hand, and said, 'If you confess, "Jesus is Lord", and believe in your heart that God has raised Him from the dead, you will be saved, Melvin.'

I felt him tremble against the point of my finger. I had him pressed against the car. I put my mouth close to his ear and repeated what I'd said.

His voice croaked a little. 'Jesus is Lord.'

I opened the front door of his car and got him into the driver's seat, then opened the back door and got in. I had my finger in the hollow at the base of his skull. We sat in the dark. A dog barked out beyond the town, and another dog answered across the distance.

Melvin had settled himself somewhat. I wasn't sure what I was going to do right then. I was on a high wire without a net.

Melvin said quietly, 'I never knew the Lord to do his bidding with liquor on his breath.'

That sort of juiced me, like he was going to do something crazy, like he knew I had no gun. I said, 'That so, Melvin, Mr Goddamn-Know-it-All? You ever read about how Jesus turned water into goddamn wine at a wedding? Well, did you, Melvin?' I pushed my finger deep into the hollow of his neck.

He said, 'Yes.'

I stopped for a moment, let things catch up with me. I whispered, 'Jesus Christ could take the cancer from your lungs if you had faith in him. Do you believe in the power of personal salvation, Melvin?'

Melvin said nothing. The night settled around us. I felt his shoulders sag. His head moved perceptibly, like he wanted to see my face. Then he coughed, so I let him cough but kept my finger at the base of his skull until he quieted, then I whispered, 'Faith is the substance of things hoped for, the

59

evidence of things not seen. It is all Jesus has ever asked of mankind. Do you have faith, Melvin? Do you believe in a second coming?'

He didn't answer.

I had my face almost to his ear. 'Earth is the insane asylum for the universe, do you know that, Melvin?' I took a deep breath. 'Drive down that alley.'

Melvin drove slowly against the backs of stores. I could hear the tires eating gravel.

I said, 'I'm going to level with you, Melvin. Things have gone to hell. I mean, they have really gone to hell here on Earth. We are losing the battle with Satan. We're going door-to-door like goddamn vacuum salesmen recruiting souls. It's come to that. I'm pleading for your soul, Melvin. That's why I am here, honest to God.'

I could see Melvin's eyes trying to make out my face in the rear view mirror, but it was dark.

I said, 'Once upon a time, you could beset a man with sickness and disease and have that man come through for you, but it isn't every day you run into a guy like Job. Or how about Abraham, and the way he tied up his only son on an altar for sacrifice, all because God told him to. Now those were the glory days, my friend. God said, "Jump!" and the faithful said, "How high, Lord?" '

Then I stopped and said, 'Yes, Lord,' and tapped Melvin with the hand that wasn't pretending to be the gun, and said, ' "Deer Creek Road", is what the Lord is saying, Melvin. You know what he means, Melvin?'

Melvin said, 'It's where I live.'

We drove off main street for the dark of a country road. I turned and looked back down. I could see the highway running against the night, and the railway track running alongside. And further back, the green neon of the Holiday Inn sign, and that pained me. The alcohol in my body just died right then and there. My body got cold. I said, 'I'm on commission, Melvin. That's how Heaven works these days. I got to bring in the goods or I'm screwed. There are no free rides, no base salary or nothing.'

I got serious again. I said, 'By the way, Carol Ann sends her love.' I said that matter-of-factly.

I felt Melvin ease off the gas. I said, 'Don't turn around, Melvin, just don't.'

He just nodded.

'Melvin, I'm going to put some questions to you, and I want you to answer me honestly, you hear me?'

Melvin said, 'Yes, Lord,' and that about blew me away. I said, 'I hope you mean that, Melvin, because the inevitable outcome of what passes between us has been preordained, and, if you die at my hand, it is not I, but God Almighty, who has pulled the trigger. I'm not beyond facing my destiny or doing the will of God, even if it means spilling your brains all over the front seat of this car, you hear that, Melvin? Religion has always been about life and death. It's that simple.'

I felt the car pull on the steep rise. A solitary light glowed in the distance along a track of darkness.

I said, 'Okay, then, which would you prefer to be, morally bankrupt or financially bankrupt?'

Melvin said, 'Financially bankrupt.'

I pinched the fat of his neck and the car slowed. 'That's a lie, and you know it. Goddamn it, I'm trying to gather customer feedback for Heaven on the current state of Christianity, and you give me this claptrap bullshit for an answer. So I'm going to ask you one more time. Which would you prefer to be, morally bankrupt or financially bankrupt?'

'Morally bankrupt.'

'That's more like it. I don't want you skewing the survey with what you think I want to hear. You have free will, Melvin. Use it. That's the governing principle of our Faith, goddamn free will.' We got closer to the light in the distance.

I said, 'I'm going to let you in on a little secret. People are not having so much of an "out-of-body experience" anymore as they are an "out-of-money experience", so up in Heaven they're discussing a second coming, where the Son of Man doesn't take on the sins of the world, like he did the first time, but instead takes on the mortgage payments of the world. What do you think of that for a pitch? God loves the world so much that he is giving his only beloved Son to take on the mortgage payments of the world, and in whose *debt* we will be redeemed.'

Melvin said flatly, 'I think it's a winner. It gets to the heart of Christian failing. Money! I think that's something people will follow.'

I hit the back of his seat rest. I said, 'A winner! Jesus H. Christ, you want to bankrupt the entire economy? Let's be realistic here. That's goddamn communism by any other name, giving people something for nothing like that. Are you out of your cotton-pickin' mind, you damn communist?'

Melvin tried to turn, but I touched his head.

'If you think the money lenders in the temple back in the Old Testament were pissed off, this would blow their tops. No. What's on the table is Heaven gives terms of a fixed rate over twenty years at, say, 5.6% interest. You think people would still be interested?'

Melvin kept driving, but he said, 'How much down?'

I sort of realized right then that this was the dumbest son-of-a-bitch in the world, or I'd been had real bad, and if I was holding the goddamn gun which was really my goddamn finger right then, I would have surely killed Melvin, because I felt I didn't know what was up and what was down. But all I said was, 'Just for that, I don't know if Jesus is going to cure your cancer. You're an asshole who deserves whatever befalls him.'

He tried to say something, but I said, 'I don't want to hear it.'

Melvin said softly, 'Jesus is Lord.'

We drove in silence. It looked for all the world like Jesus Christ might be in the house when the car stopped, the solitary light burned so against the dark.

In the house, I tied Melvin up good in the basement and blindfolded him. The basement was half converted into a TV room, with a coffee table and a big old-fashioned television set. There was an issue of *Reader's Digest* open on the table. Melvin had been playing solitaire, the cards spread in suits in descending order.

I said, 'First order of business. You got pornography here, I can smell it.'

Melvin confessed, and I went and fished around in a closet in his bedroom, and came back to the basement with a brown bag of magazines. I said, 'You like women with big tits?'

He nodded.

'I mean melons! Jesus, Melvin.'

Second thing I said was, 'You got money buried here. I'm going to ask you only once,' and that was all I had to ask him. I got over five thousand dollars in five rolls of dirty fifties and twenties from a strongbox hidden under a work bench. The figure was scrawled on a piece of paper that served as a ledger, and I could see the dates and amounts written when Melvin had added the money.

I said, 'I know there's more, Melvin, but I am a reasonable man.' I touched his back and said, 'You are delivered in the eyes of Jesus. He has sent me as intercessor and forgiver. Through him, all things are forgiven.'

Melvin flinched and said, 'Amen.' He was curled into the fetal position. Only his mouth was visible.

I said, 'I've got a survey here that I'm supposed to have you fill out that says you have done this of your own free will, but we'll dispense with that, if that's okay with you? I think, if a man has to be bound by more than his word, by some legal mumbo-jumbo, then things are in a sad state of affairs. Love, not fear, is the governing principle of a civilized and spiritual society.'

Melvin said, 'Amen,' and that killed me.

I said, 'Amen', right back at him.

That pretty much settled things. I had run out of things to say. I turned on the television. Angie Dickinson from *Police Woman* was drinking a cocktail in some sleazy bar with a guy in a leather jacket. It was a rerun I'd seen back in New Jersey. I turned up the volume and sat in Melvin's La-Z-Boy. I said, 'I could get used to this, Melvin. Whatever you think about your life, it's something special. You hear me?' I felt guilty somehow.

Melvin nodded his head.

I stayed quiet a long time. I went upstairs and poured a glass of cold milk. I shouted, 'You got chocolate powder, Melvin?'

I guess I was waiting for the end of *Police Woman*. I said, to break the tension, 'You ever watch *Police Woman*, Melvin?'

'I seen this one twice already.'

I said, 'I think reruns are fast becoming like bedtime stories. Like children, we want to hear and see the same things over and over again. We want to know the end. We want that certainty. You can drift into sleep with the foreknowledge of how things end.'

Melvin said, 'I guess you got a point when you put it like that. Carol Ann and I never did have children, none that is that ever got born. But we got them baptized here in the house when they came out. That counts against Limbo, right?'

I said, 'Limbo was officially shut down. Day care at Limbo was just a bitch. Same as here, it's hard to get good day care.'

Things hurt inside me. I didn't exactly take satisfaction in doing all this to Melvin, making him relive these memories. It reminded me of what was done to me as a kid, that goddamn hypnosis, people playing with my mind.

I sat quietly and tasted the chocolate milk. It tasted sweet like something I used to drink growing up with my uncle. I realized that this house was not unlike what I'd been used to all my life. That was a weird feeling right then. The musky mouse smell of the basement, the washer and dryer crouched in the corner, all of it, the tonal browns of the dated fifties furniture.

I looked at poor old Melvin, all tied up, and I thought to myself, we could have been friends, or neighbors, under different circumstances. Sitting there in Melvin's La-Z-Boy, I felt strangely content, like this destiny had been set out for me a long time ago, but somehow I got derailed in life. I said, 'Where did it all go wrong?'

Melvin's body shifted, so he was listening. I said, 'Where did it all go, the America of our founding fathers, as much saints as politicians: "Honest Abe" and George Washington, who "could not tell a lie", Johnny Appleseed and Paul Bunyan? How come it changed so, Melvin, so now all we hear of are the psychos: Charles Manson, Richard Speck?'

'The Devil,' Melvin said quietly.

'Maybe that's another word for progress. I just don't know.'

On the television, Angie was firing at a guy in a warehouse. He was the guy Angie had been drinking cocktails with at the bar. Angie shot him, then she went up to him in his dying moments. I could see her cleavage against the guy's face. I could tell she'd been between the sheets with him. He took her hand and said something to her about betrayal and love. Angie looked sad, with tears in her eyes that made her beautiful and haggard all at the same time. I said softly, 'Angie, my patron saint of losers.' But she just turned her back on me and the dead guy and walked away against a backdrop of crimson credits.

I said, 'The world has become a depraved and beautiful place, Melvin.' I took his bag of pornography and said, 'We are all entitled to one vice.' I said, 'What do you think about when you look at these women?'

'My wife.'

I said, 'She died of breast cancer.'

Melvin sort of choked and writhed to turn away from me.

I got low to his ear and said, 'That isn't any sin in the eyes of God. I want you to keep thinking of Carol Ann, you hear me?'

I went and put the magazines back where I found them. In a box in the closet, there was a photograph of Melvin and his wife standing before the carved relief of the presidents at Mount Rushmore. In the corner, the date read 1953.

I got him a pillow from upstairs and set his head on it. I was going to put a sock in his mouth, but I didn't.

I said, 'You want me to leave that television on?'

Melvin said, 'The radio, maybe. Television makes that whistle noise when it goes off the air.'

I said, 'That is one of the saddest sounds you can wake up to in darkness. It's like the end of the world.'

Melvin said, 'I hate to trouble you so, but I got to go bad.'

In the cold dark of the basement toilet I kept my finger against his spine. He went in dribs and drabs. 'Prostate,' he said softly. 'I don't get a night that I don't get up.'

I said, 'Maybe we can have an all-inclusive miracle here tonight.' There was no irony in my voice or anything. We were two men in the small confines of a toilet, me with a pretend gun in his back, and somehow it felt safe here. I maybe believed right then that if you thought hard enough about things you could make them so. I focused on that feeling, what I heard them call in religious circles a 'leap of faith.' Melvin had made that leap somewhere in our little chat. I wanted to help this man I was robbing. I tried that mind stuff again, concentrated on the sickness inside him. I said, 'Carol Ann is thinking about that time you and her were out at Mount Rushmore. She wants to know if that was 1953 or 1954.'

Melvin leaned against the toilet wall and sobbed, '1954.'

I felt I might have just gone too far right then. I said, 'Come on now, Melvin. This is nearly over, you hear me? Salvation. Carol Ann and your babies love you. There is no real loneliness. We are watched by the eyes of the dead. They watch over us.'

I tied Melvin's hands again and set him down on the floor. I laid my hand on his back again. 'Coincidence is when God works a miracle and chooses to remain anonymous. Do you understand that, Melvin?'

Then I said, 'And I saw the dead, small and great, stand before God; and the books were opened, and another book was opened, which is the book of life, and the dead were judged out of those things which were written in the books, according to their works.'

I tuned the radio to the late-night news. I got up then and said, 'You were saved by the power of your own faith. Jesus has many faces. He walks and lives among the righteous and the damned. You were chosen.' I made the sign of the cross on his forehead. I said, '1953, Melvin, not 1954.'

Melvin said, 'That's right, 1953.' I saw his body tense and his mouth open, but I couldn't see his eyes, though I knew he was crying inside.

'I'm going to untie you, but what I want you to do is to sit here with your eyes closed and count back from one thousand. That's how it works. You got free will in all this. I can't stop you from doing anything you want to do. God does not subjugate his followers. But like Lot's wife, I hope you don't look back. That's all I ask. Don't open your eyes, Melvin. Don't look upon me.'

I sat in Melvin's car and counted to one hundred. I had my eyes closed. I half expected him to be there with a gun to my head, to drag me from the car, and I wouldn't have resisted, but when I got to one hundred there was no sign of him. Maybe I knew that all along.

I drove Melvin's car down the hill. I felt filled with something that seemed like what preachers call the Holy Spirit. 'Hallelujah!' It just erupted out of me. At the bar, things were still hopping, but I didn't go in. From a payphone in the parking lot, I phoned Honey.

She said, 'Did you get the money wire from your brother?'

I said, 'Order whatever the hell you want off the menu. Get room service if you want, anything you want!'

And in the early hours of the morning, far down the highway at some non-descript town, I abandoned Melvin's car. I walked into a car lot and bought a rusting green station wagon with fake wooden paneling.

Along the county road leading back to the highway, I got stuck behind a school bus. Its yellow flashing lights blinked as it stopped and picked up some kids. They emerged like little toy soldiers from those miniature roadside sheds country people build at the end of long driveways to protect their kids waiting in the cold for the school bus. The kids in the back of the bus gave me the finger. One kid felt obliged to moon me, his white ass pressed against the misty glass.

It was snowing lightly when I got out onto the highway. Driving back to the Holiday Inn, I could see the northern sky in the rear view mirror, like a dark mass of grey matter, like some monstrous subconscious.

Chapter 6

It was going on eleven o'clock in the morning when I got back to the Holiday Inn. I walked slowly down the corridor. I heard the ice machine hum. At that moment it seemed like the sound of the universe.

I moved toward the glass enclosure of the pool. I saw Robert Lee sitting near a vending machine. He was leaning over with a sick look on his face. His mouth was smudged with chocolate. There were wrappers everywhere. I could tell Honey had given him the keys to the kingdom of vending. He looked up and tried to smile despite the pain inside him. He said, 'Frank, how come things taste so good when they're free?'

I said, 'Now you know the plight of Adam, of paradise.'

'Frank, just shut the fuck up . . .'

I felt his body's weight against mine. He didn't resist. I took him gently by the arm and led him across the pool area. He smelt of chlorine and his hands were withered in that way skin gets when it's been submerged too long in water. I could tell he hadn't been to bed all night.

The glass sliding door to our room was open, but the curtains were pulled halfway closed. Ernie was sitting just inside the room with his dinosaurs lined up against the glass. He smiled when he saw me and said, 'Hi, Frank!'

I kissed the top of his head.

In the room, Honey was watching HBO. She said, 'Don't worry, it's free.'

Robert Lee let himself collapse on the rollaway bed, holding his stomach. He said, 'I'm going to die is what I'm going to do.'

I went into the bathroom. Honey got up and followed me. 'Everything all right?'

I took out the roll of bills and gave them to her. She got scared just looking at the amount. 'This didn't come from Western Union. Look at it . . . Jesus, you didn't do anything you're going to regret, did you? You didn't . . . didn't kill nobody, did you?'

I just shook my head. I felt calm for the first time in a long while. I said, 'Life is not so much a matter of holding good cards, but playing a poor hand well.' I truly believed that.

Honey counted the money. She said, 'Jesus Christ, there's over four and a half thousand dollars here! What did you do, rob a bank?'

I felt like this was the longest day in the history of mankind. I took off my shirt, and then my shoes and socks, and then my pants, and then I went out and dove into the deep end of the pool, and it felt like baptism.

The truth was I could have turned away from going to Michigan right then. I had enough money to take us at least back to New Jersey or out to California. There was free will involved for once.

I came back from the pool, and Robert Lee was praying to the porcelain God, heaving up all that candy.

The television flickered and glowed in the grey oblong of our room. The heating system had kicked in, a dry static heat. The chlorine from the pool had made my skin tight. I felt smaller somehow, shrunken.

'Did you tell them we're staying again tonight?'

Honey said, 'I didn't know if . . .'

'Call reception. We need clean towels and sheets. I want the room made up if I'm going to hand over *good* money.'

'Frank, please.'

70

I said flatly, 'I got within a hair's breadth of killing a man last night.'

Honey hesitated, and her face got pale. She swallowed, her head moving slightly, 'You hit him or something? Is that what you did?' I could feel her slowly eating away at the truth. 'You told me you didn't kill anybody.' Her hand squeezed around my arm. 'Frank . . . This guy you got the money off isn't going to come after us, is he? You think we should just leave now?'

For a moment I wanted to experience what it must have been like with her and Ken; maybe there was a moment when he came home that night after killing those people when she sensed something. I said, 'Did Ken ever tell you what it felt like to be out there on the road waiting on people to rob?'

'Frank, *stop* this right now. You're scaring me!'

I said, 'What if I killed somebody, Honey?'

'Frank, don't do this to me . . . Hold me close. Hold me.'

I said, 'Nobody's dead, you hear me.'

Honey's face was white. 'Why do men feel like they have to test women?'

Robert Lee came out and fell flat on the rollout bed with exaggerated effect and Honey just turned away from me and went out into the glare of the pool.

I slept the early afternoon away and awoke to the sound of the TV. *Kung Fu*, the series with David Carradine, was on. It was the beginning of a dream sequence. Kung Fu was his former self, the juvenile monk Grasshopper. His blind master was there with those white golf ball eyes teaching him a thing or two about life. Grasshopper had walked across rice paper, but when he looked back, he'd failed the test, because there were footprints in the rice paper. The blind master was saying something about life, and then he walked and left no footprints. The dream ended in that waviness they used to distinguish past and present on *Kung Fu*. I sure as hell loved the way the master was able to make a religion out of ass-kicking. Back in the real world, a girl whom Kung Fu had been helping was rough-handled by one of the men in the saloon, and that just did it for Kung Fu, and then it started, what you wait for in *Kung Fu*, that stylized slow-motion action of scissors and roundhouse kicks, and bodies were pummeled. After the commercial break, I watched Kung Fu say goodbye to the woman he'd saved and head off over a sand dune, a lonesome soul drifting through life. I guess he had a gift that he couldn't control, but maybe that was his true humanity.

At the back of my mind I kept thinking that maybe I shouldn't go on up north, that I had this money now, like a gift bestowed on me. Having a car we owned made a huge difference. It legitimized us. I could feel my head nodding as *Batman* started.

Honey came into the room and closed the glass sliding door.

I said, 'Maybe you want to fly down to Georgia now that we have money. I mean both you and Robert Lee . . .'

Honey sat heavily on the bed. 'Don't start into me right now, Frank.'

'I'm not starting into you. I'm giving you an opportunity to re-evaluate your life.'

'Are you saying this for your benefit or mine?'

'I want to lay things out, is all. You know there isn't going to be any easy way to swing things with this will. I might as well level with you. Norman and his wife are going to fight me to the end. I've had a few hell-raising phone fights with them since all this started . . .' I took a long breath. 'Maybe you can move in with your sister, just get some sun and take stock of life.'

'Take stock of life. I know what my life is! Are you trying to say you want out, is that it?'

I said, 'I'll tell you what, I'm just going to leave the keys of the car in this drawer, right next to this Bible here, and I'm putting two thousand dollars in there. In the course of tonight, if you feel like you want to leave, do. I'm going to leave a phone number where I can be reached if you want to speak to me again.'

Honey said nothing and just shook her head.

I said, 'This isn't a test, Honey. I'm going home for my own selfish reasons. I'm going back out of *curiosity*, if you really want to know the truth. I won't say I knew that when we started out, but that's why I'm going back now.'

Honey raked her hand through her hair. 'I guess you can live cheap up there, right, Frank? If it takes some time for things to sort themselves out, that's okay by me. One way or another it has to end. You have to get what's yours, right, Frank?'

Honey got into bed beside me and I felt the carnal presence of what had drawn me to her as her arm came across my bare chest. She said, 'Hold me, just hold me.'

Just then Batman and Robin jumped into the bat-mobile and a cave opened and they sped off toward Gotham City. I said, 'Why do all crime fighters have to wear tights?'

Honey put her hand over my mouth and said, 'Shush.'

Toward the end, Robert Lee came through the door, and the roar of the pool filled the room, and I froze on top of Honey. 'Don't turn on that light, Robert Lee,' Honey said quietly. 'Just don't.'

I heard Robert Lee hesitate, then go out again and say, 'They're in there making the two-backed beast.' Then I heard this huge splash, and the window was showered in water.

We ate again down at the Holiday Inn restaurant, open faced sandwiches with thick cuts of turkey ladled with gravy and mashed potato. An old couple were celebrating a wedding anniversary, and when the guy with the guitar made the announcement we had to get up and toast this little old couple as they waltzed under a disco ball. It was a fiftieth anniversary. The guy playing guitar said they had seven kids, thirty-eight grandkids, and nine great-grandkids.

I was getting drunk fast on imported dark German beer. I said, 'What they need to come up with is a Divorce Ceremony, maybe a party where you buy a set of golden handcuffs which are opened with a symbolic key when you get divorced.'

'Frank . . .'

I leaned back in my chair and put my hands behind my head. 'Hey, if I told you I wanted to take your newborn baby and throw water over its head, would you think that would have caught on?'

Ernie smiled and kicked his small legs like he did when he got excited.

Robert Lee was also smiling, but when he saw me looking at him he said, 'I'm laughing at you, asshole, not with you . . .'

At the end of dinner, Robert Lee and Ernie wanted to go off to the pool. Honey said, 'You watch Ernie, you hear, Robert Lee?'

We got up and went through a string of beads that separated the restaurant from the bar area. We had Long Island ice teas that took us away from our troubles, in the way only alcohol can do, and I told Honey how I got the money. I showed her my finger.

We spent the rest of the evening lounging around the pool and the hot tub.

A guy with prosthetic legs came out and sat by the pool and unhooked the plastic legs and went swimming. When he finished swimming he crawled out of the pool, and dragged his torso over to a table. He toweled his hair dry, and put on a terrycloth robe and just climbed up into the chair in a fluid movement and started reading a book. He didn't put back on his legs. They were still over by the edge of the pool. It was disconcerting just looking at them.

The guy said to Robert Lee, who was looking over at him, 'Hey kid, you mind doing me a favour, you mind getting me a beer from the bar?'

Robert Lee said, 'Sure thing.'

The guy's name was Phil. He had strong arms like a bodybuilder. Phil sold encyclopedias for a living. We found that out over a few pitchers of beer we shared by the pool. Phil charged it all to his room, to his *expense* account.

Phil was in his early thirties and good-looking, and if you didn't know better you wouldn't have thought he was a guy with no legs. He looked strong and healthy and had an optimistic view of life. You could just feel that about him. He laughed at everything in a most natural way, and we laughed along with him.

I looked down at what Phil had been reading, Dale Carnegie's *How to Win Friends and Influence People*.

Phil talked about encyclopedias with a genuine belief that they brought enlightenment. He said, 'Think about it, the composite of human knowledge in twenty volumes!' He spread his arms apart to show how big or small a dimension that was.

It sounded like a real good deal.

Robert Lee was enthralled by Phil, who winked at him from time to time, even as he spoke to us. Phil knew he was being watched. He arm-wrestled Robert Lee who used one, and then both hands, and still couldn't beat him. Ernie won, but you could tell Ernie wasn't so sure he'd really won. Phil held up Ernie's puny arm and said, 'Make a muscle, kid!' and Ernie smiled.

Phil had a way of talking quick and friendly. He dispensed a hell of a lot of information in a short period of time. He had four kids and a good looking wife who had three of those kids after he came home from Vietnam with his legs blown off. He showed us the photograph of her. They were high school sweethearts. Phil was wearing a gold necklace with a jagged half of a heart, and of course his wife was wearing the other half.

Honey said, 'There's your ceremony right there, Frank,' and

then she explained the joke to Phil, who said, 'I can see Frank is a thinking man.'

I felt diminished in his presence, but not because of anything Phil said. It was just me. There were worse horrors than being accused of burning down your own house.

We drank some more, and Robert Lee asked Phil how he lost his legs, and Honey said, 'You don't have to answer any of his questions, Phil.'

Phil just smiled, and told us how he lost his legs, how they got blown off him when he parachuted into the Vietnamese jungle. He had his legs amputated in the field without anesthetic. He said all he kept thinking of was his wife. He said of the six men they sent in to get him out, only two survived. He said, 'I'm one of the lucky ones!' and he said it like he meant it.

We ended up buying a set of encyclopedias from Phil before the night was out.

Chapter 7

The town from which I came, and for which I now aimed our station wagon, was described as an apparition by early settlers, a small outpost off on one of those long dark tributaries of backwater that inhabit the northern frontier of America. It's so far north winter's breath holds life in abeyance for nearly eight months of the year. It is a town that exists between America and Canada, inhospitable and dreary in what I've always felt was a netherworld not compatible with human life or sanity. To hold onto anything up there takes savagery the likes of which only animals possess, and it's not such a good thing for men to act like beasts, to be pushed that far every day of their existence. But it's where we headed anyway, in the grip of a consuming silence that not even a pain in the ass like Robert Lee could break.

The car moved like a dark slug against the white hills, the snow coming down in a gauze. We stopped at some god-awful motel when visibility went down to almost zero. That's when Honey saw Juniper's litter box was gone. She said, 'you son-of-a-bitch,' when I tried to touch her in bed in the motel. But it passed, like all things pass. I said into her ear, 'I set him in a real nice car where the kids had coloring books and all, Honey. I got him a good place.' She still wouldn't speak to me.

It was still dark, but it was early morning when I awoke. I got out of bed. I let Honey and the kids sleep. Outside, snow was falling. I got dressed and went out and sat in a small diner connected to the motel.

The waitress came and poured me coffee and took my order. She had a nervous habit of incessantly clicking her ballpoint pen. I smiled at her, and she returned the smile. There was no menu, you just ordered what you wanted. Her name tag said her name was Janice. I said, 'Thank you, Janice,' after I gave my order.

A small town materialized as the snow abated. It felt like the previous days could have happened ten years ago, it felt that remote. I just had those stark images of Melvin in his basement, the way his face looked when I told him about his wife.

I burned my mouth on the coffee, but it felt good. I liked the simplicity of towns like this, the emptiness of a place not yet awake, the sense of hope and goodness that made us want to live out our lives in the company of others.

Janice had the radio on low. It was all news. I heard something about a storm up north. Then the story about the man who killed Ward came on the radio. It was big news this far up. And that was when I first heard Chester Green's father being interviewed, and the full impact of what I was getting myself into hit me.

I listened to Sam Green talk in a stammering manner about his son's name being implicated with the murder. His voice was forced, the words coming in a rush, then silence, and then another burst of words. He said he'd gone and seen the murderer at the hospital, that the man lying there wasn't his son. He shouted, 'My son is dead and buried!' His voice carried an accent of old Europe, a halting voice like a man not given to speaking much. And the truth was that, in his isolation on his farm, he very well might not have uttered a word for days or maybe weeks at a time. I felt his genuine bewilderment, and that made it all the more surreal.

I thought to myself, there has to be some photograph of

Chester Green to clear things up. And then I understood that there wasn't any photograph, that, in the days since Ward's murder, Sam Green would have produced a photograph of his son if he'd had one. It brought back the insularity and poverty of that time.

I just sat there. I think I hadn't really reconciled myself to the basic facts, to the idea that there was an investigation going on, that Ward was dead. I mean, I knew it and didn't at the same time.

I occupied myself by eating. I ate wheat toast slathered in butter, bacon and eggs, three pancakes, and a tall glass of cold milk. It all tasted good. Then I ordered more eggs, scrambled, and added hot sauce, and piled the egg onto the wheat bread and ate until I could eat no more, until my insides felt sore. And then Sam Green came on the radio again, the same piece they'd run before, and it sent a chill through me again. It was like he was there in the restaurant.

For a moment I had doubts about going any further. I could have abandoned everything right now, stayed away from Norman and Martha and let whatever the hell really happened up there just play itself out. I felt like maybe I was making a big mistake going back, walking into trouble like that. But that feeling lasted only a few seconds. Telling Honey we were changing plans wasn't a real option. I don't think I could have taken a fight right then.

I tried to picture Sam Green, and it was hard. Even though our farms were next to one another, in the years I had grown up with Ward I had seen Sam Green less than a dozen times, and often only from a distance, sometimes years apart, except for that one time when he came screaming to our door, when necessity drew him to us. He was a solitary figure, an anachronism even for such a backward place, a man without wife or son, a man of Protestant fundamentalist principles. Our histories, Sam Green's, and even our own family history, went back to the far North, to the days of fur trappers and explorers, to ancestors who had always shied away from humanity, who had set themselves against the dark interior of our continent. And now, looking back on things, I figure if someone had been asked to describe Ward, they would have painted him, and even Norman and I, in the same manner as Sam Green. We were what townspeople called *Outliers*.

I drank the dregs of my coffee, just thinking back on things. I remembered some nights seeing Sam Green's tractor out in his fields, watching that useless comet of light against the dark, hearing the howl of his dogs following him. I think he was demented by his own loneliness. We could see his house from our own, but somehow that proximity had borne not friendship, but suspicion and envy. Sometimes when Ward heard the tractor he used to say, 'There he is, driving over all of God's creation,' and just shake his head. He'd say, 'What I wouldn't give for that land, Norman.' He'd say that to Norman, sometimes taking Norman to the door so they could stare out toward Sam Green's land. I guess that was just Ward looking out for his son, wanting to make something bigger out of what we had, even though we struggled with what we had. Ward had a way of licking his lips when he wanted something. I thought of that right then, and that sudden image made me shiver.

Looking back on life, Sam Green and Ward had defined for me the sadness and remoteness of our ancestors. They were two hardened men, bound to their land. I thought again of Chester Green and that image of him on fire, burning like that prophetic bush in the story from the Bible, and somehow that was the phantasmagoria that fit. I thought back on us in New Jersey, me running out into the hallway screaming when Robert Lee was down with his own fever. At least I was amidst people. I had only to open the apartment door and scream for help, but what the hell was it like to be alone on a farm like that, without a wife, with a solitary son as your only link to humanity, to see your own son dying? Jesus Christ, it made me shiver, all of it, the sullen truth that there was no God watching over any of us. That's how I felt before it was all over, before I left.

Janice came and took my plate away. She filled my coffee cup, and then went and stood behind the counter and lit up. It was going on eight-thirty in the morning, but the town was dead. The light was still on in the diner.

There were only the two of us until an old man in overalls and a flannel jacket came in and said, 'God, it's cold,' shivering and blowing into his cupped hands. He ordered coffee and some apple strudel to go, but sat down at a table.

Outside, it started to snow again. The world felt small and compact. A snow truck came and sprinkled salt along the road outside, its orange light glowing against the falling snow. I knew it was going to get worse, lake-effect snow that could fall in a thick blanket all day long. During the worst of winters, snow started in October and went all the way into early May. I hugged my shoulders and shuddered. I yawned and put the hot coffee under my nose.

The radio station was one of those that repeated the same stuff every ten minutes. That was its sole purpose. Its catchphrase was 'News and Weather on the Tens.' The announcer began listing the schools in the local area that were closing for the day because of the snow. The story about my uncle came over the air again, and Sam Green was saying what he was going to say all day, like all of us were caught in a time warp.

I watched Janice wipe the counter down and look over at me. Then a cop came in, and two more men came and sat at a booth across from me.

It must have been the lack of sleep, or the proximity of what I knew was my inevitable destiny, because inside my head I was seeing that old image of myself and my uncle down at the Outreach Agricultural Facility. I closed my eyes and put my head down on the table. It felt cold against my face. The ebb of exhaustion felt like vertigo. I caught myself and opened my eyes, then closed them again.

The face of my uncle gathered inside my head, and there he was, the long face of defiance and fear, the pinpoints of his pupils staring at me across the cold light that separated us in the Agricultural Facility. His mouth opened, but there were no words. I drifted closer toward him until his utterances became audible. He was staring into an inkblot right then, telling a woman in a white coat what he saw. He said he saw me hiding in the inkblot. He looked up and saw me standing by his side. I stared down into the inkblot and felt a flushed heat behind my eyes, and there in the cloudy dark of the inkblot, I suddenly saw an incandescent blaze of light jumping against a dark night sky. I heard screaming coming from the flames. I could see shadows running against the flames. I began screaming. My uncle took me by the arm and pulled me close to him, pointing to the periphery of the inkblot. He said to the researcher, 'There he is, don't you see him, that worm, that fire starter! He's hiding there in the barn. "Come out of there, you dirty worm!" ' He grabbed me by the arm and shouted again . . .

'You asleep there?' I flinched and woke. Janice was standing over me with a pot of coffee.

I kept my head on the table and stared up at her, then I lifted my head. My mouth and cheek were wet. I wiped them with the palm of my hand. I said quietly, 'Sorry, I must have fallen asleep.'

Janice nodded. 'You okay?'

'Sure, just haven't slept much really.' I stared at the pale blue of her uniform, the white frill apron, the soft pouch of her stomach showing slightly. She was maybe somebody I would have pursued if I lived in a place like this.

I got up and went to the bathroom and washed my face with cold water. My eyes were bloodshot. I felt halfway to oblivion right then. The first hemorrhage of memory had opened up already inside me, or maybe it was just exhaustion, a matter of perception. Off to the periphery of my vision, my uncle lurked, whispering things. When I closed my eyes and pressed the palms of my hands against them, I could see stars. And even when I took my palms away from my eyes, I still felt something stirring inside my head. I splashed more water on my face. I shook my head like it was an Etch-o-Sketch, sifting away the images. But still, there on the edge of consciousness stood this other figure watching me.

Outside, I felt the cold curl around my ankles immediately. It was the beginning of a winter freeze, a time of surreal hibernation when the inhabitants of these parts fell into the torpor of an idleness and boredom that dated back eons. I shuddered at the memory of Ward and his goddamn farm, of that infinite silence and terror he maintained over me through the years.

Honey was dressed when I went into the room. She said, 'Where the hell did you go?' She had that look like she thought I might have abandoned her.

I said, 'I got something to eat.'

I gassed up in the cold morning light while Honey and Robert Lee and Ernie ate inside the diner.

We left in the snow, despite the weather report. Hours later I put down the back seat in the station wagon so it was one great bed, and Honey and Ernie got under the blankets we'd taken from the Holiday Inn. I drove further into a world where eventually even the radio only whistled and then died into static. We worked our way deep along cold impenetrable stretches of ancient forest that formed two banks of an abyss on either side of our car, a wedge of light opening up the immediate dark. We passed the solitary light at some cinderblock gas station like a tiny grotto, the ruby light of a Coca-Cola sign fizzling against absolute night. These were the bait shops for the tourists in summer, boarded up now, old world haunts lapping the edge of backwater tributaries and salmon runs, where they sold kerosene and wicks, cigarettes and can openers, woolen hats and gloves, homemade beef jerky. They kept dark cold cellars in summer with drawers full of silken earthworms and night crawlers that you bought by the shovelful.

Robert Lee sat up with me, a grim sentinel to what was unfolding, and I told him what I knew of the locality, circumscribed by the surrounding darkness. In the end, Robert Lee went over the back seat, like some marine into a trench, and got under the blankets with Honey and Ernie. They did what animals do up here. They lay low and quiet, and waited and ate the provisions we had packed.

I got out and put on the tire chains, and in the dark of night we moved slowly through sleeping, unincorporated towns, like some phantom ghost rattling its fetters. I felt the change come over me, my past life opening up again. For me, the subconscious had always been a real place, not just some nondescript darkness, but that vegetative Michigan darkness, an inner darkness of shadowy meandering tributaries that led nowhere, a place where men disappeared for ever, where there was no history, just a limbo world of things half forgotten or half remembered.

Chapter 8

We arrived finally on the outskirts of my town. We passed mobile homes set up on blocks with those second-rate beaters parked outside, a Trans Am or pickup, usually more than three cars in various states of immobility, and a snowmobile parked on a slope of snow. Yellow dirty light glowed in each trailer, until the more formidable houses that had formed the basis of the town emerged.

What was hard to believe was how the people clung to the town. There was a ferocity here like you wouldn't find in cities. After the attrition of the smartest, who left for major colleges, what remained was the tyranny of the deprived, almost a complicit acknowledgement that this was the end of the line, that this was the last refuge of the ignorant. It made these people at once simple and desperate, and that was one of the worst combinations of self-awareness you could get.

Already I felt that guarded insularity, that conservatism that comes of a people who have been abandoned in a time warp, who have not had the will to leave, to seek life elsewhere. It was a town nobody returned to unless under tragic circumstances. That usually meant a woman abandoned by a husband and left with, say, three or four kids. There was never just one. The extent of their passion, their physical lust, took them through abuse and drink for the duration it took to breed what would be considered in the animal kingdom sufficient to ensure the survival of the species.

I had no illusions about what I was facing, but emerging

from the darkness of the last few days' drive, this was civilization, an outpost of humanity, and I wanted to embrace it, for a time anyway. We had crept across half of America, left behind a season of changing autumn leaves for the stark coldness of early winter. It was a migration that would have taken literally weeks to months a hundred years ago, but that was one of the fundamental dilemmas of our age, to cope with change, to adapt in a matter of days or hours.

The falling snow was accumulating in drifts along the sidewalks. Driving slowly into town, I sensed the oblique change come over things, the growth of the town creeping out toward the edge of the wilderness we had driven through. There was a new strip mall on a tongue of frosted blacktop. I saw a barber pole turn against the cold stillness of falling snow, and a pizzeria and Laundromat, a liquor store with neon blue glowing inside. I said, 'That's new,' to Honey, pointing to a group of buildings set back from the road. There were teenagers moving between the low buildings.

Honey stared out the window. 'That's a college.'

It took me a moment to realize it, but she was right. It seemed like the Outreach Agricultural Facility had expanded into something like a real college.

Robert Lee said, 'Damn it, Frank, it's like looking at one of those plastic domes where you shake it and snowflakes start falling.'

I said, 'This is the original town they're modeled on.'

Robert Lee shook his head. 'Frank, this is the world capital of nowhere.' But even he couldn't annoy me right then. Robert Lee leaned over the seat, his head between Honey and me.

In the centre of town, I parked outside the local boarding house. It was a huge clay brick mansion from the days of the mining industry.

We got out and stretched. It was dry, bitter cold, the sky overhead the color of mackerel.

Honey held my arm, and Ernie was on the other side, holding my other hand. Honey's breath smoked when she spoke. 'We are going to have to buy some warm clothes.'

I pointed. 'There's a Woolworth's over there.'

I got us checked into the boarding house, which had served for years as lodgings for Chicago mining executives who came up north to observe operations, and to convene negotiations when the union threatened strikes. The old woman running it, Mrs Brody, gave me an off-season special weekly rate, and Honey nodded that the price was more than fair, and in truth it was cheaper than we had expected. When I signed Mrs Brody's deposit book she looked at the name and then looked at me, and I could tell she knew who I was. Instinctively, she sort of shook her head, and said in an offhand manner, 'We had some reporters from Chicago here early this week.'

I didn't open up to discussion and waited for her to show us to our room. I took two rooms with an adjoining door on the second floor, snug away in the back of the house, that shared a communal toilet and bathing quarters with three other guest rooms. There were no other guests.

We had to wind up a creaking central staircase to get to our rooms. Everything smelt of waxed mahogany and oak, a vintage spicy smell of wealth and elegance, but if you looked close, it had seen better days. Maybe things needed painting just a touch. On the landing, there was an amber-colored glass window with the image of a farmer with two plough horses out in a field. It had a long crack in it, but it still looked like it was worth a hell of a lot of money. Just to stand in the orange glow of its light made you feel like it was the nineteenth century again.

I could see the smile on Honey's face, and maybe even Robert Lee had to concede just a little right then. I had Ernie on my shoulders. I felt good for the first time in ages.

The rooms hinted at the opulence of old-world money. An old-fashioned wood-burning stove occupied the main room, and a ruby love seat faced a window looking off toward the white wilderness. An icy lace had already spread across the window. The bed, set off against the wall, was a queen-sized four poster, the legs carved into lion paws. I noticed water damage along the ceiling over the bed, dark circles of discoloration, but that didn't take anything away from the way we felt. Honey saw me looking and said, 'I think it's like a dream, all of it.'

Robert Lee said, 'It smells like moth balls.'

Honey said, 'You hush up now.'

In Robert Lee and Ernie's room there was a chest of drawers and two small beds reminiscent of a time when people were shorter than they are nowadays. I had to explain that to Ernie, and Honey said, 'That's a fact. George Washington was near a midget by today's standards, Ernie.'

The old heating system creaked and groaned, and the dust that had settled on the old radiators gave off a dry scorched smell. In the kids' room, under each bed was a porcelain chamberpot which just about killed Robert Lee when I told him what it was for. He said, 'Frank, you mind if I piss in it?'

'That's what it's for.'

'Frank!' Honey said, but I said, 'Let them be. It's what it's for.'

Robert Lee didn't piss in the chamberpot, but Ernie sat his dinosaur over one of the pots like it was taking a crap, and then pulled down his own pants. It was something to see that doughy little ass all scrunched up as he pissed into the pot. He looked like a Norman Rockwell painting. We all looked at him and just about kept from bursting out laughing.

I went into the other room and sat down on the bed and sank into the down comforter. I said, 'You've got to say one thing. A dollar goes a long way here, Honey.'

Robert Lee said, 'I'll give you that, Frank, but what does it take to earn a dollar here?'

Honey said, 'I want a truce here.'

So Robert Lee and I shook hands for what must have been the only time in recorded history.

'Frank here is going to do whatever he can for all of us, and I think that's all we can ask for.'

Robert Lee didn't quite agree. He said, 'I just realized, they don't got a damn television in the room.' Then our hands unlocked. Honey said, 'Well, maybe if you ask Mrs Brody downstairs nicely, she just might have a television we can borrow.'

The room had no telephone either, so I took Ernie and Robert Lee down to ask Mrs Brody if she rented televisions, and I asked to use the phone.

I called the operator, since I hadn't memorized Ward's number, and she rang out to my uncle's house. I realized the mistake, calling my uncle's house, but I let the phone ring. It was afternoon, getting close on milking time. The coldness of the dial tone made me shiver. I was seeing my uncle's house in my mind, the phone there in the dark passage of the hallway, remembering how in the old days voices used to echo, because people weren't used to talking into phones and had a habit of shouting. My uncle never lost that quirk all the years I lived with him.

I put the phone down. I waited a few moments and then called Norman's house. It was that patent voice of abrupt bluntness. Martha cut to the chase. 'So where are you?'

I tried to be cheery, because, in fact, I was. 'Surprise! We're in town. We just got in.'

I heard the phone drop, and it was a good ten seconds before Martha said anything.

'Before you go getting your knickers in a twist, I have my own car, Martha. You don't have to worry about me bringing shame and damnation down on you and Norman.' I said that sarcastically.

'Frank, you can turn that car right around and leave is what you can do. I told you we didn't want you here.'

'Maybe someone has yet to inform you, but your jurisdiction doesn't extend beyond your own bedroom, Martha. Last time I checked, this was still a free country.' Martha had a way of making me talk like somebody slightly deranged, so I said, 'Is Norman there? Just put me on to him, Martha. I don't think you and I have anything to talk about.'

'Why are you here, why?'

I said, 'Would you believe the very simple explanation as to why I am here is that this is as far as my money can take me? It doesn't go any deeper than that. In fact, usually things don't ever go deeper than my pockets, Martha.'

'What do you want? Money, is that it? You never change, do you? You want to extort money off us, just like you did with Ward, right?'

'What the hell are you talking about? I never extorted anything from Ward.'

'Don't deny it. I got proof. I got the letters you sent Ward. You're going to tell me you didn't make Ward send you money to a P.O. Box down in Chicago? I'm telling you, stay away from us. So help me God, Frank, I'll give them over to the police if you come near us.'

I was stunned just listening to her.

'Don't even try and deny it. I found the letters you sent to Ward hidden away in his closet.' Then her voice had come down a notch, like she was getting conciliatory all of a sudden. 'Frank?'

'What?'

'Look, how come it has to be like this every time you call, why do you have to fight us like this?'

I didn't answer her right away. Then I said, 'What do these letters say?'

'Listen, stop, just stop, don't play me for a fool.' She took a breath. 'I can't really hold anything against you. Maybe we have our differences, and I grant, maybe you got your reasons, and we got ours, and that's life, and there's not much we can do to change any of that right now. The die's been cast, and we'd be fooling ourselves if we pretended otherwise, and I'm not good at pretending is what I'm saying . . .'

I raised my voice a little. 'I don't know what you're trying to say.'

Martha stopped and took another deep breath. 'I don't want Norman to know this, but I got some money set aside that I want you to have, it's not much, but I got it set for a rainy day, and I figure this is a genuine downpour.' She waited just a moment to see if I'd take the bait, but I didn't. 'Frank, you take what I can give you, and let's call all this quits, okay?'

She said 'Frank' in that strange, haunting way she used to say it when I knew her years ago. I laughed to stave off my own feelings. I said, 'You know, you said "Frank" like you did in high school, when I took you to that dance, you remember that, Martha? I mean, if all this animosity is about us swapping spit years ago, I can tell you honestly, the affair is well and truly over.'

Her breath poured across the line. 'Frank, you got some inflated sense of yourself. That's ancient history. High school dances, sweet Jesus. You live in the past.' Her voice trailed off, and eased like I'd touched something. 'How come you even remember something like that?'

I leaned against the wall and closed my eyes. I said, 'All I'm trying to do is just establish some level ground here, is all, Martha.' I didn't say anything for a few moments. 'I'm not the monster you make me out to be, Martha, that's all I'm saying.'

'I never called you that. I never said you were a monster. Maybe Ward didn't treat you right all along, and I don't blame you for what you got from Ward, but we got nothing left, Frank, nothing . . . Take what I have. It's the best offer you are ever going to get, you hear me?'

I felt a flush of anxiety again. I said, 'I want to see these letters, Martha. If you're going to accuse me of blackmail, I want to see the evidence.'

'I didn't say blackmail.'

I felt sick to my stomach.

Martha said, 'Hear me out, please, let me just say what I have to say ... Okay?'

I didn't answer her.

'I figure whatever you and Ward had between you was your business, and God knows it took two to tangle like you did. Nobody has ever judged you, not me or Norman. Norman stopped you getting beat, right? That wasn't Norman that told me that, it was you, you told me. You told me that back in high school, how Norman caught Ward's hand one night and said, "No!" '

Just having her say it like that made me take a deep breath. Martha sensed that and said, 'You see, we got nothing against you. We didn't contact you about Ward's murder because of your mental condition, and please don't jump all over me for saying that. You might be fine now, but we didn't know. We just thought it best for it all to pass, and then call and tell you ...'

I said, 'I don't think I can keep listening right now, Martha.'

Martha interrupted me again. 'Frank, just hear me out. You ever consider what it was like for Norman to find his father dead like that?' I heard her voice break. 'He came back with blood all over his overalls. He was screaming. I heard him way before he got to the house. He was just screaming at the top of his voice.'

That image of Norman, that huge brute, just screaming like that, took the edge off things. It was the first time I'd heard something of what really happened.

'I'm telling you this because I don't think you really know what happened out here. That man that killed Ward was there when Norman went into the house. Norman told me that at first he thought Ward had committed suicide. I think that just stunned him. The gun was on the ground beside the body. Norman tried to revive Ward, but Ward was stone cold. Norman sat there holding his father. He told me that. He was sure it was suicide. He felt like it was his fault because the farm was going under. We were up to our ears in debt. I don't know if Ward wanted to see what he had struggled to keep go out from under him.

'Norman got up and phoned me. He said, "What you got cooking, Martha? I can smell something good all across the field." I said, "You over there with Ward, Norman?" I said, "See if he's going to join us for supper." Norman gave this sigh like I never heard from him before. I said, "What's going on over there, Norman?" He said to me, "You think I was a good son, Martha?" The *was* caught me as strange. I could tell there was something wrong in his voice. I said, "I'm coming over there now, Norman!" and he shouted, "No!" Then his voice got soft and he said, "Stay away . . ." and he just hung up.'

I cleared my throat, and Martha just seemed to stop. I could hear her crying. 'God, give me a moment.' She blew her nose. 'You there?'

'Yeah.'

'The reason Norman hung up was he heard something upstairs in his father's house. So he called out and said, "I got a gun here." He picked up the gun beside Ward. He shouted, "You come on down now!" But nobody came down. There was still noise upstairs, like somebody was walking around. Norman shouted again, "If I go up there, I'm going to shoot you dead. You come down now!" He shot the gun at the ceiling. But the noise just went on. Then came this wailing sound from upstairs, and something snapped inside Norman right then. He told me that. It was like a sound from another world. Norman just ran out into the fields and started screaming. I was looking out the window, because I knew something was wrong. Somehow I knew Ward was dead. I had that feeling inside, but seeing Norman coming across like a madman, it just scared me. He was shouting, "The Devil's over there waiting to take my father's soul! I heard the Devil! He's waiting on my father's soul! My father killed himself, and the Devil's waiting on his soul!" I crossed myself, I got down on my knees. Suicide . . . Sweet Jesus. Norman was raving. He had blood all over his overalls and face. He looked a horror. The kids were crying and scared. I called the police. Norman kept screaming the Devil was waiting on his father's soul. You should have heard him.' Martha took a frantic breath.

'I drove over to the house, waited for the police to arrive. I kept the car running. I didn't get out. Norman had calmed a bit. He was in the back of the car sitting there just staring at the house. And while we waited, Norman said, "There, you see him, up there by the window!" and I turned, and, my God, Frank, there was a man staring out across the land!

'I drove the car away from the house, and we stared back at the window. The man never moved. We met the sheriff and a deputy coming up the road to the house. I told them there was a man up there. They went in with guns drawn, shouting for the man to show himself, but he didn't. In the end, they said, he stood by the window, never moving, never looking at them, even as they handcuffed him.'

I said under my breath, 'Jesus Christ . . .'

'You should have seen Norman, the way he got out of the car. I don't believe I ever saw anything like it in all my life. He went toward the man. The sheriff said, "You stand back now, Norman." I suppose he thought Norman was going to attack the man. All Norman said was, "I want to see if he's real, that's all." The sheriff said, "He's real, Norman. Now just keep back, you hear." '

I said, 'That's crazy talk.' I didn't know what to say. I felt cold inside my guts.

'Now you know everything . . . I just hope all this ends soon.' She hesitated. 'The day after the murder, the police came and took Norman's overalls away. I don't know what that means, I just don't. They said to Norman, "You'd better not plan on going anywhere."'

I could feel her drifting back to the moment it all happened.

'God, you didn't see that man. He looked like the Devil when they took him out, that beard and those eyes, and dressed in this dark suit.'

I felt my head spinning from the journey and other things like hunger and lack of sleep. I said, 'Have they set a date to bury Ward?'

'I asked them when we'd get the body back, and they said, "It's state's evidence right now." They're making us feel like criminals.' Martha breathed hard down the line.

One of Martha's kids said something in the background. I could hear her talking gently. I'd never seen any of them in real life.

When Martha got back on the phone she said, 'I don't know what else to say.'

I said nothing. Then Martha said, 'I got to ask you this.'

'What?'

'How did you know Ward was dead?'

I said, 'I read it in the newspaper. Why?'

'No reason.'

'What are you driving at?'

'Nothing, Frank. Nothing.'

I said, 'I want to see those letters, you hear me?'

'I got them kept safe. You just remember I got Norman to take care of in all this. Just keep away right now. Let things pass.'

There was a noise again in the background, and Martha said, 'I got to hang up now.'

I didn't move for a long time. I went down on my haunches in the dim alcove by the phone. My ear felt cold, a vacuous silence that comes after you have listened to somebody on the phone for too long. I pinched the bridge of my nose, squeezing the tension. Something stirred inside me like sadness and regret, and at the back of that, fear of what I was capable of doing without knowing I was doing it.

Years back, during the time I was living in Chicago, after I left home, I was struggling, working shit jobs, and one morning, when I got home, I found an envelope that contained a key along with a cryptic note that said the post office address and box number, and under that a solitary word, *Sorry*.

I remembered back to that first time getting the envelope, traveling along the El down through the city where the train came within inches of people's living rooms. It was deep winter, snow swirling outside. I found the P.O. Box. Inside was a brown envelope. It contained three hundred dollars in twenties, tens, and fives. I remember looking around, like this was a set-up, like something on a late night movie. But there was nobody looking.

Over the course of the years I stayed in Chicago, every so often I got an envelope with a key. It was never much money, but something to get me by. I'd always figured that Ward felt guilty about what had happened between us, that it was his way of making amends for accusing me of setting the fire. The solitary admission of regret, the brevity of the word, *Sorry*, was characteristic of Ward. It's all I could ever have hoped for from him.

The envelopes started around the time I had a near breakdown in Chicago. No, the truth is, I *did* have a breakdown. I was hospitalized at Cook County Hospital for depression. I was working the nightshift at a hotel, delivering late night room service, and I guess sleeping away the days and living in the insomnia of night made me brood too much. I wanted to know how the hell I'd ended up working this shit existence, from goddamn Honors English, and with my aptitude in math, and there I was, a goddamn flunkey. I asked myself that question too many times, until I was asking myself out loud, until I was talking to myself on buses and subways, until people were moving away from me. I was conscious that I was talking out loud. I thought there was a difference between knowing you were ranting out loud and not being aware you were talking out loud. I thought self-delusion was the definition of insanity, and I knew what I was doing, so I thought I had things under control.

I don't remember the exact incident that got me committed for observation. That's a lie. I do. Jesus, even now, all these years later, I recoil from even the goddamn basic facts. It happened down at work. I went into the luggage room late at night just to be alone and smoke. I was in there when I had one of my visions, those waking nightmares that haunted me back then. I was looking out of the dark of the luggage room, just smoking, staring at the glow of the cigarette, blowing on it and making it throb like an ember, and all of a sudden I wasn't in the luggage room, I was hiding in the barn, staring through the slats at the glare of flames against the dark. I got that tunnel vision, and I was back at the moment my parents died. I could smell everything, the animals, the fire, the shit, every sense alive. I could see shadows running back and forth in the glow of light. I pressed against the slats and started screaming, trying to see who was there. The light from the fire was like a flare, radiating such an intense heat that I squinted and couldn't make out the shadows. But I kept screaming, and suddenly the barn door opened and my uncle was looking down at me. His face was like a jack-o-lantern, the way the flame and shadow played on it. I said his name. I saw him bend toward me, and then everything went blank like I'd been struck, just a falling sense and blackness.

They said at the hospital where I was committed, that I dropped my cigarette and started a small fire in the luggage room. It set off the sprinkler system. Firefighters found me in there, curled up like a child, shaking, with the sprinklers pouring down on me. I was screaming that my parents were in the luggage room when they took me out. I shouted for my uncle. I looked around trying to find him.

I was taken for observation, and then treatment, electric shock treatment to make me forget things, to stop me fixating on the past. I said stuff about Ward. I had listed Ward as closest relative, so he knew what I went through. I think he was the one who authorized the shock treatment. I spoke to him just once from the hospital.

I figured, given everything, he must have wanted to clear his conscience. He'd decided he owed me something and sent me the money to keep me going, or to keep me from going back home. Ward probably didn't want another Charlie on his hands, another Cassidy come home all screwed up.

I came out from the alcove. I felt a chill deep inside me. Mrs Brody had given Robert Lee a small black and white television. She said to Robert Lee, but was looking at me, 'You're going to have to get rabbit ears, most likely, and don't go trying to use a wire hanger, you hear me now?'

I was detached from everything, just watching it like it was on television.

Mrs Brody had some kind of mild tremor, and her head moved slightly every few seconds, not exactly a tic, but a quiver. Her face was old in an ancient and weathered way, but her eyes still gleamed a pale water blue.

Mrs Brody said, 'I don't remember anything like this since Mr James Parks killed his fiancée up at Beaver Lake in 1927. That was before you were born, Mr Cassidy, but Mr James Parks strangled his fiancée with the braids of her own hair is what he did.'

Robert Lee blurted out, 'You got to be shitting me,' and then he realized what he'd said, and put his hand to his mouth like he could catch his own words.

Ernie got a big beaming smile on his face and took the sucker from his mouth and said, 'You got to be shitting me.'

Mrs Brody's black shoes scraped the hardwood floor. 'I have a simple rule, boys. Every time anybody cusses they have to put a quarter in that bowl over there. So you both owe me a quarter.'

Robert Lee said, 'Yes, ma'am,' and went and put a quarter in the bowl.

'And you, too, young man.' I could see a smile lost deep in Mrs Brody's old face. She said, 'Go on now, young man.'

I gave Ernie a quarter and held him up so he could drop it into the bowl. Then we went upstairs again, and we all slept clear into the next day, until something like noon.

Chapter 9

Pale light streamed across our four-poster bed the next morning. Robert Lee and Ernie were watching cartoons in their bedroom. I could hear Tweetie Bird say, 'I tawt I taw a puddy tat! I did . . . I did!'

Honey was pressed up against me. 'You awake?'

I turned and faced her and smiled.

Honey smiled back at me. 'This is nice, real nice.'

The light was clear and strong in the room. I took a deep breath. The TV was loud in the next room.

Honey said, 'Maybe I'll head down to that college, just see what jobs they have to offer.' She moved her fingers along my face. 'A typist is always in demand.'

'You planning on living here forever, Honey?' I was still smiling.

'This is the first time in years I feel I've escaped . . . escaped everything.' Honey tensed and then forced a smile. I knew she meant Ken. 'We can live cheap here, for the time being, until we decide what we want, where we want to go, right?'

This should have been a reprieve, but then I felt the anxiety from the last conversation I'd had with Martha descend like a headache. I said nothing for a time, and we slept some more, Honey on my shoulder. When we awoke again, I told Honey about Martha and the letters. I said, 'She's under the impression I sent them, that I blackmailed Ward years ago.'

Honey shifted and came off my shoulder so she was looking at me. 'Blackmailed Ward about what?'

I said, 'I don't even remember sending Ward any letters.'

Honey looked at me. 'What? You'd remember something like that, right?'

I didn't say anything.

'Frank?'

'I don't know, Honey. I was institutionalized, so who the hell knows what delusions I was suffering back then.'

Honey raised her voice. 'You were locked up? Damn it, what else haven't you told me about your life?' I could feel her weight shift, and the springs moved.

I went about explaining the circumstances, then told her about the letters I received, about the money, and that solitary word, *Sorry*, on the first letter. I was up close to her, staring at her so it looked like she was a Cyclops, because her eyes merged into one eye.

Honey seemed to lose her indignation again. She said, 'What's this Martha want? What has this got to do with anything now? Is she going to show the letters to the police? What's any of this got to do with Ward's death?'

I said, 'It's got nothing to do with Ward's death.' I took a deep breath. 'I think I got everything settled with her now.'

Honey seemed to think for a few moments. 'She never said anything about what you blackmailed Ward over, did she?'

I got up and sat at the edge of the bed. 'No, she never said.' The light from outside hurt my eyes. I closed and opened them. I looked at Honey. 'Look I'm sorry. Like I told you, I don't ever remember writing to Ward.'

'Well you better put on your thinking cap. Not remembering isn't going to wash.'

'I know.' I lay back beside her and stared at the ceiling. I was afraid to even mention Melvin. At some gut level I felt maybe I'd done something more than I was willing to admit. Thinking back, I thought there was no way a man would wait like he did, counting backwards with me waiting in his truck. Jesus Christ, there were times when I felt a blankness come over me. I wanted to say something to Honey, but to mention my fear I'd done something to him would scare her. I'd be like another Ken. But I did say, 'Honey, did you know Ken had killed those people on the day he did it . . .'

Honey said sharply, 'Frank.'

'Just tell me, did you feel anything . . . like intuition about what he'd done?'

'I don't want you mentioning Ken again, you hear me? Don't ask me anything about him or that time, you hear me?'

Robert Lee came into the room like he'd heard the name Ken, and said, 'What are you talking about?'

Honey said, 'We were talking about how you need new clothes, how we got to get you and Ernie outfitted.'

Robert Lee just stood there looking at us, and said, 'You planning on feeding us? It's going on one o'clock.'

Down at Woolworth's, I outfitted Robert Lee and Ernie. They had a special on Green Bay Packers merchandise, so that's what I bought for Ernie, that god-awful green and yellow-gold combination. They had socks and underwear and mittens and ear muffs and caps with the Green Bay Packers logo, all that crap that plays to a kid's need to belong to something. Ernie wanted it all, and his kid sense of want and fascination trumped my sense of irony, so I sprang for the shit just like that. He took the underwear out of the plastic wrap and tore off the metal tag holding the socks together, so I was pretty much stuck having to buy that extra stuff for him, too. I even had to spring for a little backpack and an extra pair of Packers mittens because Ernie put his dinosaur into the mitten, saying it was a sleeping bag.

Robert Lee said, 'The Green Bay Packers are fags, Ernie! You name one player on the Packers, just one, and I'll give you fifty bucks right now!' He went like he was fishing in his pocket for the fifty bucks, and Ernie had that bemused kid look on his face.

I said, 'Let him get what he wants.'

Robert Lee sauntered off toward the teen section. He picked out a denim insulated jacket, Levis, a belt with Pink Floyd embossed in black on the buckle, a Rush concert tee shirt and lumberjack boots, which he insisted on leaving unlaced. Robert Lee said, 'Frank, how about you buy me one of those stainless steel whiskey flasks?' Instead, I bought him this comb he wanted that looked like a switchblade.

It was nice spending money like that on them. They both wore the new stuff and left their old clothes in the dressing rooms, like they'd molted.

In the Entertainment Section we had a fat middle-aged salesman in a brown suit show us the different sets. He sucked on mint candy. The TVs were on sale. *Jeopardy* was showing on a wall of TVs. I just listened to the questions more than the salesman.

We bought a twenty-four-inch color TV, a hot plate and a toaster. I said, 'This is the last major expense, you hear me?' Ernie was in his new clothes and smiled, and Robert Lee played with his switchblade comb. The salesman said they'd deliver the set to us at no extra charge.

We ate at a local café. It was getting dark. The lights were on over at the college.

I bought the day's newspaper. The story of Ward's murder was off in the lower right corner of the front page and continued to the next page.

Copper, Michigan – As investigation into the death of Ward Cassidy continues, police have begun to establish the movements of the alleged suspect in the day leading up to the murder.

One witness, a Greyhound bus driver, saw the suspect board the bus in Chicago. He observed the individual had no luggage. Another greyhound driver stated the suspect asked to be dropped off along exit 301. The driver recorded the time in his logbook as nine-forty a.m.

The alleged suspect, dubbed *The Sleeper*, and at this time tentatively identified as Chester Green, has begun breathing on his own. He remains in a vegetative state at Copper County Hospital.

In further developments, Mr Sam Green has made an unusual petition to have his son Chester's body exhumed, to exonerate his own name and prove his son is deceased.

I read through the article again, circling the word *Chicago*. In some ways seeing the name *Chicago* scared me. I had lived in Chicago, but it was a huge city. Still, I didn't like that coincidence, that I had lived in the same city as the man who killed Ward.

Robert Lee sat across from me and kept working on his technique, flicking out the comb before Ernie, and then just combing his own hair with this cool sneer that melted to a smile, while Ernie fed his dinosaur ketchup and egg.

By the time we got home, Honey had got an interview at the department of business at the college. If there was one thing I could say about her, she was a survivor.

The TV arrived, and we set it up in a corner of our room.

Through the course of the evening, Honey preened herself for her interview the next day. She took a long bath.

I helped Honey apply her Lee Press-on Nails, then she polished them with numerous coats of Candy Apple Red nail polish. I had to open the window because of the chemical smell. Ernie said he felt sick. I put on four TV dinners in the communal kitchen at the end of the hallway. I came back with a glass with ice cold Tab for Honey.

We watched a re-run of *Hogan's Heroes*. Robert Lee imitated Sergeant Schultz and said in a German voice, 'I know nothing . . . I know nothing . . .' and Ernie repeated him.

I was edgy as hell. The idea that I blackmailed Ward and couldn't remember it got to me.

I looked at the TV as Colonel Hogan snuck two buxom women from the French Resistance into Stalag 13. I said, 'Is this how we rewrite history, is this what our kids are going to remember about the greatest calamity in the history of mankind, a farce inside a POW camp?'

Robert Lee said, 'Cool it, Frank, we're trying to watch this.'

Honey said, 'Satire, you've heard of satire, right?' She was painting her toenails. She had tissue paper between each toe.

I went and got the TV dinners out of the oven. I could hear the TV along the hallway. I came back to the room. 'Satire presumes you know the facts first. This *isn't* satire.' One of the Parisian women climbed down a ladder. The camera focused on her ass, and Colonel Hogan pushed his hat back on his head, which was his trademark affectation, and said, 'Let me handle this.' The laugh track grew louder as the woman's ass crushed against Colonel Hogan's face in the small confines of the tunnel they used to come and go from the POW camp.

I peeled the foil off the TV dinners. I said, 'You know how Colonel Hogan died, Honey?'

Honey rolled her eyes, 'On the show?'

I said, 'No. Goddamn it, nobody ever died on the show. A show about World War II, and nobody died ... Bob Crane was addicted to pornography in real life. He was beaten to death with a crowbar in some bizarre love triangle over homemade sex tapes.'

Honey said, 'That's just what I want Ernie to hear, Frank ...'

We didn't use a table, and just set the TV dinners on our laps and ate.

Ernie wouldn't take off his Green Bay Packers coat.

Honey said, 'Let him be. He'll take it off when he gets hot.'

I wanted to watch *The Hundred Thousand Dollar Pyramid,*

but we ended up watching *Family Feud*, and, again, sleep overtook us like a drug a short time later.

Chapter 10

The next morning was that sort of clear blue day that hurt just to stare into. But with blue skies came an intense cold this far north.

Honey got ready for her interview. She was all business, walking around in her full-sized bra and big underpants, which was something she always did when she was applying makeup. It was strange to see her face all painted up and the rest of her body white and pudgy. She saw me looking sideways at her and said, 'Frank, don't burn that toast, you hear.'

Honey tried on some old things she had brought and was finally settling on the polyester suit she'd worn on the day Ken was sentenced to death, when Robert Lee, in one quick motion, just turned, came off the bed, flicked his switchblade comb in front of Honey's face and shouted, 'I don't want you wearing that ever, you hear me, you goddamn bitch!'

It freaked the hell out of me, and Honey let out a scream, since she didn't know it was only a comb. Her painted face turned almost white. It all happened in a second. And then Honey saw it was a comb, and the blood came rushing back to her face, and what happened then was one of those insane attacks I don't like to think about. Honey lost it. It was another of those strange beatings administered in almost silence, just her grunting effort. Robert Lee was curled up like something that had been extricated from its shell.

I went out with Ernie into the hallway right then, and for

the first time in a long time I went down on one knee like I was taking a standing count and just waited until there was no more noise inside the room.

Honey eventually came out into the hallway. She was still breathing hard. All she said was, 'I turned off the toaster, Frank.' She was in a different outfit, though.

The door reverberated as she pulled it hard behind her.

I stayed outside the room for a while. I could smell the toast on the other side of the door and could hear the laugh track from *I Dream of Jeannie*. Ernie was sitting by my side, and, though I didn't look in his face, I saw the white around his knuckles as he grasped his dinosaur. I said, 'It's okay,' but when I tried to touch him, he recoiled away from me. Ernie got up and knocked on the door and said, 'It's me, Ernie.'

Robert Lee came out after that and put his hand on Ernie's head. Ernie wrapped his arms around Robert Lee's waist. Robert Lee said, 'It's me and you against the world, Ernie. We're superheroes, Ernie.'

When Robert Lee breathed, blood bubbled out his nostrils. A small muscle moved in his jaw as he looked at me while talking to Ernie, then he turned away toward the bathroom. In the grey half-light, Robert Lee looked old beyond what he was, going on fifteen. I saw the beginning of manhood taking shape in the spread of his shoulders tapering to his waist.

I said softly across the hallway, 'No point stewing in your own juices, Robert Lee.'

The faucet started running. 'I'm simmering, Frank, not stewing.' He kept widening his eyes and breathing shallow. He turned his back to me. I saw the long marks where Honey's nails had torn his back.

And so it was that, with those same hands, the Georgia State typing champion got a job that afternoon. In the melancholy aftermath, little was said between any of us. The room was hot and made us sweat. The smell of grease and Salisbury steak TV dinners lingered in the air. I put down a pot of coffee in the communal kitchen.

Through the lace curtains, I could see it snowing outside in big flakes.

Honey made amends by getting me a job as a security guard at the college. Honey said, 'I told them you completed a course in criminology back in New Jersey, Frank,' which I hadn't, but that white lie got them to hire me for the night shift.

I got hired over the phone. I called the Head Dean of the College at his house, which I thought was unusual, but it was part of the dean's home-style method, his hands-on approach to life and his job in particular. He said, 'I'm not afraid to roll up my sleeves and get under the hood.' I detected an accent from back east, maybe New Hampshire, that waspish ideal of nature and learning.

The dean explained his vision. The college was in transition, moving from a Junior College to a four-year accredited institution, and had severed its ties with the Michigan Board of Education. It was a fledgling private institution with strong financial backing, part of an initiative tailored to accommodate prospective students from varied backgrounds looking for a unique scholastic experience centered around seminars in the Great Books. He said, 'We must know where we've been, before we decide where we want to go, right Frank?'

I could tell this was a recruitment speech, but I just listened in the dim alcove. The pay was unbelievably high, and the dean underscored that he felt, with my background in criminology and urban crime prevention, I would be an invaluable asset to the college. He hinted at what prospective trouble he felt this new *demographic population* of out-of-town students posed for the indigenous student body, and for the town at large. He quoted some statistic from an educational commission that approximated the crime rate increase, and listed the potential infractions. He said, 'What I'm looking for here, Frank, is a people person who can *build bridges* between *disparate populations.* Are you ready to take on that challenge, Frank?'

At the end of the conversation, the dean told me I got extra if I was willing to plow snow, which I agreed to do.

When I went back upstairs I asked Honey about my experience in urban crime prevention. She laughed and said, 'This college is basically recruiting burnout kids from rich families around the Great Lakes Region. The dean over at the Business College says there's been trouble between locals and the new rich kids. That's why they jumped at hiring you, why some local isn't getting the job.'

I told her the pay, and Honey beamed. 'This might be the best move we ever made.'

I said, 'I bet this dean is going to flip when he hears that I'm related to Ward, once the shit hits the fan.'

Honey looked at me. 'What's going on with the case?'

I shook my head. 'It beats me. I just get what's in the papers, just like the rest of us.' I looked over at Honey. 'You hear that Sam Green has requested his son's body be exhumed?'

Honey said, 'I've been too busy, and once you get working you won't have time to play cop. Just let it go for now. There'll be a simple explanation in the end, there always is.'

The television broke the silence that ensued between our sporadic talk over the next day. It was Tuesday, and I didn't have to start work until the Friday night. I did odds and ends, and called for phone hookup.

To get relief from the apartment, I took Ernie over to the campus. Robert Lee said he didn't want to go. He was holding his Richard Nixon Pez Man. He opened and closed Nixon's mouth and imitated Nixon's voice and said, 'I can take it . . . The tougher it gets, the cooler I get . . .' Robert Lee looked at me. 'The actual words of our former President of the United States, Frank.'

I felt this nagging doubt since Martha had asked me where

110

I'd read about Ward's murder, so I went by the college library and looked up *The New York Times*, scanned the previous weeks, but there was no reference to Ward's death. I felt like I was at the edge of some dark door, like I was standing on the other side of some secret. I mean, take my goddamn history of mental illness. I was a goddamn unreliable witness to even my own life, to my own consciousness.

I spent the next hour in the cold, walking the campus, numb. I passed a bulletin board that was advertising a kindergarten program at the First Assembly Church. I wanted something to occupy my mind. I went down and signed Ernie up for it. Outside the church, it said, 'How will you spend eternity? Smoking or Non-smoking?'

Back at the apartment, I watched Robert Lee, and he laughed at all the places you were supposed to laugh during the sitcoms, but somehow his laugh seemed too loud, like it was all just too funny. He didn't once leave the room except to go to the bathroom. He just sat in his underwear like some inmate.

It was like the eye of a goddamn storm, that silence.

Robert Lee said to me the day after his beating, while Honey was getting dressed for work, 'Frank, tell me honestly, who do you find more sexually attractive, *Jeannie* or that witch housewife on *Bewitched*?'

I could see Honey in the other room, and she stopped doing what she was doing and was just waiting.

I said, 'You have any interest in attending high school, Robert Lee?' and he turned and just smiled and said, 'Don't change the subject, Frank. How about I sweeten the pot, how about Ginger or Mary Ann, or how about Florence Henderson, Frank? You know who that is, right, Frank? Carol Brady from *The Brady Bunch*. You ever wonder what the hell happened to her husband, Frank? You know, Frank, if you listen to the opening song they just ignore that stuff. Did her husband die or get convicted of killing somebody? All the opening song says is, "they all had hair of gold, like their mother, the youngest one in curls," and, oh yeah, "they were all alone." '

Honey froze in the other room. I could see her just staring and listening.

Robert Lee said, 'Okay, if you won't answer, Frank, I will. I'd choose *The Invisible Woman*, that's who I'd choose.'

Honey came out and stared at Robert Lee, and he took out his comb and did that trick with it, and then just brushed his hair back off his forehead.

Honey left that day with Ernie, without saying anything.

And then sleep overtook me right through to the afternoon. I slept until Ernie woke me with a kiss, like something from a fairy tale.

Chapter 11

I called the local high school and made an appointment to enroll Robert Lee. We went Thursday morning, and Robert Lee began a morning of evaluation tests at my old high school.

It felt weird as hell walking the old polished hallways, all those same lockers, row after row, some decorated with birthday papers and ribbons. I went by my locker, 308, that small space, the sole domain where I kept everything belonging to me in high school: books, smelly gym clothes, and, most notably, my weed and pipe, before the principal started cutting locks open right around the time things started heating up in Vietnam. It still had a strange effect, even now, that institutional monotony, the maze of hallways and the sameness that confronted a teenager's emerging sense of identity.

The school was huge, like a goddamn airport, bigger than anything in big cities, one of those vast, sprawling hangars that accommodated more than two thousand kids. It was like Noah's Ark there in the morning, the way kids came from all over the county, off the isolated farms, picked up like livestock for market in the school buses. No wonder we used to flush M80s down the toilet and blow the plumbing to hell. You had to do something to distinguish yourself, to balance the solitude of farm existence with the hugeness of the high school.

Somehow the years suddenly caught up with me as I walked the corridors. I went down by my old homeroom and stared in at the eggshell-beige classroom, the desks all filled with kids slouching in their seats. Down by the nurse's office, I looked in at kids sitting along the benches, waiting for the nurse. I saw the sick table with the wax hygiene paper, the jars of tongue depressors and Band Aids, all the same crap. Kids never got to go home sick until the end of the day, since no farmer was going to come in and get their kid unless it was an emergency, and if it was an emergency, then the kid went by ambulance to hospital anyway. Mostly it was triage for upset stomachs and headaches, or feminine problems, or injuries from sports. I used to go down there sometimes complaining of my appendix when there was a test in something like biology or history. I was king of the make-up exam.

Next to the nurse's office were lab rooms where I had gone for psychiatric tests. That sent a chill down my spine. Shit, it was like another lifetime. I felt disengaged from everything, even though it was all familiar. If someone had put a blindfold on me, I could have navigated anywhere inside the school, the library, the gym locker rooms, the trophy cases up front of the school, the cafeteria, the biology labs. It was something imprinted inside my brain. Like they said years ago to me, nothing is ever forgotten inside the brain, it's all in there, just sometimes there are doors inside the brain that are locked, but all you have to do is use the right key to unlock the door.

I did close my eyes, and I got myself over by the gym, following the map inside my brain. And there was the record board, with all the school records in different sports, and all the county and state championships the school had won over the years. I scanned down through the Wrestling Wall of Fame. There was goddamn Norman in that fag wrestling outfit. He was in the heavyweight class. It listed his weight at 320 pounds.

Shit, it was weird looking at Norman there in the photograph, hunched in that quintessential wrestler pose, balanced on the foreleg with the arms out and the hands open, ready to go for some takedown move. Just looking at his big dough face, I smiled, then stopped. A surge of melancholy made my arms get goose bumps. This was all gone for ever. I looked at Norman, and the truth was, he got it worse than me in the long run, because he was a workhorse, and Ward had a way of driving him into the ground. Norman was big, like a dumb ox. I was pretty much dismissed to doing menial tasks like milking and taking in eggs, and what with Ward's wife having died giving birth to Norman, I did most of the cooking by the time I reached high school. That was one of the real reasons I took home economics, because we'd eaten like crap for years.

On the wall of fame, it listed Norman's accomplishments, All-State Freshman through senior year. He made it to the state finals from sophomore year to senior year, winning his sophomore and junior year, only to get injured his senior year with an Achilles tear that required surgery. The goddamn college recruiters who'd been after him all through high school just walked away from Norman, thinking he was washed up. He got no scholarship offers, except to a few cow-poke colleges that it was going to cost more to get to than it was worth, places in Oklahoma and Nebraska. I remember calling when I was in Chicago after the time came and went for Norman to send in his letter of intent for a scholarship. It was the year of my breakdown. I said, 'Hey, Norman, grabbing guys' balls is no sort of scholarship you'd want any part in, right? You did the right thing, Norman. You don't want to be called a fag for ever, do you?' but I felt sorry for Norman. All Norman said was, 'You never quit it, do you, Frank?' He was laughing when he said it. I just imagined his big horse teeth, the way his gums showed when he laughed.

It was hard to reconcile Norman there in the photograph with what Martha had said about him. I had that image of Norman running across the land, like some lumbering giant screaming his head off. Shit, how things change.

I called Martha from a pay phone. I said, 'I'm down here at

the high school looking at this shrine to Norman. Sometimes I guess you take a guy like that for granted. Maybe I see now what you saw in Norman all along.'

Martha sighed and let things ease. She said softly, 'God, that was a long time ago.'

I said, 'I just wanted to ask you one question, Martha.'

'What's that?'

'I'd like to see one of those letters you said I sent Ward. How do you know I sent them?'

'Frank . . . I thought maybe you would keep out of all this?'

I kept calm, cupping my hand over the phone, speaking softly. 'Listen, Martha, I want to know what I'm capable of doing, or what I *did* . . . because the truth is I don't remember. You hear me? I don't remember sending those letters to Ward. I'm admitting that to you, you hear me? That's an admission on my part. I was under goddamn psychiatric care, Martha. I was in the loony bin, drugged up good, you hear me?' I took a deep breath. 'I'm sorry, okay?'

'Frank, listen, I'm not doing anything with those letters. With everything that's gone on, I'm not going to bring up what you did to Ward. Things are already too complicated.'

'Martha, just . . .' I hesitated.

Somebody spoke in the background. I could tell it was Norman's voice.

Martha said, 'I'll be right there, Norman.' She got back on the phone. 'I have to go.'

I said, 'How do you know it was me, Martha?'

'You signed the letters, Frank. They're signed by you.'

I didn't say anything for a few moments, and the phone clicked in my ear.

I roamed the hallways until I met Robert Lee for lunch. We ate lunch down at the cafeteria for forty-five cents, a corn dog, fries, a tub of apple sauce, milk and a custard pudding with a cherry on top. The woman serving behind the counter was the

116

same as when I went there. She didn't recognize me, and I said nothing.

I could see girls looking over at Robert Lee. He leaned back with his denim jacket open and looked tough in that romantic way teenage girls find irresistible. What he was, really, was like a smaller version of the man he would become. There were kids like that in every school, and kids who looked like that always ended up in real trouble.

Robert Lee got up and went to the candy machine. He said loudly, across the cafeteria, 'What do you want, Frank? It's on me!' and when the kids turned to look at him, he hit the vending machine a hard blow, and something dropped, and then Robert Lee dipped his body and came up with a Twinkie and his quarter, like a goddamn consummate magician.

In the old days, I used to love leaving the heat of the cafeteria and going out into that cold, the dry cold gripping my throat as I inhaled. Going out through the glass of the cafeteria was like leaving the dome of some artificial life-support colony. I saw the next generation of losers outside smoking by the dumpsters.

All through lunch I kept wanting to see myself writing those letters to Ward, but I couldn't.

After lunch I sat in with Robert Lee and the school counselor, Mr Arnold Grimes, my old nemesis from high school, general asshole and purveyor of useless information. He was stuffed into an office at the end of a rat's maze of administrative cells, with books on colleges and statistical scores that figured and estimated what you might be good for in life. I think he was wearing the same blue blazer and red tie he wore when I went there. He looked like an insurance salesman on the downside of life. 'Frank! God, it's been a long time. A long time!' He had that acrid coffee breath. He patted my arms and back with an over-familiarity, like he was goddamn frisking me. 'So, how you been? What you been up to? You look good.'

I sat down with Robert Lee at my side. Across the desk, Mr Grimes was still at it. 'Terrible news about your father, just terrible.'

I didn't correct him.

'You just don't figure on something like that happening up here, you just don't, but you got to move on, and God knows it's hard, but that's what you got to do in situations like this. Move on.'

I didn't exactly light up the room with conversation, so Mr Grimes finally got round to saying, 'The kid looks just like you. Good-looking kid.'

Robert Lee said, 'He's not my goddamn father!'

Mr Grimes got that mean look that lay just beneath the veneer of affable asshole, and said, 'We don't appreciate that kind of language. You understand, young man? That sort of language lands you in detention.'

That pretty much ended things. Mr Grimes just picked out some vocational courses, along with the standard crap kids had to take, and we left.

Chapter 12

And so life began a plodding certainty after a matter of days. We just got used to the snow and cold. I began preparing brown bag lunches for all of us, peanut butter and jelly sandwiches, chips and an apple, setting everything out on the small table in our bedroom, and we each went about our own business. It was like we had lived there a long time, a routine already entrenched. Seven-fifteen, and Robert Lee had to be at the end of Main Street for the school bus. Honey started at eight-thirty.

I was back in the land of name tags. This tag said 'Frank. To Protect and Serve.' I was there almost a week without incident. The weird thing about the job was that there were no set hours. Basically, the dean told me to put in hours as *necessary*, usually at night, to check all buildings were secure, given the new presence of women on the campus. There was no clear directive other than the vague notion that the women needed to be protected. I never had a real sense of how many hours I was supposed to work, and, in that first week, I hardly ever heard from the sole security guy who ran the operation on campus. In fact, I'd never spoken to him. When he didn't show in the early hours of the morning the first few days, his girlfriend, Linda, called and told me to go home, that they had it covered. Then even she stopped calling, and I left the building unattended.

I worked the nightshift at my discretion, but was on permanent call in the event of snowstorms. In fact it became clear pretty quickly that's what I was really there for, a back-up for snow removal, and that patrolling the campus was not really in the job description, despite the dean's big speech on the phone.

There were four dorms on campus, and they were really what I was there to monitor. Of those four, two were for women, and that was the chief concern. The women's dorms were segregated from the men's and close by the security office by design. The first floor had no windows. Other than that, they were the same as the men's dorms. I was told never actually to go into the women's dorms. There were red panic buttons throughout the dorms, and, if something terrible happened, these would sound an alarm in my office.

The hardest thing I had to do was get used to living in a blur of insomnia. I developed night vision, since it was a no-no to go around using my flashlight, unless I was specifically beaming it into a suspect's eyes, except there were no suspects. Every hour or so I emerged, like a mole, going around and checking to make sure buildings were locked and checking on the student dorms. Of course, this was all made-up work I initiated myself, since, like I said, there was no real communication with the main security guy, but the first paycheck came without a problem, so I was going to keep to the directive the dean had laid out until further notice.

I walked the campus in my security outfit, my pants bunched up around my ass, since the goddamn uniform had been taken in and let out who knows how many times for other guys who had come before me.

I worked without incident until I'd been there a week. I had finished another round of checking dorms when I heard shouting coming from a car parked in the far campus lot. I shone my light on the license plate. It was out-of-state, a Volvo, and that meant it was one of the new rich kids. I had him roll down the window. Pot smoke poured out into the night air. There were two guys and a girl. I directed the light on their faces. The girl was in a bra, but one of the cups had been pulled down so her breast was visible. I said, 'You okay, young lady?'

The girl was stoned. I kept the light on her. She shielded her eyes with her arm.

I got her out of the car. I could tell she was local. She looked beautiful in the way only teenagers do. She was slim, wearing Lee Jeans and a satin jacket from an auto repair shop. She stood hugging her arms.

One of the kids got out of the car. He was squat and wearing a corduroy jacket. He was one of those hair flippers who was always sweeping the hair out of his face. He said, 'We were partaking of a little *recreational* activity.' The kid put up his hands and then ran one through his hair.

I ignored him and said to the girl, 'You want any assistance?'

The girl shook her head.

That's when the hair flipper said, 'Hey, it's our illustrious friend. Brad, it's *Frank*.'

The other guy got out of the car and looked at me.

The girl said, 'Who?'

The hair flipper said, 'Let's go, I'll tell you later.'

I left and went over to the late-night diner on campus. It closed at 1:30 a.m. I got cheese fries and a Coke and sat alone on a plastic bench, feeling self-conscious that I was the laughing stock of the goddamn campus, that my history was an open book. The kids had unnerved me. Night-time work was the kind of work where you ended up looking into your own soul, and I wasn't really up for that. It reminded me of when I had my breakdown, and I kept saying to myself that this wasn't the sort of job I should have taken. But the problem was there was nothing else right then, so I just concentrated on staying sane. For a while I thought of putting a gun down that rich kid's throat, I mean way down his fucking throat until the barrel starting choking him. I felt capable of doing that right then.

I got up and got a catalog for the college and started paging through it. They had taken a single image of an old building on the campus and put that on the cover, giving this aura of pastoral contentment and learning. It was bullshit. That building didn't represent the campus which was all new crap buildings. They had pictures of students in lab coats checking vials of liquid, serpentine apparatuses for chemical reactions. Jesus Christ, it was a real snow job.

I was on the outside. I felt that more than ever. All it took was one incident to tip the scale of my stability. I said to myself, 'Fuck those kids.'

I kept looking around me. I had missed out on a fundamental change taking place in America, the mass education of even our most rural citizens, even those with sawdust between their goddamn ears. The college still offered a variety of courses that ranged from horticulture to two-year associate degrees in things like business administration, electronics, paralegal studies, book keeping, etc., all of which I saw as merely qualifying you to answer a phone in one of those professions. The price of mere existence had gone through the fucking roof. And the thing was, these assholes had no sense of irony, no sense that this was a third-rate joke of a community college, that what they were studying for now, and taking out student loans and getting their asses in debt for, were jobs you got out of high school just a few years earlier.

Some kid tipped his tray into the trash can, and I looked up. The fluorescent lights of the diner made the kid look pale and sickly. I took a long drink of my Coke. It tasted too sweet, like they'd gotten the mixture wrong. My teeth felt sticky.

I set the college brochure aside and focused on trying to bend a spoon with my mind, the same old tricks as always, anything to keep my mind occupied. Wanting to ram a gun down some kid's throat was something I was going to have to get out of my head, because this is what nightlife was going to be like from now on.

I looked up and saw a woman in her twenties with long blonde hair, reading at a table by herself. A coffee mug steamed by her arm. She was older than most of the kids hanging around there. I guess that's what caught my eye. I could tell she was local as well.

I watched her. She was reading and marking up her book with a highlighting marker. I did the mind control thing for the hell of it, just to pass the time. I put my hands to my temples and thought hard. I said inside my head, 'Look at Frank. Frank is irresistible. You like Frank. Frank is kind and gentle. Frank is the man of your dreams.'

The woman looked up and saw me and then turned around to see who I was looking at. She realized it was her. A minute later, she closed her book and left. I figured I'd scared her off.

I sat twirling a fry in the congealing cheese. It was getting that waxy coating. I could see all these kids reading and writing and quizzing each other. I wanted to say things like, 'Shit, people, we should all be out at a goddamn bar, for Christ's sake. Life is short! It's going to pass you by! Drinks are on me.' I could have gone to a bar right then, but I didn't.

Back at the security office, I did some jumping jacks and sit-ups and push-ups. I got myself sweaty and froze when I went out into the cold night air on my rounds. I went by the prefab structure where I'd been hypnotized years ago. It was strange to be responsible for its security.

From my office window, I sat looking out at the dark sky. I could see the shapes of girls moving in the squares of light, some sitting at desks studying, others just standing around talking. Sometimes I'd see a girl smoking, the pulse of ash against the dark, or hear girls laughing, somebody talking on the phone, the sound of a radio playing low when I went outside to begin my rounds. It seemed like there was always somebody up all night studying. I can't say there was anything erotic about any of it. They might as well have been aliens from another planet.

Then one morning after my shift, in the silence of the boarding house, as I sat staring into the wood-burning stove, I got a frantic call from Martha. The others were gone. I had the curtains closed, keeping out the daylight. I was slowly adjusting to going to bed in the early morning. I had folded my pants and shirt neatly over a hanger and hung them on a hook on the back of the bedroom door when the phone rang.

Martha was crying, 'Frank! Oh God! They took Norman!'

I said, 'Martha ... Slow down ... Who took him?'

'The police. Oh God, they just came in their cars right before he went out to milk the cows.'

'When was this?'

'Just now, this morning ... Jesus, there was an almighty fight. Norman said to the police he had to milk the cows first, and the cops wouldn't wait. They insisted he go with them right then. I told Norman I could handle the cows, but Norman wouldn't go. One of the cops drew his gun. Norman took a step toward him, and, I swear, Frank, that cop cocked his gun. I had to stop Norman going any further. I said, "We got kids, Norman, you hear me? Is this what you want them to see?" That stopped him, that was all, otherwise he would have killed that cop. I could see that look in his eyes. Now he's gone. I don't know where they took him.'

I rubbed the fatigue from my eyes, trying to think. I said, 'They didn't say where they were taking him?'

Martha sniffled, 'No, they said nothing. I swear, they would have shot him down if I didn't stop him. If he gets put into some cell he's going to spook, Frank. He doesn't like confinement. He's claustrophobic. They need to know that. We got to tell them that right now, we just have to ...'

'Let me try and make a call to the guy who works security and see if he has any in with the police, okay?'

Martha swallowed and sniffled. 'I don't understand this. This is an open and shut case. I want them to leave us alone. We're the victims here, us!'

Martha stopped. Her breaths were quick. 'I don't want Norman losing what he has here, Frank, not over this. He's scared. All that crazy talk of his about the Devil. He's still convinced that's the Devil at the hospital. He's simple. He gets something like this into his head, and he won't let it go. I've told him, Frank, I've said, "A coma, Norman, is something that people fall into. It's because the man hanged himself, because he cut off oxygen to his brain, that's why he's in a coma!" But Norman doesn't listen. He sees things his way.' Martha took a deep breath. 'Please, Frank, I'm calling you as Norman's brother. You might hate me, but think of Norman, Frank.'

I said, 'I don't hate you or Norman.'

'Okay, Frank, whatever you say. I just want everything . . .' She started crying.

I waited. 'Listen, I'll call you back, okay?'

I called the security guy at work. His name was Baxter. He answered the phone with this loud, 'Hello,' stressing the *hell*.

I said, 'This is Frank.'

'Oh, the phantom night-shifter. We got to meet up, one of these mornings. But right now I've got woman trouble, if you know what I mean. God, do I have woman trouble.'

I said inanely, 'Don't we all.'

'Hey, Frank, why do men die before their wives?'

I said, 'I don't know. Why?'

'Because they want to!' Baxter let out a hoot of laughter. 'Because they want to! Jesus, isn't it the truth though!'

I felt this pain above my temple, a twitch of pain. I said, 'I got a favor to ask you, Baxter.'

'Shoot.'

I gave him an account of what had gone on with Norman and the whole investigation as Martha had told it, ending by saying Norman had been taken away by the police.

Baxter got serious. 'Shit. I've been hearing about what went on out there.'

I said, 'What did you hear?'

'Well, they removed two slugs from the scene, one from your uncle's head, and another from the ceiling.'

I said, 'Norman fired at the ceiling. He heard somebody in the upper part of the house. He fired at the ceiling. He told the cops that.'

'Yeah, well, that's suspicious as far as the cops are concerned! I mean, he's got his fingerprints on the gun, and he has an explanation all pat like that . . . Not to mention, Frank, Norman's overalls were covered in blood.'

'Goddamn it! Norman just held his father, what the hell was he supposed to do?'

'And the gunshot?'

'He was scared. He heard something and his gut instinct when he saw the gun on the ground was to pick it up and fire it!'

'Hey, lighten up. I'm just telling you what the cops see, that's all. All the cops are doing is eliminating possibilities, and your brother shooting off the gun needs to be looked into. It's as simple as that.'

I said, 'They have the guy who killed my uncle. He was in the house, for Christ's sake, what more evidence do they want?' I shook my head. 'This is bullshit, all of it. You know, my brother's wife called me up screaming the cops dragged Norman off his farm. They didn't give him time to milk his herd or anything!'

Baxter made a clicking sound like he was thinking, or getting bored. 'Look, it's all just procedural bullshit. This is a prime opportunity for overtime. That's what those stiffs are looking at, putting in overtime. You get my drift, Frank? Local law enforcement gets a case like this and they want all the flash of some TV drama, they got a script in their heads. Just let them play it out, is all.'

I settled on the edge of the bed, staring at the bedded embers of the small stove. The room was warm. I could feel the effects of fear wearing off. It was just like Baxter said, just procedure. I said, 'You know, the only reason my brother's wife got concerned is Norman is . . . he's slow in certain ways, and confinement doesn't suit him. He could be liable to do something wild if he gets freaked.'

'Listen, I got some friends in law enforcement. Maybe I'll just let them know your brother spooks easy, okay?'

I let out a long breath. 'God, I wish this was just finished.' I waited a moment. 'Do you happen to know what's going on with the investigation into identifying if the murderer is Chester Green?'

'I guess the police have checked with the Army since that tattoo has all the hallmarks of being done while the murderer was over in Korea. The army's pulling service records, checking if they had a Chester Green enlisted. They're waiting on word back.'

'Look, Baxter, thanks. I feel like an ass calling you like this . . . But . . . Maybe one of these mornings I'll stick around. I owe you a cup of coffee.'

'Shit Frank, coffee. You don't know me, do you! Listen, I've got big plans for you and me. You know we're sitting on a gold mine here. One of these days I'm going to lay out my plans on how this college is going to make us rich.'

I said, 'Sure, you're the boss,' and set the phone down.

I called Martha, but the line was busy.

The morning streamed around the edge of the curtains. My head throbbed with the need for sleep. I bedded the wood stove with another log. I took two sleeping pills I had from an old prescription for insomnia. I curled up in the four-poster bed, put my head under the covers.

Sometime later Martha called me and said Norman had come home by mid-afternoon. She got off the phone quick.

And it was that same night the first hints into the life of the man who killed Ward emerged on the late nightly news. I was working down at the college and watched it on the small set. I'd just finished watching *Jeopardy*.

A building superintendent in Chicago had called the police saying a man named Chester Green had been missing from his apartment for approximately a month. When presented with a photograph of Ward's killer taken at the time of his arrest, the superintendent positively identified the man as the same man who'd rented the apartment under the name Chester Green.

The TV camera focused a wide-angle shot on a dilapidated brownstone building, then zoomed in to a small window with its blinds drawn. The superintendent was a short fat Polish immigrant with bad teeth and a grey growth of stubble. He had the look of a guy in search of a reward. Against the backdrop of the superintendent, black kids waved at the camera.

I nearly lost it right then. I knew the area. I'd lived three blocks away from where Chester Green lived. I felt myself sweating. I kept watching. What emerged from initial reports out of Chicago was a sketchy account of the man's life. He had rented the apartment under the name Chester Green and had been there going on ten years. He had worked in construction, but had been out on long-term disability for over four years due to chronic lower-back pain from a fall. He was unmarried. The superintendent said in his broken English, 'Mr Green, he speak not so much. He was with himself most times.'

I just sat in the office for a long time, thinking about nothing and everything at the same time. I felt outside myself. Jesus Christ, looking back, Chicago was a goddamn nightmare.

I think my life paralleled the political climate of that time, leaving home for Chicago with such hope, with the message of Kennedy saying he was going to put a man on the moon, *not because it was easy, but because it was hard.* I thought, shit, let's get off this goddamn planet is right, let's head for other worlds, and off I went and left Ward and Norman and that goddamn farm behind. I was in Chicago from sixty-four to seventy-two, through that turning point in our collective history. Kennedy got assassinated in my senior year, and things spiraled after that, right on through RFK's and MLK's assassinations, through the Vietnam War protests, the riots at the democratic convention in Chicago. I lived it all in a daze of drugs, both prescribed and otherwise.

I escaped being drafted since I got institutionalized in Chicago for my breakdown. They hooked me up to a machine that burned out my goddamn memory, that made me forget things that were best not remembered. This doctor explained the principle to me, and I thought, Jesus Christ, here is a machine that could change our history, a machine that makes us forget about hating blacks and communists, a machine that could make us start over again. I said, 'You know what you got here, Doc?' I said, 'This is like a form of time travel.' I called it The Eden Machine!

And then they stuck a rubber ball in my mouth and filled me with the sweet metal taste of electricity, and my body jerked and got rigid until the pathways of memory were seared. I thought this was the answer, not just to my problems, but for us as a nation. There were things best not seen, images of war fought far away, but played out each night on our TVs, images that were going to change us forever.

But the goddamn problem in the end was that not all the memory was burned away. The machine didn't get everything, but the chronology of things had come undone. When I try to explain my thoughts when I get that feeling of disorientation, I say, 'It's like when somebody turns on a blender, how it creates that interference with household appliances, how it makes the TV fizzle and the radio crackle.' And that was at the best of times during my illness, because there were times back then when whole weeks were a blank, stretches of unaccountable time.

I wanted to call Melvin right then. I wanted to hear his voice, just to know he was still alive. I called directory assistance and asked for Melvin's number. I wrote it down on a piece of paper.

I shouldn't have called from the office, but I'd dialed the number already.

Melvin answered. 'Who's there?' The TV was on in the background. It was on loud.

I said nothing, and Melvin waited on the end of the line. The show in the background was *Jeopardy*, the same show I'd been watching earlier. It was syndicated around the country, showing at different times. It freaked the hell out of me. I just answered the next question, and the question after that, and then I asked the next question before it was even asked, and suddenly Melvin understood what I was doing. He began to say something, but I hung up.

I fell asleep, and when I awoke, it felt like I had dreamed everything. Then the phone rang. It rang a long time before I picked it up. I was sure it was the police, that they had traced the call.

It was Martha. She invited us to Thanksgiving Dinner.

She said nothing else. I felt the silence on her end of the phone out at the farm. The heat of our previous conversations had run its course.

I said, 'You see on the news that somebody has identified Ward's murderer as Chester Green?'

Martha didn't answer me. She said, 'Maybe you can bring something, a pumpkin pie if you like?'

Our relationship was as thin as that wire threaded across the land connecting our phones. I looked at the clock. It was going on 2:30 a.m.

I said, 'It's late.'

Martha said, 'I don't sleep so good anymore ...'

I should have said nothing else, but I said, 'Maybe now that things are settled, we can talk about what we are going to do about the farm?'

And the phone just went dead in my ear.

Chapter 13

The next day there was a small piece in the paper describing the meticulously kept apartment. But there was no mention of what was recovered from the apartment, no suggestion about the mystery of whether Chester Green had resurfaced twenty-seven years after his death. The article further mentioned that photographic records of the unit in which Chester Green served in Korea were being pulled, just like Baxter had told me. It didn't say anything about the exhumation of Sam Green's son, but it did say Ward's killer had been moved to the local sanitarium that had once been a polio hospital.

I read in the newspaper each day the piece on the murder investigation. Ward's killer's condition hadn't changed. He was still in a coma but was now off a ventilator. A doctor was quoted as saying, 'the longer a patient remains in a coma, the more likely it is that the patient will not regain consciousness.' I circled the name of the doctor, Dr Brown. I wondered if that was the same doctor who'd worked on me in my original hypnosis sessions after my parents died.

'An open case pending further developments' is how the paper put it. The story ground to a journalistic halt anyway, as the police followed through on leads. I was waiting for them to come and interview me, but nobody ever showed. Nobody made the connection that I had lived blocks from Ward's killer at one time in the past. And why would they?

I was in my third week of work when Ward's death was

eclipsed by Jim Jones killing his flock down in the jungles of Guyana. It came over the radio in the early hours of the morning on my shift. The reporter said Jones broadcast his spiritual message from loud speakers at all hours. His mission had been to create an egalitarian agricultural community, a utopia on Earth. It snowed heavily outside as I listened. It seemed like I was living in another universe entirely.

Baxter called me around five in the morning. 'Hey, Frank, this is going to be a big snow. If you want an hour of shut-eye, head home, because we're going to have to plow the rest of the day.' He didn't say anything about Jonestown.

I left work early, before sunrise. Snow was falling in a slant because the wind had picked up. I went home and looked in on Ernie and Robert Lee. Then I got into bed beside Honey and held her. She said, 'What time is it?' She looked at the clock. I held on to her and didn't say anything. 'You didn't get fired?'

I whispered, 'No. I have to work overtime today. There's a storm coming.'

By the time we got up, the story was all over the TV, the image of bodies strewn across the jungle utopia. We sat in the room watching it unfold. I prepared breakfast. They had a picture of the cult leader, Jim Jones. He was wearing sunglasses. I said, 'He looks like a guy out of the Secret Service.'

Honey said, 'God, he looks creepy. He doesn't look like anybody that would start a utopia.'

The recordings of the final minutes of the people's lives played through a static tape recording of cult members screaming and crying. You could hear Jim Jones speaking to his followers. Over nine hundred followers were confirmed dead in the mass suicide. Two hundred of those were children.

Ernie stood close to the TV and touched the images. I guess he didn't fully understand these people were dead. He probably thought they were sleeping, since why would a kid think that people lying around like that could be dead? He said, 'Nap time, Frank,' but his brain was considering the possibilities of what this might be. He was smart about things.

I said, 'Yeah, nap time.' Down at Ernie's kindergarten they made the kids lie down on rubber mats and pretend they were asleep. I went by one mid-afternoon to get Ernie, and all the kids were lying inert, like they might just be dead or drugged.

And despite the horror of what was unfolding on TV, they shoved in a segment on baking tollhouse cookies for the coming Holiday Season. A fat weatherman stood before the map of the United States eating one of the cookies and talked about the national weather, sticking happy sun faces on the deep south and a snowflake up north. I mean weather reporting didn't get any simpler than this. Then the weather-man listed birthdays of people who had turned a hundred years young.

We left and went out into the swirling snow, all of us to our respective destinations. Honey and I walked Ernie by his pre-school. I told Honey Martha had invited us for Thanksgiving, and Honey said, 'Let's just see, okay?'

At the office, I finally met Baxter. He smelt of booze, and his eyes were bloodshot. He was a guy in his late twenties, but he looked like he could have been forty. He rattled off his life story in a matter of minutes. He was a Vietnam vet who had been a POW and had what he called 'a gook kid' back in Vietnam. He said he crash-landed back into life here. He asked me if I knew the escape route out. He touched me when he said these things, patting my back. He said, 'I feel like a goddamn POW right now, Frank. Prisoner of Women . . .' He laughed from deep in his belly. He told me an ungodly complicated story of intrigue and romance gone bad. He gave me the blow-by-blow account of his latest misadventure.

When he was finished, Baxter sat by the dispatch radio and

got on to the State Police and National Weather Service. Everything was a 'reconnaissance mission' with him. He wanted me 'out in the field', or wanted to know what it was like 'in the line of fire' all day long as I worked the college Jeep and plowed the roads around campus. His head was filled with paranoia and the legacy of war. Something like Jonestown didn't even figure since his own life was all-consuming, a vortex of self-concern.

I jumpstarted cars with dead batteries for faculty and students after each class let out. I was dreading Baxter asking me about my tour of Vietnam. During the course of the day his two favourite subjects, his only two subjects, were Vietnam and sex. It seemed that when he wasn't killing or being a POW, he was perpetually getting high and getting laid over in Vietnam. He just talked to me over the CB, taking me right through the storm until classes let out.

By the time I got back to the office, Baxter was lit up with booze and cigarettes. He put the phone to his chest when I came back in. I could tell he was having a fight with his girlfriend. He said, 'You ever talk anybody down off a ledge, Frank?'

I shook my head. I passed out on a couch that looked like it had been rescued from some college kid's dorm room. Baxter just kept cursing into the phone.

I slept for a few hours. Baxter woke me and gave me a coffee, thick and strong. 'Night classes are getting out soon. We'll get a shit load of calls.'

I sat up and hugged myself, feeling that cold you feel when you've been woken from a deep sleep.

'Fourteen inches and counting, Frank. This is a major operation. I need you out there.' He said, 'Hey, last night my girlfriend says to me, "What's on the TV?" And I said, "Dust!" You think that constitutes a fight?' He repeated the word dust again, and laughed that deep laugh of his. 'You sure you don't want a bourbon against the cold, Frank? This is genuine medicine right here. You drink this, and I guarantee you won't come down with a cold!'

I said, 'I'll pass right now,' but Baxter poured the bourbon into my cup anyway. 'This is doctor's orders, Frank, Baxter MD ... Mentally Deranged,' and he laughed that god-awful laugh again.

I watched the TV for a few minutes up in the office. They were showing the same reel they'd showed all day from Jonestown, resurrecting the same images over and over again. It was as if I was reliving the same moment, something like clairvoyance.

Baxter looked at the TV. 'Shit, I could have told those assholes there's no such thing as happiness, there's no paradise on Earth.' He winked at me. 'Unless we're talking pussy, right?'

I said, 'Yeah.'

I emptied my bladder and came back, feeling sore inside, like I'd held it too long. It was going on 7:45 p.m. I called the house.

Honey said, 'Thank God you called.'

'What's wrong?'

'Oh, nothing big, but you got to convince Ernie that he has to leave his dinosaurs at home. He can't bring them to kindergarten any more.'

'What?'

'That Church doesn't exactly believe in evolution. The pastor was telling me that all God's creations exist as they have existed since the Ark. And, guess what, there were no dinosaurs in the Ark, Frank.'

I said, 'This is bullshit. Jesus Christ Almighty.'

'Frank, don't go blowing a gasket now. That kindergarten is dirt cheap, and, as far as I'm concerned, I think it hurts his emotional growth to be toting those ḍ-i-n-o-s-a-u-r-s around with him.' She spelled the word dinosaurs so as not to upset Ernie.

I was pissed. 'Maybe we should start telling him the earth's flat as well.'

'Frank, cut it out. He loses his place at that school, and one of us has to stop working.'

I said, 'Okay, maybe you're right. Has the theory of evolution or our understanding that the earth is round ever really impacted on our lives? Do you think we could go on living not knowing those facts?'

'Cut the crap. Ernie wants to talk to you.'

Ernie got on the phone.

I said, 'I love you, kid.'

Ernie said, 'They don't like my dinosaurs, Frank.' His voice was full of kid sadness. I could hear the television in the background. In some way, it was good to get embroiled in the sideshow of my family life.

'It's not that they don't like the dinosaurs, Ernie. Tell you what, Ernie. Why don't you leave your dinosaurs at home, since I hear the other kids are jealous, and they want dinosaurs just like you've got. And what good is it if every kid gets a dinosaur, right? They're your special friends. I'll tell you what I'm going to do for you.'

'What, Frank?'

'I'm going to hire the dinosaurs to guard our room when we're out. They're going to be just like me, Ernie. Security cops protecting our stuff. If it's good enough work for me, then they can do it too, right?'

Ernie ran that by Honey, and she got back on and said, 'Blessed are the peacemakers, Frank.' I heard her sigh. 'You enjoying that peace and quiet over there? God, I envy you. I got to give Ernie his bath now, Frank.' She said in the background, 'Ernie, don't go near that fire.'

But she didn't get off the line, just waited for me to say something. I said, 'There's something in your voice, Honey, what is it?'

Honey said softly, 'Why do life's most meaningful conversations take place across phone lines?'

'What is it?'

'I want to see the face of someone I'm talking to. I'll tell you later. I can't talk right now.' She said, 'Goodnight,' and made a kissing sound. She set the phone down, and the line died. I didn't call her back.

I told Baxter what the Church said. He looked at me. 'You ever actually seen a dinosaur? Who you going to trust, the Church or some bullshit scientists? We could be fed so much shit and what the hell would we know? I say, show me a fucking dinosaur. You want to fucking believe we evolved from monkeys, Frank, go ahead. But I say, fuck implicating the apes in this cock-up of a world we created. Shit, if that's the fucking order of things, then any goddamn scientist or person who believes we have no soul is guilty of murder when they eat meat. When some cow is slaughtered, it's no different from killing a human being. You hear me? You know, I sure as hell would like to believe that all those people I killed over in Vietnam were just that, just fucking soulless meat. It would make things a hell of lot simpler for me. But I can't! You get what I'm saying, Frank? You think I'm going to believe pussy evolved from something that crawled out of the sea? Well, do you? You want to degrade us as human beings, for what? I say, the Lord said on the first day, "Let there be pussy!" and there was pussy. That's how I see Creation, Frank.'

I had that headache again. I drank the laced coffee and didn't say any more.

'If there's one thing I am, Frank, it's religious.'

I said, 'I'll keep that in mind.'

Baxter put his hands on me and smiled. 'Shit, I was winding you up, okay? All I'm saying is, if we're going to survive, we got to believe in our position in the order of things.'

Baxter got on the other line with his girlfriend, entering into an intense discussion about the meaning of relationships within five seconds of getting on the phone.

A call came over the radio, and that saved me from listening to any more bullshit. After pulling a professor from a snow bank, I plowed the snow for something like two hours, wandering aimlessly down dead ends, sweeping through the car parks, feeling the bite of the shovel making the Jeep shake. Right then, I think I could have done that for the rest of my goddamn life, the sudden jolt as I hit the snow banks, the compression of my chest into the steering wheel. I wanted something physical, something to tell me I was alive. I reversed, and the plow scraped the road, reverberating down my spine. I punched the gas again and hit another bank of snow, the dull impact, my organs pushed forward inside my body, my head snapping back.

It was going on three o'clock in the morning. The storm had passed. The air was freezing. Stars studded the night sky. The fresh snow shone in the moonlight.

Baxter was drinking measures of bourbon inside the office. He saw me and smiled, 'What's your pleasure, Frank? Doctor's orders!'

I took my coffee mug, and Baxter poured liberally. He said, 'Say when.'

I put my hand on his, and he stopped and set the bottle down. The three bars of the propane heater burned orange.

Baxter's face shone from the alcohol. 'You can't call it winter until you get socked like this. Now for my plans, Frank, those plans I was telling you about.' He opened his eyes wide, the way drunks do. 'I figure we got it made here. Time and a half, Frank. Let's drink to that! Money in the bank!' He raised his glass, and we both drained our drinks, then he unscrewed the cap and poured again, spilling some bourbon on the back of my hand. 'Frank, I don't know how the hell you did it, but the campus is all plowed. So here's the deal. Stay at home tomorrow. I got it covered, but we're going to put down that you worked the dayshift and the nightshift. That puts you up for overtime.' He made the sound of a cash register, 'kajing kajing'. He was laughing. 'We split the overtime sixty-forty.'

I didn't argue, didn't ask which percentage I was getting. I was dazed from the work and lack of sleep.

Baxter closed his eyes and drank in silence for a few minutes. He said, 'What the hell was I talking about?' Then he said, 'Oh, yeah, you ever asphyxiate a woman near to the point of suffocation? Now *that* is an orgasm, Frank, an orgasm like you wouldn't believe for the woman.'

Baxter poured another drink. He just wouldn't let up. 'Frank, I swear to you, I envy you. I saw one of those chicks over there dancing naked in the window. It was unbelievable, Frank, un-fucking-believable. I can't believe you get to see that every night, Frank. You lucky son-of-a-bitch!' He made like he was going to kiss me, but stopped and just filled his glass again.

I went to the window just to appease him. I wanted to put some distance between him and me.

Baxter got sullen for a few minutes. I heard the clink of the bottle against his glass. He said, 'I can see you looking at me.'

I turned and said, 'How's that?'

Baxter stood up and fake saluted the dark outside. 'The way I see it, I did all the killing that was needed, and now I just want to fuck the world. I mean, I want to take all the goddamn women out there in that big beautiful world and spill everything I have inside them.'

I said, 'I'll drink to that,' and Baxter smiled and said, 'Shit, Frank, there's no more important job than fucking. Way more important than killing. I think they should give a medal for fucking.' He raised his glass. 'I see you laughing. A medal for fucking, you're thinking!'

I said, 'I'm not laughing.'

140

'Frank, I'll tell you what's goddamn funny. I got a goddamn medal for killing! You know what I want, Frank?'

'What?'

'I want...' He looked at me. 'I want to be awarded the Purple Head,' and with that, Baxter busted his ass laughing, and I smiled, and then even I lost it. Baxter's eyes rimmed with tears as he pounded the table, 'The goddamn Purple Head. Oh, shit almighty. I just made that up right now, Frank! I got to write that down. I want you to sign right here, Frank, that I made that up right now.' Baxter scrawled something on a piece of paper, and I signed and dated it. He got serious after that, folded up the piece of paper and stuck it into his breast pocket.

The alarm tripped in the office. Baxter drained the last of what was in his glass. 'You want, I can leave the bourbon, Frank?'

I said, 'You take the party with you, Baxter. I think I might just get some shut-eye.'

I went out with him to the car. He pointed to a window by the dorm. 'Right there, at two o'clock. That's where she was, dancing, naked as a jaybird, Frank!'

Baxter's girlfriend didn't emerge from the car, but she said out loud, 'Jesus, Baxter, you're as drunk as a skunk.'

Baxter got into the car. He rolled his window down and said, 'Frank. I want to tell you something.'

I leaned toward him.

'There are two things in this world that smell like tuna, and one of them is tuna.' With that, his girlfriend hit the gas, the car fishtailed, and they were gone.

I checked the campus again. It was an island of light in the dark of the surrounding woods, like something galactic, a life force of intelligence in the vastness of space above, or that's how I was seeing things that night. Taking this job had allowed me not to face the reality that there was half a day of light, and not just darkness. I made a promise to myself that I was going

141

to go out and see Ward's killer. I had come this far, now I had to witness what was out there at the sanitarium, stare at the man who had killed Ward. I had traveled halfway across the country, but for what? But in the end, I didn't have a real answer. I had just run for cover, a casualty of so-called modern existence and hourly wage jobs. That is why I had left New Jersey, or at least that is what I kept telling myself.

Chapter 14

I left before Baxter arrived and went home. The apartment was empty. I slept into late afternoon and awoke to a clear sky outside. I made coffee and called Baxter. He said, 'I got all bases covered here, Frank.' I could hear a woman in the background. It sounded like a party.

I had the operator put me through to the sanitarium. I asked for Dr Brown and it turned out he was the doctor who'd hypnotized me way back all those years ago.

'Frank! My God. I heard you were in town.'

I was taken aback he even remembered me, really. I said that to him.

'Let's say I've taken more than a passing interest in this case.'

I didn't know what that meant, if it was medical, or something else to which he was alluding.

'I don't want to compromise you or anything, Doc. I don't know the protocol, but am I allowed to go see this guy you got out there?'

Dr Brown cleared his voice. 'Well, officially, no, but for you, let's make an exception. In fact, I would like us to talk, if you have the time. I was hoping you'd call, as matter of fact.'

I said, 'Talk about what?'

I must have said it defensively, because Dr Brown said, 'Come now. We are still friends, right? You don't hold any ill-feelings, do you?'

I didn't say anything for a moment or two. 'No, Doc, I guess I'm just on edge. I've been working late nights at the college.'

'Okay. I'll see you out here.' But before he hung up, he said, 'As a mental exercise, Frank, lie down and close your eyes, and ask yourself why you came back home.' He'd hung up before I could answer.

I got Ernie from his kindergarten and took him for a soda on campus. I was out of uniform and walking toward home when the dean called me from the steps of the Administration Building. He came across and, in his affable way, shook my hand. 'Hell of a job, Frank. One hell of a job you're doing here. You were on top of this storm. I knew you were the man for the job.' The dean fished in his pocket and got out a dollar bill and gave it to Ernie. He said, 'You invest that wisely, kid.'

I didn't like the dean seeing me, since Baxter was going to put me down for the day shift. I figured on telling him to forget that idea.

At the apartment, I added wood to the stove so it glowed. The room got warm quickly. In the back bedroom, I put Ernie on his bed and read to him. He was curled up like a peanut with his dinosaur beside him. When he was asleep, I tiptoed back to the front room.

Honey had come home. She was sitting on the edge of the bed smoking a cigarette. She looked at me and smiled, 'He's sleeping?' She said it softly.

I nodded.

'Help me with these boots, Frank.'

I pulled hard, and each moon boot came off in that slow suctioning way.

Honey let the smoke gather around her. She whispered. 'I see a beautiful change in you. You're the man I married, beneath all that's happened, you are, still, inside.' I was kneeling at her waist. She touched my heart. 'In there, where it counts, Frank.'

I got up and lay on the bed, and Honey stubbed out her cigarette and lay close to me.

'I was thinking back about what you said, Frank, about when you were in high school, and how you were real smart, and I just don't think life is all over like maybe it was for people our age years ago.' She kissed the back of my hand. 'Frank, I just don't think you should let that go. You are smart.'

I said, 'I think the time's long since passed for all that.' I felt the weight of her head like a medicine ball on my chest.

'You know you can take courses at the college. I checked with the dean at the Business School, and he told me both of us are entitled to tuition at fifty percent off. In two years of night school, you could be fully qualified in whatever you want, Frank.'

I was staring at the ceiling, just waiting.

'I just feel so safe for once.'

I kissed the crown of her head.

She whispered, 'Frank, what would you do if I told you what I want more than anything else in the world is for my kid to fall in love, just once? Because, if I had one wish, that's what I'd wish, not money or fame, but to have Robert Lee experience true love.'

Her lips touched against my hand. I felt her body tense. And then she said what was on her mind. She whispered, 'I got word Ken is going to be executed.'

I felt myself tense. 'When?'

'They set a date for December seventeenth.'

I said in a soft voice, 'There's no way they're going to execute a man before Christmas, trust me.'

We were wrapped in the absolute silence of the afternoon as the light outside faded to grey and the stove burnished the room with a soft golden glow. A clock ticked on the dresser.

I said, 'There are always those stays of execution. That date will come and go. Jesus, he's got appeals that can go on for ever.' Ken was like the longest sporting event you could ever

145

imagine watching, motion and counter-motion, the appeals process, stays of execution.

Honey shook her head. 'This is going to be the end. My sister Doris got word from the state-appointed attorney that this is going to be it. He's going to die. There's no two ways about it.' She instinctively pressed my hand with her own hand. I touched the hardness of her nails.

'I never told you anything that went on between Ken and me, and now I want you to know that, if the two of you were standing here right now, I'd choose you, Frank. That's not just me telling you what you want to hear. That's not a wife lying to her husband. It's the truth.' Her mouth was hot and wet against my hand. 'He's going crazy.'

'Honey, you don't have to tell me anything. I don't have to know.'

Honey squeezed my hand. 'I want you to know, Frank.'

I kept staring at the ceiling.

'Down there in Georgia you sweat something awful, Frank. Your skin shines with sweat, and when you rub your skin, it comes off you all gritty. It's the oil from your skin is what you're sweating, and dead skin comes off. For the last few years, Ken's been rubbing off all the dead skin on his body.'

Honey hugged her knees to her breasts. She seemed vulnerable in a mortal way, like someone facing serious illness.

'He's created this thing . . . this thing out of all of that dead skin.' She stopped and let out a long sad breath. 'When Doris got the letter about his execution, she went right down and visited him, and Ken told her then about what he'd made. He said he had this thing in his cell that was the real murderer. He calls it "Bad Ken". He's told her that the thing he created is what did the killing. He wants out, he says he's ready for the afterlife. He wants to die.' Honey stopped flat and shook her head. 'I'm sorry.'

I said nothing.

'I can't say it doesn't look bad on me that I was with him,

and I was, but you know, back then I had nothing, Frank, nothing. I didn't have the opportunity to do what I wanted in life. A man comes along, and a woman takes her chances. The day it happened was just after Robert Lee's birthday, and we'd got him just this small cake. He'd wanted a bike, but we couldn't get him one, and even back then, you just couldn't not get Robert Lee what he wanted. He used to scream to all hell. This is one thing I got to say for Ken, he never once hit his own kid. He just used to take Robert Lee in his arms and hold him. He'd say to me, "We're just going to have to try harder in life." Anyway, he drank hard liquor that day and stared out of the motel we were staying at and just watched people moving around outside. It was hot. Watergate was on the TV all day long. It was this long interrogation in the dimness of the motel room. I could see Ken getting mad, see him staring out the sliver of curtain into the glare of the world. It was like a tear in reality, him staring like that into the hot sunlight, and in the background Robert Lee crying he wanted a bike.' Honey was still hugging her knees. 'I'm telling you this, Frank, because it's all going to come out in the wash. I'm going to tell Robert Lee eventually how it happened, all of it. He's got a right to know he was loved.'

Honey shuddered and said, 'We made a kid together, and that's what holds me to Ken, just that. You believe me, right? I got a kid suffering like I wish no kid ever had to suffer.'

I said, 'Shoo. It's okay.' Her voice had risen.

Honey kissed my hand, put it against her cheek and kissed it again. 'I swear to God, Ken believes in that thing he's created. He was talking to Doris like a crazy man. He was screaming to Doris that it's a medical fact that all the cells in our bodies die and that we're different people after something like eight years. Jesus Christ, can you believe it? And so Doris asks the guards, and they said it was true about him having that thing in his cell. They said, "Oh, Bad Ken. Yeah, there's something in there with him in the cell."'

Honey slept after that, and I got supper started.

In the back of my head, there was Ken and Bad Ken, that furtive creature in the corner of the cell. I sensed what it must have been like for him, locked into that cell with the memory of a murdered couple down in Georgia all those years ago. I really believed he couldn't reconcile the person he was now with the person who had done the killing. The way I saw it in life, there were only two states. Either you're seeking to recapture the past, or trying to escape the past. The real agony for someone like Ken was to be prisoner to a past that was going to get him executed. His life stopped on the day he was convicted. He was defined by a single action in his past. I felt some parallel ghost life with him, a sameness of situation, stuck in the eternal rerun of the past. And then there was Robert Lee, coping with the image of his father's future execution. At times, I thought he was experiencing what I'd seen, but in reverse, envisioning the death before it happened. We swirled around the same vortex.

That night I made a tent out of sheets, and Ernie and I pretended we were old time trappers out on some expedition. Ernie put a cooking pot with a black handle on his head which was supposed to be a raccoon hat. Honey heated some beans right in the can, and Ernie and I ate them and drank plain black coffee, though Ernie's was really Coke.

Honey sat staring at the TV, chain-smoking and drinking can after can of Tab.

Robert Lee came home late. I could tell he'd been smoking pot, that same smell from that rich kid's car, but I didn't say anything. Robert Lee set down a quiz he'd taken in math. When Honey saw it, she said, 'Hey, you got an A+ in Algebra!'

Robert Lee said, 'I cheated.' He still wasn't talking to Honey since his beating. He came under our fake tent and put his hand on Ernie's head. He said, 'I got you some Pop Rocks, Ernie.'

Honey made popcorn and handed it into the tent. She sat

on the bed and painted her toenails. I could smell the nail varnish.

Through the flap in the tent, we watched *Starsky and Hutch*. Huggy Bear was wearing a pimp hat with a feather and drinking a cocktail. His teeth showed in the dim ruby light. He said, 'Cops coming in through the front door give the place a bad name.' He flicked his finger and dismissed one of his women in the way only a pimp can dismiss a woman.

Of course Huggy didn't talk until Starsky flicked a ten spot before Huggy's big nostrils, which flared like he could actually smell money. It was pure racist bullshit, all stereotypes, but it was entertaining in the way I guess we wanted blacks and whites to get along.

Honey said, out of the blue, 'Hutch is real cute. I like him better than Frank Cannon. I don't see why they have Cannon on at all. He's gross.'

Robert Lee said, 'Shhh. We're trying to listen.'

Honey shouted, 'Don't shhh me, you hear?'

Robert Lee said, 'You can forget Hutch. You couldn't get a date with Ironside,' and right then I just busted my ass laughing.

Honey shouted, 'That better not be you laughing in there, Frank!'

In a way, I wanted it just like this for the rest of my life, I truly did.

But the humor died during the nightly news when we saw the grainy image of Chester Green in uniform with his platoon in Korea, and alongside was a mug shot of Ward's murderer at the time of his arrest. The two men were not the same, not remotely similar.

Chapter 15

The mystery of the Sleeper was the big news again in the area after the revelation that he might not be Chester Green after all. Sam Green seemed vindicated and said in that indignant way of his that he wanted his son's body exhumed. He wanted to know why the police hadn't responded to his request. His voice carried a hint of hysteria. He said, 'I went and looked at the murderer when all this started, and I told them that wasn't my son!' The story was playing when Baxter arrived.

Baxter looked at me and set a coffee and some powdered donuts on the table. He was uncharacteristically quiet, waiting until the report was over. He looked at me. 'This gets creepier all the time.'

I said, 'Did you ever hear anything about Norman, about how things went?'

Baxter sat and drummed his hands on the table. 'A lab report came back, and there was gunpowder residue on Norman's hand and on your uncle's hand.'

'Meaning what?'

'When a gun is fired, it discharges gunpowder that gets ingrained on the hand of the person who fired the gun. So it seems that both Norman and your uncle fired a gun according to the report.'

'And the Sleeper?'

'Inconclusive ... What with the Sleeper hanging himself, things got screwed up, and when they swabbed his hand after the ER worked on him, the results were inconclusive.'

'That's bullshit! Jesus Christ, that's the cops' mistake, not something Norman should be strung up over! Goddamn it, I can't believe this!' I looked at Baxter. 'What about the Sleeper's clothes? Was there ... residue or whatever the hell there could be on his clothes?'

Baxter nodded his head. 'Shit, Frank, you cover all bases. You know, as a matter of fact, the Sleeper's clothes were analyzed.'

'And?'

'Nothing ... They got nothing.'

'What the hell does that mean?'

'It means exactly what I said. Right now there is no physical evidence that supports the theory that that man, that Sleeper they got out at the sanitarium, killed Ward.'

I got up and stared out into the gathering light. I said with a hint of fear in my voice, 'Norman took the gun and shot at what he thought was the Devil! That's why he shot at the ceiling.' I turned and looked at Baxter. 'There's no way my uncle fired a gun. The cops have to be mistaken. It doesn't make sense. What are the cops saying, it was a suicide after all?'

Baxter shrugged his shoulders. 'They're saying nothing right now. I'm just telling you what I heard came back in the report. There were two shots fired, and it seems like both shots have been attributed to your uncle and Norman.' Then he put up his hands like he was surrendering. 'There is one other thing, Frank.'

'What?'

'Norman said the body was cold when he touched it. When Norman was interviewed again, he said the body was cold, and the medics confirmed that fact.'

'So?'

'It means Ward was killed earlier in the morning, maybe two hours previous to Norman calling the police. You got to ask yourself, why did the Sleeper stay out at the house?'

I said, 'You think he was looking for something?'

'I don't know, but it's something that has to be considered.'

I left after my night and headed out of town toward the sanitarium where the Sleeper was being held. I had permission to take the College Jeep, since there was no storm forecast, and I hadn't started my own car in over two weeks. But mostly, I wanted it so I could present an official aura going out there to the sanitarium. I even stayed in my security cop uniform.

It was warm inside the Jeep. The radio was on low as I drove through the deserted campus. A pale morning sun hung low on the horizon, spilling a weak light into the grey shapes of fading night. I drove through Main Street, past our boarding house, past the war memorial in the town square. I was going to go in and see Honey, but then I decided against it. I wanted the solitude of the morning drive to clear my head.

I could see the peak of my uncle's house in a dip in the hillside. It was the first time in years I'd seen it, barely visible, just the rooftop. If I hadn't known where to look, I wouldn't have seen it. The grain silos were off to the south. Further back, a ribbon of smoke came up from Norman's house, shrouded in a belt of pines frosted with snow. Martha had started breakfast, the crackle of bacon and smell of corned beef hash frying on a pan filling the cool air of her kitchen. Norman would already have been out milking the cows. It was a meager existence.

I turned slowly up to Ward's house. I had time to kill before meeting Dr Brown up at the sanitarium. The Jeep moved slowly. I was watching for Norman off in the distance, because I didn't want to bump into him right then. When I got to see him, I wanted it to be a long talk. I wanted it to be away from Martha.

I drove down the road as it rose slightly, then dipped into obscurity. What lay at the end of that solitary road was the origin of my existence, the very act of my conception and birth occurred out there in the ruins of the old house. That sent shivers up and down my spine.

Just like I couldn't quite grasp the idea of my parents being dead when I was with that psychiatrist in the old days, I now had that same feeling looking across at the rooftop of my uncle's house. I expected him to be there, that cantankerous asshole, tinkering with his old machinery, or wandering his property with his hands deep in his overalls. Even though I knew he was dead at a conscious level, somehow he went on living. I guess he'd been alive inside me for years, or some variant of what I thought he was anyway. Now what physically remained of him was down in some icebox at the coroner's.

I had spent almost half my life out there with him. In my mind, it was the place from which everything emanated. There was never anything more real than that farm. What constitutes life is laid down in childhood, the physical surroundings, the people you meet, and somehow the isolation and the fierceness with which my uncle clung to things impressed its sullen madness on me. It was all about survival and hard work.

Maybe that's why things were so dull in my mind, why there were memories I could not fully recall, because, even in those sad days in the wake of my parents' death, there was work to be done. I think the true reel of my consciousness starts right after my parents died. There was only my uncle and me out at the farm for nearly two years before Ward got himself a wife and Norman came along.

I pulled into the open yard in front of the house. I killed the engine and parked close to the barn, so the Jeep was obscured from view, so Norman couldn't see it from his house. I got out and went to the front door, but it was locked. I went to the back window and stared into the kitchen, and, just like in the movies, there was this chalk outline of a body. It was like a ghost image. I realized I'd touched the window and wiped off my prints and stepped back from the house. At the far side of the house, a pipe had burst along the gutter, and a crystal chandelier of ice caught the morning light.

I got back into the car and set the blower on high. But I didn't drive off. I stayed and stared out through the windscreen, looking between the house and the barn. I leaned the seat back a bit. I took my coffee cup from the cup holder and took a long drink. Then I settled and felt myself drift for a moment, and that old world resurrected itself . . .

A fire burns strongly in the kitchen. I see myself and my uncle in there. We do not speak. My uncle warms milk. Eggs tremble in a pot. I see myself sitting at the small table. I am biting my nails, waiting. Outside it is still dark. I look at the door from time to time, like I'm expecting someone to knock. I can see the look on my face, staring out as I stare back in on myself. It's like I have a secret I want to tell myself, but I just sit still and wait, biting my nails, looking between the window and my uncle.

'Stop!' my uncle says when he sees me biting my nails. He slaps my hands. 'Don't.'

'Eat!' My uncle sets the breakfast before me. He eats standing. I look at him and then at the window, and he goes and checks the window and cups his hand against the glass to peer into the dark.

I turn my eyes down and eat, but when he sees me staring again, he says, 'There's nothing there. Now eat.' But he looks out the window from time to time. It is still dark. I hear the animals outside in the barn. Then I hear a noise upstairs, the sound of feet, and I look at the ceiling, and my uncle says, 'Eat!'

Under the glow of a kerosene lamp, I see myself wriggle between the stalls. But across the yard, I can see a light on up in the attic. My uncle pushes me forward, saying, 'Mind your work.'

My breath smokes against the cold. I dip a brush into a warm bucket of water and wipe down the stiff, rubbery udders. My uncle follows with a bucket, milking. I see his face against the cow's hide, the shift of light from our kerosene lamp. He milks with his eyes closed. I hear the hiss and spurt of milk against the metal bucket. I move on down the line. A cow stomps nervously, pisses and farts shit into the half-dark, covering me. It is a warm spreading feeling . . .

I started back awake. The coffee cup had tipped onto my lap. I felt the warmth seep against my groin. I set the cup into the cup holder. I wiped tiredness from my eyes, blinked and yawned mechanically. I checked my watch. Thirty-five minutes had passed. This was a hazard of the night shift. Waves of hypnotic exhaustion lapped and ebbed at the edge of sleep.

I put the Jeep in gear and turned it slowly to face the house, seeing the upper windows of the bedrooms. I had an image of a shadow upstairs in the back room of the house, waiting for my uncle's soul, and I could see Norman, that behemoth of a man, reduced to superstition, to believing in the Devil. It's what I wanted to believe. What the hell must it have been like to be inside his head at the moment when he snapped and believed that the noise upstairs was coming from something otherworldly? What did he envision up there in that room, some traditional creature with glowing eyes and a pitchfork, or something less defined, some winged shadow crouched on the bed waiting patiently to claim a soul for Hell?

And then I had an image of him pulling the trigger against Ward's head. Martha was standing at the door. She was telling Norman what to do. I saw the gore, Ward's head torn open. I watched Norman take the gun and put it around Ward's hand and shoot at the ceiling. I could picture all that. I could understand the desperation, the hopelessness . . . But where was Ward's alleged killer, when did he enter the house, what was he there for, why did he submit to waiting in the house hours after the murder?

I drank the dregs of the coffee in the cup holder, then pulled away slowly. The Jeep slid, then the tires caught the bite of the lane, and I left.

Chapter 16

I thought of Charlie and his polio right when I saw the sanitarium. Its bleakness had not changed, a stolid, featureless building on a hill overlooking the flatness of an icy inlet. I had this kid book back then about the Pied Piper of Hamelin, and in it was this picture of the Pied Piper leading kids up the side of the mountain when the town screwed him over and didn't pay him for leading all the rats into the river. That's how it felt looking up at the sanitarium, then, and even now. Whatever went up that hill was trapped forever.

I stopped the Jeep at the bottom of the long rise and stared at the building's austerity, the lack of windows on the first floor, and the bars on the few windows on the second and third floors. It gave you a glimpse into a dark past, something conceived in a time of fear and panic, in an era of plague and disease.

Two huge wooden doors without windows led to a gloomy vestibule, cold as a meat locker, where there was a solitary black phone on a waist-high table. A sign above the phone said *Pick Up Phone.* I picked the phone up and said who I was. A locking mechanism turned slowly, and a door opened into the cold, clinical light of the inner sanctum.

A pudgy man in a white uniform and white nurse shoes looked over my uniform, and that set a tone of formality, but, shit, I knew the guy from high school, Bob Gilmore, an asshole a few years older than me, a lowlife who used to affect a greaser pose smoking out back of school. I was just glad he didn't recognize me. Bob still had the jet black hair slicked back off his forehead, but it had thinned so the pink of the scalp showed. Bob said flatly, 'Follow me.'

On a faded beige wall were black and white photographs of staff and doctors standing behind children, either in wheelchairs or with legs locked into a scaffold of wires connected to black cripple shoes. I instinctively slowed, staring at the still life images of an age captured in one definitive yearly portrait. God, what the hell would I have done if my kid Ernie had come down with some disease like that? There was something arbitrary and cruel communicated in those grim portraits, something about our utter insignificance.

Bob seemed to slow and wait patiently. I saw he had the blackened stub of a cigarette between his thumb and index finger. He must have been smoking when I called, and flicked off the head of burning ash.

The central feature of the sanitarium was a square courtyard, something like a greenhouse with a high glass roof. It was filled with institutional looking chairs with leather straps on the arms and gurneys lined against the far wall. There were some ethereal looking patients in white gowns sitting quietly like abject saints in the chairs, some bound both at the feet and hands, others seemingly free. I could hear the clink of cutlery in the background, the smell of greasy breakfast food in the air.

Bob coughed, and I moved after him.

The elevator, this big industrial style box, needed a key to unlock it. Bob had a jailer's chain of keys on a ring. He set his cigarette behind his ear and turned the key. Bob pulled closed the accordion-metal gate, and the elevator jolted, then groaned with an almost human effort, and we rose off the ground.

The elevator's interior liquid light washed uniformly over us. Our eyes met for a brief second, and then Bob's eyes seemed to brighten in a flash of recognition. 'Frank Cassidy! Oh, my sweet Jesus, look what the cat dragged in!'

I gave a flabbergasted, 'Bob!' I raised my hand. 'Don't tell me, Bob ... Bob ... Bob Gilmore!'

Bob said real loud, 'The one and only! Bob Gilmore, ladies and gentlemen!' He shook my hand. 'You son-of-a-gun, Frank Cassidy, the uniform threw me, but I'd know that face anywhere.' He play-punched me in the arm. The elevator shuddered. 'Frank Cassidy, impersonating an officer of the law! Jesus Almighty, if that don't beat all. What did Frank Cassidy do, steal it?' He still had that same god-awful laugh and dimwitted way about him.

'I'm working security down at the community college.'

'Well I'll be a monkey's uncle! Jesus, we got to catch up on old times. I won't even go into Bob Gilmore's sorry-ass life. This is it, Bob Gilmore, Custodial Engineer at the loony bin.' Then he punched me hard on the shoulder. 'You son-of-a-gun, Frank.'

The elevator came to a jolting stop that punctuated our bullshit conversation. Bob pulled back the railing, and we stepped out into the stream of light in another long hallway.

Bob lit his cigarette, inhaled deeply, then exhaled out the side of his mouth, and raked his hand through his oily black hair like the greasers did years ago. He was still going on with the same bullshit. 'Goddamn it, the one and only Frank Cassidy.' He touched my shoulder again, like some Doubting Thomas, like he wanted to make sure I was real.

I droned back, 'Bob ... Bob Gilmore, of all the people in this world.'

Bob grinned, and his lips collapsed into the dough of his face. 'I bet Frank Cassidy's got a story to tell. I bet Frank Cassidy's got one hell of a story to tell.'

His face had deflated, so there was no real definition, just a rounded fatness, and somewhere in there the old Bob Gilmore was becoming re-absorbed. Bob smiled as I looked at him, impervious to life in the general way I always wished I could have lived it. Don't get me wrong, guys like Bob Gilmore were

158

the sages of how you had to adapt to your own demise, guys who lived in the twilight of their high-school years and reckoned with what they may have wished for, and what they ended up with, guys who stared down the crosshairs of middle age and still managed to get their asses out of bed each morning.

'So, you married, Frank? Shit, of course Frank Cassidy's married, a good-looking guy like that. You look like a guy that's married. I saw that in the way you were looking at those portraits downstairs, Frank. Only parents stare like that. Oh yeah, you got marriage written all over your face, Frank.'

I said, 'Guilty as charged,' and held up my ring finger and showed the band. And of course, that obliged me to ask, 'So who's the lucky woman in Bob Gilmore's life?'

Bob shook his head. 'Bob Gilmore has been playing the field. I don't think Bob Gilmore is a one woman man.'

I said, 'Hey, I hear you. Bob Gilmore might as well keep his options open.'

'That's what Bob Gilmore figures on doing, Frank, keep his options open.' A vine of smoke rose from Bob's finger.

He unnerved the hell out of me with that bullshit of referring to himself in the third person, like he'd cleaved into some distinct alter ego or something. There was something heroic in using the third person. We were like Titans, or glorious goddamn stereotypes. If we'd been in a movie, I'd have wanted us to wear big placards that said things like 'Loser!' or 'Fuck-up.'

Extracting myself from Bob's presence was like pulling out one of my own teeth. Finally, Bob took me to an office door and said, 'I'll get your number when you come on down. Bob Gilmore wants to know the Frank Cassidy story, from beginning to end.' He spread his arms wide in the manner of Vaudevillian showbiz, suggesting amazing wonders behind a tent. But before he left, he stopped smiling, stubbed out his cigarette, dropped it on the ground and, pivoting on the ball of his foot, came real close to me and whispered, 'So, you going to tell your old friend, Bob Gilmore, who the Sleeper really is?' and suddenly the charade hit me, and all the time he had that solitary question in the back of his head. He had known me since I had come through that door. He'd been playing with me.

I didn't say anything, and Bob leaned even closer. 'I heard tell Frank Cassidy can hypnotize people without them ever knowing it. They say that's how Frank Cassidy did it. I suppose Frank Cassidy could even hypnotize Bob Gilmore here, and he'd be none the wiser.'

That left me sort of stunned, but thinking back, it's what that blonde had feared, me staring at her back at the campus diner. Maybe it was true, people thinking I had those powers.

Dr Brown's room was bathed in the yellow light of morning, the air gleaming with dust. The office smelt like ether, something you'd use to put somebody under. It was heavily laden with wood beams, reminiscent of the hull of a ship submerged in deep water.

Along the wall was a glass cabinet with a light glowing around its edges. I waited a few minutes, listening for Dr Brown, since there was another room connected to the office, but there was no sound. I went and stared at what turned out to be a collection of exotic butterflies mounted on a green felt background. The butterflies had labels identifying them by their long unpronounceable scientific names.

The butterflies had their wings held apart by small pins. Some were small, but others had big crêpe-paper wings, butterflies nearly as big as both the palms of my hands held open, like they were out of the Amazon or something. I could see the detail of the head of this one butterfly, the coiled tongue and compound eyes, the torso with its dark glossy armor. I leaned closer, staring at the sheer complexity of the black alien face.

When Dr Brown's hand touched my shoulder, I jumped out of my skin, thinking something had escaped captivity and landed on my shoulder. 'Jesus H. Christ!'

Dr Brown said, 'So you've discovered my collection of butterflies.'

I had to swallow my goddamn heart before I could speak again. Dr Brown stood right beside me and put his hand on my back again, shoring up the quarter century it had been since I'd been under his care. His eyes, set deep in loose pink-rimmed sockets, had aged considerably. He turned and pointed at this giant African butterfly, like we'd been talking a long time on the subject of butterflies. 'After procreation, she eats the male.'

I said, 'We call that alimony in the human species.'

'Ah, Frank, you haven't changed a bit.' We stayed looking at the butterflies. Dr Brown seemed to wheeze between breaths. He touched me with the tactile sensation of an insect examining me with its feelers.

Dr Brown went behind his mahogany desk and beckoned, 'Sit, Frank, sit.' He didn't look at me as he spoke.

'So, did you ever get to the bottom of those dreams?'

I followed him to a chair across from his desk. I sat and said laconically, 'Can't say I ever did.'

Dr Brown said with his characteristic frankness, 'Do you still get those nightmares?'

I said flatly, 'It's all water under the bridge.'

'Ah. I detect a note of fear.'

'No, just boredom.'

'And hostility too.' He wrote something down in a notebook. 'So, you haven't answered my question.'

'The nightmares still resurface sometimes.' I looked around the dark, vaulted ceilings of Dr Brown's office, breathed the smell of wood polish. A heater made the curtains flutter in a current of hot air.

'I find it curious that a man ups and moves his family all the way back home. I say that from both a personal and medical perspective. It suggests something latent in the subconscious.'

I smiled and said, 'Should I be lying out on the couch for this, Doc? Is this officially a session? I didn't bring a checkbook.'

Dr Brown said, 'What I find most peculiar in all this is that Chester Green was a name you mentioned under hypnosis when I first worked with you. Did you know that, Frank, that you mentioned Chester Green?'

I lied and said, 'No.'

'Well, you did.' Dr Brown took off his stethoscope and hung it around the neck of a blanched skeleton like you'd see in some high-school science lab. The skeleton had been fashioned into a damn coat rack. It was wearing what I presumed were Dr Brown's winter coat and hat. 'So you're back to pick up farming, is that it?'

He drank a glass of water, then loosened the knot of his tie around his neck, and then refilled his glass and drank again. His lips made a soft smacking sound as he finished.

I didn't answer the question, and Dr Brown let it go. There was a book open to a technical sketch of a man with a hangman's rope around his neck. Dr Brown caught me looking down at it.

'Ah, *The History of Hanging*. Interesting book. I think people should know that hanging isn't just tying a rope around your neck and kicking a chair out from under you. Hanging is more complicated than that. I really think that's something that should be highlighted in health education, that and trying to blow your head off with a rifle. It hardly ever gives satisfactory results!'

I said, 'I guess I never thought about hanging being really complicated.'

'Oh, Frank, on the contrary. In fact, there's a whole science to hanging. Think about it, hanging has been one of the great spectator sports in our civilized history of Western culture. It has defined how we dispensed justice. Right? How did the state execute prisoners?'

'Hanging.'

'Exactly.' Dr Brown turned a page in the book. 'Look here, there was even a table of formulas which detailed for executioners the appropriate size and length of rope for a given weight of a prisoner, and instructions on exactly how to position the knot so the neck broke instantly when the prisoner was hanged. Think about it, the lives we live, that committees of brilliant men actually spent a good portion of their life devising a means to kill people.'

I said, 'That is something.'

'Well, you see the fundamental dilemma for the state when it executed prisoners, right?'

'What?'

'Imagine a crowd gathered for a public execution, and a prisoner is decapitated due to a botched hanging, or a prisoner strangles on the end of a rope and wriggles and writhes for minutes. How does that affect the public gathered to watch?'

Dr Brown tapped the table, making his point. 'It instills a sense of horror. It shakes people's sense of justice. First and foremost, execution is not about torture. Execution is about quick justice. The state cannot be seen to be exacting revenge, or causing prolonged suffering. That's a cornerstone of our judicial process: clinical justice that is devoid of unnecessary suffering. That's a fundamental element of any judicial system. And so, to that end, execution has to be quick and rendered uniformly in each instance.'

A brief silence settled. Dr Brown smiled and laced his fingers together and formed a small cathedral with his two index fingers. 'So, to the business at hand then.'

I began talking at a million miles an hour. 'I really appreciate you seeing me like this, Doc, and I want you to know I don't mean to come off like I don't respect what you did for me over the years, because I do. But I got on with life in the end. To be honest, I just don't think about the past. Maybe it was traveling around the country or something. Somehow things lose their importance when you start moving around the country, when you get the responsibility of a family. I got two kids and a wife now, Doc, you see where I'm coming from?'

'Sure, but it still begs the question why you are here, Frank?'

'You mean at the hospital here?'

'That, and, more generally, what made you pick up and come back? On the phone, you told me where you'd been living. New York?'

'New Jersey.'

'That's quite a change to just up and leave.'

'I feel like I've had to answer that a million times already.'

'And what's your answer?'

'I don't have one, if that's an answer you'll take.'

'Well, I'm not asking for a reason, but if you stay here, and things stay as they are, you know you've landed yourself in the middle of a regular mystery, and you have to expect people to talk, no matter how absurd their theories.' Dr Brown stopped and looked at me across the desk.

I looked straight at him, 'If I come up with a real answer, you'll be the first to hear about it, okay, Doc?'

Dr Brown winked. 'Sure, well, we have that settled then. So what did you want to see me about, Frank?'

I told Dr Brown about Norman and the gun residue and how it was on Ward as well, but inconclusive for the Sleeper. I kept talking in circles. When I finished, I felt like I was coming up for air. I waited and then I said, 'Listen, Doc, can I ask you a question?'

'What?'

'I want to know if the Sleeper is ever coming out of his coma.'

Dr Brown drummed his fingers on his desk. 'Why?'

'To clear Norman.' I hesitated. 'And maybe for my own . . .'

'Sanity?'

I shrugged my shoulders. I looked at Dr Brown, 'That's a pretty harsh assessment of my mental state,' and then I smiled, and Dr Brown smiled back at me and said, 'Okay, but to your question as to the prognosis. Do you want the long or short explanation?'

'However you can best explain it, Doc.'

Dr Brown swiveled around in his chair, and took down a plastic brain. It was something he obviously used to help people understand what the hell was going on with their loved ones. I watched as he took apart the brain. It looked like it belonged in a kid's science kit.

I leaned toward the desk as Dr Brown started talking. 'Well, this sort of takes us back to our previous discussion about hanging, actually. Like I told you before, sometimes, when someone tries to hang themselves, they end up with a broken neck but don't die. They usually end up paralysed, because the spinal cord is damaged.'

'But in this case, the Sleeper didn't injure his spinal cord when he hanged himself. His injury was above the spinal cord in what's called the brainstem. You can see here that the brainstem sits above the spinal cord, right?' Dr Brown touched the plastic brainstem with a pencil. 'This area here, Frank.'

I nodded.

'When the Sleeper tried to hang himself, the shirt he used tore away from the ceiling. The force wasn't strong enough to break his neck, but the knot crushed his airway, and he was basically strangled until he went unconscious. However, there was enough air getting into his body to keep him alive.'

Dr Brown pointed at a red artery running along the brainstem. 'The force of the strangulation damaged what is called the basilar artery. You can see it, along here.'

'I see it.'

'Well, the Sleeper was recovering the first night. He had a breathing tube in his throat, so he couldn't speak, but he was able to respond appropriately to commands and yes or no questions, so there seemed to be no apparent brain damage to his higher thought processes. He had function of his arms and legs. However, by the next morning, a clot had formed in the basilar artery, blocking blood flow to his brainstem, and that's when he went into a coma. You got this so far, Frank?'

'Yeah . . . but how did the blood clot put him into a coma?'

'Well, for one thing, the brainstem houses the alarm clock for interrupting our sleep or a period of unconsciousness. We need some mechanism that basically turns us on and gets us functioning. Technically, it's called the reticular activating system. The clot that formed in the Sleeper's brain injured his brainstem, and that in turn affected his waking mechanism. So he remained in a coma for the first two weeks he was here.'

I raised my head and looked at Dr Brown. 'You say for the first two weeks. So what's he like now . . . I mean, is he awake now?'

Dr Brown took a deep breath. 'Well, no, Frank. It's more complicated than that.' Dr Brown looked at me. 'I think the Sleeper may have what we call "Locked-In Syndrome". Granted I'm not saying there is conclusive proof, but I've been researching the disorder, and there may be manifestations of cognizance.'

I shook my head. 'What?'

Dr Brown put a finger to his lip and seemed to think for a moment. 'Let me explain again. People with Locked-In Syndrome are like statues. That is the best way I can describe them. They are mute and paralysed in not just their arms and legs, like somebody with a spinal cord injury, but in their heads too. They can't grimace or smile, speak or swallow, nod or shake their head. Like I said, they're just statues. They may as well be made of stone. They're effectively locked away inside themselves.'

I leaned back in my chair for a moment, trying to digest

what he was saying. 'Okay, but ... so ... so how's that different from a coma?'

'Ah, good point. Locked-In Syndrome is very different from a coma, and much more tragic. In a coma, patients are unconscious and unaware of their body or their surroundings. They merely exist as a biologic entity, but there's no conscious thought. But in Locked-In Syndrome, the patient is *conscious*, Frank. They live the nightmare of hearing and sensing everything. They are literally awake and as conscious as you and I, but they don't have the ability to move, to let the outside world know they are in that state. The paralysis is that profound. They are stone people, statues in every sense of the word.'

'So how do you know they're conscious if they can't communicate? I don't get how you can tell the difference between a coma and this Locked-In Syndrome, if there's no way that they can communicate.'

Dr Brown leaned forward and nodded. 'You see, eye movement is controlled in the cerebrum, not the brainstem, so, even though the brainstem is injured, eye movement is stored elsewhere, and, by the grace of nature, this is the one clue that lets us know that we're not dealing with people in a coma, that this is different. If there's no major cerebral damage in a patient with Locked-In Syndrome, then higher thought processes are intact, and there is the possibility of establishing communication with the patient. I've been reading up lately, on rare documented cases of patients who were able to communicate through a sort of Morse code of eye movements, like blinking, or, in some instances, there's not even the ability to blink, and the code is devised by either horizontal or vertical eye movement – basically, any discrete conscious repetitive action that forms the basis for creating a code.'

I said softly, 'So the eyes become the window to the soul.'

Dr Brown nodded. 'But the key is to recognize this condition, and begin trying to communicate with the patient.

The patient can make the first step, but you have to realize what you're dealing with to understand that they are communicating. You see the horror of this? There may have been literally thousands of people in what was perceived as a coma who went through their life, and nobody ever tried to establish communication with them.'

I interrupted Dr Brown. My heart was racing at this stage. 'And you were looking up these rare cases, why?'

Dr Brown withdrew his head and stayed quiet for a few moments.

'You got through to him?'

Dr Brown said, 'Frank!'

I was breathing quickly. 'You've been communicating with him?'

Dr Brown put up his hand. 'Frank, just listen to me. I'm saying that I have examined the patient and there may be signs of cognition. There's nothing conclusive. A person has to want to be found, they have to want to let us know that they are inside looking out.'

I stopped and shook my head. 'So he could hear everything we're saying but just be unable to speak?'

'Exactly, a man locked away inside his body.'

The day shone behind Dr Brown. It was hard to distinguish his face. My eyes couldn't adjust to see him clearly. I said, 'So why are you letting me see him, Doc?'

'Well, you called me, Frank, right? You asked me.'

I nodded.

'Frank, let me say that, of all the people who might be tangentially involved in this case, in this tragedy, I think you might come closest to understanding that maybe there are things you never want to find out. Maybe there was too much pain and loss and not enough gain to be had for what I put you through years ago. Maybe this man wants to be left alone, I don't know, but you might have the empathy inside you to communicate your feelings, just to speak with him.'

I felt my head spinning. I said, 'That doesn't seem like a reason.'

Dr Brown looked at me. 'You don't have to go in and see him.'

I said, 'I don't get it, but I'll see him.'

'Good.'

'So, let me get this straight. The Sleeper can communicate, right?'

Dr Brown looked at his watch. 'What I said, Frank was that the possibility exists medically.'

'That's not an answer to my question.'

'You decide. Give me a second opinion.'

I just looked at Dr Brown. I said, 'I don't know what I'm doing here.'

Dr Brown raised his eyebrows. 'Well, you are here.'

I said, 'Did you tell the cops about this Locked-In Syndrome?'

Dr Brown shook his head. 'After my dealings with the police in your case, I lost faith in the law. I always thought that maybe it would have done you better if I'd never gone to the police after you were hypnotized.' Dr Brown touched the bridge of his nose and his head tipped almost imperceptibly. 'Right now my sole directive is to keep this patient alive, nothing else. I'm a caretaker, that is my sole role.'

I nodded.

'Good. I have your assurance that what we discuss here does not leave this office?'

I felt something between us that I didn't quite understand.

'Can these patients ever recover, Doc?'

'There are cases where patients recover partial or even total use of their body. It runs the gamut.'

'So, what do you think are the chances of recovery?'

'I think you're ahead of the game. I haven't said the Sleeper even has Locked-in Syndrome, you understand that?'

I nodded and waited. I broke the stalemate of the next few moments and said, 'Well, I better go see him then?'

'Okay.' Dr Brown rose from his chair. 'Frank, despite what happened to you years ago, I still believe in the power of the subconscious, that there are realities behind realities, things we are afraid to look into, but they are there, repressed memories.'

I knew he was talking about the fire. He came around and faced me. I didn't look into his face. He touched my back, and we left his office and went out into the cold corridor.

Dr Brown walked slowly with a limp, a vestige of his own battle with polio. He wore the shoes of a polio victim.

I could see down onto the icy inlet through the big barred windows. I said, 'This looks more like a prison than a hospital.'

'Well, at the time of epidemics, this sanitarium was both a hospital and a prison really...'

We arrived at a door to another wing. 'Well, Frank, I'll leave you here.' Dr Brown took my hand and held it. Through a porthole in a locked door I could see another long expanse of corridor.

We lingered a moment longer. The long finger of a branch tapped a window behind us. I said, 'I remember from when I was a kid, there was a room of iron lungs here.'

'All gone, I'm pleased to say, gone for scrap metal, consigned to the history books. We have won many wars this century.'

I said quietly, 'You know I had an uncle here years ago who came down with polio.'

'Charlie, wasn't it?'

'Yeah.'

'He was a school teacher, right?'

I said, 'You got a memory, Doc.'

'That's my line of work,' and with that he smiled weakly.

I smiled back. I said, 'God, I remember coming here with Ward and how Ward used to ask Charlie some question, multiply this and that number, and Charlie had the answer.

170

He was a genius with numbers. I mean, I'm not just saying that. It's a fact. I think Charlie liked to be quizzed. He used to wink at me when he got the answers right. Ward used to write out all the numbers, the addition and subtraction of this and that number, and I used to sit with Ward and he did the math, then he'd say, "Okay, Charlie," and he'd list off the numbers, and God almighty Charlie got it right every time. And Charlie used to have nickels and dimes out on a metal tray beside his iron lung, and he'd say, "That's for you, Frank. Take it."'

Dr Brown didn't say anything.

I said, 'Shit, it's amazing what you remember and what you forget, how things stick in your head like that.' I said, 'I got a kid like that, with that genius, Doc.' I said, 'You get a kid like that, and you're set for life, Doc. A kid like that can carry you through old age. A kid like that is money in the bank. It's the best retirement package you can hope for.' I waited a moment or so, and then I said, 'But you know what I remember most, Doc?'

'What?'

'I remember Ward saying to Charlie one evening we were there and Charlie had finished answering his questions, "Oh, you got it all figured, Charlie. So how come you never figured out how to keep that wife of yours, tell me that Charlie?" Jesus Christ, I remember Charlie crying, but all Ward did was say it again. It's something he said even after Charlie got out of the sanitarium. Charlie had no peace, Doc, not coming to stay with Ward anyway. I mean Ward rode all us hard. Jesus, when I think about it, Charlie was still limping with a cane when he left. I remember him doing this Charlie Chaplin imitation like it was all fun and games, but it wasn't. I guess Charlie would have crawled the hell away from Ward.' I stopped abruptly. I said, 'This doesn't amount to a hill of beans, Doc.'

'Talking is a way of remembering. It's the first step.'

I didn't ask to what.

171

We had run out of things to say. An orderly was to come and take me. I said, 'Doc?'

'Yes?'

'You've analyzed me. Would you think I'm capable of doing things I could blank out of my conscious mind?'

Dr Brown said, 'Give me a for instance, Frank?'

I told him about the letters Martha said I'd sent to Ward asking for money.

Dr Brown coughed and then swallowed. 'How does she know you sent them?'

'She said they were signed by me.'

Dr Brown took off his glasses and began cleaning them, nodding his head slightly. 'Signed by you . . . interesting. The answer to your question, is I don't know, I honestly don't know what you're capable of doing.' He looked at me with those loose wet eyes of his.

The orderly unlocked the heavy door.

Dr Brown touched my arm. 'We'll speak, Frank. Call me in a day or so.' I watched him turn. He dragged his leg badly. He stopped and turned, like he was going to say something, and then didn't.

The old quarantine ward was in a remote wing of the hospital. It had been transformed into a rehabilitation ward. I had to go through three separate doors to reach its inner chamber. I passed an obsolete rusting communal shower room like you'd see in a men's locker room, where those who cared for patients must have scrubbed in the old days. It had a haunting aura of desolate abandonment and cold. There must have been a leak in the upper piping because the enamel was stained with long brown fingers.

I walked slowly by a series of large rooms that looked for all the world like torture chambers. There were patients connected to a scaffold of metal contraptions undergoing various treatments. A system of pulleys and rollers ran along a track in the roof. I could hear the clank of metal. Two nurses stood out in the hallway, smoking with those impassive faces of people who have worked too long and too hard, faces of institutional monotony.

Halfway down the corridor, the ward opened into a large communal room. I saw paraplegics and quadriplegics and men without legs, urine bags on metal hooks that connected through the pajamas of patients. Some patients lay flat on their stomachs on gurneys with sheets draped over their buttocks.

The orderly stopped and surveyed the room. I could see him pick out a nurse standing at the far wall, drinking coffee. He nodded, and she smiled and raised her cup. The orderly mouthed something to her, and she smiled again. So we waited there for a few moments for some reason.

The patients were watching a soap opera on one of those institutional black and white televisions mounted to the ceiling in the corner of the room. The curtains had been drawn to cut out the glare, so it was dim, like evening, and quiet, except for the voice of a beautiful young woman on the television who was holding on to this guy in a turtleneck who looked like a million bucks. She was sobbing into his shoulder.

I just stood at the back of the room and looked out over the wheelchairs. It was like I was on a goddamn pilgrimage.

The woman was starting into one of those improbable soap opera speeches. I just listened.

'I came back here to live with you, that's what I've always wanted. I came back here because I want to be with you forever. I want to wake up with you. I want to make love to you and make babies. I want all of it. I want you! If there were a thousand guns lined up outside, I would want to face them with you. Love me enough to know that I'm your life.'

Someone in one of the wheelchairs shouted, 'Crystal, don't do it! The guy's a scumbag.'

That sort of broke the moment, and the orderly motioned for me to follow him.

Off a narrow passageway that had served as an isolation unit in the time of TB, I finally saw this thing they called the Sleeper. I walked unceremoniously into a cold rectangular room devoid of anything but a bed and chair and laid eyes on an inert statue. But that was not entirely true.

The eyes were wide open.

Chapter 17

The Sleeper looked insubstantial, a mere outline of a body under the covers, like a relic. The weeks of immobility had withered his body. The hands had atrophied, the fingers curled like animal claws, the nails unnaturally long, the color of candle wax. But it was the head that held me, unnaturally big, like a creature of alien origin, a head on a thin stalk of neck with a raw tracheostomy.

A bell sounded out in the hallway, and the orderly said, 'I got to get that.'

I sat on a wooden chair beside the Sleeper and leaned close. He smelt of illness, an odor like sweating cheese, pungent and faintly rotting. White flecks of foam had formed around the corners of the mouth. Cold sores were slowly opening. Even the open eyes that betrayed this was something living had that sunken appearance of a blind man.

The Sleeper looked older than I had imagined, and frail.

I touched his arm.

No reaction. The eyes stared straight at the ceiling.

I got close and whispered, like I was a priest reciting the last rites into a dying man's ear, and said softly, 'Dr Brown told me your secret. Blink once if you can hear me.'

But there was no reaction.

The tracheostomy made a sound like a leak from a bicycle tire.

I watched the eyes. I waved my hands over the eyes. They followed for a millisecond and then adjusted back to the same

175

cold stare. It was a reflex, because the same thing happened each time. It wasn't communication.

I stared directly into the eyes. I said quietly, 'I'm Frank Cassidy.' A moment's silence. Nothing registered. I said, 'I'm the nephew of the man they say you killed.' I felt at a loss for words. I sat beside the bed just thinking. I had nothing to say, after all this time. I just stared blankly back into the Sleeper's face. I couldn't see why this man would communicate with me. I was, after all, the nephew of the man he'd supposedly killed. Why would he confide in me?

I leaned over and said softly, 'I can tell you things about the case if you help me. I assume you haven't heard anything about the case, but I can tell you what's happening if you just let me know you're in there, okay?'

But there was nothing, no hint of what Dr Brown had intimated I'd find. Maybe there had been brain damage. I stood up. 'Dr Brown told me he thinks you might have what's called Locked-in Syndrome. I wouldn't wish that on anybody, you hear me, not even you.' I ran my hand through my hair. It was hot in the room. I felt myself sweating. I said, 'I don't hold any resentment toward you.' I raised my voice just a notch. 'Listen, if you can hear me, we can work something out. Like I told you, this isn't all cut and dried. Maybe you didn't really kill Ward. That's right, there were two shots fired in the house, and, you know what, the police aren't sure you pulled the trigger on any of those shots. You hear that?'

The orderly had come back and was standing behind me. He said, 'He's in a coma. He can't hear you.'

I turned and faced the orderly and shook my head. He struck a match and lit a cigarette. He looked at me and said, 'It's creepy as hell, isn't it?'

I just sat there looking at the Sleeper. The stalemate lasted a few minutes. I watched the IV drip bag and feeding tubes, the monotonous drip drop of fluid. Sound filtered from the communal hallway.

There was no expression on the Sleeper's face, just the eyes as always, open and staring at the ceiling. He lay motionless, the breath so shallow it reminded me of hibernation, a sleep so natural for this part of the world.

Silence persisted for a time. My back was warm, a greenhouse warmth from the window. The sun sat low on the horizon, a yellow eye staring in through the window.

A nurse, thin in an unattractive way, like Popeye's girlfriend, came and said, 'Clifford, we need you back up front.'

The orderly left.

In the ensuing silence, I just sat there and looked into the Sleeper's eyes again. The eyes blinked, not like a person blinks, but like the shutter of a camera lens. A solitary tear formed a perfect drop that gleamed in each eye, and then one tear, and then the other, rolled down the side of the face and pooled in each ear. The eyelids opened again, but the eyebrows didn't rise. Nothing. The face was a mask in which the eyes stared out. I used the sleeve of my shirt to wipe the eyes. They fluttered and then stopped as I withdrew my hand.

I said in a subdued tone, 'Look, I know this all seems strange, that Dr Brown would send me after you supposedly killed my uncle, but he did. Let's just say that I'm not exactly broken up about Ward dying . . . You hear me? I don't know what you know or don't know, but I'm on your side. I might like to help you for my own selfish reasons . . . You hear me? I'm telling you the truth. The cops have no proof you killed my uncle. Maybe Norman killed his own father. He shot the gun that killed Ward.' I felt I was saying things all wrong, so I stopped speaking.

I took the Sleeper's curled hand. It was like touching stone, and I squeezed gently, working my thumb through the Sleeper's grip, kneading the pad of muscle beneath the thumb, slowly opening the hand, feeling the tendons beneath shift and move as I pressed the flesh against the tendons, working each curled finger from its stiff clawed grasp. I took the wrist, and with my other hand, turned the Sleeper's hand on the pivot of the wrist. His hand turned a flush of red. I could see the veins along the wrist, a network of subterranean blue beneath the translucent skin. All the time I watched the face. The blue irises stared at the ceiling.

I did the same with the other hand, warming the ashen flesh, kneading the muscles until the hand was warm, until it relaxed and opened. I massaged each finger. I whispered, 'I'm giving you the opportunity to come out from behind that mask. Is this how you want to spend the rest of your life?' I bent the arm at the elbow, working my hand along the cold limb and that is when I saw the faded tattoo that told you that it had been there a long time. I think, that more than anything else sent a shiver through me, that this had to be Chester Green.

I set its dead weight back across the bony ridge of his hips, so he looked like someone lying in state. I went to close the eyes, like I heard people do when they come upon a dead person. The eyelids closed over the eyes. I stepped back and took a deep breath. I went to leave, but the eyes opened again and blinked, then blinked again. I stopped and waited for the reflex to stop, but it didn't. It went on that way for a time.

I stared down. I said, 'Can you hear me?'

The eyes kept blinking.

I said, 'Listen to me. Blink once if you can hear me.'

The eyes stopped blinking for a few moments, then blinked once.

It took a second to register. I asked the question again, and the eyes blinked once. The wet wound of the tracheostomy made a noise, the diaphragm rose slightly, and then a bubble formed over the hole and quivered before popping without sound.

I felt faint just standing there. I could sense there was life behind the mask. I said, 'Who are you?' but of course that was not a yes or no answer.

The eyes remained open.

I stood staring down at the still face. The eyes wavered in that reflexive way, then the eyes shut and opened again. I felt myself shaking. I said, 'Listen, one blink for yes, two for no, you understand that?'

The eyes blinked once.

I still didn't believe I was really communicating with him. The eyes stared up at me through the eyeholes of the impassive death mask.

I said nothing for a time, letting the errant noises from the hallway find their way down to the room. I didn't know if tears were an automatic response, or if they betrayed emotion. Two red marks traced faintly from the outer edge of the eyes disappeared in the dark hole of each ear, like the Sleeper had been perpetually weeping. I took the edge of the sheet and gently dabbed one ear and then the other.

I stood up and felt lightheaded. I went to the window, and stared across the dark growth of woods beyond the steel railings. I could see whitetail deer in a gathering near a stream.

I turned and faced the Sleeper. I said, 'Is two plus two five?' and the eyes blinked twice, and then I said, 'Is two plus two four?' and the Sleeper blinked once, and with those inane questions that you might ask a child, I knew the Sleeper was in there looking out at the world.

I said, 'You are Chester Green?' but right then I heard the orderly and the nurse coming down the hallway. I felt lightheaded. I said, 'You want me to come back?'

The eyes blinked twice.

The orderly came into the room and said, 'We got to clean him up now.'

The blood had drained from my face.

The orderly looked at me. 'You okay?'

I looked at the Sleeper. I said, 'You mean yes?' but the eyes opened and closed twice.

The orderly looked at me, but saw I was looking at the

Sleeper. He saw the eyes. 'What the . . . did you see that?' The orderly waved his hand over the Sleeper's face, but the eyes just flickered in that automatic response that wasn't communication.

I said, 'See what?' I looked down at the Sleeper, the cold statue of his body laid out, betraying nothing in his perfect hiding place.

Chapter 18

I felt cold and shaky, like what I'd witnessed couldn't have happened. Why would a man who revealed himself to me tell me to stay away? The further I drove from the sanitarium, the more I believed nothing had happened.

Back at Mrs Brody's, Honey was home. It was the beginning of Thanksgiving vacation. Honey had a typewriter set up facing the side of the hill where the last mining pit operated. I listened to the rapid firing of the keys, like what I thought distant machine gun fire must sound like. The radio was turned low, to a Fifties radio station. Light pooled beneath the door frame. If she had been anybody else, I could have found comfort in her, but I decided not to tell her what had happened, that, until Ken was dead, it was better for us to live parallel lives, to cope with our own personal demons alone.

I came in behind Honey, softly, and she didn't hear me. She was topless. The red marks from the elastic of her bra straps showed. She was still in high heels.

I coughed discreetly and Honey turned. Her breasts hung almost to her navel. The right breast pulled to the side.

'Frank!' She smiled at me. 'I got extra work, typing up college kids' papers.' There was a notebook open to some scrawled essay.

I just stood there. The potbellied wood-burning stove gave off a faint smell of wood.

Honey had printed up signs advertising her typing services. She said, 'Look!' I looked at the poster. She had a picture of herself from high school centered underneath her rates, along with her phone number. It was a photograph from when she won the Georgia State Typing Contest. It said that on a banner above her head, but the year had been rubbed out. She had the same long hair she had now, combed to the side and falling the length of her bare arm. She was wearing braces. I could see that because she was smiling.

I turned and looked back at Honey. She looked like the mother of the girl in the photograph, but I didn't say that out loud.

In bed I kissed the underside of her breast, the damp warmth where her heart beat. She was still talking about typing in her intense way. She said, 'This is money in the bank. Term papers.' I plugged her mouth first with my finger, and then my tongue. I felt her ease and give in to me, the bigness of her hips beginning to move. I crawled slowly toward orgasm, through the ambush of what I'd seen, those eyes staring at me out at the sanitarium. Her fingers moved on my back, like she was typing something, transmitting something into my back.

In the aftermath, Honey breathed heavily.

I got up, since it was close to time to pick up Ernie. The room was hot. I looked at the poster. I said, 'How long after this photograph did you meet Ken?'

Honey was lying on her side, but she raised her voice. 'What did you say?'

I knew I should have said nothing. I said, 'Forget it.'

'No, what did you say?'

I turned and faced her. 'How long after this photograph did you meet Ken?'

Honey started in a low whisper that suddenly flared like a wildfire. 'You come home and sweep me off my feet, and then you pull this bullshit, Frank!'

'Shoo, Mrs Brody will hear you. It's nothing. I didn't mean anything, forget it.' I put my finger to my lips. I was standing naked in the middle of the room. I was self-conscious in the way Adam must have felt after he'd eaten from the apple in the Garden of Eden.

'Goddamn you. You want to know, Frank? You want to know the truth? In that photograph, I was already pregnant with Robert Lee. Is that what you wanted to hear? Ken and I dated way back, even when I was a sophomore. Maybe I never told you that. Now you know! He was my first, in the back of his car. I was in love with him. Love at first sight. Real love, like when you're young and you won't compromise on what you want! That kind of love. The kind of love that makes you not able to eat, that puts butterflies in your stomach!' She was shouting all of this. I heard a door open downstairs. 'You want to know it all? I'll tell you. You want to hear how Ken came in my mouth when I first got my braces? You want to hear it all? Well, do you?'

I winced and felt my scrotum turn. I took my shorts off the floor and stepped into them.

'Don't you ever touch me, you asshole. Never! Never, ever again! You hear me? I could make it without you. I got talent, more talent in my pinkie than you'll ever have! I could get on without men in my life, you hear me, Frank?'

Honey went out to the bathroom. I saw her wiping herself clean with a cloth like she was wounded. Honey finally stopped and dropped the wet cloth and just stood there. She was still in her high heels, and the size of her legs on top of the high heels made me think of some huge prehistoric flightless bird, something Ernie could probably identify. I swallowed and said, 'Ladies and Gentlemen, I give you Honey Wainscot, the Georgia State Typing Champion!' I said it like Bob Gilmore would have said it, with the fanfare of a three-ring circus, and somehow Honey just stopped dead, her head bowed, and her long hair fell in a curtain, obscuring her face. I could hear her sobbing. She sat down on the toilet and put her elbows on her knees.

I wanted to touch her, but she said, 'No, Frank. You go on

down and get Ernie from school. Just go.' She waved her arm, dismissing me. She looked for all the world like a beauty pageant queen who had been dethroned. I went and touched the back of her neck, but she shook off my hand. 'Don't!'

'Everything you do brings me closer to you, Honey. I want you to know that.'

'Frank, just leave it. Go get Ernie, okay?'

I took a step back and stood at the door. 'This is all going to be over soon, Honey.'

Honey pushed the hair out of her face and rubbed her eyes and looked through me, then turned her eyes down. 'I got a letter from Ken yesterday.'

I kept my distance.

Honey sniffled and wiped her nose with the flat of her palm. Her breasts floated in her lap. She shuddered and said, 'Frank . . .' She let out a long breath. 'It wasn't anything you did. You hear me? It was just . . . just that I was trying to keep it out of my head is all. I was typing like the old days, Frank, finding that place where I think about nothing, where everything just turns out right.' She opened and closed her hands. 'I was the best at something once. The best in the whole state. That meant something.' She cried like she had lost a loved one. It lasted minutes. I said nothing.

I heard a door in Mrs Brody's part of the house open and close.

Back in our room, Honey put on her nightgown and lit a cigarette and used a saucer as an ashtray. I could see she was still thinking about Ken. I wanted to see a cartoon bubble pop up out of her head that showed a picture of Ken strapped into an electric chair.

Honey's eyes got glassy, and she squinted with thought. Things were racing through her head. Sometimes her eyes got big, her lips moved like she was following some conversation. She wasn't even aware I was there, or that's how it seemed. Then she said, 'You know that photograph . . . that

184

photograph I got on that sign I made, well, Ken sent it up to me.' Her eyes opened wide and her head nodded. 'I think Ken knows it's coming to the end. He kept that photograph of me all these years, but he sent it back to me.' That made her voice choke. She cleared her throat and exhaled two tusks of smoke through her nostrils. 'I've been looking back, Frank, over so many years. You know what I was thinking, when I saw that photograph that Ken sent me?'

I shook my head.

'I was thinking I look like the mother of that girl in the photograph.'

It was like I had put the thought into her head.

I said, 'It makes you no less beautiful.' I looked away from her. On the refrigerator, I could see Robert Lee's test, the A+ circled in a big looping circle, and beside it something Ernie had made for Thanksgiving, a turkey standing beside a house. The turkey was as big as the house. Kids didn't get the dimension of things at any real level. I said that to Honey. 'Do you think he really sees a turkey as big as a house? Jesus, is that how the brain works when you're a kid?'

Honey was having her own conversation. 'I think if I practiced again, I could beat my old record. I know I could.' She held up the finger that had been snapped back in New Jersey. 'Everything heals with time, right?'

The telephone rang. It was the church where Ernie went to kindergarten. I could hear an organ playing in the background. They wanted him picked up.

Honey got up and plugged in the kettle. She took out a bag of tea and spooned four teaspoons into a teapot. She had her head turned away from me. She leaned and opened the garbage can, and a hot smell of garbage filled the air for a moment. She scraped off a plate, then set the lid back on the garbage. 'Frank?'

'Yeah.'

'Maybe I might go back to Georgia with Robert Lee. I got vacation coming with this job.'

I didn't answer. I felt the beginnings of a headache that I thought might never lift once it settled.

Honey said, 'Maybe when Ken sees me, he'll want to be executed.' She kept her back to me, but I could imagine the look on her face. She was miles away from me right then. She was staring at the high-school photograph of herself and how Ken would see her now. Honey said, 'I got a suit picked out for him, a light blue suit like Bible salesmen wear.'

'Robert Lee?'

'No, Ken.'

I said simply, 'I could have a nervous breakdown right now, but I just can't afford it at the present time.'

The kettle whistled, and it was like we had come to a train station in some remote and quiet place.

Chapter 19

It was the Tuesday before Thanksgiving. Sam Green looped through the day's news and weather, shouting, demanding his son's body be exhumed.

I went down to the office. Honey left with Robert Lee and Ernie for Sears just to look around.

The college was officially closed. Baxter was watching *The Newlywed Game*. He looked up at me and said, 'It's amazing what couples don't know about each other.' A husband had guessed the wrong answer to a question and the wife mock punched him on the arm.

'Turn that crap down, Frank.' Baxter had our timesheets strewn on a small table. The small gas heater was pumping out heat. 'We did well out of the storm.' He was smiling. He took a beer from a small cooler he had beside him, pulled the tab on the can, slurped the foam, and said, 'Avoid reality at all costs.'

I told him about the dean seeing me out of uniform. Baxter dismissed it. 'Shit, Frank, you think the dean has time to go checking up on our timecards? Come on, Frank. You got an inflated sense of your own importance.' He looked at me and smiled. 'Come on, Frank, let me handle the financial side of things for us.'

'Sure.'

I sat down on the sofa. It was soft, so I sank and my legs came up to my chin.

Baxter went back to adding up figures, and drank in between adding up columns. I was about to leave when he said, without looking up from the timecards, 'So, you want to know the latest developments, Frank? That's why you're here, right?' He winked at me.

I looked up at him. I said, 'I guess.'

'Hey, don't sweat it. Whatever I find out, I'll tell you, okay? You and I got a nice thing going here, and you scratch my back, I'll scratch yours. We're going to make this goddamn college pay out the ass, Frank. My goddamn sanity and soul are worth a hell of a lot more money than this job pays.' Baxter took a long drink of beer, tipping his head back so I could see his Adam's apple bob as he swallowed. He finished with a belch that he pulled from deep in his throat.

I said, 'I'll play it however you want to play it, Baxter.'

Baxter rubbed his mouth with the back of his hand, his head bobbing back and forth like he was thinking. 'Okay, Frank, I think we got a deal. I think you and I are from the same side of the tracks. So here's what I know, Frank. Get this, late breaking news. It seems like the military fucked up. They pulled a record on a C. Green, and they just assumed it was the right Chester Green, but it wasn't. It was a Clifford Green. They fucked up big time. It looks like we're back to square one. What the cops have to go on now is simply that statement by the superintendent down in Chicago positively identifying the Sleeper as the same Chester Green that rented an apartment in Chicago. I think the plain reality is that the Sleeper is Chester Green.'

I said, 'The military is going to keep checking, right?'

Baxter shrugged his shoulders. 'Get this, nearly eighty percent of military personnel service records were destroyed in some big fire in St. Louis in 1973. Chances are, the military doesn't have squat on Chester Green.'

I was shaking my head. 'Why the hell didn't the cops just go out and dig up Chester Green's grave way back at the beginning of all this? I mean Jesus Christ, this could all have been set straight long ago.'

'They will now, but originally they didn't want to be seen following Sam Green's demands. Cops don't just go digging up graves, Frank. They were following other leads, and waiting to see if the Sleeper came out of his coma first.'

I said, 'Well, they better dig up that grave and end this goddamn mystery.'

I'd got up to leave when Baxter said, 'There's one other thing.'

I looked across the room at him.

'Did you know you lived three blocks from Chester Green?'

I didn't answer that. I looked at the floor is what I did.

'Hey, Frank, you might as well sit down. It gets worse.'

I still didn't move.

'I hate to rain on your parade, but the cops know you mentioned Chester Green's name at that hospital where you were committed down in Chicago.'

I felt a flicker of fear, like there was something just beyond my comprehension, or my willingness to admit. I turned, and outside the light was clear and hard.

Baxter opened another beer. I heard the tab click. He said, 'It was that sister-in-law of yours that started the cops looking, Frank. She gave them a few letters you sent your uncle asking for money. They got it all, Frank, the Chicago postmark, all of it.'

I kept looking out the window. I said under my breath, 'That bitch.'

Baxter took another drink of his beer, and wiped his mouth with his sleeve.

'Come on, Frank! What was she supposed to do? I heard you started pushing her about meeting to split up the farm. You did that just the other day. Did you do that, Frank? Is she lying?'

Again I said nothing.

'She told the cops you called her the day after Ward was killed and said you read the account of the murder in the paper. She said you were like a rabid dog, saying you were going to get Norman off the farm, that everything belonged to you.'

I still said nothing.

'Jesus, Frank, say something,' but I didn't.

'Okay, Frank, but you can't just hide from the facts. The cops checked the local papers from the metropolitan area around New York and New Jersey, and you know, there was no mention of your uncle's murder in any of those papers.'

I turned and shouted, 'Goddamn it, I read it. I swear to God . . .'

Baxter cast his eyes downward. 'Read it where, Frank?' Then he smiled. 'Look, I'm not out to bust your chops, you hear me? I'm just telling you what I know.'

I said, 'What are you trying to say, that somehow I knew Chester Green was alive, that I had something to do with Chester killing Ward?'

Baxter shrugged his shoulders. 'Look, as long as Chester stays in a coma, you're in the clear one way or another. The way I hear it, your uncle fucked you over, so you deserve whatever you can get away with. My advice is play it cool, Frank. You screwed up calling that witch sister-in-law of yours, gloating like you did over Ward's death, but maybe you can still save your ass. Maybe some jury is going to buy that you read about Ward's death in a paper. I mean, it's not beyond a reasonable doubt, right?' Baxter winked when he said that. 'And that's the margin we all live within, a reasonable doubt, right Frank?'

I couldn't speak right then. I turned and looked out the window again.

'Shit, Frank, late night TV tells you don't ever go back to the scene of the goddamn crime. You know what percentage of murderers return to the scene of the crime?'

I shook my head.

'A shitload is how many, Frank. Listen to me. This is a war

of wills. You got to keep your head about you, and just pray to hell that Chester Green doesn't wake up out of that coma. You jumped the goddamn gun was all. You should have waited back in New Jersey, you shouldn't have just come charging out here like you did.'

I kept looking out across the campus. I could see the administration building. It was covered in snow and looked like a postcard. 'So why haven't the cops interviewed me yet? If there's all this goddamn investigative work going on, why the hell hasn't anybody come and got me?'

'All in good time, all in good time. A good poker player doesn't show his hand, does he?'

I said, 'What about the fact that Chester Green didn't have any gun residue on his hands or clothes? You said the evidence was inconclusive, right?'

'Like I told you before, your uncle was cold when the cops arrived, so maybe there had been somebody else there earlier with Chester.'

'Sam Green?'

Baxter waited a moment. 'Sure.' Then he said, 'I'm going to level with you.'

I didn't turn around.

'I gave the cops a sample of your handwriting, just a report you wrote up.'

I turned, and Baxter was staring at me. 'Look, Frank, I'm giving you a running start, okay?'

I called Dr Brown from a campus phone. It took ages before he came on the line. There was some kind of echo on the line, but I didn't want to hang up. I kept my voice under control. I pre-empted him and said, 'I got to talk to you, Doc.'

'What is it?'

'Listen, I don't want to talk on the phone, okay?'

'Okay. Are you working tomorrow night?'

'Yes.'

'I'll come down and see you at the college. Say ten o'clock?'

And so I waited out the monotony of the morning, and by early afternoon, just like Baxter said, news reports began retracting the earlier statement regarding the photographs.

Martha called me that same evening. She said nothing about the reports. All she asked was if we were allergic to anything. But I figured she'd heard the news. I could tell she'd been crying, her voice had that sound of someone coming down with a cold.

I resisted the urge to say anything to her about the letters. All I said was, 'We're not the kind of people who can afford to be allergic to things.'

She sensed nothing in my voice, or betrayed nothing. She just went on about Thanksgiving. 'I got a big turkey, Frank. I want this to be something special.'

I said, 'How's Norman doing?'

Martha didn't exactly answer me. She said, 'When you come out, be kind.' It was simply said.

I said the first thing that popped into my head. 'Honey's got more work than she can handle typing up term papers. There's money in typing term papers,' I said. 'You type good, right, Martha?'

'I haven't typed in years.'

'But it's like riding a bike, right?'

'Yeah.'

'It's good money, Martha, and you get to work out of home. Honey says it's money in the bank. It's a new requirement that kids have to turn in all term papers typed. And I figure she has more than she can handle right now.'

Martha said, 'That's real nice of you.' Her voice had lost all bitterness. 'You think we're ever going to be friends again, Frank?'

I laughed at the irony of that question, but I let it pass. I resisted the urge to say anything about the letters. I said, 'You know I always think of you as that smart sister on *Little House on the Prairie*, Mary, the one with glasses who's always doing her homework.'

Martha said, 'At least you didn't say Nellie Olsen.' I could feel her take a long moment to let things ease between us. And then she did cry, I mean sob in that heavy way people overcome with grief cry.

I said nothing, and Martha went through all those things people do, the deep breaths and sighs, and then she blew her nose, and I just waited until she said, 'God, Frank, you still there?'

'Yeah.'

She sniffled again and then half-laughed. 'Oh, I don't know why I'm even crying. It's over, thank God it's over. You saw the news, right?'

I said, 'Norman is in the clear.'

Again, Martha had to take a moment to blow her nose. 'I don't know why they put us through what they did. I'm just glad it's over is all.'

I waited a moment. 'So what do you think is the story?'

And suddenly Martha raised her voice. 'Frank, don't, you hear me? There is only one story I'm interested in, Frank, and that is Norman didn't do anything wrong, that's all, you hear me?'

I let things settle for a few moments. Martha said, 'I got to wipe my eyes, Frank, wait, okay?' and she set the phone down.

And in the brief silence I think I was smiling for Norman. I could see him tucked into bed, like something from a goddamn nursery rhyme, that monster in his bed, that gentle giant, that goddamn simpleton.

Martha got back on the phone and I said, 'You know, I got nothing but good memories of Norman, really.'

Martha said, 'I know, Frank, I know you are good inside. I want you to know that, you hear me?'

I felt self-conscious. I said, 'Did I ever tell you about

Norman winning the State Meet in tenth grade?' I didn't let her answer, even though she was in school the time Norman won. I said, 'That was a first in state history. A tenth-grader won the heavyweight division. I came back up from Chicago for the finals. Jesus Christ, I remember it like yesterday! Norman looked like Lenny from *Of Mice and Men*. He gave me this big smile and came over and gave me a bear hug that lifted me off my feet. I said, "So, Norman, what's it like to have squeezed every guy's balls in the state?"

'Then, ten minutes later I saw Norman destroy this senior in the heavyweight class. I mean, he took this guy down with brute strength. I could see the senior trying all those wrestling moves, but Norman just slapped off the guy's grip, breaking holds just like that. Norman had hands like shovels. Then Norman pile-drives the guy into the mat. He just lifted this huge guy off the mat, and down he came like a house. I mean the whole gymnasium shook. I swear it was like an earthquake.

'Late that night Ward and I went and got Norman off the school bus. It was like two in the morning. Norman was holding this big-ass trophy. Someone had sprayed "State Champ!" on the side of the bus. Norman had on his letterman jacket. Ward was all stiff, like he always was, but he kept touching the trophy.

'We took Norman out for a feed of pancakes and a jug of milk at one of them all night diners, because he said that's what he wanted. I said, "My treat!" I sat there the whole meal, making spitballs and blowing them through a straw at Norman, hitting him on the forehead, but he did nothing. He was just hungry. I mean, here was the goddamn man-child state champion I was toying with.

'Then we all went down to a bar, and Ward and I had a few drinks to celebrate. Norman was under age, so he had to stay out in the car like he was our pet gorilla. We got drunk toasting him, one of the only times Ward and I ever drank together. We got a booth so we could see Norman out in the car. He was just sitting there holding his trophy. I don't think he even had the radio on or anything. I went over to the jukebox and played Jimi Hendrix doing "The Star-Spangled Banner". Shit, it was something to just look at Norman out there in the truck. He was fifteen years old and the strongest human I'd ever goddamn seen in all my life. He was a freak of nature, like something you'd take to the 4H County Fair and put up there with the world's biggest cabbage!'

Martha said, 'Frank?' I stopped talking. 'Maybe you could tell that story tomorrow at dinner. I want my kids to hear that story. But leave out the spitballs. Leave out the cabbage and all that. Tell it like how it must have felt to be Norman coming home with that trophy. You think you could do that? That's what Norman needs to hear right now, Frank. Tell it simply how it was, how he won.'

But at the end, I spoiled everything. I couldn't resist saying what was in the back of my mind. I said, 'You lied to me, you bitch. I know you showed the police the letters,' and just hung up and left the phone off the hook.

I tried to sleep but couldn't. Every time I closed my eyes I was staring at the Sleeper laid out on the bed. His eyes opened and closed. I kept trying to make him respond to this and that question, and, just when I was sure he was communicating, the eyes would rapidly blink and I'd feel lost again, unsure. I kept thinking it was all just because of the sense of suggestibility Dr Brown had put into my head, making me want to believe I could get through to the Sleeper. Maybe he was working with the police, and this was all part of some elaborate plan to freak me out, to convince me that Chester Green was still conscious, even though he was in a coma. I mean, I'd never even heard of this alleged syndrome.

The longer I stayed in bed, the more paranoid I felt. I went down and got Mrs Brody's Scotch and took it back up to the apartment and got loaded, and some time later sleep overtook me.

I slept for a few hours. Then I woke and stared at the TV, watching a rerun of *Leave it to Beaver*. I'd seen it about five times. Another lesson was been learned by the Beaver. He was sitting on Ward's knee. Beaver had owned up to the fact he'd broken a window with a baseball.

Honey and the gang came back. I could hear them mounting the creaking stairs. Robert Lee was up to his antics again. He said, 'So, Frank, we finally get to meet the better half of the family!' He said 'better half' and used his fingers as quotation marks. He'd been down with Mrs Brody after he'd been to Sears, cutting wood for her. He'd eaten something she'd baked that must have been laced with booze. He smelt of booze. He'd also gotten two pumpkin pies from her for our visit out to Martha and Norman's. Robert Lee said, 'The old bird gave me ten bucks for Thanksgiving.'

Honey was flouncing around in a floral dress that looked like it would have made a good set of bathroom curtains. She seemed dissatisfied with the dress.

I said, 'More diets start in clothing stores than in doctors' offices.'

Honey just glared at me. She had pinned the price tags to the inside of the Thanksgiving dress, which meant that she was thinking of returning it after Thanksgiving. She told me that's what she used to do back in Georgia; buy clothing, and then return it after she attended whatever the hell she had to attend. I wanted to say, 'Let's just keep the goddamn dress, just this once!' but I kept my mouth shut. Ken's illustrious blue suit was wrapped in plastic, and I didn't even bother to say anything, but that was something I'd have returned after they'd laid Ken out. It wasn't like Ken was ever going to wear it again.

The tension was electric there in the room. Honey wouldn't make eye-contact with me after she saw me look at the suit.

I said, 'I just might start this shift early, if it's the same to you?'

Honey said, 'I got typing to keep me busy. You do what you got to do, Frank.'

Ernie was watching TV, standing two feet away and looking into the screen the way kids have a habit of doing. *Sesame Street* had started. Ernie's namesake was in some tub with a rubber duck and a saxophone. Bert was saying to Ernie that he had to put down the duck if he wanted to play the saxophone, but Ernie kept trying to squeeze the rubber duck and play the saxophone at the same time. There were bubbles coming out of the saxophone, and the goddamn rubber ducky squeaked, and then the saxophone made some god-awful sound. Bert was getting wild, like he always did, that indignation all centered in eyebrows that arched when he got real mad. Ernie just started with that laugh of his. I wanted just once for Bert to pull an automatic weapon on Ernie, just like on the cop shows. I wanted Bert to say in that stern cop voice, 'Step away from the saxophone, now! Assume the position!' Children's TV had a way of eating away at my brain. But all I said was, 'You know, I've never seen Ernie and Bert's parents.'

Robert Lee said, 'They were burned in a fire, Frank,' and that sort of took my breath away for a moment.

Even Honey stopped dead and waited. I could see her looking at me in the mirror, but I let it go.

Chapter 20

The night passed. I awoke to the shift of the TV light in the early morning just as Wyle E. Coyote was squashed by a two-ton metal anvil. The weight was written on the anvil. Outside, I could hear the whine of snowmobiles off on the hillside near the mine.

I stayed in bed for a long time just thinking. I'd come to the sullen possibility that maybe I had gotten Chester Green to kill Ward. I mean I didn't really believe it, but it was something that had to be confronted, my own unreliability. I had, in the light of Ken's impending death, in the hard way that Honey had treated me back in New Jersey, felt the need to reclaim our humanity, to get us the cash that it was going to take to live a normal life. I felt I'd lost Honey back in New Jersey. She and Leonard had a thing going, or at least Leonard was pushing the issue as her manager and confidant. That goddamn hickey he gave her when she left, just doing it to humiliate me. Looking back I think I had lost my mind. At the back of everything, I must have fixated on the farm as the key to money. And still I kept waiting for the cops to come forward with some irrefutable evidence that I'd called Chester Green, or that he'd called me, some thread of evidence that was going to make me understand that I lived two lives, that there was a stranger inside me who went about his own business.

I got dressed and left without waking Honey. Robert Lee and Ernie were sharing the same bed, still asleep.

Main Street was busy. An army of rich out-of-towners had come up to the hunting lodges along the lakes that still survived from the early forties. They moved around in their luminous orange vests over their plaid shirts, and all wore caps with ear flaps. They looked like Elmer Fudd in their ridiculous gear. They didn't look like locals, who still wore army surplus that had actually seen action in foreign wars.

Hunting was a timeworn rite of passage. They came with their college sons, packed into 4x4's loaded with gleaming new weapons and amber bottles of booze, whole battalions of males wanting to capture the bloodlust that had propelled their ancestors to the top of the food chain. They preserved that aura of the age of robber barons, of wealth and power and corruption, once-fine-faced men now gone fat with drink and eating, deal makers who reveled in the monstrosity of their own physical size, men with barrel bellies and booming voices.

Every few years, somebody ended up mortally wounded. Some businessman was pulled from the forest with a hole in his back, and that curiously legitimized the hunt, a human kill. It made a good story for the boardrooms in the cities. By the holiday's end, the fat cats would turn and leave with gutted bucks strapped to the fronts of their vehicles, taking them down to the freezers in their rich men's clubs, to make deals months later in summer's heat, drinking champagne and eating the rare, bloody sinewy venison of their own winter kill.

The campus was emptied of students, save the few stragglers who still hadn't turned in their term papers. I moved on my rounds through the desolate corridors. There were boxes laid out where the students were to turn in their term papers in sealed envelopes. It was some kind of honors system because, shit, you could have taken someone's paper and read it over and got the answers just like that. But I think they were teaching things other than knowledge there at that college. I guess that was it, teaching people not to take the easy road. I think it went under the general title of 'Self-Respect'. I felt on the verge of screaming my head off, but I didn't. In each building, I used thumb tacks and put up Honey's sign.

I went back over to the security office and made some coffee, but felt tired. Baxter had left a pack of cigarettes, and I smoked one all the way down to the butt and lit another and did the same thing again. I closed my eyes from time to time, and there on the periphery of consciousness lay the Sleeper staring at me. He said, 'You going to leave me here, Frank?'

I abandoned the office. Outside the snow had abated, but it had turned sharply cold. The sky was getting dark, studded with shimmering stars. I could hear the ice down near the river groan and creak, the stratum of each ice layer distinct, freezing ever deeper as winter set in, freezing down to the dark murk where walleye, ling, and sturgeon lurked in sediment beds and reeds. I remembered going out with Ward and Norman for nights of ice-fishing. Dusk and deep night were the prime time for walleye. Dusk triggered the walleye night bite, then there was that lull for about an hour or so, before the night bite resumed. It was in that no-bite hour that inexperienced fishers abandoned the ice. That was our coveted secret, so if you waited for absolute night, you'd feel the pull on the lines. It had something to do with light gathering rods behind the walleyes' eyes. It took an hour before that mechanism kicked in. There were secrets up here that had been passed down from Indians through the French trappers and down to us.

I salted the college roads against the coming frost, cleared back the snow in the main parking lot. It wasted almost an hour and a half. I stopped only because the low gas light came on. I got the Jeep back to the security office. I checked the doors over by the science hall and moved close to what I knew was my eventual destination, toward the small prefab structures of the psychology lab. Inside, only a string of emergency lights faintly lit the path to the exit doors. It was strange as hell to move past the room where I'd been hypnotized all those years ago. I stopped and stared into the room. I wanted to see myself in there, but I couldn't resurrect the image.

I could hear the sounds of animals in cages, the smell of alfalfa and rodent feed, the squeak of a hamster wheel turning somewhere. I opened a door and shone my light on a cage of mice. Their small pink eyes glowed. It sent shivers down my back.

I went down by the administrative office and put in my skeleton key, felt the tumblers move and fall into place.

I checked through the records, but I didn't come across anything concerning me. I figured, if there was anything, it must have been archived by this time. But in among the files under C I saw a file labeled Martha Cassidy. I took it out and sat down. I used my flashlight to read. She had been receiving counseling for manic depression since the birth of her twins. Under a list of complaints, it listed financial stress as the principal cause of her depression. She had a bleeding ulcer which was being treated. The psychologist who'd examined her had written and circled 'Suicidal Ideation' in red ink and starred it. At the end of the file, it listed medication Martha had been prescribed.

I went back to the filing cabinet and set the file back. It was weird looking in on someone's life like that, reading the professional opinion of somebody trained to look into the mind. I felt sorry at one level for calling Martha a bitch, for undoing the peace she had offered on the phone. In giving those letters to the police, she was doing nothing other than protecting Norman and everything she held dear to her. I mean, you couldn't fault her for that.

The truth of it was, her relationship with Ward was just as bad as mine was with Ward. Martha ended up pregnant her Senior year of high-school. She had a kid and didn't reveal the father until two years later, when Norman came forward and married her. Martha had been tutoring Norman in remedial math. Norman was in summer school, going into his Sophomore year when he got her pregnant. In retrospect, I think he won that State Meet out of sheer rage, or fear, that year. The realities of life lay behind every goddamn move. He was wrestling with demons. They married right after his graduation. She was living in a one-room apartment on goddamn food stamps. And I think Norman could have walked away, he could have taken that scholarship, but he didn't. He owned up to what he'd done. I know Martha would have let him go. She loved him that much. You know I could see Norman, dumb as he was, faking an injury, ending his own dreams. I don't know that for a fact, but Norman always had a way of dealing with things in the simplest of ways, and sometimes that was the best way. He got no real scholarship offers because he was a risk college coaches weren't willing to take on, and that made it all the easier when he married Martha. There was no sense of anger of regret over the kid they made together. It was plain and simple that Norman got injured bad, that was it, just an act of fate. And shit, of course Ward probably knew all this. The son he'd pinned his hopes on went nowhere. I guess Ward must have hated Martha from the moment she came and moved in.

I was thinking a million miles an hour. Shit, Martha was a manic depressive. Her life was screwed, Norman's life was screwed. I could see it, some fight with Ward, Martha lashing out at him. And God, Ward had a tongue that could cut. He could fight his own battles. I could see Ward make a lunge at Norman. I could see Martha go for the gun they kept. I could see her screaming. Shit, a gun can go off just like that. I stopped dead. No, that wasn't it at all. Whatever happened was real for Norman. He well and truly believed the Devil had come to sit and wait on Ward's soul. It was just like he said, he showed up and found Ward dead. That was the truth.

I left the office and checked on the other buildings. Over by the library, I checked the catalog index of microfiche for our local paper. I took out the reel from a slot labeled 1951.

I went over to a cubicle with a microfiche reader and scanned the film. I found the date Chester Green died. It was two weeks before the fire that killed my parents. In the article it described Chester's sudden illness. He was just seventeen. I leaned back and let my eyes adjust to the dark background of the library. I could have sworn on a stack of Bibles that Chester Green had died after my parents died, since that image of him burning up in bed must have stemmed from my hypersensitivity to the memory of fire. That's how I aligned the memories. I sat still, sifting through the reality that I had it backward all these years.

I got up and went through the library, through the canyons of shelves, losing myself in the labyrinth of study cubicles. In a small alcove I got a Coke for free. I felt a sting of pain in my hand. I'd hit the machine hard.

I went back to the microfiche reader again, turning the small wheel, and the stories flew by my eyes. I got up to the story about my parents' death. The house had been totally consumed in the fire. The bodies of my parents had been burned beyond recognition. There was a picture of the house ruins, a solitary finger of chimney black and crooked against the sky. It mentioned that our family had already suffered misfortune earlier in the year, when Charlie had gone to the county sanitarium, a victim of polio. It was just another of those oblique coincidences that let me understand that remote and tragic time.

I put the microfiche back.

I went and put a dime in the payphone.

Honey answered. She said she was watching *The Mary Tyler Moore Show*. That's what we talked about, the show. Honey said, 'I like the way Mary throws her knit cap into the air and twirls it around. I thought I wanted to be that woman once, you know.'

I said, 'She can sure turn the world on with her smile.'

Honey sighed into the phone, 'Frank, you're not mad at me, are you?'

'No. I think we just might make it after all.'

'Frank, stop, please. You hear me? Don't push me away. Why didn't you wake me this morning?'

I said, 'I put up your signs all over campus.'

I heard a noise in the background. Honey said, 'Frank, wait.' There was something on the television. Honey said, 'Quit it, Robert Lee.'

I waited on the end of the line.

Honey said, 'Frank, they're digging up Chester Green's grave. They got a court order or something.' She described the scene. There was a TV camera crew on scene. 'They're digging right now.'

Honey held the phone to the TV, and I closed my eyes and listened to the subdued but melodramatic voice against the sound of what must have been a gasoline generator lighting up the grave.

Back in my office, I turned the heater back to low so that only one bar glowed. I turned off the overhead lights in the main office and waited in the dark for Dr Brown. At some gut level I felt there was no syndrome, that there was only Chester Green in a coma out at the sanitarium, and that Dr Brown was here to make me confess to being part of the conspiracy to kill Ward. I felt like calling Dr Brown and telling him not to come, but I didn't and just waited.

On the police radio I listened to the dispatcher talking back and forth to the cops out at the grave, just to calm my mind. The sense of mystery was subsumed by the fact that it was the eve of Thanksgiving, and the cops and reporters wanted to get back to their families. The night had been carefully chosen. I listened to the dispatcher say, 'Happy Turkey Day' to a cop who checked out early. He explained he was heading off to be with his divorced wife who had agreed to meet him at a lodge so he could see his two kids. The cop was paying for everything. He told the dispatcher how much it was costing him. The dispatcher made a soft whistling sound and said, 'Ouch,' like she'd been pinched. She lost her formal sharp voice and said softly, 'Patty still has a thing for you, Harold. I don't think it takes anything from a man to beg a little.'

The cop said, 'What eats me is she wanted a separate room for her and the kids, like I couldn't be trusted all of a sudden, like I was a damn stranger. What I said to her was, "Mr Checkbook says he isn't going to just piss away money like that! Mr Checkbook don't have money to piss away on lodges and fancy Thanksgiving dinners!" I said that to her.'

The dispatcher sidestepped the issue. 'You make sure you try the duck at the lodge, Harold. They got the best duck I ever tasted. If you get the chance, I highly recommend the duck. They do it in a glazed orange sauce.'

The cop said, 'Well, guess what! Surprise! Mr Checkbook says there's no second bedroom. Mr Checkbook is pretty much finished with this bullshit!'

I could have listened to that all night long.

I got up and made some coffee. I turned on the television to one of those UHF channels where there was no news, just trash. Long-legged girls in star-spangled red, white and blue shorts and knee-high tube socks raced around a ring in Roller Derby. When they whirled by, they looked like something in a blender if you just half-looked out of the corner of your eye. They went that fast. I sat and watched a big breasted brunette body check a skinny blonde with big fawnlike lashes. The blonde went over a railing and landed on her ass with her skates up in the air still turning. The brunette got two minutes in the penalty box.

The audience consisted of fat guys in Hawaiian bowling

shirts and shorts and black socks and shoes. They were drinking beer from plastic cups. It was live from Los Angeles. You could tell it was hot there. It was Thanksgiving Eve all across the greatest country on the face of the earth.

I lay on the sofa in the main office. I closed my eyes and felt the heat of the coffee cup against my hands and listened to the distant rumble of skates on the wooden rink.

Chapter 21

Dr Brown arrived just after ten o'clock. He had on a heavy parka with a fur collar. He looked old and small, his face like a wrinkled raisin. He coughed and put his hand to his mouth, and waited, then swallowed. He said, 'Frank, have you heard the authorities have an order to exhume Chester Green's body?'

'I caught it on the radio.'

Dr Brown shuffled with his characteristic polio limp, dragging his leg across the room. He had on brown polyester pants that hung just above his ankle so the white spidery hair of his legs was visible, as were the metal rods drilled into his black cripple shoe. He passed me and gave off a faint fecal odor of infirmity. He stared at the TV. The Roller Derby was still on.

I felt on guard, but I said, 'You want some coffee, Doc?'

He nodded.

I killed the TV and the room darkened. I went and poured two cups of coffee. I needed the caffeine hit.

Dr Brown took the cup. His head made a slow turtle movement, rising on the thin stalk of his neck, then settled again into the shell of his parka. His body trembled inside his parka. The cripple shoe moved of its own accord.

Dr Brown said simply, 'So, did you get anywhere with the Sleeper?'

'No.'

Dr Brown's brow frowned. He looked directly at me. 'The

orderly said he thought he saw the Sleeper blink to something you said.'

I stared back stone-faced. 'The eyes open and close all the time. One moment you think he's in there, and the next . . . nothing.' I pressed my hands against my thighs.

Dr Brown's body moved with that faint subterranean tremor. 'At least you tried.' He took another drink of his coffee. 'Maybe you might go back there again, try again?'

I said, 'What I don't understand is why you think he's going to communicate with me? Why do you think he would? Is there a reason?'

Dr Brown set his cup on his knee and shook his head. 'No, there's no reason in the world, not if you don't see one. And you don't see one, do you?'

I felt I was being tested. 'No I don't.' I looked away, and the darkness of outside pressed up against the window.

'So, Frank, you asked me to come and see you?'

I took a drink of coffee. I could see my reflection waver in the cup. I didn't know what to say. I looked back at Dr Brown. I felt my heart racing. I took a shallow breath, and said, 'I hear there's a theory going around that I blackmailed Chester Green into killing Ward.'

Dr Brown nodded. 'I've heard that.'

I said, 'Come on, Doc, you've been with me since . . . the beginning.' I stopped and started again. 'There's no syndrome, is there, Doc? Chester Green is in a coma. You sent me in there to . . . to freak me out. That was it, right? You got something against me, Doc?'

Dr Brown wanted to say something, but I just shook my head. 'Don't.' I had to sit before continuing. 'The police have tied me to Chicago around the time the letters were sent. They cross-checked the dates with the postmarks on the letters.' I bit the side of my cheek, my eyes staring at the floor. 'I mean, it's airtight, isn't that what they call this type of evidence?'

'What's your version of things?'

'My version! Shit . . . I don't know if I'm capable of that kind of repression. Was my hatred of Ward so deep that I could do something like that to him and dissociate myself from the fact?' I said, 'That's a question, Doc. I'm asking for your medical opinion.'

Dr Brown's eyebrows raised in his wrinkled brow. 'It depends . . . If there is something locked away inside you that you remember and hold Ward accountable for . . . maybe his accusing you of setting that fire, then maybe your psyche could cordon off that memory, and use an avoidance or repression mechanism to cope with that trauma at a subconscious level. You could have struck out at him, and maybe you wouldn't remember.'

I shook my head. I said, 'Who the hell lives at that level of goddamn repression? I can't believe . . .'

'Frank, don't do this to yourself. Repression is a legitimate psychological phenomenon.'

'Are you asking for a confession, Doc?' I felt flush for a moment. 'You want to know if I blackmailed Chester into killing Ward? Isn't that the question? That's the million dollar question the cops want you to get me to answer, right, Doc? That's why you let me see Chester, isn't it?' I was shouting by the time I got it said.

Dr Brown said, 'That's not it at all.'

I looked at him. 'I wish you could be goddamn honest for just one minute with me, Doc. You know what?'

'What?'

'I hold you responsible for what happened to me and Ward. You dragged the police into something I never understood. Shit on you! You ruined my life, ruined Ward's life. That's what you and your goddamn science did to me!'

Dr Brown stood his ground. 'You're worked up. Maybe you're right to be paranoid, but I'm not working with anybody. I give you my oath as a doctor, as a healer, or as a friend if you believe in nothing else about me, do you hear me?' Dr Brown extended his hand. 'Frank, I've been with you since the beginning like you said. I was there to try and help you, and if I failed, I am sorry, Frank, sorry from the bottom of my heart. I'm on your side.'

I eased a bit. 'I didn't mean that last remark, okay?'

'Sure, you have a right to be mad, to be paranoid, but it's not my doing. There are other forces at work, there have always been other forces at work.'

I didn't know what the hell that meant really. I shrugged my shoulders. I said, 'I feel like a stranger to myself, Doc. There are times when I look in the mirror and I don't recognize who I am.' I hesitated for a moment. 'I want to level with you, Doc. The police checked the papers in the metro areas of New York and New Jersey, and there was no mention of Ward's murder. So how the hell did I know Ward was dead?'

Dr Brown sat back in his chair and set his glasses back on his face. 'So how did you, Frank?'

I told him about the way truckers brought papers from far-flung areas, hauling through the night.

Dr Brown said, 'Well, there's your answer, you read a paper brought by a trucker. Accept that reality.'

'And what about the Sleeper coming from Chicago, and the fact that I lived there. You don't see that as . . .'

'As coincidence, Frank.'

I said, 'This seems like legal counsel, like a criminal defense pitch, not psychiatry.'

'Take it as you will.'

I said, 'I'm looking for answers, here, Doc. I want to know what I might be capable of doing.'

Dr Brown said simply, 'Let's go to the gravesite. Let's start there.'

I turned off the lights in the office and, against the dark, bluish sparks of static electricity came from Dr Brown's foot as he dragged it on the carpet.

Chapter 22

Dr Brown was silent as we went through town, heading toward the graveyard. I saw a light at the back of Mrs Brody's house. Honey was still up typing. I told Dr Brown about Honey and the typing.

'I'm glad for you, Frank.' He said it in that same quiet voice that must have hypnotized me a hundred times over the years. It had that hint of suggestibility and calmness that lets you release yourself from the natural order of self-preservation and suspicion.

We left the town behind us. It glowed in the rear view mirror.

A snowplow worked in front of us. We slowed, and the driver put his hand out the window and waved us on. Salt sprayed the truck and rattled in the undercarriage.

Dr Brown slowed and turned off the main road, working hand over hand to take the hard turn. The truck lights washed over the dark woods on either side of us. The road rose steeply in a switchback roadway that had originally been an old mining road. The graveyard was located up there, since this was where most of the early deaths occurred, down in the depths of the mines.

Dr Brown drove slowly. The truck cut back along the switchback. He shifted and missed a gear, and the clutch ground and then caught. Our bodies bucked forward in the dark. He said, out of the blue, 'What are you thinking about now? Free associate, say anything that comes into your head . . .'

'Sleep . . . my wife . . .' I stopped and said, 'Nothing . . .' It was the truth. I said, 'I'm not much good at this, am I?'

'There are no wrong answers. Keep going.'

'Money, house, car, vacation, pay raise, money . . . no wait, I said money before.' I said, 'A bigger house, a longer vacation, a bigger pay raise.' I ran out of things to say after that, and began again, saying 'An even bigger house . . .' but just stopped.

Dr Brown said, in almost a whisper, 'There's another level beyond those things.'

I said, 'I guess, but this is the level at which I exist.' I felt the tires crush against the snow, the slow cradling, the shift of the truck as it moved through the dark.

'Tell me about the nightmares, Frank, the nightmares you mentioned back at my office.'

I looked at his profile. He stared straight ahead into the cone of light outside.

'It's always the same, just the same fleeting images of fire and being in the barn hiding from my uncle, or at least it feels like I'm hiding. I cry out, and my uncle hears the noise and turns and peers around and then fixes on the barn. I hear him shout to somebody, and then the barn opens, and he towers over me. It ends in darkness, like a reel coming undone.' I leaned against the door while I spoke, the rumble of the truck making my insides tremble. The glass felt cold. I said softly, 'You know, now I don't even really remember that night any more, what I remember is memories of memories of that night. I have memories of waking up in motels and apartments after nightmares about Ward, and what I remember is the feel of those rooms, of the sense of isolation, of the TV show playing against the dark. Sometimes I'll have incorporated something on a show into the nightmare . . . all things disconnected from the fire. I remember sitting in the luggage

212

room of a hotel in Chicago, smoking alone, and just the act of lighting a match, of blowing on the ember of the cigarette, transported me back to the farm. The luggage became the cows, the cloakroom the barn.'

Dr Brown said, 'And that's what got you institutionalized in Chicago?'

I stopped talking all of a sudden and felt my body tense. Dr Brown knew about that. Right then, I felt certain he was working with the police. They had already consulted him as to my mental stability. I said quietly, 'How do you know about . . . about the mental institution in Chicago?'

'One of the doctors in Chicago taking care of you was reviewing cases of repression, and he came across your name. I was listed as the author of the paper, and I got a phone call wanting a consultation on your history.'

'Why didn't you tell me that?'

Dr Brown said softly, 'You never asked. I don't read minds.'

I said, 'I thought that was your specialty.'

We turned the last switchback and drove toward the old mining pit, along a ridge of hillside that gave a view of the land. Across the landscape I could see in the surrounding woods the dim undercarriage of light, hinting at small enclaves of life spread across the land. A ribbon of quicksilver water meandered against the surrounding dark toward the distant invisible life source of Lake Superior. It was a sight that had not changed in eons, something timeless against the passing of our own lives. I was thinking that in my head and said simply, 'Does it matter what happened almost three decades ago?'

Dr Brown whispered, 'That's classic avoidance, Frank. What did happen?' His face was obscured in the dark of the cab.

But I didn't answer him, and he didn't ask again.

If I'd been driving, I would have turned around and gone home. My life was elsewhere, it was with my wife and my kids. I truly believed that right then. Or maybe it was just fear, a reaction against what was outside the truck.

Dr Brown turned off the lights but kept the truck running. In the distance, through the dark silhouettes of trees, we stared at an aura of stark lights, their white chemical brilliance burning away the dark. It looked like the set of a movie, with tripods of lights angled toward the ground.

It was almost like some extraterrestrial ship had crash-landed into the mountain. A generator throbbed and sputtered, giving power to a television crew who had finished whatever shots they'd needed. They were inside their van filled with a wall of small screens and controls.

I moved away from Dr Brown. Phosphorous flares hissed along a walkway that led to the grave. Light emanated from the grave. It seemed like the body had been exhumed already, and the job was done. The mouth of the grave was black and dirty against the surrounding snow, as though the grave had literally vomited up the mound of dirt. A piece of excavating machinery with a claw stood off to the side.

I was stopped at the edge of yellow police crime scene tape. It rimmed a perimeter around the grave.

I said to the cop dressed in a heavy parka, 'So what did they find?'

The cop said, 'You are going to have to step back ...'

Dr Brown moved slowly and came up behind me.

The cop said again, 'You'll have to clear this area now.'

Dr Brown identified himself.

The cop called over to a guy in a long coat, some plain-clothed cop who shook Dr Brown's hand. He ignored me.

Dr Brown said, 'So what's the verdict, Burt?'

'They got the coffin, but there was no body in it.' The cop pointed over to the large mound of dirt, and there, outside the blaze of light, was the dark shape of a coffin.

Dr Brown put his hand on my shoulder. I didn't look at Dr Brown. I just said, 'I think I'll wait in the truck.'

I turned and walked away from the light. I heard Dr Brown

tell the cop who I was. I sat in the truck. I wanted to leave right then, not just this hillside, but the town.

Dr Brown did not come back immediately.

I felt a physical pain. I was shivering inside the truck from cold and shock. Chester Green was alive, and I must have known that in my subconscious all along.

Outside, the world glowed in the cold clinical light of the spotlights. Off to the side I saw a stooped man raising his fist. I could tell he was shouting, and I knew right then that it was Sam Green.

I felt the undercurrent of exhaustion take me under so there was only darkness, and the blonde from the Roller Derby flashed across my consciousness, and then there was Honey typing. She was naked, and when she turned it was Honey with the face of adolescence from the poster. She was pregnant. Her stomach showed in a smooth mound. She smiled and said, 'I love you. I will always love you, Ken.' I shouted, 'No,' and turned to run, and right outside the door of our bedroom was the farm, and there was Norman in his wrestling outfit, up in a tractor with all his trophies. He waved to me as he went by. He looked like the Jolly Green Giant. I followed him across the land, back toward the barn. We passed Charlie in his iron lung. He was in the middle of the yard shouting out answers to mathematical problems. He saw me and shouted at me to ask him a question. Norman just drove right by into the barn. I ran in after him. And there was Ward inside shouting, 'Where are you?' It was night. I was hiding with the cows. The barn glowed against a blaze of fire. I could hear a man screaming in the background. He shouted Ward's name, and Ward stopped. I stood up to watch and felt the force of him hitting me ... I could see myself asleep in the corner near the fireplace in Ward's house. My head hurt. There was noise upstairs. I could hear Ward shouting. I struggled slowly up the stairs and turned the knob on the door to the room from which the noise was coming. The door was locked. Ward said, 'He's awake. Stop!' He said, 'Go downstairs now, you hear me, Frank? You're dreaming, Frank, go downstairs.' I tried to turn the knob again. Ward shouted, 'Go downstairs.' I heard another voice behind the door. I put my eye to the keyhole, and there was Ward's eye staring back at me.

Dr Brown came back slowly, with that polio limp, a silhouette against the stark light. He didn't say anything, just shuddered and revved the engine, and turned in a labored circle. We got a sweeping glance of the excavated grave, and the gravestones in the background.

We came off the hillside in silence, like something had finally been decided. The radio was on low, but Sam Green came over the airwaves, shouting, 'I swear to the Almighty, my son died and was buried! I put him in the ground. Where is my boy's body?' I felt if I rolled down the window I would be able to hear him against the night. I wanted to put my hands to my ears to stop him shouting.

Dr Brown reached and turned off the radio, but he looked at me for a moment. I said nothing. In town, the light at my apartment was off, but the TV flickered against the dark. I checked my watch. It was close on midnight.

We passed the town church. I said, to try and ease things back to normal, 'I think a church steeple with a lightning rod on top shows a lack of faith.'

Dr Brown said simply, 'Stop, Frank!' That upped the tension.

I said, 'You can let me out here.'

'Wait.'

Dr Brown drove to the college, and put the truck in park. He just stared straight ahead, 'What now, Frank?'

I said in a monotone voice, 'You have Chester Green out there at the sanitarium.' I staved off looking at him. None of this affected me the way it should have. For a moment, I contemplated that reality, that maybe I was functioning at the level of a low-grade sociopath beyond real redemption.

Dr Brown said, 'Frank! Tell me what you remember!'

I said flatly, 'I remembered the name Chester Green, if that's what you are asking me . . .'

Dr Brown nodded, 'So now we're getting to the truth! You said Chester Green's name at the hospital where you were sent for treatment. Do you remember Chester Green? You saw him the night of the fire, right?'

I shook my head. 'Just the name. I associated Chester's name with fire. Sam Green came to our house screaming that his son was on fire in his bed, burning up with a fever.'

Dr Brown made a noise of feigned disgust. 'That's not right. Your uncle put that idea into your head, didn't he?'

I said, 'No.' I took a breath. 'I remember it. I remember Sam Green coming to our house.'

'No, Frank, that's not it at all. What you saw was Chester Green on the night of the fire, and you told that to your uncle, right? And he went about brainwashing you, trying to plant that image of Sam Green coming to the house into your head, right? That's what happened, isn't it?'

I felt numb just sitting there.

Dr Brown raised his voice. 'You don't think that your uncle planted the association with fever in your head to confuse you, to confuse me . . . to throw off the entire investigation, to make a sham of me and my methodology? Think, for God's sake, Frank. There's nothing that can hurt you now. You're not that child that came to me. You're a man. You've already been damaged! There's nothing else that can be done to you!' Dr Brown hit the steering wheel. 'Don't you want to heal, don't you want forgiveness for yourself? Do you want to live the rest of your life in fear of some phantom subconscious, Frank, believing you are capable of actions you cannot remember?'

I said, 'But maybe I did blackmail Chester into coming up here?'

'Ah, now we're getting somewhere. And what if you did, Frank, what of it? Listen to me. You are the victim here, do you hear me?' Dr Brown's glasses caught the light outside and gleamed. 'What of it, Frank, they deserved what they got, all of them!'

It was right then that I understood Dr Brown was here for reasons beyond any police investigation. He trembled when he spoke. He had lost any sense of decorum. He looked demonic, his face in shadow, crouched against the dark, shouting.

Dr Brown glared at me, 'You want to know my motivation in all this?'

I didn't get to answer.

'I'll tell you, Frank, *revenge*, for both of us, for you and me. Justice, Frank, that's what I first felt when I heard about your uncle's death at the hands of Chester Green. This thrill like electricity went through me!'

Dr Brown put his hand on my arm and squeezed. 'You see, I knew I was right . . . right about my belief in you all along, that you saw something out there the night your parents died, that you didn't start the fire. I said to myself, "That boy saw something!" That's right, Frank. I believed in your innocence. I wasn't wrong all those years ago. My *intuition* was right.' Dr Brown coughed and cleared his throat, and his hand squeezed tighter around my arm.

I said, 'What did happen?'

'You tell me. You were there.'

'No, I want to hear what you think happened.'

'Okay, we'll do it your way. You tell me if I'm wrong. I think your uncle found out Chester never died, and he blackmailed Sam and Chester. He got Chester to set the fire that killed your parents. He wanted that farm to himself, Frank.'

I raised my voice. 'Jesus Christ, you're out of your . . .'

Dr Brown shouted, 'It's all on those tapes, all of it. You mentioned Chester Green's name so many times.'

'What tapes?'

'Tapes of you under hypnosis.'

I said, 'So why didn't all this come out? If you had proof, if you had me on tape . . .'

'Don't think I didn't try. I pushed the State Attorney's office to prosecute your uncle after the fire. I had the police drag him in off his tractor, and I let him see you, Frank. I let him know that he wasn't getting away with murder! I gave the police all those tapes of you under hypnosis. I had the proof on those tapes.'

'So what happened?'

'I'll tell you, Frank. Those parochial hacks didn't understand my methodology. In the end, the State Attorney's office rejected everything. "Inconclusive," Frank, is what they said, "the ramblings of a child," they said my science was a sham!' Dr Brown took a shallow breath, racing to say it all. 'I was ruined by it. The research I'd done on hypnosis was rejected as unsound. I lost credibility. You should have seen your uncle, that damn yokel in his overalls and boots caked with dung, grunting denials that he didn't know what I had against him! I might as well have brought a case against an ox! This is why I'm still here, reduced to a third-rate town on the edge of wilderness. And the truth is, I was right all along! I was right! This night vindicates me. It vindicates both of us. Chester Green is not *dead*!'

I felt Dr Brown's hand on my arm. 'Just tell me I was right, Frank.' He came closer, so his breath was hot on my face. 'I want to share in your secret. I want you to tell me *I* was right all along.' Dr Brown still had his hand on my arm. 'You don't have to keep up this charade with me any longer. Tell me I was right.'

The vents were blowing hot air. I said nothing, sitting in the silence that lapsed between us.

'Don't you believe in providence, that their deception all those years ago has come full turn, and now we are in control. Think of it, Frank, an old man who won't even come and be with his son, and a son who will not reveal himself. They will take this to the grave, understand that!' Dr Brown nodded his head. 'Listen, we have our hostage.' Dr Brown's hand came to rest on my knee.

Things had come to an end. I went to open the door. Dr Brown said, 'You did know Chester Green was alive all along, right, Frank? Tell me that much, tell me I was right all along?'

I didn't answer his question, and just got out.

I watched the taillights bleed against the snow until he was gone.

In the office, I mixed some of Baxter's bourbon with boiling water and added a measure of sugar. It warmed me instantly. I wanted to watch the morning light form in the east, but it was only going on two o'clock, and I wasn't going to last all through the night. The buzz from the drink was losing its edge.

After a time, I noticed that the answering machine in the main office was blinking. I went in and pressed play, thinking it would be Honey. I hit 'play'. But it was Sam Green. He was shouting that he was going to get my kids. I was standing in the dark with my bourbon, listening to him shouting. His voice filled my head like he was there in the room with me, but that was just from the bourbon.

I rewound the message and played it again, and then took the tape and put it into my coat pocket. A half-hour later the phone rang, but I didn't pick it up, and there was no tape in the machine. It rang for a long time.

I drank the last of the bourbon, but, despite being drunk, I felt scared. I locked up and walked home across the dead campus, huddling against the cold. I had this image of Sam

220

Green eyeing me down the barrel of a gun and waited for my head to explode.

Chapter 23

I was alone in the apartment the next morning. I didn't even remember coming home. Robert Lee, Ernie and Honey weren't there. I checked the time. It was going on ten o'clock. I heard muffled music coming from beyond the door.

The news that Chester Green was not in his grave filled the airwaves throughout the early morning. I thought of the tape I had of Sam Green, how he'd threatened to kill my kids. I should have called the police right then, but I didn't. I guess I didn't want to have anything to do with the police. I didn't want to tempt fate.

I heard Mrs Brody's record player blare polka music when Honey came into the bedroom with a plate of pancakes, sausage links, scrambled eggs, and a small glass of grapefruit juice on a tray. She was smiling.

I sat up. The door was still open. I heard Robert Lee singing, and Mrs Brody let out a shout.

Honey laughed, 'Frank, you got to see this! Mrs Brody is down there doing the polka with Robert Lee.' She set the breakfast on a side table and sat down beside me, touching my face.

She was wearing a floral dress ruffled and puffed at her forearms and embroidered with white lace around her neck.

I watched her with a level of suspicion but kissed the back of her hand and said, 'Happy Thanksgiving.' Then I turned her hands over and kissed her fingertips. They were red from typing. 'How many pages?'

Honey put her index finger to my lips and said, 'Shoo. This is a holiday.' Her eyes looked glassy, like she'd been drinking all morning.

The record player was still playing loudly downstairs. I could hear feet stomping on the hardwood floor. 'That's quite a party down there.'

Honey smiled and curled her hair behind her ear and whispered, 'This is the kind of Thanksgiving you always see on television, snow and mountains and small towns.' She got up and went to the window and pulled back the curtains. 'All my life growing up in Georgia, I wanted a Thanksgiving like this.'

Everything had an antiquated feel to it, and maybe it was the music from downstairs, but it was also the way Honey was dressed, like an overgrown Alice in Wonderland. She looked incongruously young and old at the same time, standing against what looked like a backdrop of fake winter.

I said, 'You hear Chester Green wasn't in his grave?'

Honey didn't answer me. She just turned her back on me and went to the closet and took out a box. 'I got something for you!' She took it to me. 'Open it. Go on.'

It was a stars-and-stripes terrycloth robe, just like the one Sylvester Stalone wore in *Rocky*.

Honey said, 'Put it on, Frank.'

I got out of the bed and put the robe on and tied the belt loose around my waist.

'Walk over by the light. Make like you're . . . smoking a pipe.'

I made like I was smoking a pipe and put on an English accent. I said, 'I'll take a spot of tea.'

'God, you cut a good-looking pose.' Honey smiled and said, 'I think money can change everything up here.' She touched her head. She lit a cigarette and took a long pull and held it, and when she smiled the smoke came out of her mouth and nostrils. She blew again to clear the smoke. Honey said, 'I want you to eat your breakfast, and read the newspaper and stare out the window.'

It was like she was giving stage directions. She produced a newspaper.

I tried to eat and read at the same time.

Honey said, 'How are the foreign markets doing, Frank?'

I was actually going to look that up, but then I understood and said, 'Holding steady, though I think precious metals are the safest bet, what with the fluctuating dollar.' I felt like an ass. The breakfast had cooled, and the coffee was stone cold, but I ate it. The pancakes were like cardboard. I said, 'Chef has outdone himself.' I dabbed my mouth and crossed my knife and fork on the plate.

Honey said, 'Oh, good help is so hard to find these days.' She stressed the 'so'.

I stared at the paper again for effect. Outside the day was framed in the window. I remembered then about Sam Green threatening Robert Lee and Ernie. I said, 'Honey, there's something I want to tell you.'

Mrs Brody let out a shrill yell, and the record skipped, and then something broke, and Honey walked in that awkward way big women walk in high heels and shouted, 'What the hell's going on down there?'

I got up and went to the toilet. My bladder hurt with that low-level pain you get from holding things inside too long.

In the bedroom I turned on the television low. A guy dressed in a pilgrim's outfit threw confetti into the air and advertised an adjustable bed. You could try it risk-free for sixty days, and, if it wasn't the most comfortable bed you'd ever slept on, then you got your money back. It sounded like a great deal.

I debated whether I'd change or go down in the robe and decided on the robe, since it was the path of least resistance, and Honey would be expecting me to wear it.

I stood on the stairs and listened, the music filtering

through the grey light. I touched the ornate bear-claw carving of the stair post. I wanted to lose myself in believing I owned this house, that I was coming down to my family gathered around a Thanksgiving fire. I saw the fire casting shadows even before I turned and entered the room. The living room was filled with a luxurious heat that smelt of cedar and smoke, an aroma of bygone days.

Nobody saw me enter the room or actually, Honey did, but didn't acknowledge me. She was watching Mrs Brody dancing with Robert Lee. They were doing an old-time slow waltz.

Ernie was sitting in a big leather chair so his legs dangled in mid-air, with his dinosaurs beside him. He was smiling like I don't ever remember him smiling before. He clapped his hands in that excited way kids do. He had on a new sports coat and grey pants and a white shirt and a red bowtie. He looked like a ventriloquist's dummy. He was perfect and complete in the way you hope your kids will be.

Robert Lee turned in slow circles with Mrs Brody. He had the steps down, following her lead. He was wearing a suit he'd gotten out of a box left by one of the old miner immigrants who'd died years ago. He had his hair in a severe part. He looked like something that had come through a time machine.

Mrs Brody was tipsy. At the end of the record, she held out her hand, and Robert Lee kissed it and led her to a high leatherback chair. She was wheezing and putting her frail hand to her heart, but you could tell she was happy. Robert Lee went and poured two measures of red punch from a crystal bowl and smiled a wry smile at me when he passed. He smelt of mothballs and hair lacquer.

Robert Lee looked me over in the robe and turned and said to Honey, 'Who invited the Heavyweight Champion of the World?' He said it like an announcer introducing a fighter to the ring. He was as tall as me in his shoes. He turned to me again and said, 'Can I interest you in a libation, Champ?'

Ernie was just taking it all in. He said, 'Champ!' when I looked at him.

Honey changed the record. She downed a glass of punch and then poured herself another.

Robert Lee ladled another glassful and brought it to me.

Mrs Brody asked for the music to be turned down. She took a glass of punch and wanted to toast all of us. Her eyes were wet as she stood up and cleared her throat. She was wearing those mannish black shoes old ladies wore in the forties.

She went on about the miner immigrants who had stayed with her over the years, about the meals she prepared three times a day, how she used to clean each room. She told us about how she sewed their clothes and even wrote letters for those of them who couldn't write.

I sat looking between the fire and Mrs Brody and the goddamn giant bear looming behind her. Its fake amber eyes caught the glow of the fire.

Mrs Brody was gone all soft with remembrance.

Honey was standing like this was the national anthem or something, but it was too late for me to get up now.

Mrs Brody was telling about how the house became a makeshift hospital in 1932 when a mine shaft collapsed and buried eighteen men alive. Or really it was eighteen boys, all around Robert Lee's age, all immigrants. Mrs Brody touched Robert Lee's arm.

Nine of them came out of the pits and stayed upstairs, and some had to have legs and arms amputated, but only two survived in the end, because the others got gangrene. She wound down eventually and put the glass to her weak, trembling lips and drank with her eyes closed and blessed herself and the dead and the living. 'We had great Thanksgivings here once upon a time.'

Mrs Brody went between laughing and crying so many times, sniffling and blowing her nose. She told us stories about how her young immigrant men got snowed in some holidays and didn't get down to the cities to see their girlfriends who worked as domestic help. But it didn't kill their mood. She said the men danced with one another on Thanksgiving, Christmas Eve and Christmas Day, old style waltzes from Russia and Poland.

Robert Lee said, 'You sure you weren't just keeping fags?'

Ernie kicked his small legs and laughed. I kissed the crown of his head.

Honey said, 'Robert Lee! You're a heartbeat away from getting it good, you hear me?'

Mrs Brody said, 'It was one of the most beautiful things to see, young men dancing like they did, the way they could dream with their eyes open.' Her face was cast in shadow, so it was only the outline of her face that was visible, not the wrinkles or imperfections. I watched Robert Lee looking at her and smiling. Her voice was soft against the crackle of the fire. She looked at Robert Lee and said, 'Can you imagine what it was like down in those mines in the dark? It was like they rose from the dead each evening, resurrected.'

I thought of Charlie for some reason right then, the sullen horrors that befell us only one generation ago, what it took to survive. I even had pity, at some level, for Dr Brown.

Robert Lee looked at Mrs Brody and said, 'How come you never got married?'

Honey said, 'You don't have to answer any of his questions.'

Mrs Brody stared at the fire. 'I let life pass me by. I got scared of all that death out there. I was here so many times when men died out at the mines that I got scared of ever . . .' Mrs Brody took a deep breath. 'I didn't let myself fall in love. I didn't see the beauty of life until it was too late.' She turned her head from the fire and looked at Robert Lee. He said, 'Hey, it's not all bad! You got us, right?'

She smiled, 'When you least expect something good, it just comes like that.'

Robert Lee looked at me and said, 'Frank, what's the legal age for drinking?'

I poured whiskey from a decanter into a glass and handed it to him.

Honey said, 'Just a quarter of a glass. We got a history of problem drinking in my family.'

Mrs Brody went under fast.

Honey put on another record but kept the volume low. We stayed like that for a good half-hour. Honey topped up her drink again and stayed by the lace curtains looking out into the quiet street. A church bell rang down at the Church where Ernie attended kindergarten.

Mrs Brody began snoring.

I left with Ernie and Honey. We went back upstairs single-file.

Robert Lee stayed behind.

There were three hours to kill before we had to go out to Norman's house. I felt the stalemate of how things stood between Martha and me. She hadn't called me back after I called her a bitch.

Honey sat at her typewriter, staring out the window. She laced her hands together and cracked the joints in her fingers, but she didn't start typing. She had a ruby glass of port next to the typewriter. She turned to me and said, 'Why do people always invite you over to celebrate the holidays? Is it because they're bored stiff looking into one another's faces all year?'

I didn't answer her, because she started typing with that rapid-fire motion.

I knelt before the television and went through the stations and stopped on Channel Thirty-Two. A log burned in a fireplace, taking up the whole screen. I left that on for a bit, watching the same looping footage every few minutes, no real sound except the crackle that approximated what a fire sounded like. Ernie came and stood looking at the screen.

Honey turned and said, 'Now I've seen everything.' She continued to type even as she looked at the screen.

The fire was there for the benefit of those lost souls over in Traverse City who lived in apartments without fireplaces. It was a fire that seemed like it would elicit suicide and not comfort, the crimson flicker like an open wound in the center of the room if you squinted your eyes. We were fast approaching a world in which there was no such thing as the real thing, or the real thing was being redefined, until the thing represented was more real than the real, since the real didn't exist. It was a higher order of human consciousness, a reality into which we were moving.

I said, 'The audacious power of human longing . . .' but didn't get to finish my train of thought. Honey said, 'Put a lid on it, Frank.' She was coming down off whatever high she'd been on.

Slats of mid-morning light fell across the floor.

I went to the bathroom and showered and shaved.

I changed the station from the burning log. The Patriots were playing Buffalo in an East Coast game. It was snowing hard in Buffalo. I turned the volume to mute.

Honey ignored me and typed for a good hour, even though she had declared it a holiday.

I filled a bowl with milk and Coco Puffs for Ernie and filled myself a bowl as well. The milk turned brown and sweet. I felt what it must be like to be a kid for a moment. Ernie wanted more. We had a second bowl.

It was late in the second quarter since it was an East Coast game. It all seemed distant and remote, and pointless without the sound. Men piled on one another and then got up, one at a time, and there was the ball, like some primordial egg, as though this was all some elaborate mating ritual.

I washed the bowls and stretched out on the bed, and Ernie curled against me and slept against the hollow of my armpit. I watched the game unfold. And through it all, Honey kept up a constant pace on the typewriter.

I had fallen asleep when the phone rang. Honey said, 'Let me get it, Frank.'

I opened my eyes and felt half in this world and half in the next. I heard Honey say, 'Yes, I accept the call,' and it was like the air had been sucked out of the room.

I sat up, holding Ernie. He yawned and wiped his eyes.

Honey put the phone to her breast and shouted for Robert Lee, and then looked at me like I should leave.

I knew it was Ken on the line. 'You want me to take Ernie?'

Honey nodded and cut her eyes away from me.

Downstairs Mrs Brody was nursing her head with a tall glass of water. Robert Lee left without saying anything. The fire had died in the grate to glowing embers, but it was still hot in the room.

We could hear Honey talking loud upstairs.

Mrs Brody looked at me and then at Ernie and said, 'You want to play Snakes and Ladders?' and Ernie nodded his head. Mrs Brody made me take down a jar of wheat pennies she had collected, which she used for parlor betting.

Outside, I worked on digging the car out of the snow.

The sun was warm if you stood out of the shadows. It was good to do some physical exercise. When I'd cleared the snow, I got into the car, and it started immediately since I'd plugged a heating pad over the battery a few nights before. I set the heater on full blast. A web of ice covered the windows so everything was a darkish grey.

I turned on the radio, but there was no real news this late into the day, nothing about last night, just tapes of music, pre-recorded and set to loop through the afternoon and into the night, a music filled with trumpets and choir voices. It sounded just right for this cold, clear day, shrill rejoicing like Judgment Day for the saved. I imagined that music playing out in the parlors of the small farmhouses, the white expanse of fields spread around them, animals fed and chores done, men washing earnestly in tubs, getting the grit out from under their nails and wiping away the dirt behind their necks, putting on starched white shirts and pleated black pants, preparing for this singular holiday of Thanksgiving, a collective history threaded back to a single act of defiance by people in search of religious freedom. I could see in my mind women working hard setting the table, lighting candles, stirring pots of mashed squash and sweet potato, the smell of turkey sifting through the farmhouses.

I kept wanting Martha to call me, but of course Honey was on the phone.

I looked at my watch. It had crawled toward the time we were to leave. I got out of the car. Ernie had come out and was standing at the back door. He was dressed in his Green Bay Packers jacket and mitts.

I smiled at him. 'You hungry, Ernie?'

He nodded.

The curtains billowed up in our apartment window. Robert Lee stuck his head out the window. 'We all ready down there, Frank?' His voice belied the fact that he had just spoken with his father, and that scared me.

I used a brush to clear off the windshield and hood of the car.

Robert Lee came down and stood with Ernie. He called up to Honey to come down. Mrs Brody came to the back door and stood with the boys.

I said, 'Remember those pumpkin pies, Robert Lee.'

I had my back turned to him when he said, 'Hey, Frank, what's the difference between snowmen and snowwomen?'

That's when I got hit in the back of the head. And for a moment the image of Sam Green flashed in my mind, his threat on the tape the previous night.

But Robert Lee shouted, 'Snowballs, Frank!'

The snowball hurt like a son-of-a-bitch, but I sucked it up

like a Christian at a public stoning. Melting snow trickled down my neck.

Honey came down with the pies, and we got into the car. I could tell she'd been crying.

Ernie said, 'Snowballs,' and Honey turned her head and said softly, 'What's that, sweetie?'

Robert Lee came close to my ear and said, 'I'll teach you yet, Frank. The rules of engagement dictate you never turn your back on the enemy, never.'

Chapter 24

The journey out to the farm was interrupted by Honey. She had me stop, and she got out and just stood at the side of the road. I watched her through the windscreen, like I was staring through a TV, like this was not really happening. It was sub-zero cold, and Honey's coat was open. She was tall in her high heels. She had a hand to her face, like she was trying to stop the grief coming out of her.

Robert Lee kicked the back of my seat.

I turned slowly and said, 'You do that again, and I'll kill you.'

He stopped.

I got out of the car and went to Honey and put my hand on her back.

'Jesus, Frank, I just want all of it to be over, all of it.'

'It will, soon.'

A crow perched in sharp relief on a fence, black against the white background. I looked back, and there were Ernie's and Robert Lee's heads just looking at us. I could tell Robert Lee was saying something to Ernie, even though his lips were obscured by the back seat. I turned away from them.

Honey kept her back to me. 'You know what he wants to do, Frank?'

'Who?'

'Ken!'

'What?'

'He wants to donate all his organs to medicine.'

I thought they couldn't kill Ken quick enough for my liking, but I said, 'That seems like something noble, right?'

Honey shrugged her shoulders. 'I don't know, Frank.' She kept staring off across the cold fields. She was shivering from the cold and other things. 'What's going to happen on Judgment Day, Frank? Ken's going to be all cut up and in other people. How's that work?' She turned and looked at me for the first time. Her eyes had a glazed look.

I said, 'Salvation and resurrection are a mystery Honey, but I'm telling you, if Ken does something like that, then Jesus has a way of putting him back together when the time comes.'

Honey sniffled and rubbed her nose. 'Frank, where do you think badness exists inside us?'

'I don't know.'

'What if they put all those bits of Ken in somebody else and it's passed on? I mean, killing those people like he did . . .'

I said, 'Jesus Christ, Honey, you don't actually believe that, right?' I could feel the cold gripping around me. I thought this was the most stupid conversation I'd ever had in all my life.

'I don't know. Would you take the heart of a man who'd killed two people?'

'If I was dying, sure I would.' I put my hand out to touch hers, but her hand just clenched.

I let her say nothing for a bit. It seemed like silence had become the motif of all our lives. I just looked out over the snow. The sky was a marble color, and I knew it would snow again by evening, a heavy wet snow. Across the fields I could make out light in houses even at this hour. The houses were small islands of humanity lost amidst the vast coldness of winter. It was a life I had lived for so long, and it made me shudder just remembering.

Honey had her coat open, and her breasts hung heavy in her floral dress. The cold made her neck and face mottled. She said, 'Frank?'

'Yeah?'

'You think somehow, if Ken was cut up and put into other people, that . . .' She hesitated. 'Frank, I know what you're going to say, I know how you feel about religion and all, but I just want to tell you, Ken never forgave me for leaving him, for going off and getting married.' I could see the tears in her eyes. She put her hand to her nose and sniffled. 'You think he might . . . might come after me?'

I said, 'No, that's not going to happen. It's not.' I kept my voice level. I looked into her eyes and shook my head.

Honey's voice was weak and shallow. 'He told me on the phone that he was going to come see me, like that's what he wants more than anything else in the world.'

I turned, and Robert Lee had made his index finger and thumb into the shape of a gun and had it trained on me, but when he saw me looking he took his hand down. Ernie was there, too, doing the same thing. Robert Lee said something, and Ernie took his hand down as well.

I kept staring at them and said to Honey, 'How about we don't go out to Norman's for Thanksgiving? How about we just take a drive? I know this lodge that serves Thanksgiving Dinner. How about we just go there and spend the time by ourselves? We have the money for the first time in ages. You've been working, and I've been working, and, no matter what's going on around us, it can't touch us, Honey. You have to remember that, not Ken, or what's happened with my uncle, none of it. You hear me?' I smiled at the end of saying that. I said, 'Life's what you make it,' and I believed that at some gut level.

Honey took a deep breath and leaned her head back and blew a plume of hot breath into the air. 'I know you think I'm crazy, but you don't know Ken. He'll do anything to go on living.'

We got back into the car and just drove aimlessly along lanes that led to farms. We stopped and watched some deer close to a dark knot of woods. They sensed our presence and turned their heads to us and watched. They flashed signals to one another with their tails, a silent language across the frozen land.

We rolled down our windows, just to feel the coldness that they endured. The day had settled, and the wind carried a mist of windblown snow that made things look almost like a sketch.

I stopped at a gas station that serviced the highway. It had a neon 'Open' sign glowing against the dappled sky. It was going on three o'clock already. There was a row of pumpkins in descending order each carved with the face of an American president, or that's what it said on this sign, but it was hard to tell one president from the next, except for one that was just a smashed pumpkin, and I guess that was JFK, after he was assassinated.

Honey and Robert Lee and Ernie went in to get soda and chips and candy bars. I pumped gas and looked out at the highway. It was desolate, like there'd been a plague that had killed all the Earth's inhabitants. They used to talk of nuclear winters, of grey ash and a world without sun, and that's how the day felt. The east was already surrendering to a dark bruised color.

Out back, there was a public toilet and a phone. Everything reeked of oil and old cars. I called out to Norman's house, and, while the phone rang, I saw a black bear in a cage. It was under a tarp held up by tent poles. The bear was sitting up and just staring out at the road.

Norman answered. I could hear a football game in the background. The first thing Norman said to me was, 'You think I could play professional football?'

I was still staring at the bear. I could smell the dampness of its fur, an acrid animal odour.

Norman repeated his question, and before I answered, I heard a click on the line and the breath of someone else

236

listening. I figured it was Martha. I said, 'You never played football in school, Norman.'

'That's not what I'm asking you. You seen what I did on the wrestling mat. Now, I want you to tell me if you think I could play professional football!'

I said, 'Yeah, I think you could play professional football,' and, by the time I had that out of my mouth, Martha shouted, 'Frank, don't you encourage him, you hear me? Norman is twenty-five. He's not eighteen anymore. You got to go to college to get drafted, isn't that right?'

Norman said, 'You hush now. I'm strong. You know me, Frank, you seen what I can do?'

I said, 'Yeah, you are the strongest man I've ever known, Norman.' And it was the truth.

I could still hear the football game in the background. The television was on real loud, louder than was normal for a television.

Martha said, 'Where are you?'

I was looking at the bear. He got up on his hind legs and sniffed in my direction.

'Frank?'

'My kid's come down with a fever.'

Norman said, 'Frank, I know I could play professional football.'

Norman sounded like a dumb shit. I said, 'I don't think you can play professional football just like that, Norman. You have to get an agent, and you have to have a time for the forty-yard dash, and you have to have documented what you can bench press and dead-lift, some huge weight. You have to have a physical that shows that you're not concealing any injuries. You have to have all that before anybody is even going to let you have a tryout.'

Martha said, 'You see, Norman, it's like I said. It's not like you can go on over to Green Bay and just put on a helmet. Frank is right, it's not that simple.'

Honey and Ernie came around to see where I was, and I put my finger to my lips, and Honey nodded. Then they saw the bear, and Honey said, 'Jesus Christ,' and took a step backward. The bear rose again and rattled its cage.

I waved frantically for Honey to stay back from the bear. It made a growling sound and shook its cage again.

Martha said, 'What's that growling noise?'

'That's my stomach, Martha. Like I said, I was set on a real feed.'

Norman cut in and said, 'I wasn't thinking of Green Bay. I was thinking the Miami Dolphins. That's my team, Frank. I want to get away from the cold.'

I just rolled my eyes. The bear was sitting again. It yawned and showed a pink mouth against the black tarp.

Martha said, 'Did you call a doctor for your kid?'

I said, 'I just might yet, Martha. I figure, everybody's eating now, so maybe I'll wait a bit. Fevers in kids can flare and then just drop off, but I don't want to bring anything out to your kids, since my kids were back east, and who knows what the hell they might have brought with them.' I could feel myself beginning to talk in circles.

Robert Lee came around the corner. He looked at the cage and then at me. He went toward the cage. I waved my hand, but he ignored me. I said, 'I have to go now. I just wanted to wish you a Happy Thanksgiving.'

Norman said, 'How fast do you have to run the forty to make it in professional football?'

I said, 'I don't know. That's what an agent would tell you. They have all the facts and statistics. The best thing to do if you're thinking of a career in professional football would be to write to the Green Bay Packers and ask them if they know an agent that could work with you. That's what I would do, Norman.'

I was just getting off the phone when Norman said, 'I don't want to farm no more.' He said it with such a simple fatalism

238

that it sort of stunned me, more than if he had screamed it. 'I just don't want to.'

Martha said nothing either, and I knew something had come undone in their lives.

I said, 'It's over, Norman. Listen to me. There was no Devil, you hear me? Chester Green never died. You hear me, Norman, nobody is looking at you as having done anything wrong!' I swallowed and felt the cold wrap around me. 'Whatever the police said to you was just scare tactics, Norman. You fired that gun, and they had to be sure you really just fired at the ceiling. Are you listening, Norman?' I said, 'Martha, you tell him!'

Martha said nothing.

'I'm going to come see you Norman, not today, but it's not good that brothers haven't seen each other in all this time, you hear me?'

Norman said, 'If you're coming out this way, look into a stop-watch for me, okay?'

'Sure.' I hesitated for a moment, then said, 'Do me one favor, watch out for Sam Green, okay? He called and said he was going to get my kids. I want you to watch your kids, you hear me, Martha?'

Again she said nothing.

The football game blared in the moment of silence before I set the phone down.

I shouted, 'Keep the hell away from that thing!' Shouting startled the bear, and it seemed to get submissive and went on all fours and lowered its head.

The yard was strewn with bits of cars, and the ground was a stew of mud and snow with deep grooved car tire marks heading toward a swayback barn that was on the verge of collapse.

We moved slowly toward the bear. His head was huge, bigger than you would think when you see a bear from a distance. The bear's breath came in heavy sighs and steamed in the cold air. His black nostril holes opened and closed. I could see the fur was matted with mud and frosted with ice along his back.

Standing a few feet from him, the smell was terrible, since the cage was littered with decaying pieces of cabbage and carrots, a rotten putrid mess.

The bear's leg, which was chained to a hook in the ground, was raw and red against the black of his fur, and he stopped every few minutes and licked at the wound with his long pink tongue.

For four bucks you could get your photo taken with the bear. It said that on a cardboard sign leaning against the tarp.

The owner came out the back door and said, 'You interested in a photograph?' He was thin, like a cricket. He had big dentures that showed when he opened his mouth. He said, 'That bear was hit by a semi a few years back. He's got a bum leg.'

Robert Lee looked at me and at Honey like he wanted his picture taken, but he said, 'You mind if I get one of just me with the bear? I got my own money.'

I said, 'My treat.'

The owner told Robert Lee to get a pumpkin from around front, and he went inside and came out with a pilgrim's hat, which he gave to Robert Lee, and that's the image that materialized minutes later for posterity, Robert Lee as somber as a Lutheran standing next to the cage. The owner had thrown something at the bear so it stood high on its hindquarters and looked ferocious. It pained me to see that.

Then Honey, Ernie, and I got a picture taken, and Ernie wore the hat and stood between Honey and me, holding a hand each. The owner made me hold a pitchfork, like in that American Gothic portrait.

Inside, the owner had a small television with rabbit ears on a crate close to the window. The reception came and went in a grey static. *It's a Wonderful Life* was on and Jimmy Stewart was just about to jump off the bridge, and his guardian angel was watching him. He was about to get his wish, to have never been born, and now he was going to see how life turned out without him. It was one of my all-time favorite movies.

The owner said, 'You hear about them digging up that grave and finding no body?' He showed me a newspaper with a picture of the excavated grave.

I bought a wad of beef jerky and paid for everything and left just as Jimmy Stewart touched his lip, and it wasn't bleeding because he had never been born.

Out back of the gas station, I gave the bear the dark tongue of jerky. It looked straight into my eyes. I said, 'Eat,' in a soft voice.

I called The Cedar Lodge and booked a room and dinner. Then I changed that to two rooms. I felt magnanimous in some strange and pathetic way watching the bear eating, giving it a few minutes of pleasure. I think if I'd had a gun and I was by myself, I might have taken the owner out and locked him in with the bear and just seen the vengeance that animals can exact.

We passed the Polaroid shots around, and Honey laughed to see us. It looked like the pictures had been taken years ago. It was one of those moments we were going to look back on over our lives, and that gave our movements some dramatic portent.

It snowed in big spiraling flakes as we headed off again along the moraines, where the ice fishers were out in their tents. The evening died slowly. We stopped and watched the ice fishers for a while. I turned the heat up high. It was like watching a movie, just staring out into the world.

I felt overwhelmed by a sudden sadness. I could see Norman out there cutting into the turkey with Martha and the kids sitting around the table. He was talking the finer points of professional football with his kids, and that hurt in the pit of my stomach.

Chapter 25

We had worked up an appetite by the time we arrived at the Cedar Lodge gate. We drove down a long canopied corridor of trees strung with orange lights. The main lodge glowed in the distance.

Honey put her hand on mine and smiled. Ernie leaned forward and put his head between us. He was fascinated by the lights. Our faces glowed amber.

I stopped the car, and two doormen dressed as elves came and waved at us.

Robert Lee said, 'Check out the fags,' but I think he was saying that because he felt he had to, and I could see the look of awe on his face.

I said, 'I'm offering a reward to anybody who behaves.'

Ernie said, 'I'll be good, Frank.'

I could see him in the rear view mirror. 'I know you will.'

The lodge looked like an amalgamation of every dream you have ever had about winter, the aged wooden beams interlocked in the old world fashion. A huge fire blazed, making everything shift and glow. The interior was decorated with animal hides, and a collection of Indian artifacts hung on the walls alongside the heads of bison and bucks and a huge murky tank that held a collection of fish native to the dark waters of the region. There was also a small souvenir store where you could buy seasonal portrait calendars and coasters with the faces of famous explorers, along with produce like smoked meats, fruit preserves, Indian moccasins, headdresses, beads and earrings.

A bulletin board listed the winter activities. Ice skating and ice fishing were offered. The featured event of the evening was a horse-drawn sleigh ride out to an old barn for hot apple cider tasting. I signed us up for that. The day's menu was posted in a script like it had been written with a quill pen. There was an embossed wax seal on the bottom of the menu. We read it with an eagerness that underscored our hunger for food and so many other things.

Our bedroom was designed like a barn, our king-sized bed up a ladder on a second floor where you couldn't quite stand up since the roof formed an A-frame. A fire was burning, and there was a complimentary bottle of wine and a fruit basket.

The theme of Robert Lee and Ernie's room was *The Old Woman who lived in a Shoe*. The door was like a boot tongue, and inside everything was miniature. The room was done in a pastiche of eggshell blue and scarlet. Ernie's bed was a teacup and Robert Lee's was a peapod. Ernie looked normal-sized, but Robert Lee seemed like a giant. There was a complimentary bottle of Coke and a coloring book on each bed.

Robert Lee had been eerily accommodating ever since he got the photograph with the bear. He said he would eat with Ernie in a room reserved for kids.

Honey and I showered together and held each other for a long time in the hot steam. We touched each other with the tenderness you might use to tend a wound. Honey leaned back against the shower and cupped her breast, and I leaned forward and took the nipple to my lips and took the weight of her breast in my hand and felt her heart beat. She pressed into me, and I felt the soft balloon of her breast roll and fill my mouth. The shower hissed, the steam rising in folds around us. I opened the glass shower door and lay flat on the damp floor. Honey materialized from the steam and straddled me. She pressed the bigness of her legs along my legs and rocked back and forth. Then, slowly, she hoisted herself and for one moment stared down at me, and then sank on to me as if this single moment could vanquish the aimless wandering of our lives.

In the aftermath, we grew cold and went into the loft and held each other. The built-in radio console was playing Gordon Lightfoot singing, *If you could read my mind*, and it did what music does best, saying what we can never say, forming those invisible bridges that bring us closer together. I closed my eyes and followed those melancholy words. Honey rolled over and pushed her back against me, and I leaned against her like a piece of a jigsaw puzzle that had found its purpose.

The room phone rang and brought us back from the blankness of sleep. It was reception to confirm our dinner reservation. The shower was still on, the steam condensing in the room below us like a bank of fog. It was like descending in an airplane through clouds.

We lingered again in the shower. I said, 'I sometimes think Christianity would be a far greater ministry if Jesus had sex while on earth.'

Honey just put her finger to my lips and said, 'Frank, no words . . .'

We ate dinner, and suffice it to say we got stuffed. I had to unbuckle my belt a notch right there at the table. It was the kind of food that's a drug, that takes you under. The wine was included. Honey had Martinis, since that was what she drank when she was young. The room was crowded with people, but there were some older couples who maybe never had kids, country people dressed like they had come from church, having done good Christian deeds. They were dressed in that parsimonious way the truly devoted subject themselves to. I wanted people to know what Honey and I had done.

And then I saw who I presumed was the cop from the radio the previous night, the illustrious Mr Checkbook. He was big and had one of those brush-cut State Trooper haircuts, and his pants were too short and showed his steel-toed boots, a dead giveaway. Then I saw his wife. It was the blonde woman I'd stared at down at the college diner. She didn't see me. From a distance, she looked young and pretty, like someone who got caught in high school in a bad relationship, before she knew the meaning of life. I could tell she wanted to be anywhere but there with Mr Checkbook. She had been crying. Her eyes looked glossy, and her kids, dressed in matching shirts and pants, looked gloomy, like they had been shouted at. Just looking at her, I wanted to believe she had another man who was waiting for her, a quiet guy who maybe had liked her in high school and was willing to take on her kids like they were his own. But Mr Checkbook was never going to let her go.

I told Honey the story of Mr Checkbook as he sat down at a table. In a way, I think he was the kind of husband I would have picked for Honey. All she said was, 'He's big,' like that was something she liked in a man.

Mr Checkbook saw us looking at him and stared at us hard, until we looked away and pretended we were talking about something else.

I found myself telling Honey about Norman and what he said about wanting to try out for professional football and wanting to get out of farming. I said it in a monotone way, but it sent a chill through me, like this feeling had been there behind the sex, waiting patiently to surface.

Honey said, 'Professional football isn't something you just pick up. I hope you told him that. He's how old?'

I said, 'Twenty-five. He's committing slow suicide, is what he's doing.' I told her about Norman swearing it was the Devil who had been waiting upstairs for his father's soul. 'The cops took him and grilled him about shooting the murder weapon.

For a time, before they dug up the grave, Norman was a suspect, or at least the cops weren't exactly buying his story.'

Honey kept eating through everything I was saying, making the occasional face. She used her fork to take some turkey off my plate. She said, 'Isn't it all over now? Doesn't Norman know he's in the clear?' I could tell she had a certain impatience with the whole episode.

I said, 'I think he's having a mental breakdown.'

The waiter came and poured more coffee. Honey wanted another dessert, and I just waited while she decided between New York Cheesecake and a custard pudding topped with glazed fruit.

The alcohol was affecting me. I thought about telling Honey that Chester Green could communicate, and next thing I found myself saying, 'I've got a secret, Honey.'

She was eating her custard pudding, and, with half-interest, she said, 'What secret?'

I stopped short and said, 'I love you,' and she held her fork over the pudding and said, 'You want to tell me the real secret?' but I just said, 'I love you,' with such a trembling honesty that she smiled and touched me with her fork on the back of my hand, like I was something she could eat, and the dinner was saved again.

Honey pushed her plate away and said, 'You know, I have a hair color that won't ever need to be dyed.'

We moved on to after-dinner drinks and had what was called a Golden Cadillac and a Velvet Hammer, and finished with Irish Coffees.

Robert Lee and Ernie passed the dining hall and didn't look in at us. It was like seeing them in a dream. Honey said, 'They came out of me, Frank.' She pointed at her stomach, and I can tell you that was the craziest notion you could have had at that moment.

Honey said, 'That look right there. That's why I married you.'

Out in the lobby, I felt I was in a sort of suspended animation. *It's a Wonderful Life* was playing again. Jimmy Stewart was frantically looking for the money his uncle had misplaced. His Savings and Loan bank was on the verge of going under. I watched Jimmy Stewart losing his mind with terror and grief. He was shaking his uncle and calling him names. It was truly sad to see a good man at wit's end.

Honey took Robert Lee and Ernie off on the horse-drawn sleigh out to an old barn for the cider tasting. I stayed behind. It was close on 9 p.m. The snow was falling hard.

I went out and stood for a time in the cold, to let the heat of the dinner cool inside me, something Ward always did at meal's end, and something Norman did, too, as he got older.

I stood listening to the sound of the wind in the trees. I got so I shivered and hugged myself, and stayed standing in the cold until my skin stung and my teeth chattered. I remembered a story Ward told me, about how he got caught in a storm with my father and Charlie on the way home from school, and how they dug a hole in a bank of snow and lay down and hugged one another for warmth through a long night of howling gales, taking turns to be in the middle. It was not until the dying evening of the next day that the storm cleared and they dug themselves out and followed the light of the farmhouse across the fields. They went on home to a feed of raw onions and bread dipped in bacon grease, washed down with black coffee. Ward said they felt that their mother half believed they were ghosts, because she had this strange, fearful look in her eyes, and she backed away from them. At first she was afraid to touch them, but when she came to understand they were alive, she sat at the table and cried like he had never seen her cry before or afterward. It was one of the few things Ward ever told Norman and me about his life as a child.

I think reality is something we in the modern world take for granted, but something that people years ago struggled to maintain, and why ghosts and superstitions permeated the membrane of so-called real life.

I went back into the lobby and called Baxter and asked if he'd work the next day or so, and he agreed, since the college was officially closed, though I knew he probably wouldn't go near the college but would put us down as having worked.

I called Norman's house. Martha answered. Her voice was almost a whisper.

I said, 'You have to speak up. I can't hear you.'

'You should have come out.'

'Martha, you never called me back after . . . you know, after I accused you of giving the police the letters.'

'I called your apartment an hour ago, and there was no answer. Where are you really?'

'Cedar Lodge.'

Martha said nothing.

'You have to understand, Honey wants no part of any of this. She's got her own problems.'

'He's sick.'

I said, 'Where is he now?'

'Sleeping.'

'So how long has he been talking about professional football?'

'He watched a game last Sunday, and he's been talking about it since then.'

I said, 'You know, stranger things have happened. I once read this story about . . .'

'Frank, don't, just don't!' Martha lowered her voice. 'You haven't seen him. He's lost his will to live.'

'You're in the clear, Martha, you and Norman. This is now on Sam Green and Chester, not us. What the hell does Norman have to be afraid of now?'

'Something just turned off inside him. I don't know what.'

I should have gone out there right then, but it was snowing hard. I would have if I'd had the college Jeep. 'Maybe he needs to just get away for a week? Maybe I could come out and do the work on the farm, milk the cows and such, and let you and Norman get away. I work the nightshift, and I bet I could work it with the guy I swing shifts with. Tell me that's not the best offer you've had all week, Martha?'

'Who's got the money for that?'

'We can work something out.'

Martha said, 'Frank, wait, I got the kettle on boil.'

I heard her put the phone down, but there was still the sound like someone breathing on the line. I said, 'Is that you, Norman?'

'I seem to remember you dated Martha back in high school, right, Frank?' It was Norman's voice.

I said, 'Norman, I'm not even going to dignify that with an answer,' which is something I heard in a movie once.

Norman said, 'I bet you kissed her on the mouth. I bet you did.'

I said, 'You're talking about the Stone Age, ancient history, Norman.'

'I think she still likes you.'

It was a conversation two juveniles might have, but it was right then that I could sense what Norman was coming around to, not jealousy, but talking like he wanted to know that, if something happened to him, I might still have an interest in Martha.

I said, 'You know, the minimum salary in professional football is something like eighty thousand bucks, Norman.'

Norman made a smacking sound with his lips, like he was thinking. I imagined him sitting by his bed in the dark in his long johns.

I could hear Martha's shoes on the cold stone floor as she came down the hall and picked up the phone.

I stopped her saying anything by saying, 'I was just telling Norman that the minimum salary is eighty thousand in professional football. Isn't that right, Norman?'

Then I went and told that story about Norman winning the State Meet when he was in tenth grade. By the time I finished, Martha was crying softly. It was like a eulogy.

Chapter 26

Thursday through Sunday night, Thanksgiving passed and we escaped the pressures of life in the way only people with money can. In the TV room at the lodge we watched a Disney special about kids finding a box of treasure in a cave. The kids thought it was the secret treasure of Bluebeard. But, of course, it wasn't, though the crooks who had stashed the treasure pretended they were Bluebeard and his pirates when they came across the kids playing dress-up with the treasure. It was a wild caper, with the kids and their dog, Scamp. The kids lived in a middle-class neighborhood and had a secret tree fort that said 'No Adults Allowed!' Ernie didn't seem to know if the crooks were really pirates or not. He was caught in the flux between fantasy and reality, between knowing the truth and wanting to remain in the domain of childhood. I watched his small hand grip the chair arm, watched him hold his dinosaur close to him when Bluebeard roared with his fake old English accent. The kids caught Bluebeard and the crooks in the end with sling shots and jump ropes. When the show was over, fireworks shot from the Disney castle, and that gave us a melancholy sense that things were ending, since the Sunday night Disney movie was what marked the end of the weekend and the beginning of real life. Disney was the sole illusion you took with you into the week. Life seemed all the more cold once the colors of Disney dissolved and the evening news emerged.

By the time we got home, Ernie and Robert Lee were asleep. Honey stayed awake and looked at me from time to time and smiled. It had snowed heavily. The road was reduced to one lane with the drifting. I said softly, 'I'm going to work through the night plowing.'

Honey said, 'We overspent ourselves.'

I put my hand on her leg and whispered, 'No regrets.'

Back at Mrs Brody's, we got the fire going and put Ernie to bed. He asked me if Bluebeard was real, if there was really buried treasure in caves.

Honey set herself up with her typewriter and started typing without saying anything, but with a certain mania that she needed to make back what we'd spent. I made coffee and cut up some of the pumpkin pie we hadn't brought out to Norman and Martha. Robert Lee stayed up and watched a late-night creepy movie. He had the volume real low. I left just as Lon Chaney was turning into the werewolf.

The college driveway had been cleared, but in erratic lines that wove here and there. The Jeep had plowed into a pole. The pole was bent so the light fixture craned toward the ground like one of those creatures from *The War of the Worlds*.

There were some lights on in the dorm rooms, since some kids had come back for classes the next morning.

I followed a set of footsteps stitched across the hard snow. Inside the office I found Baxter sleeping in a heavy down coat on the sofa. The room was freezing, but the smell of liquor cut the air.

I didn't turn on the light and was reaching for the keys to the Jeep when Baxter opened his eyes and said, 'That you, Frank?' He said it in the contrite voice of a man who was very drunk but coming round.

He sat up slowly and planted his feet on the floor. We were still in semi-dark. Outside, yellow lights glowed like a small galaxy. Baxter pointed at me. 'I got it all covered, Frank. All of it!' He spread his arms apart. His head came forward, and he caught it with a jerking halt and then lifted it again. 'Overtime, Frank. I put you down for ten hours yesterday.'

I felt slightly worried that he was going to get us both fired.

I turned on the propane heater, and the blue flames flared and licked away the dark. Baxter looked ghoulish in the shadows.

I said, 'You remember crashing the Jeep?'

Baxter scraped his feet on the cold floor. 'Don't you worry. That's all part of the plan.'

I felt obliged to ask, 'What plan?'

'My plan, Frank. I split it seventy-thirty with Herb Hansen down at the garage for fixing the Jeep. He overcharges the college. You see, this college has so much goddamn money, Frank! If they don't spend their budget, then the next year their budget gets cut. That's what they call "a fiscal reality".'

I put on coffee and turned on the police scanner. It was just static at this hour. I waited until the coffee was ready, then I gave Baxter his coffee and sat down across from him.

Baxter looked at me. 'Do you think a man can have too much pussy, Frank?'

I said, 'I don't know.' I wanted to get up and just go out into the cold.

Baxter said, 'Shit, Frank, these are fundamental questions we must face in life.'

I said, 'Okay, no, you can't have too much pussy.'

'Right answer, Frank.'

I could see him coming back from the melancholy that had made him crash the Jeep. He looked across at me and said, 'What do you call a lesbian with fingernails?'

I didn't even get to answer.

'Single.' Baxter hit his knee when he said that.

I was thinking of Honey's nails, about her finger and her getting mugged. I wanted to say something about that, but I didn't. Baxter said the joke again, more to himself than to me.

I started talking for no real reason, just to break the ensuing silence. I told Baxter about the lodge and about the bear I'd seen and kept talking about New Jersey and Honey and Ken, and my kids, and about Norman and pro football. It was the longest single conversation I'd ever had with Baxter.

Baxter cut in. 'I remember your brother real well. Shit, he put this town on the map way back when. If anybody could go pro, he could.'

'Yeah, maybe he could,' and for a moment I tried to see Norman in a big house and with jewelry on his fingers. Why the hell couldn't that happen? Shit, Norman was big like no other man. If I had one wish right then, it was for him to succeed.

The propane heater had made the room hot. Baxter said, 'Frank, I plan on seeing this holiday out with due festivity.' He took out a fifth from his coat and unscrewed the cap. I got up and got two cups and went out and scooped up snow in each cup and came back and set them on the small table before the sofa.

I downed two quick shots and then settled back into the sofa and felt things ease just like that. It had almost an instantaneous effect, or that's what I wanted, so it's how I felt.

Baxter stared into the amber of his drink. He turned his glass so it made that noise ice makes against glass. It was a comforting sound.

I liked being there with Baxter at that moment. When we got good and drunk, I said finally, 'Maybe I should pull out the Jeep and see how bad it is.'

Baxter said, 'Here's to pro football! Here's to goddamn Norman, that goddamn lunatic!'

I said, 'Here's to dreams,' and I proceeded to watch Baxter fall asleep.

I cleared the snow around the college and spread salt along the walkways. I used the old Jeep. Eventually, I parked it and left the heat running on high. I was drunk. I reclined the seat and closed my eyes. I could feel the vent blowing over me. I was going to give myself fifteen minutes rest.

I thought back to the profound silence that surfaced after our day's work at the farmhouse with Ward and Norman, the curtains drawn, darkness all around us, the way Ward would begin his prayers. He always asked God for forgiveness, for exactly what, I never knew, perhaps for the mere act of existing, for what he had to do for us to survive, for slaughtering the cow that gave the least milk in a season, a grim statistic kept in a ledger out in the barn after each milking. That was the single event that hinted at what we were capable of doing, leading the cow away with a handful of alfalfa out in the cool October air and knocking it unconscious with a club, always after the last of the Indian summer, and on a glorious clear morning. I remember going in and staring at the carcass that had to hang for forty days down in a small pit our ancestors had dug for storing perishables. That sudden memory lapped against the truth of where Ward lay now, like one of his own carcasses, in cold storage, unburied.

It was 3:15 in the morning. The guts of the Jeep throbbed. I put it in gear and started working again, the monotonous back and forth. But in the back of my head, I could see myself opening the P.O. box in Chicago where Ward's check would come. I leaned over and stared into the dark hole, and there on the shelf of the locker was Ken, like he was in solitary confinement in his death row cell. He was miniature, wearing a white tank top and sitting on this tiny bed. There was a small porcelain toilet. Ken looked out at me. He said, 'How would you like that, Frank, in twenties?' Then he burst out laughing. He said, 'See the cashier,' and on the cell bed, Chester Green opened his eyes and said, 'Help me! Help me, Frank!' I felt that jolt as I came to an abrupt halt in an embankment of snow. I rolled down the window. The goddamn old Jeep had a leak. The window seals were cracked, and the exhaust fumes were getting sucked into the back. I took a few deep breaths. The air was freezing. My breath fogged.

Inside the office, I felt tired and worn. There was a rerun of *Police Woman* playing. I felt as if I had meandered through a string of nondescript apartments over the years, seeing reruns of reruns of shows I had seen, a strange weighted density of not just the shows but now my memory of watching what I was watching again and again, an induced déjà vu, except, I really had lived these moments before. I could tell with exact clarity, if pressed, what was going to happen, maybe even quote a line here or there, or a catch phrase, 'Just the facts, ma'am,' 'Book 'im, Dano!' or 'Who loves ya, baby?' What do you call all that shit, the past, or the recurring future? Or was the future the recurring past? It was a mechanical pattern of insomnia that had afflicted me over the years. That was how I lived for many years, and even into this marriage, staring at the shifting shadows of a TV set.

Chapter 27

The light fell soft across the small room inside the Sanitarium. Chester Green had his eyes open as always, bearing his solitary vigil. Serpentine tubes gargled. Alongside the feeding tubes, a catheter with yellow fluid siphoned urine from under the blankets.

I told him about the police finding nobody out at the grave. I told him about Norman wanting to become a professional football player. I told him about Ken. Sometimes I closed my own eyes when I talked. Then I looked at him, and I told him Sam Green said he was going to get my kids. I sort of lost it. I said, 'You son-of-a-bitch! Is this how you want to live out your life?' I said it inches from his face.

I squeezed his hand, but nothing, no response, just the eyes staring at me. The hand was white except for a small crescent mark on the back. I lowered my voice and said, 'I'm sorry . . .' I looked at Chester. 'Is this how you want to end your days, alone?'

I was working up to what I really wanted to ask. My heart was beating fast. I swallowed and said, 'Do I know you Chester?' I was holding his hand again. 'I think I *must* know you . . . . Am I responsible for you coming back here?'

And in the ensuing silence there was nothing for a long time and then a solitary tear formed and rolled down the left side of the face, but there was no answer.

I got up and walked out into the long corridor. It was

lunchtime. I could hear plates and trolleys moving out in the main room. It smelt of institutional mashed potato and meat loaf, overlaid with the menthol odor of Ben Gay rub.

I went up to the main hall and got the daily newspaper. The orderly who'd taken me to the room was standing around. He was big in a way they needed orderlies to be in places like this, with the strength to lift wasted bodies between contraptions, big enough to subdue or scare those who went over the edge. I could see him strapping people into straitjackets. I could see him manhandling me like the orderlies did in Chicago when I had my breakdown.

But because I was on the outside now, not one of the patients, the orderly smiled when he saw me. He said, 'You want a tub of mashed potatoes and sliced beef? It's on Uncle Sam.'

I said, 'No thanks.'

The orderly said, 'They're not contagious,' so I took a tray and got in line and got the day's special. In a small revolving glass case at the end of the line, the desserts circled slowly. I got a slice of pound cake.

The TV was on permanently. It was another soap opera, *Guiding Light*, I think. There was a buzz of tension in the air. A woman was making a speech. She was down by some pier, and it was foggy, and she was talking out loud to herself, but there was a man standing behind a pylon listening to what she was saying. She was talking about revenge. The guy listening to her was wearing one of those improbable black coats with the collar turned up. He was like something out of a spy thriller. It required a total suspension of disbelief, but if you gave yourself over it sucked you right in.

The patients' faces were craned like flowers seeking the silvery light of the screen. The curtains had been drawn. Maybe it was like propaganda, the essential good versus evil of the soaps that made them so easy to watch. The people on the screen seemed more beautiful at that moment, and their troubles seemed all the more important.

The orderly mixed his mashed potato with milk. He was scooping out the mash from a small bowl between telling me things. Then he put the spoon flat against his tongue and ate with his tongue licking the potato off the spoon. He said, 'This is good.'

I looked down at my lunch and picked through a tub of green beans and a plate of beef and caramelized onions. I said, 'Any change with Chester?'

The orderly turned the mashed potato in his mouth and swallowed. 'No.'

I said, 'Does Dr Brown go and see him?'

The orderly looked at me and said, 'At night he goes in there.'

'And does what?'

'Stuff . . .'

'What kind of stuff?'

The orderly shrugged his shoulders, 'Just stuff.'

The room was filled with a haze of smoke. Cigarettes pulsed in the grey light. Some paralysed guy in a wheelchair with a tracheostomy was having a fellow patient hold a cigarette to the hole in his throat. Then the patient put the cigarette to his own lips, and they did that in silence, sharing the cigarette like it was the most natural thing in the world.

The orderly got up and came back with coffees for us. I ate the pound cake. I can't say it tasted like anything. The onions had overpowered my taste buds.

The orderly took out a pack of cigarettes and tapped the pack against his palm. He lit his cigarette and waited, like he had something to tell me, which he did. 'You know what?'

'What?'

The orderly looked at me. He was one of those dumb types who could work these jobs at a surface level and not become affected. 'You friends with Dr Brown?'

I answered in a noncommittal way, just shrugging my shoulders.

The orderly drank his coffee and picked up his cigarette and smoked. 'I think . . . this is just me saying this . . .'

I waited.

Tipping his nose with his index finger, smoke scrolled into the grey around the orderly. 'I think maybe Dr Brown is doing things . . . sticking Chester Green with needles.'

I waited, hiding my own emotion.

The orderly took another long pull. 'He doesn't let us go in with him or anything, and after he comes out I've gone in and . . . put it this way, I was washing Chester and I was doing his feet, and there are all these . . . pinpricks, these red marks on the soles of his feet.' The orderly stubbed his cigarette on a saucer, and looked at me and seemed to change his mind, 'You know what, forget it!' The orderly stopped dead and squeezed my arm. 'What the hell do I know about anything, right?' He let go of my arm and half-smiled to ease the tension. 'I think I got too much time on my hands, okay?'

I said, 'I think Dr Brown was testing Chester's reflexes.'

The orderly said, 'That's it right there. You hit the nail on the head.' Then the orderly stood up and excused himself.

I took a copy of a newspaper and went back down to Chester's room and sat and read the first page, catching up on what was going on in the world.

I resisted looking at Chester's feet and kept reading. I must have read for a good ten minutes before I stopped abruptly. I pulled the sheets back at the end of the bed, and looked at the soles of his feet, at the pinpoint redness of where he'd been pricked repeatedly. I looked directly into Chester's eyes. 'Are you there?'

There was no response. I took a damp cloth and a bowl of water on the steel desk beside the bed, and I wiped Chester's face, cleaning the flaked lips, wiping the crusts of sleep from the corners of his eyes. His body had grown more cadaverous, more atrophied in the time he had lain immobile. The hands had curled again into fists. He had been abandoned to die. There was no directive for physical therapy, nobody to act on his behalf. His father had decided to let his son die out his days alone. I began kneading the muscles and tendons in the hands. The skin was almost an ash color, like the blood had been drained from the body, except for the dark crescent mark where the thumb and index met.

I said again, 'Are you there?' and the eyes opened and closed once.

I had to catch my breath, that sudden sense of recognition that he was in there again. I said, 'Is that yes?'

Chester Green blinked once.

Out in the hallway, the heaters hissed.

I said, 'You can't hide away like this, you hear me? Dr Brown wants revenge, you know that, right? Did he tell you his theory of what happened?'

The eyes blinked once again.

I just stood there for a long time. I said, 'Do you know me?' and for the first time Chester Green blinked yes, and blackness, like I'd been hit with something, filled my head, and for the first time there alone with Chester Green I feared him, I feared what he might say if he ever communicated with the outside world. And at that very moment I thought how it wouldn't have been hard to put a pillow over his face, to have this mystery end in death and silence. In fact, I did reach for his pillow, but, when I turned, there were the orderly and Dr Brown.

The orderly pointed and said, 'See, he pulled the covers back. He did something. I saw him.'

Dr Brown said, 'Okay, Clifford, thank you, I can handle things from here.' Then he said, 'Frank . . . Frank,' and made a tsk-tsk sound. 'I've been hearing some disturbing things about what you're doing here.' Dr Brown looked at me.

The orderly waited at the door.

I felt my heart racing.

Dr Brown said, 'Clifford, don't we have other things to keep us occupied?' and Clifford walked away silently in his nurse's white shoes. Dr Brown went and looked out into the hall, then looked at me. 'Clifford has told me in good conscience what you did here, Frank, that you stuck Chester with pins. I could, this very instant, call the police, and have you arrested for what you did here. Needless to say, I'm shocked at you.'

I half-laughed, more out of fear than anything else.

Dr Brown trembled as he covered Chester's legs. 'I have a witness, Frank. Clifford came and told me what you did. Tell me, can you honestly say, looking at those feet, with the blanket pulled back like this, that you didn't do this to Chester? This might just be like those letters you can't remember sending your uncle, Frank. You might be as sick as we've always suspected.'

I was staring at Chester, staring at his hipbones and knees, mere wrinkles in the covers, like he was slowly vanishing to nothing.

Dr Brown shuffled to the hallway and shouted, 'Clifford!'

Clifford cast a long shadow across the room. He grabbed me by the arm and twisted it behind my back.

Dr Brown followed down the hallway. He said, 'You are a witness to what he did, Clifford. I want it duly noted.'

Downstairs, Bob Gilmore was waiting. He made a whooping sound. He said, 'Bob Gilmore thought Frank Cassidy had checked in for good.' His laugh was loud in my ears. He helped Clifford, taking one of my arms. I gave no resistance. Bob Gilmore said, 'Clifford, if someone with multiple personalities threatens to kill himself, is it considered a hostage situation? Think about it, Clifford.'

The orderly said in my ear, 'You motherfucker, stay away!'

Chapter 28

I spent the rest of the early afternoon driving around with a strange sense of relief and regret all mixed into one. I had nearly killed Chester Green. I had that coldness of guilt, or maybe it was just the coldness of the land, the whiteness of everything, or simply because Chester Green knew I wanted to kill him. I had been so close to putting that pillow over Chester's face, to ending that nightmare forever, silencing the only person who could speak against me. And I knew in my heart a sense of fear was never going to leave me until he was dead.

At the office I saw Baxter passed out cold. The office smelt of pure alcohol. I went across to the Psychology building and asked the secretary to see one of the professors, and, when I was led into an office, I said I was looking for tapes of my sessions under hypnosis.

The professor made a call while I was there. He asked me the year and who had carried out the sessions. He related the information to whomever he was speaking to on the phone. Over the course of a few minutes the conversation focused on the legality of who really owned the tapes, and *if* they even existed. I just stared out the window at the security office and thought about Baxter. I think if I had breathed deep enough I could have smelled the booze coming from the office.

The upshot was simply that I left my address with the professor, and he said that, if there was anything archived at the state college, and if there were no statutes on right of ownership, etc., he'd have the tapes sent to me.

I think I shook his hand. I didn't even catch his name, and I didn't ask him. I knew where to find him. I just left and got into the Jeep again and started driving.

After driving aimlessly for ages, I drove to Ward's house. I could see the smoke rising up by Norman's house. I should have gone up to see him, but I didn't. The time for meeting had come and gone. I had let Thanksgiving pass, and there was no going back, no real reconciliation.

The police tape around Ward's house had been obscured in a drift of snow. The house was all but abandoned, the clapboard paint peeling in curling tongues. A padlock knocked against the door with the cold pull of wind through the barn. There were no tractor marks or any sign that Norman had been over looking after the house. I went around the side of the house where the snow hadn't drifted. I got in through a window, tapping out the glass and undoing the window latch.

It was as cold as outside, but still and grey inside the house. The chalk outline of Ward was still there on the kitchen floor.

The pilot lights had gone out. I noticed that just staring at the range. The stillness was absolute, like nothing you could imagine in a city. This was the natural order of things, the true coldness of the world.

In the bathroom a faucet had burst and formed a frozen crystalline waterfall. The floor was glazed with ice.

I moved against the cold shadows.

In the dining room, kept for special occasions, the ancient blue china plates were on the shelves, the drawers lined with wax paper and the silver all there. Martha and Norman had scavenged nothing.

I went into Ward's bedroom. I stared at the wedding photograph of Ward and his wife, the solitary photograph people up here conceded to posterity. Photographs were considered a vanity in the old days. It was easy to think of her as never having existed. She died in childbirth with Norman. I had this one image of her ironing near the fire, that's all, not even the image of her face, just her presence.

I looked at her in the lace dress, holding a floral arrangement. She looked distant, no trace of romance, defiantly staring at the camera, but then again, that's how all people back then seemed to regard cameras.

I looked at the small wooden bed with the thin mattress. It's where Norman was created. I think whatever was consummated there was done in this coldness, at least in the heart anyway.

Outside I could hear the padlock tapping against the barn door. It was one of those sounds that was filled with old memories. I had lived here for years. That feeling overwhelmed me. I sat on the edge of the bed, and my breath fogged in the cold.

I climbed the attic stairs. The attic was dark except for seams of light showing where the wood had warped. Through a small porthole window I could see the chore light out in Norman's work shed growing stronger as the day waned. I felt like I was staring back in time, like a ghost roaming a dead past.

The boards creaked under my weight. Snow had blown in through the cracks in the wood.

The attic was filled for the most part with things that had broken on account of Norman's size, a few armchairs with their backs broken, a bed frame of his that had cracked in half. There was a porcelain toilet that Norman broke when he was in seventh grade. It made me smile just thinking back on that. And then I stopped and realized that's what killed Norman's mother, his size. He got stuck, and he ended up coming by caesarean operation. She bled to death with the complications.

I felt cold just thinking about that, just how things come to an end, how death is subsumed in the pull of daily life, how a man or woman dies, and life goes on. There were no irrevocable losses. In time, Ken was going to be forgotten, just like my parents, and my uncle, and Chester Green.

I found an old chest in the corner of the attic with a tarp draped over it. It was filled with old newspapers, yellowed with age, containing the birth and death notices of our family, and other newspapers with stories about World War II battles in Europe and the Pacific. There was a faded picture of a ticker-tape parade down the canyon of New York's Fifth Avenue. Under the newspaper were baptismal vestments and baby clothes from what looked like the last century. I took them out of the chest. The lace vestments were brittle. I set them aside. There were other small boxes within the chest. A strongbox contained farm receipts divided by year, each parcel of receipts wrapped with twine. Underneath that box was another that contained immigrant letters written in a foreign language with dates on them going as far back as 1865. The paper was hard and cold, like parchment. I felt slightly ashamed of what I was at that moment, what I had amounted to, considering what had been endured to get us to America.

There were other letters littered throughout the chest. They were not letters really, but scrawled notes. Some were from the Korean War. The envelopes had marks from the Army. I read through one letter. It was short and simple.

Life goes on. I have seen men shot dead and still I go on living. I don't really understand the ways of Almighty God. Maybe this is hell right here. Maybe I am already dead. I feel dead.

C

'Charlie! Jesus Christ.' Just seeing the signature hurt. My God, just to glimpse into the desperation of Charlie's life made me just stop and sit. A man like that abandoned by his wife, stricken with polio like he was. Jesus Christ, I thought, what the hell could he have served as with that bum leg of his? But I guess they took what they could get back then.

I saw one of those postal orders, just like I'd received in Chicago. I looked at it. It was made out to Ward. The postal order had a red receipt stamp imprinted over it with the word 'cashed' written in pen. It was dated eleven years ago. I went through the rest of the chest. In a strongbox at the bottom of the chest, there were bundles of postal orders, all with the same red receipt, dating back into the sixties.

My God, it had been Charlie all along who had been sending money. Charlie was living in Chicago when I was living there, but he kept to himself. We never did meet.

I looked at the amounts Charlie had sent to Ward over the years, sometimes over six hundred dollars, even back in the sixties, when a sum of money like that meant something. Charlie had tried to make amends for his infirmity, for having come back to the sanitarium when he got polio. Ward had always called Charlie's original departure from the farm to make a living elsewhere a sin of vanity.

I felt this strange sense of something sacred, finding this small secret that a dead man never intended to reveal. And right then I felt tears well up inside me. I thought, here was a legacy I could give to Ernie at least, and so, with the light of the evening setting toward dusk, in the eerie light of moon on snow, I took what I considered my heritage, wrapped, the letters and postal orders and some of the paper clippings in a sheet and stole away from the house.

I felt myself letting the simple truth sink in. Charlie had sent me the money, not Ward. Jesus Christ, to think I'd never even gone near Charlie. I'd treated him like some goddamn pariah. I was just as bad as Ward in the end.

I was driving home when I saw a man running in the distance toward me. It was like nothing I had ever seen before, a man running out there. As I got closer, I saw the man was dressed in only his long johns and big boots and was wearing a football helmet. He was huge, and his mouth steamed against the coldness of the dying night. The man had a hunting dog with him that wove along the narrow road, sniffing. As I passed him, the man didn't even look at me.

I drove on a few yards, and it finally clicked. It was Norman. I stopped the car abruptly and looked in my rear view mirror. Norman didn't turn around. He was huge and tragic, just running in his work boots like that. It was one of those indelible memories that I knew was going to stay with me until the day I died.

I think the full gravity of what was happening just struck me, the calls and his voice and Martha all filled my head. And there was Norman now, like something from a parallel universe, unreachable.

Chapter 29

I think I was no closer to understanding anything. I had reached a point of profound sadness, and the only place I put my mind was with my family. I did think about Norman from time to time, but could not bring myself to call him. I didn't say anything to Honey either about what I found out at the house. She was facing Ken's demise. I found a phone bill one morning in a drawer and saw Honey had been speaking with her sister in Georgia.

We got a crate of oranges and grapefruit from Florida, sent up by Honey's sister in Georgia, which brought the issue of Ken to the fore again. Honey had told me over the years how her family always got a crate of oranges and grapefruit each year near Christmas. I guess they were reminiscing about the past.

The fruit was sweet against the dull starch of processed food we ate mostly during that winter. Honey devoured five grapefruits in one sitting. I cut up oranges into halves and then halves again for Ernie, who smiled when he bit into them.

Robert Lee pretended he was a boxer with a mouth guard, biting on the orange and pressing the peel over his teeth and shadow-boxing against the morning light. Ernie did the same.

I felt taste buds I didn't know existed inside my mouth. Just looking at the crate of fruit, the bright orange and the hugeness of the fruit was the most exotic thing set against the monotony of snow outside. It was hard to imagine you could get to a place where things like that grew, and that it was part of America, and not some dream.

But at the back of things, despite the sweet taste, Christmas loomed just three weeks off, and with it Ken's execution.

I got a brochure sent by mail about Disney World. I was going to ask for time off. But Honey said no when I brought up the idea. She had decided against going to see Ken. She didn't exactly say that, but I could tell she was never going to let him see her any way except the way she was in his dreams.

Then one evening she came home late from work. She'd had her hair dyed black and cut short. She said, 'Surprise!'

I have to admit, it took a few seconds to realize that it was Honey. I mean, I knew it was, but it stopped me cold.

'I bet you don't even recognize me, do you?'

Ernie basically answered that by starting to cry. We had been sitting on the end of the bed watching TV and eating TV dinners when Honey came in.

Honey said, 'It's me, Ernie,' and Ernie looked at me, and I nodded. I saw him grip his dinosaur and bite his upper lip.

Then Honey looked at me and said again, 'You wouldn't really recognize me, would you?'

It was then that I understood what she was doing. She was hiding from Ken.

I gave Ernie a bubble bath. He kept looking to the door like he didn't really believe it was Honey. Sometimes he sniffled like he was going to cry, but he didn't.

Honey came by the bathroom and said, 'I was just fed up with all that hair, was all. You know long hair can make a woman go bald. Did you know that?' She looked at Ernie.

I kept my mouth shut for the most part. Honey kept catching glimpses of herself in the mirror in the bathroom.

I told her about seeing Norman out on the road, just to change the subject.

Honey said, 'In his long johns?' but she wasn't really

listening to me. She went into the bedroom and typed for a while until Ernie was ready for bed.

Honey said, 'I'm the same on the inside, Ernie. I love you.' She etched the words in the air when she said love. Ernie smiled, and she took his hand, and she helped him form the word. Then they made me do it as well.

Honey and I got into bed. I was watching *The Bionic Man*. It always reminded me of Ken, 'a man barely alive ... we can rebuild him. We have the technology,' and that computer-processing sound in the background. I said, 'I could see Ken as a secret agent.'

Honey said, 'What?'

'I could see Ken as bionic, you know, if he wasn't ... an organ donor. He could be a government weapon, something they might send into Russia.' I knew I should have shut my mouth, even as I was speaking.

'Go on, Frank!'

I said, 'Forget it. It was just a joke.'

Honey raised her voice. 'Do you think it would be a joke if Ken was bionic and he came up here to get us, and we were driving at like eighty miles an hour, and Ken was running right beside us, and we couldn't escape, do you?'

I said, 'I never thought about it like that.' Right through the rest of *The Bionic Man*, I kept seeing Ken's face, or what I thought would be Ken's face, because, the truth is, I'd never actually seen Ken in all my life.

It was during the credits that Robert Lee came home. He just looked at Honey.

'Who's the kid, Frank?' Honey said it like she wasn't Honey, like I had another woman in bed with me. She said it again, 'Who's the kid, Frank?' and started laughing.

Robert Lee looked hard at her and said, 'You can run, but you can't hide.'

Honey stopped play-acting and half-laughed. 'What the hell does that mean?'

Robert Lee said, 'Figure it out yourself,' and disappeared into his bedroom.

Honey looked at me, and I played dumb and said, 'I honestly don't have a clue.' I said, 'You can run, but you can't hide. What the hell does that mean anyway?'

Honey pulled back the covers and got out of bed and stood in the doorway to Ernie and Robert Lee's bedroom and shouted, 'You don't got to make a Federal case out of it. You hear me? I'm still the same person inside, you hear me?'

I just turned over, and Honey got back in beside me and said, loud enough for Robert Lee to hear, 'You know any good military schools, Frank?'

I really wished she wouldn't implicate me.

Robert Lee said, 'Fuck you!'

And then Ernie's voice said, 'Fuck you!' and that hurt deep inside. I could hear Ernie crying, but I didn't go in, and neither did Honey, but she was crying. She said, 'It's just a haircut, right, Frank?'

I dressed in the bathroom later that night. When I went to leave for work, I could see the silvery shift of light under the doorway. I put my eye to the keyhole. Robert Lee and Ernie had taken out their comforter from their bedroom and formed a teepee at the end of Honey's bed. The TV was on again. It was a *Star Trek* rerun. I watched Captain Kirk dissolve in the transporter and get beamed down to a planet that was ruled by green women. I'd seen the episode before. The women didn't fight with their hands but with their minds, which wasn't that different from Earth.

Just crouched there with my eye to the keyhole was like staring into my own conscience.

I went through the stuff from Ward's house down at the office. I didn't want Honey to see any of it, or let anything on to Robert Lee.

272

Baxter stayed at work, since he was working overtime, even though it wasn't needed. He was on the phone, having some heated discussion with his girlfriend. I tried not to eavesdrop and turned on the scanner and heard hardly anything he was saying.

Baxter hung up. 'So what you got there, Frank?'

'Odds and ends. Letters. War letters I found out at my uncle's place.' I showed him the pile. 'My uncle Charlie fought in the Korean war.'

Baxter took a letter out and read down through it. 'This is some troubled shit, Frank.'

The phone rang. Baxter got it. He said, 'So you had a change of heart?' Baxter leaned back in the swivel chair. I knew it was his girlfriend.

I gathered the letters together.

I went outside to stand and feel the cold on my face. My heart was beating hard like I had done exercise. I didn't want to even think of Charlie, about how things ended up for him.

Charlie never got real work again as a fulltime teacher after the polio, because he was a cripple and he scared kids. He got a stint as a substitute teacher, which was hell for just about anybody who had to come in and take over a class when the real teacher was out, but it was worse for somebody like Charlie, a cripple. You wanted to say, 'What the fuck do these administrators think when they do something like that?' Of course, the kids just went to town on him. There were rumours about Charlie molesting kids, which was bullshit. It was just that he had the braces. Some kid recanted what he'd said against Charlie, but that was years after Charlie was dismissed, when the damage was done. I got that story down at Charlie's funeral, from a priest who had found him a halfway shelter that let him live there because he was real smart with numbers and helped with the parish accounts. I kept thinking, why the fuck hadn't Charlie taken some accounting course or something and got a job like that? I said

273

that to the priest standing there talking to me, but I think he was pretty much finished talking to me because I was drunk, or fast getting drunk.

The priest told me Charlie had been run down by a car. He said, 'I guess he couldn't move too well in his braces.'

It's what you wanted to believe, anyway. There were never any charges filed against the driver of the car.

I got shit-faced drunk that night at a Holiday Inn. Charlie had an insurance policy to cover funeral expenses and something over to get us free drinks and a food platter. The rooms were covered by him as well, which I thought was pretty noble, considering how his life had gone. It was the last time Norman and I had really talked face to face. It was right after he graduated and married Martha. Shit, it was seven years ago, the year Norman graduated high school. I remember Norman saying, 'Charlie took my father real good,' but I didn't know what the hell that meant, though Ward didn't show up for the funeral, which of course spoke volumes. I figured he meant about Charlie leaving the farm and abandoning everything, and then coming home after his wife of a few months left him when he got polio.

I told Norman the plain facts, so he got both sides of the story. I said, 'Charlie gave up his share in the goddamn farm, Norman. He signed it over to my father, who left it to your father, or that's what happened anyway after the fire, so I don't think you and your goddamn father have anything to complain about. That's right, Norman, I think in the end your father got what the hell he wanted. He got rid of me, and he got the farm for you!' I was drunk off my ass. I think Norman might have been drinking as well. I don't even know, but I do remember how Norman kept tapping his big fat finger into my chest. It was like getting poked with an iron rod. The fucker just didn't know his own strength. I said, 'It's typical of that asshole of a father of yours not to come down to his own brother's funeral!' Norman said, 'Somebody had to milk the cows,' which was true, but I said, 'So why the fuck did you come down and not Ward?' Norman told me to keep it down. We were in this reception room with bright lights, and some of the hapless souls who had shared Charlie's last years were standing around.

I said, 'Fuck you, Norman, you didn't know shit about Charlie. Charlie was gone by the time you were born.'

Somewhere in the course of the evening, Martha told me about Norman getting her pregnant, about him coming to rescue her even though she told him he was free to do as he pleased. I remember saying, 'Is this some kind of goddamn love story that's supposed to make me cry or something? What do you want me do, declare this "Great Guy Norman Day?"' I think Martha went to hit me.

Norman butted back in and kept tapping me with his goddamn finger. The priest came over to break things up. I was off my rocker. I said to him, 'I think Judgment Day is going to be in a reception room just like this. We are all going to wear name tags.'

I had the mother of all hangovers the next morning. The funeral, even thinking of it, makes me think raging, fucking headache.

I stomped my feet against the cold. Baxter was still talking. His steel-toed work shoes were propped up on the desk and he was wearing white athletic socks. His pants bunched at the crotch.

I took out the letters again, and scanned through them. I found one dated 1951. I stuck it in my pocket and got up.

Baxter said, 'Hey, Frank, my girlfriend's gone into the joke business.'

I just looked up at him.

'Here's her latest. How many men does it take to paper a room?'

'How many?'

'It depends how thin you slice them.' Baxter said, 'Suck my

fat cock, you hear me!' and that made me wince. He grabbed himself for effect, even though his girlfriend wasn't there to see it. 'You think that's goddamn funny?'

Baxter looked at me and gave the finger to the phone. His eyes looked tired, like he'd not slept in a long time.

I said, 'I'll see you later, Baxter.' I was wondering how much of all this was the war, and how much was just Baxter, or maybe that was something that could never be answered.

I left and went over by the library. Something was there at the back of my head, nagging at me.

I scanned through the years in the microfiche filing cabinet. I took out the microfiche reel for 1951 and went and sat in one of the desks. I turned the small wheel until I found the article about the fire. I read down until I found the reference about Charlie that I remembered reading last time.

I took out the letter from my pocket, and I shook my head. Jesus Christ, Charlie was in the iron lung in 1951. I withdrew my head from the microfiche reader and just sat still for a long time.

I spent the rest of the night looking over the letters back at the office. I'd assembled the letters, fanning them out before me.

Baxter said, 'You look like a guy with a bad poker hand, Frank. You better lie down. You look like shit.' He cranked the heat. 'Frank, you got to keep warm. You can't just go out wandering in the snow like that. Shit, you got that look, Frank.'

'What look?' I went and lay down on the couch.

'A look I saw in combat soldiers who were losing it, Frank. Guys who started talking crazy, not crazy like they were seeing things, but crazy for simple things like their girlfriend or talking about when they were kids, about tree forts, about a new bike they got once, about a snail they poured salt on one summer, about the taste of Kool-Aid and ice. Or guys talking about the future, about the what-ifs, what they were going to do when they got home. I'll tell you, Frank, it meant they couldn't be trusted. They were looking back or forward, and you can't look at life like that. You got to look at the enemy out there in front of you. I saw guys survive two tours of duty and then, wham, they got picked off just like that, because the past or the future don't account for shit! You tell that to the bullet that blows your fuckin' head off!' Baxter stopped abruptly, making his eyebrows arch on his forehead.

Things had just unraveled inside my head. I didn't want to think about anything right then.

It was early Saturday when I woke. I made a pot of coffee.

Baxter was sleeping in the back room with his girlfriend. She was awake, smoking, when I put my head into the room. She had on only a bra. Baxter was somewhere under the covers. I heard him snoring.

I said, 'You want coffee?'

Baxter's girlfriend said, 'Bed and breakfast? You could sweep me off my feet.'

When I came back in, Baxter was wriggling under the covers. He said, 'Hey Frank, I'm doing a little undercover work!' and he burst his ass laughing.

Baxter's girlfriend said, 'You bite me, Baxter, and I swear to God I'll kill you!'

I was sitting alone outside when it struck me. 'C' was the initial not only for Charlie, but also for Chester.

Chapter 30

I got to work again by 6 p.m. Baxter had disappeared. The phone was ringing. I answered. It was Martha. She said, 'We got served with papers. We're bankrupt.' Martha swallowed, and I knew she was crying.

I tried to say something, but Martha cut back in. 'These two men came, like two ravens. That's what they looked like against the snow.'

'Why didn't you tell me you were going bankrupt?'

'I told you. We've been going bankrupt for all our lives.'

I closed my eyes and just waited.

'You know what Norman did, when the men came out and served us?'

I said softly, 'What?'

Martha laughed and sniffled. 'God, I don't even know why I'm crying. It was the damnedest thing I've ever seen a living human being do.' She sniffled again and breathed deep. 'Norman upturned the car the men from the bank came in, Frank. The men were at the door serving me the papers, and Norman had come back from running, and he just knew what the men were doing. The men didn't see him, but Norman just went over to the car and squatted, and he let out this roar, and by the time the men turned around, Norman had tipped the car on its side! What's that show, the one about the doctor who changes into a monster?'

I heard a kid's voice in the background say '*The Incredible*

Hulk.' It was eerie thinking of her kid standing close to her, listening to everything.

'The Incredible Hulk, Frank. That's what Norman was like. And the men, God Almighty, you should have seen them run away into the fields. It's all too easy to pick on women, but they ran when they saw what Norman did. The car teetered on its side, and then Norman pushed it again, so it just upturned on its roof. The windows didn't smash or nothing. It was just that the car was upside down.'

I heard the kid laughing in the background. He made a sound like the Incredible Hulk made on the show. He kept doing that until Martha said, 'That's enough now.'

I waited and then said, 'Where's the car now?'

'It's outside.'

'They're going to make you pay for that if you don't set it right.'

'Pay with what?' In the background I heard her kid say, 'Pay with what?' And then Martha repeated it again, 'Pay with what, Frank?'

I said, 'I went out there, Martha, to Ward's, and I found letters up in Ward's old chest.'

Martha's voice got heated. 'What were you doing? What are you looking for? What did you take? None of that stuff belongs to you, Frank, you hear me?'

I said, 'I think whatever legacy is left is between Norman and me. I want something . . . something to remember. I got kids who deserve to know about me and where we all came from.'

Martha eased a bit. 'I just want whatever there is up there to be divided equally between you and Norman, that's all.'

I knew what I wanted to say, and so I closed my eyes, and, despite the consequences, I said, 'Chester Green is conscious, Martha.'

Martha said, 'He's in a coma.'

'No, listen to me, I've been speaking with him. He can communicate with his eyes. He blinks yes or no to questions.'

'Frank, you're making this up. Tell me you're making this up!'

I went into the long explanation of how Chester was hiding away to protect his father, and I told her what Dr Brown was doing to him.

Martha cut right in. 'You should leave things alone, you hear me? I don't believe this, and nobody else will either! This is all settled and done with. Sweet Jesus, speaking to a man in a coma!'

I said, 'What are you afraid of, Martha?'

'Stop, Frank. I'm afraid for you, that's what I'm afraid for!'

'I think we have to face the truth that maybe . . . I think Ward knew Chester Green never died.'

Martha shouted, 'Stop, Frank! You hear me? Don't do this to yourself. Don't do this to Norman. Why are you going after Ward, even in death? Is this what Chester Green told you?'

I said, 'No, he's told me nothing.'

'That's the only sensible thing you've said yet. Chester Green is in a coma. He couldn't tell you anything! Don't you go making things up, making up how you see things in your head, you hear me? I want you to think about your own family. Are you going to expose yourself as mentally ill? Going around telling people you can communicate with Chester Green is going to get you fired from that beloved job of yours. You hear that? Even if you got no love any more for Norman, think of your own family.' Martha put her hand over the phone and then whispered, 'Norman's coming. God Almighty! Look, I have to go, Frank, but please, please, I'm begging you, don't spread something like this about us, please. Don't do this to your parents' memory, not to Ward, not to yourself!'

Outside it was dark. The lights in the dorms had come on sporadically here and there.

Somehow just that image of Norman broke through all the

other dark shit that was inside my head. It was a story for posterity, something that maybe exactly defined our heritage, one last colossal feat of strength.

It was going on ten o'clock at night when I drove over to Ward's house. I had fought an irresistible urge all evening to go see this car Norman had upended. I left the Jeep at Ward's and walked over to Norman's place and stopped when I was close enough to see the upturned car out in front of the house. The lights were on in the living room. I could make out Martha sitting in the kitchen. The TV was on loud, and the laugh track carried in the coldness of the night air. Snow swirled around the window.

I turned away and went back along the road. The sky was dark overhead, so I had to use the flashlight inside Ward's house. I went up into the attic, and I pointed the flashlight where the chest should have been, but it wasn't there. I scanned the dark. Everything else had been left undisturbed. I shone the light near the door and saw the tracks where Martha had dragged it down the stairs. I wanted to go over to her right then and have it out with her, but I didn't.

I spent hours driving aimlessly. By the time I got back to work it was Sunday morning, after midnight. I saw the light on in the apartment but didn't go home. The war memorial glowed like a grotto, the lifelike figures frozen and fringed in a mantle of snow. The wind blew drifts against the storefronts, and eddying snow swirled in alcoves.

On campus the snow had flattened everything, obliterating the demarcation of parking lots and the winding ribbons of paths and roads.

Baxter was inside, since we were both going to be needed to clear the snow right through the storm. On the police scanner, it predicted over sixteen inches of snow.

Baxter was sitting before the heater in his coat and boots,

warming his hands. He said, 'I got this shift, Frank.' He was drinking straight bourbon. He looked at me. 'So you getting any closer to solving your mystery?'

I shook my head. 'There is no mystery.' I said, 'It's been Chester Green all along, all of it, the letters, the postal orders, shit, even that letter he sent to me saying *Sorry*.'

Baxter nodded his head. 'I figured as much, Frank.'

I called Honey. She was up typing. It was going on 1:45 a.m. Honey said, 'I'm real busy.'

I said, 'You sure you don't want to go on down to Georgia?'

Honey said, 'I found a way back inside myself.'

I said, 'You heard anything about Ken?'

Honey didn't answer, but she didn't hang up. She just set the phone down beside her. I don't know if she did that on purpose or not. I didn't hang up either. And so I listened to Honey typing in the background. I lay down on the couch and cradled the phone close to my chest until I fell asleep.

Chapter 31

The storm had abated overnight to reveal a sparkling world of clear blue sky and freezing cold temperatures. But the snow was to come again by afternoon. Up north in Canada, power lines were down, and over two feet of snow had paralysed a string of small towns that grew more isolated, detached from the modern world and left to their own devices as the winter progressed.

The dean called and said simply, 'From now on, I want you and Baxter to both clock in using the timestamp machine inside the door of the office. I want you both to sign your names for each shift on the timesheet. We need to keep proper accounts as we expand our security presence on campus.'

That last remark didn't allay my fears that we had been caught. Baxter was talking like a paranoid nut. He said, 'They're watching us!'

I said, 'How much did the Jeep cost to repair?'

Baxter said, 'Are you with me or against me, Frank?' He handed me a cup of black coffee.

'I'm with you.'

While he bedded down for the morning, I worked the Jeep, clearing snow, and then started a few cars. It was bone-chilling outside, and most students elected to stay inside or congregate in the student hall that was done like a hunting lodge A-frame. The lodge was half-full of students where a huge fire blazed. TV had been banned from the hall, and it was devoted to intellectual pursuits like poetry readings, chess club, bridge club, and clandestine meetings related to politics, women's rights, human sexuality, pacifism, and religion. In the centre of the A-frame was a kitchen unit where students prepared hot cocoa and a variety of herbal teas, all provided free of charge by the college.

Over by the college chapel, services were taking place. Mostly it was professors and their wives who made the modest attempt at keeping a level of civility and normalcy despite the weather. There was a pancake breakfast advertised after services. I could smell spiced sausage in the air.

I called Honey about lunchtime and she came down and used the typewriter we had at the office, since hers was out of ribbon, and nothing was open on Sunday. We had one of those typewriters with the golf ball at the office. Honey said it was a crime for us to have something like that, since all we could do for reports was hunt and peck.

Honey was dressed in a ruffled blouse she wore to her job and had on her high-heeled shoes, which made her as tall as me. She was wearing lipstick and blush and perfume. I wanted to tell her she looked good, but I didn't. We didn't get to talk, since Baxter was pissed as hell about the dean. I knew he was running scared.

I said, 'How much did that friend of yours stick the college for on the Jeep?'

Baxter ignored me. He went out a few times and said, 'All present and accounted for, sir!' and saluted the administration building.

I got burgers and fries, and Robert Lee and Ernie came over to the office for the first time ever and ate with us.

Robert Lee said to Baxter, 'You ever shoot anybody?'

Honey said, 'You don't got to answer any of his questions.'

Baxter was working on forging my signature, because, according to his new master plan, we were going to beat the system. He'd been doing that all morning and into the early afternoon. He hadn't touched his burger or fries.

Honey and I went out and drank our coffee. The snow had held off most of the day. A group of girls in sweaters were building a giant snowman. Their shrieks carried on the cold air.

I said, 'Twenty years, shit, five years ago, there was nothing like this. You were a woman, and your destiny was sealed tight. You got yourself married quick or you stayed at home and worked the farm until some prospect came and took you off a family's hands. And shit, it wasn't much better for me either.'

Honey hugged herself against the cold. She didn't look at me. She said, 'When I was that age I already had Robert Lee, and Ken . . . Ken had already killed those people.' The mouth of her coffee cup smoked in the cold. She turned and looked at me. 'What are they raising here? Twenty-year-old women that don't know shit from shinola.'

I said, 'I guess this is daycare at its most profitable.'

Honey shuddered against the cold. 'Is there that much we got to learn just to live these days?'

One of the girls stuck something into the crotch of the snowman, and another girl pretended to straddle the snowman and fuck him. The snowman had that classic smiling face and a hat cocked back on his round head.

Honey watched the girls. She said, 'Ken's stopped trying to use the courts to prevent his execution.' Honey didn't look at me when she said that. She said, 'I wish we could just go into a coma for the next week, both Robert Lee and me. I want it all behind me. What did I ever do to have my son held prisoner his entire life for a crime he didn't have a part in?'

I tried to touch her.

'No, Frank, don't. They're killing Ken, for what? To save the state money, to save them feeding and sheltering him?' Honey rubbed her nose and squeezed her eyes and wiped them. 'I'd work my whole life to pay whatever the hell it costs to keep him alive. Not because of Ken, but for Robert Lee! They don't have the right to kill my son's soul, they *don't*!'

There was nothing I could say, and Honey just turned around and went back inside. She got back to typing, into that dark space inside her head.

I took Ernie and Robert Lee out in the Jeep. Out back, where there was nobody, I let Robert Lee drive and clear part of the back lot. Then I put Ernie on my lap and let him make like he was clearing another lot.

The vent was blowing hot. I think I was having a nervous breakdown in slow motion, if that's a medical possibility. I felt time collapse and gain density. Ernie had his small hands on the wheel. He had his dinosaur between his legs. I could feel the excitement in Ernie's body.

I told Robert Lee about what Norman did to the car.

'What kind of car was it?'

'Ford Fairlane.'

Robert Lee said, 'You're shitting me, Frank?'

'No, I'm not. A Ford Fairlane. The kind of car bank men drive.'

I let Robert Lee work the south lot across from the office. He beeped the horn so Honey looked out and saw him driving.

It was beginning to snow hard as the evening dragged on. The sky got mottled. The sun vanished, and then everything turned dark in a matter of minutes, and lights came on all over campus.

Back in the office, Baxter's girlfriend, Linda, had come and joined the party. It was claustrophobic with all of us in there.

Time just seemed to pool in these useless hours. Ernie smiled at me. Maybe this was where we retreated, to the foothills of middle age, a silent calamity without atom bombs or invasions. Ernie said, 'I got to pee, Frank.' I took him to the toilet.

I came back into the room. Baxter's girlfriend called

whatever she was drinking 'a cocktail'. She kept saying that, 'cocktail'. She was lit up good.

Robert Lee was taken with her right away. He told the story about what Norman had done, but he was looking at Linda while he told it.

Honey said, 'Why do you have to go telling him lies like that?'

I said, 'Because it's true.'

Linda poured another cocktail for herself and Baxter. The room smelt sweet with booze.

Linda said, 'He can't be yours, he's too good-looking.' She looked at Robert Lee and said, 'I can make room for you on my dance card.'

We didn't get out of there before Linda made Robert Lee and Baxter arm-wrestle for her. The prize was a kiss.

Baxter let Robert Lee win. Honey butted in and said, 'He'll take a rain check, Linda.'

We ate over at the diner on campus. At the end of the meal Robert Lee said, 'Why don't we just go on out and see that car your brother upturned Frank?'

Honey said, 'Frank made that up.'

It was going on nine-thirty, but I said, 'Maybe this is a lesson in life he just might want to see.'

Honey looked at me. 'Honest to God, cut it out.'

From the road I didn't see any lights on out at Norman's house.

I expected to see the glow of a hurricane lamp, or a candle at least, but as I drove with just the dim orange of the parking lights, I saw only blackness off where Norman lived.

At the end of the long rutted road up to Ward's house, the blackness consumed everything. The snow was falling thick around the car in a billion flakes.

Maybe Honey sensed something about me because she said,

'I think we should just turn right around. This is crazy, showing up like this.'

Robert Lee said, 'So where's the car, Frank? I don't see any car.'

I leaned back and said, 'Norman's house is over there.' I pointed to the dark and then moved in the direction I'd pointed.

Honey said again, 'We should go back!'

The Ford Fairlane was exactly how I said it was, upturned. It showed against the house in the dim glow of my parking lights, like something dropped from outer space.

Honey said, 'Jesus Christ.'

I made everybody stay in the car. I kept it running to keep them warm.

The house was quiet and dark, desolate. I took out my flashlight and scanned the property. I moved toward the barn. The smell of ammonia cut through the cold. I pointed the light to the ground. The snow was crimson all around me. I moved the light along the barn wall. It was as though the barn was bleeding through its slats.

I looked back at my own car. I shouted, 'Stay there.'

I pulled back the barn door.

In the wide beam of light I witnessed the grim carnage of slaughter. It was a lake of sticky blood covered with a coat of ice. Norman had slit the herd's throats. The huge barrel bodies had collapsed in their stalls. Some had been hooked up for milking, I assumed, to calm them, so that they stood patiently as was their habit. The light washed over the dark. The shift of shadows gave the illusion that some cows were still alive. The huge bovine eyes were wide open, the big tongues pressed forward and swollen purple in the cold, and around each neck was a pink crescent wound drawn from ear to ear. One cow had succumbed to collapse only in death. Its hind legs had slipped outward, tearing the abdomen into an open seam of gelled gore. The milk sac protruded under the dead weight like a balloon, bloated, the udders frosted where milk had leaked.

I closed the barn door.

I turned and looked at the grey bulk of the Ford Fairlane in the yard. Robert Lee and Ernie had gotten out of the car. Robert Lee had opened the Fairlane's door. The small light still worked. They were laughing, and Robert Lee was trying to gain leverage to see if he could budge the car, but he couldn't.

I shouted, 'You get back in the car, now!'

Robert Lee looked at me. 'Where are they, Frank?'

I shouted again, 'You get back in the car, now!'

Honey said, 'What is it?' She beeped the horn in agitation.

I shouted again, 'You stay put, all of you!'

I expected to see Norman with his brains blown all over his bedroom, and his wife and children in their beds with their throats slit like his prized milkers.

I opened each door throughout the house and stared into the grey still-life of domestic settings. The kitchen table hadn't been cleared, and the remnants of the Sunday roast surrounded by shriveled potatoes remained the centerpiece on the table. Two gallon jugs of milk had been downed over the course of the dinner. A pie had been consumed, leaving only the baking dish. Martha had made coffee.

It was a Sunday meal like I had eaten for so many years. I lingered in a coldness that robbed the air of any odor. A clock ticked out in the hallway.

In the living-room, an old rolltop desk was open with the farm receipts stacked and impaled on a nail and a notepad Martha used to do the accounts. The letter of foreclosure was a mere few lines, a form letter no doubt. In the cold hallway, I stared at the phone from which Martha had spoken to me.

My eyes adjusted to the grey murk of their lives. I went upstairs. It was like walking through a giant doll house.

Honey beeped the horn again and startled me.

I kept thinking, surely here I will find them, but each room held no profound horror, or the horror that finally settled was the cold inevitability that they had gone. They had abandoned the farm our family had held for over a hundred years.

Outside I checked for Norman's truck. It was gone, but I could see the embossed mark of the tire threads. I figured they'd left right after dinner.

Across the cold I could see luminous snow give back the dull light of an unseen moon. It was still snowing, but it had eased off. The dark shape of the woods in the distance merged with the sky.

When I got back into the car, Robert Lee said, 'How big is this guy, Frank?'

'Big enough to play pro football.'

Honey smoked silently and shook her head. She didn't turn around. 'What's back there?'

I could see Robert Lee's eyes in the rear view mirror.

I was crying without sound, seeing those animals in my head, the carnage of Norman's rage. I had to stop and open the door and dry heave.

All the way home, we said nothing. I turned on the radio to break the silence, and that's when word came across the airwaves that Sam Green had been found dead on his farm.

Chapter 32

I turned on the TV early in the morning. *McCloud* was starting. He was ludicrously riding his horse through New York City in the opening sequence. Then the morning news came on. The storm of the winter was forecast for later in the day.

I prepared breakfast for Honey. The sound on the TV was real low. In some ways the weather eclipsed Sam Green. There were just a few moments of footage of his ramshackle home. It was snowing hard out by his farm. It didn't say how long Sam Green had been dead on the TV, or how he had died.

I didn't want to think that Norman had any part in it. But I knew that when the police saw what he'd done to his own animals, they were going to start hunting for him. I blamed myself for not going to rescue him from his madness.

The TV broke back to *Good Morning America* with Joan Lunden. She didn't look like any woman I had ever known. She was talking with another woman about a recipe for Christmas cookies. The woman was baking in a gleaming kitchen set. It was six in the morning, and Norman was a fugitive.

I got out small individual boxes of cereal for Ernie and Robert Lee. They liked choosing from the variety pack. It cost extra to buy it that way, but it was worth it. I kept rationalizing everything I was doing, trying to suppress that image of the animals. I wanted to lose myself in routine like Honey could. I warmed a saucepan of milk, all the time expecting the police to call me, but there was no call.

I waited for the bacon to cook in the pan. I turned off the TV, since the reception just fizzled, and turned on the radio. Every ten minutes they listed school closures. I figured, with the snow, school might be cancelled, but it wasn't.

I took down the bottle of Flintstone multi-vitamins and set a small dinosaur-shaped vitamin on Ernie's tray beside his juice cup. I felt my hand tremble. I did everything slowly and deliberately. I saw Norman's face illuminated by aqua dash controls. He looked sinister, shadows making his eye sockets dark and cavernous. Outside, the mile markers went by, except they were the lines demarcating a football field, and Norman was inside driving and shouting, 'He's to the forty, the thirty, the twenty, the ten . . . touchdown!'

I set the breakfast on a tray and entered the room.

Ernie said, 'Hi Frank.'

Honey sat up in bed, and Ernie went and got in beside her, and I gave them their breakfast.

Robert Lee stayed inside the teepee. He said, 'School cancelled yet, Frank?'

I said, 'Not yet.'

I changed to the local network station on TV. A guy out ice fishing over in the next county had caught a prize sturgeon. He was out on the ice in something that looked like a public toilet. Then the local TV ran a trailer for the late-breaking news on Sam Green's death and cut to a commercial.

Honey looked at me, 'Where's Norman?'

Robert Lee looked at me.

I looked toward our window. A veil of snow was illuminated by the street lights.

Only Ernie seemed oblivious to what was going on. He wanted to wear his Spiderman underwear to kindergarten.

The local TV broke live to Sam Green's farm. A reporter bundled in a parka gave a brief synopsis of the recent tragedy surrounding Ward's murder and the mysterious reappearance of Chester Green. The reporter interviewed a detective who said Sam Green had apparently died of a single gunshot to the head. The camera cast a long shot across the land, and, in the distance, despite the snow, you could see the dark smudge of Norman's house.

Honey looked at me. 'How did the police know to go out to Sam Green's?'

I didn't answer her, and Honey just turned and got changed in the back room.

Ernie stayed looking at the TV that broke to a commercial advertising Stretch Armstrong. Two kids were pulling Stretch Armstrong apart at the arms and legs. I guess I was in a daze. I think I was shaking. I looked at Ernie. I said, 'I sympathize with Stretch.' I extended my arms and said, 'Pull.'

Robert Lee just looked at me. He knew I was scared.

Ernie got up and pulled. He put his foot on my foot and pulled my arm.

Honey came back and stared at me.

I didn't explain and Ernie stopped and let go of my hand. I turned and pulled my sleeve down over my other hand, and when I turned I showed Ernie. I winked at him, and he tried to wink back, but just blinked his eyes, and of course that made me think of Chester Green just for a moment. I felt myself losing it. I had to sit down for a bit.

The TV listed school closings on a ticker tape across the bottom of the screen, but it didn't include the high school.

Robert Lee said, 'You know what they make us watch on days like this, when the teachers don't show, Frank?'

I looked up at him. 'What?'

'Health Ed sex movies.'

I just nodded.

'Yeah, I'll probably see two shadows humping today, Frank. They'll pack us into the auditorium and teach us about sex.'

293

Robert Lee took out his Nixon Pez dispenser and held it toward the lamp by the bed. The shadow materialized on the wall, and there was the unmistakable profile of Nixon. 'That's right, Frank, the former president of the United States is going to make a little visit to the projection room at school today during the sex movie.'

Ten minutes had somehow passed, and the ticker tape of school closures came on again, but still school wasn't cancelled.

Ernie left his dinosaur behind to guard the apartment. We waited as Ernie spoke into the dinosaur's ear and made it nod its head. He set out a box of cereal next to the dinosaur.

Honey and I watched Robert Lee leave on the school bus, then we walked Ernie down by the church. It was snowing slantways.

We walked across the road toward the college.

I said, 'Out at the house...' I could hardly get the words out. 'Norman slaughtered his own cows.'

College classes were cancelled at noon. I got that over the radio. Then the secretary from the college administration office called and said college evening classes were cancelled. Over eighteen inches of snow had fallen in the past twelve hours. The secretary said I was to use the PA system that was connected directly to all classrooms and to direct all faculty to move their cars out of the parking lots.

I made the announcement over the PA system. It sounded ominous somehow, doing it that way. I was thinking someday I might have to say something like, 'The World is at war. School is out!'

I called the high school after that. Robert Lee was coming home on the bus. Then the church called me. They wanted Ernie picked up right away.

I called Honey. She said, 'Frank, you sounded like God

Almighty on that PA system.' She said it without irony. 'I thought it was God Almighty.'

'I need you to be with the kids, Honey. This is make or break with the dean. He knows Baxter's been scamming him.'

I worked for two hours against the backdrop of mayhem, against the insanity of what had gone on out at Norman's farm, against the knowledge that Sam Green had a hole in his head. I felt like Chester Green, hiding behind his mask, waiting. What if he found out his father was dead, what then would keep him from trying to end his own silence, and that made me stop the truck and have to take long deep breaths. I didn't know if anybody else ever went out to Chester, or if Dr Brown was solely responsible for any updates on his condition. But right then, I could do nothing about any of it. I tried to put everything out of my head.

The college kids had kegs of beer and were dressed up in togas and out in the snow. Music blared from open windows. Christmas lights flashed in the windows and the trees outside the dorms. Some kids got up on a dorm roof and set up a Santa Claus on his sleigh with reindeers heading toward the sky. Bing Crosby was singing about a White Christmas over at the girls' dorms.

I went by the administration office, the oldest building on campus, originally built by the mining company. And there was the infamous administration secretary, Barb Kiester, the centerpiece of a festive Christmas grotto of her own creation. I didn't want to have to deal with her right then.

I told her I was thinking of getting the Resident Assistants to get kids out to clear the snow.

Barb said, 'That's not your call. Wait.'

Barb was one of those middle-aged unmarried women who celebrated each holiday with a tragic zeal, bowls of M&Ms and jelly beans always in the color of the season, the red, yellow, and browns of fall, autumnal orange for Halloween and Thanksgiving, the red, white and blue of the Fourth of July, heart-shaped Valentine's Day candy, along with jars of lemon drops and malted milk balls, Hershey's kisses, and the powdery coated Bazooka bubble gum with the little jokes inside. She was a celebrator of traditional and obscure holidays, mindful of Lincoln's and Washington's Birthday, of Columbus Day, Veterans' Day, of Arbor Day and Sweetest Day and Flag Day, of all occasions religious and secular or otherwise, and those invented by greeting-card companies, Secretary's Day, Boss's Day, Father's and Mother's Day.

Barb spoke to the dean, who was at his desk and didn't get up. Barb just talked loudly about what should be done. The dean nodded. I could tell Barb held the purse-strings of the college. The dean was a mere puppet.

Barb called the weather service.

I felt like an asshole just standing there. Barb had a mug that said, 'World's Greatest Secretary.' It was marked around the edges with the pucker of lipstick stains. I looked down, and Barb was wearing fuzzy bear-claw slippers, and in the back of my head, I was screaming to myself, 'My fucking brother's on the run! What the hell am I doing here?' But, of course, I stayed.

After speaking with the weather service, Barb got off the phone and shook her head. The dean peered over reading glasses and said, 'Let's ride it out a while longer.'

He kept looking over his glasses, holding me in his gaze. 'Everything okay over at security, Frank?'

I said, 'Sure.' I felt my toes curl in my boots.

The dean said, 'You think we can get by this year with just the one Jeep?' The dean didn't let me answer. He said, 'The thing is, Frank, I got some product literature on next year's model. It's a major redesign.'

I said, for something to say, 'How major?'

'Major, Frank! Believe me, *major!*'

I said, 'Oh, major.'

The dean said, 'We've got to sit down one of these days and just talk.'

'About what?'

'Campus security. As we expand, we need to formulate our policy on campus security. I can tell you're an idea man.' With that, the dean turned his eyes down to whatever it was he was reading, and that ended the conversation, but he did say under his breath, 'What we got over there now is a dog and pony show.'

I'd turned and started to leave when Barb said, 'Sucker . . .' It stopped me in my tracks, and I sort of wheeled about, but Barb was just holding a sucker out to me.

The sun, lost in snow clouds, never showed, but the day's light was surely waning, inevitably sinking toward oblivion.

Across the campus, music blared from speakers set in windows. I watched kids playing co-ed football. Some smartass threw me a pass, which I caught, and the kids whistled and cheered. Norman came into my head right then, and the call from Martha.

Back at the office Baxter said without missing a heartbeat, 'Hey, Frank, what we need now is a major snowball fight.' He said nothing about Sam Green or Norman.

I said, 'Why's that?'

'I'll tell you why, Frank! I got a guy who repairs windows. I got a deal with him if something like a major snowball fight breaks out here and windows get smashed. We split it twenty-eighty.'

I flopped down at my desk. I said, 'We're not getting that new Jeep.'

'Bullshit. We're getting that new Jeep.'

I said, 'There's a major redesign coming out next year. That's what the dean told me.'

'How major?'

'Major.'

Outside, it had turned dark without me even noticing. I could see my reflection in the glass. Beyond that I could hear the music from the dorms.

The phone rang. It was Barb Kiester. She said, 'Do you know how to thread a reel of film through a projector?'

I said, 'Yes.'

Baxter said real soft, 'Is that Barb Kiester?'

I nodded, and Baxter walked out, leaving the door open.

Barb gave me some directions. I was to open up the auditorium, start up the projector and then announce we were running free movie night starting at six p.m. The college owned three movies, *The Graduate*, *Love Story* and *Airport 75*. Barb and the dean decided on *Love Story*. They had that whole conversation in my ear while I stared at myself in the glass. I wanted to hang up, but I didn't.

Baxter came back in with a snowball. He was working it back and forth in his hands until it was round and solid. He took the microphone for the PA system, and then he walked out again. The door was still open.

Barb said into my ear, 'Have you ever made popcorn professionally?' I knew what she meant, but she said before I could answer, 'Forget it, we're getting the manager from concessions over there to run the soda and popcorn.'

That's when the campus resonated with this voice screaming, 'Snowball fight! Snowball fight!' I heard a window smash. Barb screamed. Then another window smashed and then another. Baxter started screaming again, 'Snowball fight! Snowball fight!' And within a few minutes the world's greatest snowball fight erupted. It spread like a contagion.

The line to Barb Kiester went dead in my ear.

I ordered a pizza for pickup and left and hid away from the world, from everything.

Chapter 33

The power was out all over the town, but it felt warm in the room since I'd bedded down the fire. I turned on the transistor radio. It listed affected communities. School was cancelled, as was the college. Then the news announced again that Sam Green's death was under investigation. The news mentioned the disappearance of Norman and his family.

Jesus, Norman was just stupid enough to run from the police. If there was a chase, I didn't know if he was going to come out alive.

I heard Robert Lee and Ernie talking in the next room.

I got up. We had a stock of candles and a hurricane lamp, which I lit. I said, 'School's cancelled,' into the dimness of Robert Lee and Ernie's room.

Ernie said, 'I'm hungry, Frank.'

We left Honey to sleep and went into the kitchen. It was eerie seeing Robert Lee and Ernie in the shifting light, the shape of their shadows on the walls. It was like we'd gone back in time. They said nothing throughout breakfast, eating their cereal by candlelight.

The firewood burned, a spicy odor that filled the house. I heard Mrs Brody moving downstairs. I thought about asking her to watch Robert Lee and Ernie. I said, 'I won't be long, you hear? I just need to check on things at the college.'

Robert Lee looked up at me and said simply, 'We got TV, Frank,' but then he remembered there was no TV.

It was daylight outside when I went downstairs. Mrs Brody was sitting in the living room by her own fire to keep warm.

'Everything all right?' She was sitting quietly, playing patience on a small game table that had the markings for backgammon. It was from a time when parlor games were all there was, when people had to confront the silence of their own lives.

The white light of the morning had an ethereal quality, like something spiritual that hurt to stare at too long. The world seemed colder than it had ever felt before. I wondered how far Norman had gotten before the storm really hit.

The college was a disaster area, broken windows everywhere, some patched up with cardboard and tape. I could see the Christmas lights in some rooms, weak beacons against the morning light. I realized then that our backup generator had kicked in. At least we had power.

The trees near the dorms had been toilet-papered, the garlands of white paper fluttering in the cold. Disheveled snowmen had lost their form, some decapitated, others mere mounds where the drifting snow had gathered. Things had been abandoned, the portable barbeques from the previous night out in front of the dorms, paper plates littered everywhere. Across the quad, near the girls' dorms, sheets weighted down with shoes hung from the trees, billowing against the blue sky overhead. It looked like some Armada run aground.

I checked the main route into campus. Baxter hadn't done anything about plowing. The cars were stuck in drifts of snow. I went and scraped away the snow from each car to make sure nobody was trapped inside. Then I made my way toward the security office. I hugged my shoulders against the freezing air.

The phone rang right as I went inside. It was Barb Kiester. She was over in the administration building. She told me neither she nor the dean had left the building since yesterday. She said, 'The dean wants to see you, now!'

I checked the back room. Baxter was lying with his girlfriend. They were both asleep.

I went over to the administration building. The tension of the previous night had deflated like after a revolution. Some students with hangovers were making their way toward the dining hall, which was open.

The administration building had been pummeled with snowballs. All the windows facing the quad that housed the dorms had been broken.

Barb Kiester was wearing her down coat. The cold from outside seeped through the broken windows. The dean was standing behind Barb. He had a five o'clock shadow. He said, 'What is there to say, Frank?' He looked at me. 'I could have Baxter arrested for inciting a riot.' But before I got to say anything, the dean said, 'But what would that serve, right?'

I looked away and didn't answer.

The dean looked at Barb. 'How about you make some hot chocolate for us, Barb?'

The dean and I went into his office. All the windows had been smashed. He had pulled the curtains, but they billowed against the draft of circulating air. It got hot and then cold depending on the wind inside the office.

The dean was dressed in a plaid polyester coat and fat knotted tie. He looked like a defunct clown who had stopped being funny. He sat behind a mahogany desk with a string of diplomas mounted behind him. He said nothing about Norman.

He looked at me. 'I'll get to the point, Frank. I take full and absolute responsibility for what happened last night.' He said it like he was taking on the sins of the world. 'I am the *head* of this *body*, Frank, and what happened last night was symptomatic that there is something wrong with the *body*, that is the student body . . .' I followed along with the forced metaphor. I was a million miles away from the office at that moment. I focused on the dean again.

He kept touching his head when he said *head*, and his torso when he said *body*. 'As the *head*, I need to instill a sense of respect in what this *body* stands for. Are you following me?'

I said, 'Heavy is the head that wears the crown,' but the dean was talking right through what I said.

The dean said, 'I think the fundamental dilemma is that we outgrew ourselves. We built the three new dorms this fall, and frankly I don't think we were logistically and psychologically prepared for what that entailed, for the bigger picture. *Infrastructure*, Frank, both the physical and psychological have to come together, and that didn't happen. We were under-manned. We weren't ready to cope with a resident student body, not in its current form. We moved from a purely commuter campus to a resident campus. That's a different *ballgame*. It's a different *league*. We need to re-engineer our concept of *what* our college is offering, re-evaluate what we *want* to accomplish as *educators* . . .'

I didn't really know what any of this had to do with me, but I pre-empted him by saying, 'Are you telling me I'm fired?'

The dean was dead serious. 'No, Frank! No! I'm not blaming *you*. I'm addressing the large issue. I'm just articulating the problems facing the college as we move forward. We have reached a juncture where we must decide if we *want* to be players in higher education. Right now we're in violation of state law, because the college doesn't have an on-campus fire department. We have ninety days to comply.' The dean had read that last fact from a piece of paper. It seemed like he was preparing a defense for what had happened on campus. 'The dining hall also needs an automated dish-washing machine. We've outgrown our current setup. And laundry services . . . we have no facility to accommodate students, Frank . . . if this were a bigger town, then maybe we could rely on private enterprise, but right now we need to come up with a plan to become . . .'

The dean went on about how the college was staying closed, and all finals were 'take-home'. The state highway authorities were also going to plow the college this one time to help out.

He'd been busy. He showed me a brochure of a snow blower that was also a leaf blower. 'Dual purpose. That's the kind of equipment we need. Am I right?'

'Yes.' I felt like I was going to faint. I kept seeing Norman out on the highway, driving fast.

Barb Kiester came in with a tray and set down two cups of hot chocolate sprinkled with marshmallows, along with a plate of cookies. The cookies were the shape of Santa Clauses, sprinkled with frosted sugar.

The dean took a cookie and said, 'These are made from scratch.'

I said, 'They're good,' even though I hadn't actually tasted them.

When Barb went out, she left the door open.

The dean bit into the cookie and drank from his mug. 'Shortbread. I got a weakness for shortbread.' He looked to the side of me, and shouted, 'How many sticks of butter in this, Barb?' He said that loud, jockeying in his big leather chair so he could see her.

She said, 'It's a family secret.'

The dean said, 'That's it, don't tell me. I don't know if my cholesterol could take it.' With that, he laughed real loud and said the exact same thing again, 'That's it, don't tell me. I don't know if my cholesterol could take it.'

I swiveled around and bit the head off the Santa Claus, and it crumbled in my mouth. I turned around again. The dean had an array of photographs of his children, seven all told, and his optimism had infected his children, who had spawned forty grandchildren. They were all clustered together in a family

303

portrait taken against a backdrop that suggested it was either Sears or Montgomery Ward.

The truth was, the dean and Barb were having a love affair right under everybody's goddamn noses. I wondered how the fuck you get so high in life that you can do what you please, that you dare others to unmask your façade. I was beginning to lose it. The slaughter at the barn surfaced again. Norman looked at me. He said, 'Everything passes, Frank, everything . . .'

The dean was still talking. I looked at him. 'Let me show you something, Frank. I want your opinion.' He pushed a piece of paper toward me. It was a job description. It said things like, 'the *successful candidate* will possess *interpersonal skills*, be *detail oriented*, be committed to the mission statement of the institution.' At the end, it stated there was a negotiable salary, commensurate with a candidate's qualifications and experience.

The dean looked past me to Barb, then at me again. 'I'm in the people business, in the commodity of *human potential*, that's what I'm all about. This college is dedicated to serve the *will* to succeed, to engender an environment that fosters the goals and aspirations of those who want to succeed, *winners*, Frank.'

He was talking like a glossy brochure. The dean said, 'You know, I liked what I saw when you came and interviewed.'

I hadn't been interviewed in person, but I said nothing.

The dean said, 'I think we might be looking at a potential candidate who meets the criteria right here.'

I turned and looked at Barb and said, 'Congratulations, Barb!'

The dean said, 'Ah, *self-effacing*. That's the sure sign of *personal integrity*, Frank.' He leaned and stared at me, '*You*, Frank have the *skills* to succeed.' He referenced my background in criminology, the courses I had supposedly taken. His eyebrows arched when he said that. The dean pushed another paper toward me. He beckoned for me to come closer, under the aura of his banker's light. A current of cold air circulated past my feet because of the broken windows.

I leaned toward the desk and set the job description down, and the dean retrieved it, then pushed a letter toward me. 'Read it.'

It was my application to the college, and a letter of acceptance signed by the dean. While I was reading it, he said, 'Honey is *in-process* over at the Business College. I have it on good authority she'll be part of our spring enrollment. I think we can put an attractive financial aid package together for her.'

I said, 'And I can enroll and still run the security office?'

'Frank, this institution is a *living* organism and, if we have people who grow with it, that only serves to further our mission of *self-realization*.'

I said, 'I assume that means yes?'

The dean tapped the back of my hand with his index finger. 'This is what we are looking for, someone with ambition, somebody who has a vested interest in this institution, somebody who understands what continuing education *is* all about. *Work-study initiatives* are the backbone of an institution.' He enumerated a list of things like *self-esteem, personal fulfillment, self-worth*, which were basically names for the same thing. It was like he was speaking English but not English.

I cut in and said, 'And a *pay* raise.'

When the dean smiled, his dentures showed in a wide, false smile. 'That's the *intangible* we're after here, a sense of humour . . .'

I said, 'I'm serious about the *pay* raise.' I felt like you feel when you take a deep hit of pot and hold it deep in your lungs.

The dean's hand settled on the back of my hand. It was warm from holding the hot chocolate. His breath smelled sweet. A gust of wind pulled the curtains apart. They billowed then went limp, and the sudden brightness of outside was subsumed in the room's weak light. You could see in that brief glimpse that the campus was destroyed.

The dean retrieved his hand, like no matter how he wanted to hide from reality it was there outside the window, and no amount of words was going to change it.

He looked at me and changed his tune. 'We had a call early this morning from a dubious outfit that said they'd been hired to fix the windows. It seems Baxter had commissioned their services, but we have declined their proposal.'

'I see.'

'We need to institute fiscal financial accountability. From now on, *all* work orders must be cleared through Barb, okay? Barb has negotiated with an outfit from Traverse City that's coming to replace the windows. They should be here first thing tomorrow. I want you to oversee the job.'

I took the opportunity to get up to leave.

The dean also rose. 'By the way, Frank, you did see Baxter throw that first snowball, right?'

It was like signing an armistice in a bunker, but it was something I did for my kids and Honey.

It was mid-morning before I got the sidewalks cleared. I used a winch and got the stranded cars out and into the south parking lot. Some of the students helped me.

Baxter came to me and said, 'My window guy got stopped coming on campus, Frank. That's bullshit!' I pretended I didn't know anything about it.

I stayed outside the office. I passed it numerous times. I could see Baxter inside walking back and forth, talking on the phone. I knew he was screaming at the top of his lungs. I had sold him out.

I checked the buildings and shoveled up glass just to kill time. I kept myself occupied, but there was no hiding from my own conscience.

The highway authority showed around lunchtime and

plowed the main road onto campus and some side roads. It was amazing what the right equipment could achieve. By two o'clock, a caravan of cars was ready to head south for the holiday break. It was agreed that groups should leave together to ensure everybody's safety.

The dean came and presided over their departure.

I had taken the initiative somehow, despite everything, and had the dining hall set up a table that offered free coffee and hot chocolate to all students who were heading out on the road.

The dean looked at me and touched my shoulder, and, Jesus, the guy was almost crying. 'This is what we're about, Frank, *family!*'

I thought the dean and Jim Jones would have a lot to talk about.

Chapter 34

That evening, a cop car arrived without its siren, but the red light turned against the dark outside like I was staring at my own heart outside my body.

Two detectives in heavy coats came to the door. They managed in a discreet way to separate me from Honey.

The detective closed the door. He said, 'Take a seat, Frank,' but even though he used my name, there was nothing friendly in his voice. I could tell the detective was from Traverse City. He was fat and worn in the way you think of detectives in movies. When he sat, his thighs spread into two pear-shapes.

The detective asked me to tell all the details, how and why I'd gone to Norman's house. I told the man I'd taken Honey and Robert Lee and Ernie out there to see what Norman had done, upturning the car like he had. The detective said, 'So you'd been out there by yourself, and then you went back out with your family?'

I said, 'Yes.'

Then the detective said finally, 'Where are Norman and his family now?'

I said, 'I . . . I don't know.'

The detective looked me in the eyes. 'Why did you go out there?'

I raised my voice. 'I told you, the car.'

The detective resettled himself on the chair and wrote something into his notebook and then said, 'If we can just establish some facts. I'm just trying to account for everybody right now.' He said again, 'Why did you go out there?'

I shook my head, and the detective just repeated he was establishing facts, so I said, 'Norman's wife told me what he'd done to the car. I went out just to see it with my own eyes. Later that night, I was telling Honey about what Norman had done, and one of my kids didn't believe me. I wanted to show him.'

The detective wrote again in his notebook. Then he lit a cigarette and cupped his hands like people do when they're outside in the wind. He pulled a few times, then flicked his wrist and extinguished the match. His mouth formed a small 'o' when he exhaled. He looked at me again and said, 'Where are Norman and his family now?'

I said, 'I don't know.' Then I looked at the detective and said, 'He's gone to try out for a pro football team.'

The detective took another pull and blew out of the side of his mouth this time, looking down like he was reviewing his notes. He didn't look at me. 'Which pro football team, do you remember?'

I said, 'The Miami Dolphins.'

The detective looked at me. 'How would you describe your relationship with Norman?'

I struggled to say something and couldn't.

The detective kept looking at me. 'How many times would you say you visited Norman?'

'I never went to see him.'

'But you went out to his house twice on the evening he disappeared? Is that what you're telling me?'

I said, 'Yes.' I didn't have it in me to keep talking.

The detective closed his notebook like the interview was over and said again, 'I'm just establishing all the facts, just accounting for everybody.' He inhaled the last of his cigarette before getting up to go.

I said, 'Is that it?'

'Unless you left something out, Frank?'

Honey waited until the detectives had gone and said, 'What was that all about?'

I said, 'I don't know.'

Honey looked at me, 'Why did you go out there, that first time?'

I said, 'Is that what they asked you?'

'They wanted to know where you were all that day.' Honey lit a cigarette and went into Mrs Brody's living room. 'Jesus Christ, I got my own troubles to worry about. They know everything! They know you were in an institution. They wanted to know how you've been acting.' Honey was trembling. 'Frank, I can't do this. Not again, you hear?' She put a hand to her stomach like she was going to be sick.

I tried to touch her.

'Don't!' She looked at me. 'What the hell have you done?'

'Nothing. I've done nothing.'

I could see the fear in her eyes.

'Where were you? Where were you the day Norman went missing? You were out there, Frank. The police know you were out there . . . my God, you took us out there that night.' She was starting to hyperventilate. 'You son-of-a-bitch, what have you done?'

I tried to touch her again, but she put her hand out to stop me. 'Tell me you did nothing to Norman and his wife!'

I felt everything crashing around me. Ken's execution was a week away.

I left without explanation. I guess you go cold when shock fills your body. I went across to the college and got the Jeep, but no matter how I heated the interior I was still cold inside. I drove out of town.

I stopped at the bar where I had my first and last drink with Ward, after Norman won the State Wrestling Championship.

310

It was near empty, despite it being Saturday night. There were some men dressed for ice fishing, like giant grubs pushed up to the bar.

I played 'We are the Champions' on the jukebox. I didn't want to acknowledge the reality that maybe Norman wasn't going to be playing pro ball, that it was just something I made up, that I had been talking to myself all this time. The men in their suits turned and looked at me, like I'd disrupted the mellowness of their mood. The man behind the bar had a master control, and the sound from the jukebox diminished.

I left and went out by the old farm, driving through the lunar cast on the hard-packed snow. Ward's house was abandoned, a two-dimensional stage prop flatness against the eerie backlight of the moon. It didn't seem like this could ever have contained human life, let alone mine. I now wondered how Martha got that chest down by herself. It was big, too big for her to have moved. I was talking to myself. I shouted, 'I *never* wanted the goddamn farm!'

At Norman's, there was no upturned car. I checked that against the previous reality by which I had sworn up until then, but there were footprints and the grooves of tires under the bedding of new snow. Police crime tape circled the shed. But I crossed the line and opened the shed door. The cows were all there. They had become glazed, frozen carcasses hidden away in the dark.

It was evening when I showed up at the sanitarium. Bob Gilmore wasn't there, just another guy I didn't know. I asked to see Chester Green, and the guy who worked the desk made a call to the upper ward, and I was let through.

A nurse was waiting for me. Clifford was there, but he just sat with his elbows on his knees and a cigarette in his mouth.

The nurse took me down to Chester. She said he had pneumonia.

When we got to the door, Chester was back on a respirator. The nurse stayed while I stood there.

Chester's eyes weren't open. He looked like he was dead. I suppose I should have been glad, but I wasn't.

As I was leaving, Dr Brown opened his door and looked at me. I could tell then that he'd let me come up. He said, 'I heard you made inquiries into those tapes?' He shored up the distance between us. He looked at me and said, 'Chester Green is mine, Frank, mine alone.'

I just left. In a way it solved so much for me. Dr Brown was never letting Chester out. He would do in the end, what I had nearly done, he would take Chester Green's life before it was all said and done, or this pneumonia was going to kill him.

And then I thought, Jesus, it could have all just ended like this in Chester's quiet death. I wanted to know why the hell Norman had to go and kill Sam Green, why he had to destroy himself like that. I said, 'Norman, you crazy son-of-a-bitch, why did you do it?' but of course Norman was long gone. He was out there somewhere on the highway. That is what I believed inside my heart, because whatever else I might have been capable of doing, I would never have hurt Norman. I just wouldn't have.

Baxter was working the night shift when I went by the office. The TV was on. It was Alfred Hitchcock week. Baxter ignored me. I mean, what I did to him just reared up before me. It got my mind off Norman just long enough.

Baxter kept his silence.

At this desolate beach community, the birds were lining up along the wires surrounding a schoolyard where kids were playing. There was no apparent main character in the way of most films, no identifiable hero or villain, just a sense of gathering fear pervading the town. I stared at the TV, through the silence that persisted between us. We were just waiting for everybody to get their eyes poked out of their heads, the inevitable ending. There was never going to be an answer to why this was happening, and that made it all the more real and sad.

The soundtrack spooked the hell out of me, just that sound of the birds, the flapping wings and that throaty coo birds make.

When the movie was over, I turned and looked at Baxter and said, 'That movie would be vastly improved if there was more pussy in it.'

Baxter nodded his head and said, 'You're catching on, Frank.' But he didn't look at me.

We drank straight bourbon. The campus was dead. The term had come to a close, as had so many other things.

Baxter closed his eyes and withdrew his hand. 'You know, Frank, I should fucking kill you, you know that?' He winked at me when he said it, then got serious. 'No, really, Frank, I should kill you, but, you know what? It turns out you might have done me a favor. If I sign up for psychiatric treatment, I get half-pay and full medical benefits, with the prospect of returning to my current position.'

I didn't say anything.

'Let me just say this, Frank, I wouldn't like to have fought alongside you in Vietnam, that's for fucking sure.'

I said, 'My kids . . .' but Baxter said, 'Hey, Frank, I don't want to hear it, okay?'

Baxter rubbed the tiredness in his face and leaned forward. 'But I want to bend your ear for a few minutes, Frank. I want to tell you a little story, just to set the record straight on who the hell I am.' Baxter pointed at his own chest. 'In here. I want you to know how I got to be like this, Frank, because I changed from what I was once upon a time.'

He took a drink and held it and then swallowed. 'Before I went to Vietnam, Frank, my father and I used to go out winter hunting. We had this cabin up on Prescott Lake, nothing really great, but something we had in our family for years. We went up around this time in sixty-eight. There was hardly any snow on the ground. It was too damn cold to snow. It got dead still as we walked. We could feel the cold tighten around us. This dry powdery snow fell down from the high pines like frosting. It was eerie as shit.' Baxter made the motion of snow falling with his fingers.

'My father says, "This is bad trouble." The temperature dropped something like forty degrees in a matter of an hour or so, and we were far enough into the woods that it was better to make for the cabin than try and turn around. I remember that cold like nothing else, Frank. You can lose it just like that out in nature. You get scared like an animal, Frank.' He looked at me hard and took another drink, and I followed his lead. He filled my cup again. The bourbon burned all along my neck.

'Our eyes stung. We got so we couldn't see right. We couldn't hardly breathe air that cold. It burned our lungs. We warmed the air by cupping our hands over our mouths. Our legs got numb fast, so it was like we'd been injected with morphine or something. You start thinking about salvation, Frank, just like that. Mortality sneaks up on you all of a sudden.' He swallowed and went on.

The gas heater made the air taste sweet. The orange bars glowed.

Baxter talked in a low, sustained voice. 'So we barely got to the cabin. We were frozen. It was hard just trying to start a fire. Our hands were like claws, but we got one started eventually. I just followed my father's lead. I was good at taking orders. I was a follower. I wanted to be led the right way.'

Baxter took a long breath and leaned forward and drank again. 'A crust of ice formed quick out on the lake. You could hear it crackling as it formed. It was like the world was going to splinter into a million pieces. Jesus, it was weird. You ever feel like ... like you've survived something terrible even though nothing's really happened, and maybe that's what makes it all the worse, to feel like you do?' Baxter stopped and looked at me. 'Am I speaking like a crazy man, Frank?'

I said, 'No.'

'Shit, Frank, now I think back and know that was the moment I stopped thinking like a child. We were feeling good in that way you get when you're just glad to be alive. I could see my father looking at me like he knew I was changing into a man. You feel that connection, that blood connection. We didn't talk at all.

'The cabin groaned, and the wood expanded. We got the fire roaring. It got dark and, Frank, the whole universe appeared just like that over us. We got drunk good and fast. To my father, it didn't matter what age you were in numbers, it was in here that counted.' Baxter touched his head and then his heart. 'My father used to say, "Whiskey drunk with ice can bring you to a whole new level of compassion."' Baxter clinked his glass against mine, and we drank. I felt my head throb from the heat and the alcohol and from concentrating on what he was saying.

Baxter started again. 'The fire was going so strong we were sweating. We had to crack open a window, it was that hot in there. I watched my father in his long johns and wool socks staring out in the dark. He opened the door. He set his face to the cold and his back to the heat. He made me do the same. My father had a way of turning the whiskey with a slow movement of his wrist.' Baxter showed the motion.

'That's how I remember him, if I want to think about him, the sound of ice tinkling in a glass. He called me once when I got shipped out to boot camp, and it was that sound of ice in his glass as he spoke to me that made me see him like he was standing with me.' Baxter smiled and turned the glass again, and, in his head, I knew he was staring at his father. 'I'm losing the thread of this, Frank. Where the hell was I? Oh yeah, it was the last year I went out there with my father.' Baxter shook his head and looked deep into me.

'Well, sometime after we fell asleep, it warmed, so the snow fell thick like cotton wool. It was a near whiteout when we got up. We ate scrambled eggs and milk and nursed our heads the way you do after a night of drinking. There was no talking after a night like we'd had. That was a rule, no talk. It was a silence that made my ears ring, maybe worse than noise really. It was like penance, Frank. Then the snow stopped, and it was like . . . like a curtain had been drawn back on the world. It hurt our eyes just to look outside. The light poured in through every crack in the wood, rays of light like Jesus Christ was outside waiting on us.'

Baxter leaned forward again and drank and kept the glass to his mouth and stared at me. I could see his Adam's apple bob.

'My father said to me, "Get all the guns we have ready. *All* of them." And so we set about oiling up the guns and loading them. In the distance, I could hear some sound that I couldn't quite catch. We strapped on snowshoes. Outside, everything was flat, nothing had any dimension. We went in the direction of the noise, out around the lake to where it was sheltered from the wind that was blowing up a storm. We were out an hour, and the mercury dropped again. The world froze around us, Frank. I could feel my legs going numb again. And that's when the noise grew louder, like the crying sound of babies. In the clearing, close along the lake, we emerged.' Baxter drew a breath. He leaned forward and whispered, 'It was like somebody had painted the world red. And then I saw it, Frank, hundreds of geese flapping and pulling against the snow, trying to escape the ice that had trapped them. You see what I'm saying, Frank? The thaw and then the freeze, it locked them into the ice! There were foxes and wolves, and coyotes, circling through the geese, tearing them to shreds, but they weren't getting anywhere really. The ice cut them up bad. It was a lake of blades. Nothing was going to survive. We'd come across nature left to itself, Frank. I don't think I ever saw anything so sad and beautiful in all my life. By then, my father

316

had started discharging his gun, pop, pop, pop. We emptied every round of ammunition into that flock of birds until our arms were dead tired, until my father went down on one knee from exhaustion. I used to think like that sometimes over there in the jungle, in Vietnam. I used to say, I'm doing this for their own good. Pop, pop, pop . . .'

Baxter trailed off and finished up his drink and got up and stumbled and nearly fell against the table. 'I never saw my father alive again after I left. He died when I was off in Vietnam.'

He stayed quiet for a short time. Then he yawned and rubbed his face. His eyes were red and weary from the booze. He got up unsteadily and put on his heavy coat. He looked at me. 'Maybe sometimes it's better to put something out of its misery. Right, Frank?'

I felt the burn of the accusation, but I don't think he was really blaming me for what I'd done.

'I'll see you around, Frank.' Baxter went over to the PA system, and it made that feedback noise. He cleared his voice and, winking at me, said into the speaker, 'Elvis has left the building!'

Chapter 35

It turned out the police had held back a suicide note written by Sam Green for a few days after his death. Norman was stopped down south, on the border of Tennessee, questioned, and then released. There was no call from him, nothing. I ended up reading accounts of events in the paper, just like everybody else. The article served as a pitiful epitaph to everything that had unfolded since Chester Green had shattered his secret history:

> Copper, Michigan – Police have released a statement confirming that Mr Sam Green's death was a suicide. According to police reports, Mr Green went to Norman Cassidy's barn and slaughtered his livestock prior to his death.
>
> Mr Cassidy, the son of recently murdered Ward Cassidy, called the police when he heard a commotion in his barn. Police arrived to find Mr Green outside the barn in a distraught state. Despite the evidence indicating Mr Green had killed Mr Cassidy's livestock, Mr Cassidy elected not to press charges, stating he was planning on retiring from farming and had requested Mr Green assist him with the slaughter. Several hours later, the police officer went to check on Mr Green and discovered his body.
>
> Forensic evidence, along with a suicide note, have led police to rule Mr Green's death a suicide. The handwriting has been verified as Mr Green's.
>
> Released to the press today, the suicide note provides a glimpse

into the tormented and steadfast denial Mr Green continued to maintain in the face of rumours that he staged his son Chester's death for insurance purposes. Mr Green's last line reads, 'I am going into the afterlife to find my son at the right hand of God.'

Chester Green, the primary suspect in the murder of Ward Cassidy, continues to lie in a coma at Copper County Sanitarium. Medical experts hold little prospect of him ever regaining consciousness.

Norman Cassidy and his family have relocated. His farm and property have been foreclosed. The Cassidy family had been residents in Copper County for over one hundred years, as had the Green family.

I just stood in the background at Sam Green's funeral, the snow falling in specks like bad reception. I went alone. The funeral started at 10 a.m. There weren't many people in attendance, but Dr Brown showed. He dipped his head in brief acknowledgment of my presence.

Chester Green's open grave had not been filled in. They set Sam Green into it, since it was a family plot.

Two nephews of Sam Green had come back from California for the funeral. They were his only surviving family. Somebody pointed to me in the background, and one, and then the other, nephew turned and looked at me. Both were tanned. Even from a distance, I could see that. The big news of the day was that the nephews had been seen jogging early in the morning. That was considered sacrilegious.

After the funeral, a reporter followed me toward my car. I kept walking, but the reporter was one of those persistent types from one of the major stations in Chicago. He said, 'Your wife's ex-husband is scheduled to be executed this week, isn't that right? How is she coping with everything?'

That was how Robert Lee learned the date of the execution.

That's what Honey told me when I got home. I watched the footage on the one o'clock news in the kitchen on the small portable TV.

Robert Lee had gone out somewhere.

Back in the bedroom, I noticed a package from the Department of Psychology at the State College. It must have come early in the afternoon, after I'd left for the funeral. My childhood had arrived in a small box, but there was no rush of emotion, nothing. I just left it sitting there.

Honey stared at me and then at the box.

Outside, people moved against the cold, wrapped up like they were deformed or injured. I said, 'Florida sounds good right about now.'

The phone rang. A bank official asked if I wanted to remove any family belongings from either property.

I said I did. I'd received another call from the medical examiner a day earlier, asking if I wanted to claim Ward's remains. I told him I was waiting for his son to call me, so the body lay in cold storage somewhere, unburied.

Ernie was holding his dinosaur close to his chest, his small hands gripping the dinosaur's neck. He was watching *Lost in Space*. The robot was getting abused by Dr Smith.

I looked at Honey and said, 'You want to come out with me to clear things off the farm?'

Honey was smoking a cigarette and drinking coffee, sitting on the bed. She looked at me. 'Those sons-of-bitches! Why couldn't they have left me out of this?' She got up and went to the bathroom.

I lay flat on my back. When the show ended, Ernie came over to me and made his dinosaur walk on my stomach. He made that deep rumbling sound of something huge stomping the ground. It felt good.

Honey came back into the room and said, 'Damn it, quit it, Ernie,' and Ernie stopped.

I said, 'Don't speak to him like that.'

Honey said, 'Don't you speak to me like that, Frank, ever!'

I took Ernie with me to Ward's farm. It was freezing cold, but we got out. He was bundled into his Green Bay Packer coat. I told him I'd lived here once upon a time. I showed him my bedroom. The outline of Ward was still sketched on the floor. Ernie looked at the outline and then at me, and I realized that he knew what it meant. He'd seen enough crime scenes on TV.

I took nothing from Ward's house.

Over at Norman's, we walked through the shadows, the cold yellow light pouring through the windows. The house had southern exposure, and it felt warm, like a greenhouse if you stood facing the glass.

In the attic, I found the chest Martha and Norman had retrieved. It was emptied of almost everything of personal significance, only old newspapers left scattered about the attic, along with old farm receipts. Further back in the attic, I found another chest that had been gone through. I found wedding photographs of Norman and Martha. There was another of Norman from the State Meet his sophomore year. And among those shots I found another wedding photograph. The names of my parents and the date of the wedding were handwritten on the back of the photograph. I just stared at the photograph, felt the tears in my eyes. I took the photograph with me.

Ernie had found a wooden rocking horse and was rocking back and forth. He said, 'Giddy up.'

I looked at him, and he smiled. He wanted the rocking horse, so I took it.

Down in the living room, we stood before the warmth of the sun streaming through the window. Ernie continued to rock on the horse.

I checked the phone, and it was still in service. I called Honey and said the first thing that came into my head. I said, 'I hope you will never give up on me.'

Honey said softly, 'I won't.'

That's all she said, and in the ensuing silence I heard the daytime TV in the background. It was the *Dating Game*. Then the line went dead.

I came back into the room and took out the photograph of my parents. Ernie got off the horse and came and sat on my knee. He put his arms around my neck. I was crying without sound. I tasted the salt of my tears. Ernie looked at me and then looked away, and then back at me like he thought maybe he had done something. I smiled and kissed the crown of his head. I took a deep breath, and Ernie smiled in that shy way kids smile. I showed Ernie the photograph of my parents. I told him who they were. I said, 'Your grandparents, Ernie. They lived out here on the farm with me.' I said, 'This is when they got married.' My father was placing the ring on my mother's finger, his index finger and thumb spread apart and her delicate hand extended.

Ernie nodded and looked up and curled his lip. He squirmed and said, 'I got to go, Frank.'

In the bathroom, Ernie pulled his pants down like kids do and sat on the toilet. I stayed in the doorway, waiting. I heard the small plops, then the wheel of the toilet paper turning. Then he stepped on to a small stool Norman had bought for his kids to reach the sink. I watched him like he was something some toy-maker had created. He knew I was watching him. When he was finished, he said, 'Why are you sad, Frank?'

I said, 'I'm not. Sometimes people cry because they're happy.'

In the kitchen, I found the foreclosure note on the table. I called the bank and spoke with a man about taking over the farm, but it was too far in arrears. It was going up to auction. The voice on the end of the line told me a cooperative had an interest in the land. The voice said the Green farm was being offered as part of the same holding. The voice said it was out of my price range. This shithole was out of my price range! I just laughed, and I shouted, 'This is the greatest fucking irony of my entire life! You hear me, the greatest fucking irony of my entire life!'

The man at the bank hung up.

Ernie had come back, and when I turned he said, 'This is the greatest fucking irony of my entire life,' and stomped his foot like I must have done.

I drove away without looking back, like Lot leaving behind everything he ever knew.

Chapter 36

The governor ordered a stay of execution into the New Year, and so Christmas passed with the spectre of Ken's death still looming. We ate way too much and drank too much. That's the meaning of holidays, I guess. I think I was in a daze most of the time. No call came from the police. I was never questioned again. Everything ground to a halt.

I waited for word from Norman or Martha, but, again nothing. I stayed away from Chester Green. I don't think I would ever have gone to the sanitarium again, but then I got a call from Baxter. He was recovering from treatment at the sanitarium. He said, 'You ever planning on coming out here to see your old friend, Frank?'

I said, 'Sure I am.'

Baxter said, 'You see where the Bionic Man is married to one of Charlie's Angels?'

I said, 'I thought you were getting help out there?'

'Hey, Frank, that's a fact. Lee Majors is married to Farrah Fawcett.'

I said, 'I guess they got the right guy for the job.' I felt uncomfortable. 'You okay, Baxter?'

'There's nothing in my head that can't be burned out of me, Frank. Pretty soon I'm going to be a man without a past.'

The college reopened, and Honey and I enrolled, like two goddamn teenagers. We had to line up, just like all the other kids on campus, and get our classes authorized, first by the professor and then by the administration office. It was a bureaucracy unto itself, presided over by middle-aged secretaries like Barb. Honey kept saying, 'I'm not that much older-looking, am I? I got good skin. That's something I was blessed with, good skin.'

I thought of those heartfelt graduation stories they had each year about some ninety-year-old graduating from either high school or college, due to circumstances of war or some personal tragedy. I said that to Honey, and she said, 'You lack self-esteem, that's your big problem.'

Daily life usurped everything, like it always does, eclipsing Martha and Norman and his kids. The papers didn't even mention Chester Green out at the sanitarium any more. The reopening of the college was big news, the parade of cars coming back for term, the free movie, *Love Story*, playing continuously over at the auditorium. Honey and I went to it, and Honey said, 'Thank God we don't have cancer.'

We got outfitted for school at Sears, new clothes and school supplies that set us back a pile of money. Mrs Brody was firmly entrenched in our daily lives now. She rode up front when we went out, like a grandmother.

Walking through the campus after dropping Ernie off at kindergarten, I felt the invigoration of hope and youth, of expectancy and love, of ambition in the students. I existed sometimes as a student, other times as an employee of the college. I felt that sense of self-consciousness, like I was having the most constructive mental breakdown possible. That's how I described it to Honey one evening, after we'd finished studying. Honey looked at me and said, 'Think of life as a terminal illness, Frank, and then every day you survive is a blessing.'

The college felt like a secular religion, a commune of practicality, the American way. Set this life against the nightmare of Mrs Brody, awaiting the bodies of her immigrant men buried alive, afraid to take a husband, or Charlie, blessed

325

with genius, ending up a cripple, falsely accused of molesting kids, or of good Ken and bad Ken, the dissociation of all those years between the crime and punishment, truly a new creature grown in captivity. I thought maybe all Ken had ever needed was a good Junior College, a portal to another dimension.

I said to Honey one afternoon, as we were walking back to get Ernie, 'Can there be salvation in a Godless world?' and she said, 'Sure, I guess you just have to save yourself.' Then she told me she was joining the bowling team, without missing a heartbeat.

I said, 'It's hard to believe that our national security is based on a policy of mutual and total annihilation with the Russians. Our existence is supported by an arsenal that could kill every living thing on the planet, except cockroaches.'

Honey said, 'Don't fight happiness.'

But of course, Ken was that migraine that visited me each night, until finally Honey told me he was to be executed, that the final date was set. He was to die at midnight. In the eyes of the law, that was the beginning of a new day, but, in human terms, it was the very end of the day.

On the morning of Ken's last day on earth, Honey had her high heels in a bowling bag, one of the only possessions she'd taken with her from Georgia. It looked like something an executioner might put the decapitated head in. She showered for going on an hour. I could tell she was doing all her crying right there.

I stared at Robert Lee's poster of Pink Floyd's *Dark Side of the Moon*, the point of white light hitting the prism, splitting into the spectrum of its hidden colors against the intensity of the blackness of outer space.

We all left the apartment together. Robert Lee didn't exactly know Ken was going to die today, or at least I didn't think he knew. He left without saying anything to us.

We dropped off Ernie, and then I walked with Honey

toward campus. I said, 'You okay, Honey?' I tried to touch her. She stiffened.

She said, 'I'm riding the cotton pony is all.'

I said, 'You don't have to go in today.'

Honey said, 'I'll see you later, Frank,' and left me standing in the falling snow.

I spent the morning trying to figure our take for the week on parking fines. We had just instituted parking fines on campus, and parking stickers were now required, which was something the dean had learned about while attending some conference on College Life. He had a shit-load of schemes that were a benign form of extortion. We set our fines at ten dollars. The catch was, a student didn't graduate until all accounts were settled, so we were basically printing money every time we wrote a ticket. The parking tickets were going to finance the new Jeep.

Over at the Business School, I called in on Honey to see how she was coping. Mrs Brody was minding Ernie through the afternoon, and Robert Lee could take care of himself.

Honey had spent the day on the phone with her sister who had gone to see Ken, or that's what I was told, among other things, like, for instance, that the dean of the Business College was letting Honey talk for free, and the college was picking up the tab. That was all told to me in a furtive whisper by a woman who ran the mimeograph machine. Her hands were stained blue. I didn't catch her name.

I went along a corridor to where Honey had her desk outside the dean's office, just like the operation over at the administration office with Barb and the head dean. The dean was out where Honey should have been sitting, reading through some files.

The dean stopped me from going any further. The door to his office was closed. He got up and directed me back out to the hallway. He put his hand on my back, like you might comfort the bereaved. He said, 'I think we have it handled, Frank.'

I was dressed up in my security cop outfit. I felt insignificant in the way only a uniform can make you feel. The dean smelt of bologna. He'd been eating a late lunch when I showed up. I said, for lack of anything else to say, 'What's in bologna, Dean?'

He knew not to answer me. Instead he said, 'Maybe Honey might just see this out in my office. We're covering the tab on the calls, so you don't have to worry.'

The dean had gotten a bad hair transplant job. Under the light, you could see where they'd woven the hair into his scalp.

Honey happened to come out of the dean's office and broke the tension. We both turned and looked at her. She looked like she'd been crying. I hesitated to go toward her.

Honey said, 'You know, Frank, the dean has a stationary bicycle in his recreation room that he rides when he watches TV. He's covered something like a thousand miles while he's watched TV.'

The dean interjected, 'Fourteen hundred and counting.'

That really impressed Honey, or at least she pretended it did right then. We were all dancing around the obvious, as they say.

I said to the dean, 'That's something. I bet you could cook your dinner under your own power, Dean.'

He ignored me and said to Honey, 'How are you holding up?' He took her hands and said, 'You ever see someone type as fast as this woman?'

I said, 'No.'

The dean said, 'And a bowler, too.'

I said, 'A better bowler than typist, or so I've been led to believe.'

Honey looked dazed, but she tried to smile.

I said, 'You want some water, Honey?' and she nodded.

I filled a paper cone of water and gave it to her, but as she reached out for it she stopped and said, 'Ken has requested cheese fries, a hot dog, and Coke for his last meal.' That made her cry, just saying that. She said, 'That's my son's favorite meal, Dean. Right, Frank?'

'Yes.'

The phone rang, and Honey jumped and ran back into the dean's office, but it was for him. Honey insisted he take it in his own office. She dabbed her eyes, which were red from crying.

Honey and I waited at her desk. She told me a team of doctors had come with coolers, ready to take Ken's organs off to awaiting recipients. I didn't say anything.

The air smelt of vomit, but it turned out to be a can of Chef Boyardee that the dean had been eating. There was also a plastic bag of carrots and celery sticks.

Honey told me her sister told her Ken worked out and watched his weight over the last month of his imprisonment, after he signed a consent form giving his body to science. He wanted his body parts strong for his hosts. Honey said, 'That's what Ken calls the people who're getting his body parts, "The Hosts".' Honey said that word, 'hosts', a few times, and each time I could see the fear in her eyes.

In the end, I said, 'You want to take these calls at home? This isn't a time to worry about what things cost, you hear me, Honey?'

Honey said, 'I got to compose myself first, Frank. We'll see, okay?' She took my hands and kissed the back of each. 'I think Robert Lee knows. Not the day, Frank. I never told him that. But he's watched me. He knows.'

I drove out by Ward's in the interim. A bulldozer had already crushed both Ward's and Norman's houses, along with Sam Green's. On a signpost, it listed the new owners.

Just knowing Martha and Norman were gone made me feel alone, alone in that strange way when you understand something has come to an end, or, more exactly, that it has been over for a long time, just like Ken had been dead since the day he got convicted and sentenced to death.

I poured coffee from my thermos. It tasted bitter and hot. I felt it invade my chest with its warmth. I just sat facing the gouged space where I had lived, my reflection an unsettling ghost staring back at me in the dying evening light. I think I was waiting to understand everything, for revelation, but there was nothing, only the dark growth of the distant forest. Only Chester Green remained.

Back at the apartment, I looked in on Ernie. He was riding the rocking horse we'd taken from Norman's. Mrs Brody seemed drunk. She said, 'I think having a child would be like a love affair that never ends.' I knew she was thinking of Robert Lee. She had out an album of photographs of her when she was young. I stopped and took the album off her lap, and she looked like one of the most beautiful women I'd ever seen. I think she saw what I was thinking in the look in my eyes. Under the photograph, it said, 'Hope 1912.' Mrs Brody smiled and said, 'That's my name, Frank, Hope, a child born at the end of the nineteenth century.' She looked down at the photograph. 'This is my fifteenth birthday. The same age as Robert Lee . . .'

I said, 'I think he'll like it.'

Mrs Brody whispered, 'All before there was ever a World War I or II, before atom bombs . . .' Her eyes were glossed over. 'We found cures for so many things, then we went and found other ways to die . . . to kill ourselves.'

I got the tapes from the apartment. I kissed Ernie before I left.

I walked the perimeter of the campus, hearing the whine of snowmobiles far up in the hills and looking to see the beams of weak light off to the east, the snowmobiles heading along the old railway tracks that led toward the mines and the old graveyard. I could see the twinkle of lights from the last remaining copper mine. There was the dull thump of some compressor, digging. It felt like the earth had a heartbeat.

I went over by the psychology building, went through the old prefab structure, back to where the tapes had been made, the only source of light the crimson of the fire exits. I made my way through the labyrinth of passages, like a journey through my own subconscious. I didn't turn on the lights, just let my eyes adjust.

I continued through the prefab structures, got to the small room where I'd seen Ward sitting all those years ago. I could see that look in his eyes, the fear, knowing that I was speaking about him, about what had gone on out at the farm.

I found the AV room and got out the reel-to-reel tape player. It was chained to a metal cart, like they always are. I pushed the cart out into one of the small experimental labs and locked the door behind me. I was shaking. I had to hold my hands out and steady them before I could take the cold spool of the first tape and thread it. I hit 'Play' and sat back and listened to that small, tremulous voice of my own innocence. I will never forget the loneliness crushing my lungs as I lay in the dark and began listening to myself speak across the ages.

It sounded like old-time radio, a crackling static. My memory aligned with the sound. I listened. There's a man near the fire, but I can't see him. He's shouting about Charlie. I hear myself on the tapes say the name, Charlie. Dr Brown intervenes and asks me who's talking, and I hesitate and don't answer his question, and he says again, 'Who's talking, Frank? Who is it?' He describes what I've already said and pushes me to identify the man, and he ends up saying, 'Is it your father?' and I say, 'Yes,' and then he asks the question again, and asks if it's my uncle, and I say, 'Yes,' and Dr Brown grows agitated on the tape. He seems to talk with somebody in the background and then repeats the question, and I answer as before, answering yes to his leading question, never telling him outright. Another voice says, 'Is it Father Christmas?' and I say 'Yes,' and Dr Brown shouts, 'Turn it off!'

There is a renewed sense of calm, like time has passed. When the tape begins again I am describing my mother lying on the kitchen floor. I never say her name. I am hiding upstairs, looking down. I describe myself hiding. I use the third person. I say, 'Frank is scared.' I describe my own fear in this way. That's what is apparent, my own fear, the dark horror that has made me close my eyes to what I am seeing. I can situate myself in the house, but I am unable to stare into the face of the people who are there with me. I talk about somebody moving in the kitchen. I say, 'Frank sees the bad man.' Then I say, 'Frank wants his mommy. Frank is good.' You can hear Dr Brown saying, 'Frank *is* a good boy.' Dr Brown is on the tape pushing me for a name, trying to define attributes, to narrow my choices, to force me to look closer into my memory in order to see this bad man, but I stop so many times and start again with nonsense. At one point I tell Dr Brown I want a puppy right after he asks me to describe the man, for what seems like the hundredth time, and you can hear Dr Brown shout at me. He says, 'Puppy! There is no puppy, you hear me, Frank? I want you to listen, Frank! Who is the bad man? What did the bad man do, Frank? You are safe now, Frank. Tell us, Frank. If you are a good boy then you'll tell us who is the bad man. Who is the bad man, Frank?' There are long pauses where there is either static, or those murmurs of a conversation taking place in the background.

On another tape, I describe two men talking, but I don't hear the words. They're drinking. At times they roar, and they go quiet. I describe a strong smell in the room. I come back over and over again to this smell. Dr Brown tries to establish the smell as sour or of something burnt. He says, 'Of charred wood?' but I don't answer, and the assistant's voice says, 'I don't think he understands charred wood,' and Dr Brown groans and describes wood that has been burnt, what it smells like, but I can't identify the smell. Then Dr Brown tries to establish if this is before or after the fire, if the woman is still there on the kitchen floor, if the smell is coming from her, but I can't answer that. He pushes me for an answer, and I eventually say, 'Yes,' but it's a concession at the end of repeated questions. Further on in the tape, I describe my uncle turning and seeing me hiding, and this time I do say his name. I say simply, 'Uncle is mean. Frank is a good boy,' and Dr Brown tries to establish if this is before or after the fire, and I seem confused and can't answer and lose the thread of where I was, in what I was telling, and Dr Brown has to repeat what I previously said, and there's that sense of dissociation evident on the tape, that I can't, as a child, process that Dr Brown is repeating what I've said on the tape, and, when he asks me to continue, I can't. Dr Brown seems confused.

There are minutes where you can hear Dr Brown trying to lead me back to seeing the two men. Then there are long periods of silence. I identify one of the men as my uncle on another tape, but can't see the other face. I fix on the smell again, and Dr Brown asks if it's of chemical cleaner, of pine scent or bleach. But all I do is hesitate, and I can't answer and just say, 'Frank doesn't like the bad smell.' Again, Dr Brown cannot establish when the bad smell occurs. I talk of worms. I say worms on numerous tapes. In fact, worms is the word that begins two of the tapes. I say, 'Worms are icky. Frank doesn't like worms.'

On another tape, Dr Brown asks if my mother is still lying on the floor, since I describe a woman lying on the floor, but after persistent questions to establish if this is my mother, I ask, 'Who is lying on the floor?' and Dr Brown goes to great lengths to repeat what I've already said about the woman lying on the floor, and I say, 'The floor?' Then I talk about the worms again, still using the third person, always talking of Frank like he is not me. I say, 'Is Frank going to bed without supper?' and Dr Brown says, 'No, Frank is a good boy.' Then I say, 'Worms are icky. Frank doesn't like the worms.' It drives Dr Brown over the edge. He says at one point, 'Frank better be good or the worms will get him!' and the assistant says in the background, 'Dr Brown, my God!' and the tape shuts off. You can feel the exasperation Dr Brown feels, the futility of what he is doing.

Later, I hear myself talking, but it's a distant sound, and Dr Brown speaks over it, and then I speak, even though I'm speaking on the tape. It seems that they're replaying what I've previously said on a reel-to-reel. It's a strategy that backfires, because I don't understand what they've done, and Dr Brown questions me about the story the voice on the tape is telling. I can't identify it as me, or connect with the story. I say, 'Who's speaking?' Dr Brown says, 'You are speaking,' but I don't understand. Still Dr Brown persists and lets the tape play and stops the tape at critical points and asks me to continue, and I don't. But I come back again and again to the bad smell, and Dr Brown says, 'It must be the smell of burning,' to his assistant, who says, 'Do you know what smoke is?' and I say, 'Yes' and Dr Brown seems to get upset with the assistant and asks the question himself, and I answer 'Yes,' and then he says, 'Is the smell like smoke?' and I say, 'No.' Then he goes on a long litany of things that smell, and by the end of the list I've lost track of what we're talking about, and I say, 'What smell?' and the tape stops abruptly. I can just imagine Dr Brown's anxiety.

On tapes dated weeks after the initial interviews, I describe Frank hiding among the cows. The barn glows against a blaze of fire. Dr Brown asks how Frank got there, but Frank doesn't remember. I say, 'Frank's head hurts.' Out in the dark, Frank hears a man screaming. Frank identifies the man as his uncle.

I feel the cleaving apart of my own consciousness, just listening to that voice, to the fear that comes across, the subconscious will of a child to hide behind the third person, even at that age, to have the instinct to hide from what was seen.

I describe seeing my uncle against the fire which burns strong and lights up the night. There is another man running back and forth. 'Two men or one man?' Dr Brown asks the question twice before I answer 'Frank sees two men,' but I can't see either of them together or identify the other man, just my uncle, because he comes into the shed at one point and sees me standing up looking out at the fire, and he screams, and then I remember nothing, not until I'm off in a room and there is no fire anymore. It's not the barn. Dr Brown establishes that fact. I describe hearing my uncle shouting, and again the protracted cross-examination by Dr Brown continues, interrupting what I'm saying, asking if my uncle is shouting in the barn and if the fire is still going, and I seem confused, and again Dr Brown becomes agitated. After another prolonged silence, I speak of leaving the room. I go slowly toward where the voices are speaking. I turn the knob to go into the room, but the door is locked. My uncle says, 'Jesus Christ!' and then goes silent. I am crying on the tape. I say, 'Frank wants his mommy.' I describe how Frank tries to turn the knob again, how he hears a voice behind the door, how he puts his eye to the keyhole, and sees his uncle staring back at him. Dr Brown waits until the surrogate voice of Frank is finished and asks if this is before or after the fire, and the voice of the other Frank, the small child locked into the laboratory says, 'What fire?' The split in personalities between the two voices is evident. The voice of the surrogate Frank is more breathless, more scared.

Just listening to the tapes, I sense the inevitable perplexity of Dr Brown, the inexactness of his methods. There is no chronology to the events, nothing of real substance. I am an unreliable witness, the two personae exist, each coping as best it can. That comes across, the inaccuracy of the subconscious, the collusion of wills, of Dr Brown leading me toward what he believes. My fear permeates the tapes, but there is nothing that implicates my uncle, nothing that could have been used in a court of law, that is. I say at one stage the name 'Chester Green', just out of the blue when Dr Brown asks me on one tape about who my uncle is talking to. He says, 'Is Chester Green there?' and I say, 'Yes,' but later I don't remember Chester Green's name. And so begins the protracted method of having me listen to my own testimony again, and Dr Brown says, 'You see Chester Green, right?' and I say, 'Yes,' but you get the sense, listening, that I have been primed to answer yes. Again the nameless technician says something muffled, and Dr Brown says, 'Who's there with your uncle, Frank?' but I don't answer the second or the third time, even with their prompting, even as Dr Brown lists a host of people's names. I say, 'Frank doesn't like the bad smell,' again, out of the blue, and it is this Frank voice that talks about worms, but Dr Brown grows agitated and says, 'Forget the goddamn worms!' and then says, 'Edit that, you hear me?' and the assistant says something, and, by this time, even Dr Brown has lost his line of questioning. Finally, Dr Brown says, 'I want Frank to stop hiding. I want the real Frank to come out.' But it is pointless, and finally Dr Brown says, 'Turn it off!' and the tape goes to static.

I stayed sitting, and minutes later the reel unspooled.

Nothing materialized from the tapes, only the sad fact that I had been ruined, that I was a child who was suffering.

Something stirred inside my head, that smell. I hadn't remembered that before, but now I found myself sniffing the air, seeking out that smell.

Later I saw my mother in brief flashes at the foot of the stairs, face down. That sent a chill through me. I felt weak and stayed sitting, letting the voice from the tapes sift through my mind. I closed my eyes, and I saw her head turned and her eyes open, but when I spoke to her, she didn't answer. She was staring like Chester Green out at the sanitarium, that dead stare.

I shook my head, the dull impact of her death or dying coming back into my head. I see her lying at the foot of the stairs. Her stomach is huge, like she is pregnant under her dress.

And maybe in that first memory, I began to understand things.

I gathered everything together, put the reel-to-reel away and locked up the building.

At Dr Brown's office, I opened his door, and he looked up from a book, his eyes distorted by his reading glasses. I shouted, 'You ever touch the Sleeper again, and, so help me God, I'll kill you! You hear me, you son-of-a-bitch? You're not God Almighty!' I hadn't even checked to see if the Sleeper was off the respirator.

Chapter 37

By the time I got back to the campus, it was eleven o'clock. Outside the snow was falling. The notion of my mother pregnant chilled me. I could see her dead. The years folded in on themselves, and I felt the sadness of a child. I shouldn't have listened to the tapes on this night, but I had.

I found Honey sitting alone at the Business Dean's office. She was on the phone.

I spoke to Honey's sister for the first time ever. She had a voice just like Honey, but she used Southern expressions that Honey had long abandoned. She said, 'Y'all are having a storm up there, I hear?'

I said, 'What's it like down there in Georgia?'

Honey's sister told me the temperature.

I said, 'That's good sleeping weather.'

Honey had her hand out and wanted the phone back.

This was Honey's sister who had married a black guy called Seymore Sykes, when things like that weren't done down south. I guess Honey and her sister were cut from the same cloth, two Southern beauties who reached a maturity of body, if not mind, when things like that could hurt a woman.

I waited out at Honey's desk while she finished talking.

When Honey put the phone down, I said, 'Did he ever admit to killing those people?'

Honey shook her head and whispered, 'No.'

I said, 'He never said anything?'

Honey whispered, 'I remember Robert Lee sitting before the

338

TV, watching the news about Nixon, and Ken said, "What the hell do you expect from a nation that spies on everybody else? Why the hell do people think Nixon was going to do anything other than wiretap his goddamn enemies!" Ken felt cheated somehow about everything.' Honey put her head down. 'Jesus, 1973 was the single worst year of my life, the year Ken got sentenced to death.' Honey took a moment and swallowed. 'All Ken ever said was it was like a conveyer belt out on the highway outside our motel. That's how he described it when we used to sit out on the balcony facing the highway.' Honey had her eyes closed. 'At a certain point, all he saw was not people, not cars, but money driving by. Everybody had the face of George Washington, everybody had that face on the dollar bill. That's what he told me. Things had changed inside his brain.' Honey stopped and then began again softly, 'And I believed him, Frank, inasmuch as you hear people say they can be filled with the Holy Spirit or can speak in tongues. I don't think he ever really believed he killed those people.'

Right then, I started calling everything associated with Ken 'Kengate'.

We left for home. Honey tried to hyperventilate in Mrs Brody's hallway to get whatever final tremors of emotions out of her. It was hard to watch her lean against the staircase railing and pant like she did. Honey said, 'God, how can people survive this cold.' She was shaking.

Mrs Brody stood on the opposite side of the bubble-glass door in the small apartment she kept for herself. In the drawing room, she had a fire going, just in case we might want to come down and use it. I stood in the doorway. I could see she had out her best china set. Honey stood beside me. She squeezed my arm, then looked away.

I said, 'You want Robert Lee and Ernie to come down here?'

Honey shook her head. She said, 'I got so much work to catch up on.'

We went upstairs, and Honey went into the bathroom and locked the door behind her.

Robert Lee and Ernie were in the apartment inside their makeshift teepee. They were watching a rerun of *The Brady Bunch*. Robert Lee didn't say anything to me. The volume was loud. It was right around that time when rumours were spreading that Greg had fucked Florence Henderson in real life. It was a time of loss of innocence.

Honey came out of the bathroom. She had gotten into her housecoat. She said like this was just any other night, 'Frank, turn on the kettle.' I plugged in the hotplate. Honey sat at the electric typewriter and started typing.

I blew on the window to make a peephole and saw the moon against fast moving clouds.

I watched time crawl toward the day's end. I felt a sense of relief that Ken was finally going to die, that the years of appeals and waiting were over. In all the years I'd been with Honey, I'd never actually seen Ken. He existed as some dark, invisible force, like gravity, pulling at me. I remembered back in school hearing about how scientists predicted the presence of Pluto by studying the elliptical irregularity of Neptune's orbit. Maybe that held for my own parents and Ward, and Norman and Martha, and now that image of my mother dead, all just tangential forces on the periphery of my life.

I looked at Robert Lee's face. His hair was long and stringy, the way kids wore it. He looked like a young Jesus Christ, the Jesus Christ in his adolescent years who is not mentioned in any of the Gospels.

A rerun of *Gilligan's Island* started. It was the episode where the Harlem Globetrotters were somehow marooned on the goddamn island. You pretty much had to check your brain at the door to watch that crap, but Ernie was glued, and even Robert Lee seemed interested. It required a suspension of disbelief we seemed willing to give to TV, but not to other things, not to real life, or even religion, but we abided by the rules of the show. We conformed to the storyline. I was thinking, here is the island to which Ken should be sent, some mysterious island where the castaways could never escape, but you could get to them if need be.

Honey typed right through Ken's execution, but it was a staccato typing, fast, then slow, as her brain processed what was going on over a thousand miles away in the heat of a Georgia night. Ken's warm body was being flayed open and scavenged in some backroom for the resurrection of so many hapless, waiting souls.

Chapter 38

Robert Lee just went off to school the next day, and we all acted like nothing had happened. We took Ernie down to kindergarten. At lunchtime, Honey and I came back from class and went to the apartment. I think if you forget how to forgive, then you have lost your humanity. We made love with our eyes closed. Making love when you know you should be someplace else can be the greatest feeling in the world.

In the silent aftermath, in the yellow glow of the world outside, with the light streaming across the room, I imagined Robert Lee sitting in the glass house of the dining hall, coping with the image of his father's death. I saw him dispensing free Cokes and candy, doing that trick with the vending machine, like the miracle of the loaves and the fishes. Robert Lee a messiah of the cafeteria.

I felt at a turning point, that we were moving in the direction of redemption, that we had suffered for whatever original sin we had been born with. On the cathedral radio, 'Raindrops Keep Falling on My Head' was playing.

Honey turned and kissed the damp softness of my inner arm.

I whispered, 'You ever see that movie, *Butch Cassidy and the Sundance Kid*?'

Honey said nothing.

I whispered, 'That's my favorite movie of all time, maybe because of the name, Cassidy. Who doesn't want to be associated with Paul Newman, right? In the opening scene,

Butch is surveying this bank that's turned modern, something beyond what he can manage to rob, and he says to this guard, "What happened to the old bank? It was beautiful." And the guard says, "People kept robbing it," and Butch says, "That's a small price to pay for beauty." '

Honey opened her eyes, like she was listening. She touched the side of my face.

'You hear Butch, this aging outlaw, going on about Bolivia. He says at one point, after he tells the Kid about Bolivia, about its riches, "I got vision, and the rest of the world wears bifocals." I love that line. This posse followed Butch and the Kid, driving them all the way to Bolivia, that posse, always seen at a great distance, like some remote authority, like fear gathering.' I took a deep breath. 'That's how all this has felt.'

It snowed less through the latter part of January. There were more clear blue skies, but the temperature stayed below freezing, which kept the students indoors.

There was something melancholy underlying the normality that settled in around us. It was like the claustrophobia of a storm's eye, but the truth was, the storm had passed, and that sense of calm was something I had to grow accustomed to. We didn't have to think about Ken any more. Robert Lee seemed to let the pain go deep to some remote place inside him, and Ernie was just Ernie.

Some nights during my shift I went back to the apartment, just to look at Ernie. One night he was awake and wanted to go to the toilet, so I took him. Ernie stood like an apparition, clinging to his dinosaur. We ate cereal in the kitchen off the main bedroom. It was 3 a.m. I had to make a small bowl for Ernie's dinosaur.

I said things like, 'You like Frank, Ernie?' The light was stark in the kitchen, like an interrogation room against the blackness at the window. I used that third person I used on the tape, saying the name, Frank.

Ernie looked at me like he didn't understand that question. He looked at his dinosaur. He dipped his head, like he and the dinosaur had things to say to one another. Then he nodded. He had his spoon hovering above his bowl. A drip had formed underneath.

I said, 'Go on now. Frank wants you to eat.' I felt embarrassed, asking my kid questions like this in the early hours of the morning. I got up and poured myself a coffee. I just looked at Ernie. He was complete, a miniature person. His feet were dangling off the chair. He had that secret smile he sometimes gave me, like he knew I needed something to keep me going, not words, but just that look he kept for me. He was like that blank slate on which our history was written. There were times when I wanted to ask him what he thought about everything, to hear the unadulterated truth from a child's mouth. In some dynasties they had kid rulers.

And at the back of things, I was slowly coming to understand my own past. I listened to the tapes over at the prefab psychology building some nights. I now knew my mother had died in a fall. I saw the blood near her waist. When I went to her and touched her, I saw this thing, this thing with eyes between her legs. She had fallen, the child inside her partly born.

At times I looked at that single wedding photograph, my father putting the ring on my mother's hand, a last surviving image of their existence.

We visited Baxter out at the sanitarium in the aftermath of his treatment, in the weeks after Ken died and was buried.

Baxter had lost who he was to a large extent. He smiled at me when I came, with a faint hint of recognition, and then he did know it was me, and he said my name. Honey and Robert Lee and Ernie waited in the communal TV room.

Baxter smelt of sickness. He was in a robe and matching slippers his girlfriend had brought for him. I could see where he'd been shocked, the soft indentation of two marks on either side of the head, where the threads of memory had been burned out of his brain. His hands trembled on his lap. They had him facing the glorious evening. I could see clear out to the humpbacks of small islands along the great lake, where small banks of fog hung.

Robert Lee and Ernie were watching *Superman* out with the war veterans. I kept turning and watching Robert Lee staring between the TV and the veterans.

Baxter saw them and said, 'Bring them in, Frank.'

In the communal room, Superman was spinning the world backward, reversing time to change history to save Lois Lane, who had died. I watched the blur of actions in reverse.

Honey whispered, 'I don't see how Lois never can see that Superman and Clark Kent are one and the same person.'

I said, 'I guess we see what we want to see.'

In the mid-afternoon light, everything took on a gel quality, like staring though a jelly mold. Everything smelt of hospital pine and bleach, the clinical sanitized odor of sickness.

Baxter had Coke and candy. He poured the Coke into five plastic cups, but his hands shook with the effort, and he spilled the Coke on his robe, but he persisted, and I resisted the urge to help him. I could see the blue of his veins along his white, hairless hands.

We toasted his health, and a strange sense of quiet settled over all of us. Baxter made a smacking sound with his lips. 'Next time you come, Frank, bourbon would be appreciated.' Baxter cleared his throat and said, 'When you're high, you fall down easy! You know who said that, Frank?' Baxter winked at Ernie and said, 'Humpty Dumpty said that, just after he cracked up!'

We all watched a deer move across the snow. The moon was already in the sky.

Baxter said, 'I got a kid over in Vietnam. I'm having the Veterans Administration track down my records. I think a kid might be just what I need.' He looked at me. 'Linda had a pap smear that didn't turn out real good a while back. I think she's open to the idea.'

In the stalemate, Baxter said, 'Hey, kid, I want that rematch,' and Baxter and Robert Lee arm-wrestled, and this time Robert Lee let Baxter win.

In the end, Baxter said, 'Here's one more, Frank, for the road. Adam and Eve had an ideal marriage. He didn't have to hear about all the men she could have married, and she didn't have to hear about the way his mother cooked.' He smiled at me. 'It's the cleanest one I got, considering the company, right, Frank?'

Along the narrow passage of the sanitarium, the pipes hissed and knocked. The trapped heat made the windows mist as always. I knew, at some gut level, the truth in all this. Something had fallen into place on the nights listening to the tapes. The image of my mother's death stuck with me, that beatific look on her face, the way I moved around her like a scared animal, staring at the sack of membrane and blood that poured on to the floor. It was not something I had let myself see before, but now it haunted me.

I stopped in the hallway and thought of the Sleeper in the purgatory of his own condition, like something God had forgotten to take care of, something that just went on living at a cellular level, or that's what I hoped had become of him, something without consciousness.

I turned to Honey and said simply, 'I want to show you something,' and we went in the direction of the small cell-like room, past Clifford, who looked up from reading the newspaper and looked like he was going to stop me but didn't when he saw my family.

We crowded into the small of the room, the solitary porthole window letting in the last of the day's light. In the

346

dimness, we just stood there looking at the man laid out on the bed.

Honey crossed herself. Ernie drew close to her side and held his dinosaur. Robert Lee looked at me.

It was as though I was staring through the wrong end of a telescope, that long tunnel vision feeling. It was like a rip in time, being here with this man, this atrophied thing that bore only the merest trace of something human, an etiolated stalk of humanity, the clawed hands turned inward toward some fetal origin.

I took a deep breath. I said, 'I brought my family to see you.' I said all their names, like a slow roll call. I told the Sleeper that Robert Lee was named after a general and was defiant, like a war hero. I made Robert Lee stand forward for a moment. Then I said, 'Ernie's named after a character on *Sesame Street*.'

I said, 'But this is the way we name things.'

I said, 'You know how Ward got his name, "Ward"?' I looked at Honey, and she said softly, 'How?' She had the look of someone searching to know what I was doing here.

I said, 'Ward was the first in his family born in a hospital. When my grandfather went to get him, he got lost, and they kept saying at the hospital, "Which ward is your wife in?" When he was leaving, they said, "So you found the right ward!" and that's what my grandfather decided to call the baby, "Ward"!'

I continued slowly, 'And this is Honey. Her name represents what she is, sweet, but she can also sting,' and Honey said, 'Frank...' but I had gone down on one knee, like some penitent, and I whispered, 'And I'm Frank, as always, and I am named after *you*.'

I opened the Sleeper's clawed hand, and in the fold of the skin between the thumb and index finger lay the solitary secret of who he was, the crescent mark.

Honey whispered, 'Sweet Jesus...'

My father wept without sound, like one of those religious statues that are from time to time purported to bleed and augur things like the end of the world. I had the wedding photograph with me, and I took it out and showed it to my father. I pointed to his hand, and to the mark on the hand of the man in the photograph.

I said, 'It is you in there?'

And through the grey death mask, the eyes opened and closed once.

The Jeep was freezing. I had the vents on high. Honey huddled against the cold as we pulled away. All Honey said was, 'How, Frank?'

I said, 'That's not the hard part, but the why.'

From a distance, the gas station that held the bear looked like a spaceship set down in the wilderness. I turned off the lights and drove the last mile along the narrow scar of the country road. Everything was devoid of color except the aura of hazy bluish light at the gas station. We fed the bear in the dark, until a light came on out back where the guy who ran the gas station lived. I saw the shadow of the guy inside. He was holding what I presume was a gun.

I pulled back on to the road and drove out by the bulldozed property. I used the Jeep's shovel to break down the sign.

Robert Lee was smiling, and so was Ernie.

Honey said, 'No more, Frank,' but I drove up along the road to the non-existent house one more time, back to the nightmare of the slaughtered animals, and back further to what Ward and my father had done, those Resurrectionists, digging up the fresh grave of Chester Green, taking his body to the farm, setting fire to the house, setting Chester Green in with the remains of my mother in some primitive funeral pyre. Two brothers bound by poverty and hopelessness, and another brother abandoned to the sanitarium with polio, the prodigal prodigy. I bore silent witness to their work, hidden away in the barn all those years ago.

In the moonlight, we could see far. It was that sort of moon, big and bone white, an Arctic moon. I said, 'It's as though we never existed.'

Honey stayed in the car with Robert Lee and Ernie.

I got out of the car and howled like an animal, like a creature communing across the ages, across space and time.

Chapter 39

The coroner's office called a week or so later and wanted me to claim Ward, since the investigation was over.

I called the State Police. They told me Norman was staying at a motel called The Gator.

I went to the window of the office and stared out into the night. It was nearly seven o'clock. It had warmed up outside. The campus outside was slick and shining in the suffused yellow campus lights. I picked the phone up and called the number.

Martha answered, and she was caught off guard. She coughed and cleared her throat.

I spoke simply. I said I was going to get Ward from the coroner's office and that he was going to be put in the ground in a week. That's all I said.

Martha must have gotten up and opened the door to the outside, because all I could hear was the sound of insect nightlife. Martha seemed like she was having her own conversation. She said, 'It's sixty-two and clear skies, and it's eight o'clock at night. We got a pool here, Frank. All the rooms are centered around the pool.'

From the room number, I could tell she was on the second floor. I pictured her standing against the railing of her motel in the warm evening air.

One of Norman's kids said something to Martha, and she said, 'Okay, but only for ten minutes or so. You stay in the shallow end.'

Martha got back to me. 'You know, the reception is done up like the mouth of an alligator, Frank. You walk into this big open mouth to register. It's something to see.' Martha just went on talking in the Florida night air. She said, 'We got a woman friend named Delores who's a mermaid at Water World. She lives at the motel here.'

I said, 'In the swimming pool?'

Martha laughed out loud. 'That's real funny. In the pool. That's funny.' Then she stopped laughing. She said, 'You know, Frank, it seems only right that this is where they launch things into outer space.'

I said, 'Listen to me.'

But Martha pre-empted me. 'You know, they got rockets launching into space on the TV down here in the morning hours. They interrupt the regular broadcasts to show it live. I was watching a launch the other day, and it's strange just to see all that it takes to get something into orbit, all those fuel tanks and rocket boosters, but how all that stuff just falls away, and all you're left with is the capsule, with just what you need to survive. I went outside during a launch, and there was the rocket against the blue sky, heading for outer space.'

Martha got quiet. The night insects made a piercing sound in the background. I heard the sound of water splashing. 'You've got to see them swimming. They look like tadpoles when you're looking down on them. You can see their legs under water, opening and closing.'

I moved the phone to my other ear.

Somebody said Martha's name, and she responded. She said to me, 'It's the mermaid, Frank. She swims in the evening.'

I said, 'Where's Norman?'

Martha waited and said, 'Norman's out. Norman is Neptune at Water World. It's just short-term, before Spring training, before he gets signed up to play pro ball.'

I said, 'It's like you are speaking from a distant galaxy.'

Martha said, 'I feel dispossessed of everything, and that's a good feeling. I want you to know we've found paradise.'

Ward was buried out at the family plot, in a private ceremony. I put notice of his funeral in the obituaries. The funeral was attended by a few people. I mailed the notice to Martha, but got no response.

Norman ended up playing pro ball in the fall with the Dolphins. It's something to see him on a Sunday afternoon. I saw him at a post-game interview. He had on an orange shirt and a gold chain around his neck. He was leading the league in sacks early in his rookie season. I assume he has a big house and a fancy car.

During that summer of seventy-nine, the sky fell to earth, or actually Skylab fell to earth, disintegrating upon entering the atmosphere. I watched it with Ernie on the TV, a daylong coverage. I got a sense that earth was just a departure pad for the human race, that we would end up spread out across the galaxy. That night we all looked up at the stars on Mrs Brody's roof. I tried to explain what light years were to Ernie. Robert Lee was with us. He said, 'New Jersey, Ernie. That was light years ago, right, Frank?'

Ernie looks at Robert Lee in the way a big brother wants to be looked up to.

I can't say I will ever be Robert Lee's father, but we don't fight like we did. He was taking Driver's Ed and Geometry at the high-school that summer. He left on his bicycle each morning. Honey used to watch him leaving from the window. She said so many times, 'Life moves so fast, Frank.' It was the last summer he'd ever ride a bicycle like that. We worked the finances so we could offer Robert Lee a deal, that if he kept his grades up, we would buy him a car.

It was beautiful that summer, hot and blue skies. Honey and I took summer school classes and still worked. Our world was small, everything within walking distance. I was happy for the first time in my life. I guess there is nothing like working toward something, toward self-improvement.

My father died in the late fall of that year. We became friends, my father and I, in the sense that I came and read to him during the afternoons before work. Sometimes I brought my homework. My father emerged slowly over that summer from his Locked-in Syndrome to where he could sit in a wheelchair, but his limbs were so atrophied he never recovered any real mobility.

During the initial recovery, an investigator came and sat with my father, but in the end the investigator gave up because my father continued to hide behind his mask, never revealing he could understand anything.

When I went to see him, he was usually sitting in his wheelchair. He still wore the feeding tubes and had a catheter, all that scaffold of equipment gleaming in the bright light of the coming long days of summer. They set him facing the vastness of the world outside.

On occasion, Dr Brown watched me pass through the corridors on my way to my father, but we never spoke. Sometimes I nodded my head, a conciliatory gesture, or just watched him shuffle through the corridors of his own imprisonment. I sometimes wonder if he knows my secret, if he understands this intimacy that draws me to the small room, if he realizes he got it all wrong. He's a smart man, after all.

And in a slow, protracted way, over the course of the months, the tracheostomy healed, and, in a wheezing voice, almost a whisper of breaths, I learned the sad history of our hidden secret, the long, suffering nightmare of how, in those mad hours of darkness after my mother's collapse and death in childbirth, things transpired, how Ward and my father came up with the idea of the insurance scam to save the farm, how they set upon the idea of setting the fire. I learned how my father, on the verge of suicide, submitted to the madness of disinterring Chester Green so two bodies would be found in the fire, and how he disappeared days later for the purgatory of Korea, a war nobody wanted to fight, assuming Chester's identity and facing what he felt would surely be his own death. But death had not come.

It is a conspiracy equal to that age of fear, a détente in the Cold War of that solitary existence, where my uncle got what he had always wanted, the farm, and my father, who never wanted the farm, finally escaped, if that's what you could have called his existence. By morning, when the night pulled back its curtain of dark, the pyre of ash bore testimony to the desperate acts of desperate men in desperate times.

Of course, in the telling of all this, I have put my own spin on things, given a tragic density to the telling of the story.

We didn't speak only of that time, because the past was behind us, something that could never be recovered, never fully understood, and I saw the pain it caused my father. I simply wanted us to start sharing the present, to sit by him, absorbing his mere presence. We followed the baseball season that year on the radio, right through the glorious days of summer, and into the fall and the World Series. There is a secret code between pitcher and catcher, a sign language of nods and twitches, and, sometimes, alone at home, I turned a baseball game to mute on the TV and watched that silent language, and it was like myself and my father, the intimacy we shared beyond mere words.

In the fall, I took Ernie with me to the sanitarium to be with my father. We spent the time listening to the pop of bats, to the din of crowds screaming in stadiums. Ernie had Charlie's genius for math, and he knew all the percentages and statistics, the ERAs and RBIs, him and his dinosaurs sitting on the floor amidst my father's entombment, three generations threaded together. I asked Ernie questions about batting averages, and my father smiled weakly, knowing we Cassidys lived on.

We listened to a series that year that went all the way to an improbable seventh game and to the ninth inning before the World Champions were crowned. We followed along as Willie Stargell took his Pittsburgh Pirates to the promised land with his bat, and it was not unlike the suspense of my entire existence, the not knowing until the very end.

I do know that my father came back to see Ward, who was in the last stages of cancer. He told me that. Ward picked him up, and, in the quiet of the house, I can only imagine the faces of two brothers at the end of life, sitting in the cold autumnal light, wondering what the hell it was all for, reckoning with eternity, with the barn door latch knocking in the background, like death itself beckoning them to cross over to the other side. I don't know who pulled the trigger. I didn't put that question to my father, because, in the end, it doesn't matter. Both men had been dead a long time. Forensic evidence suggests that Ward blew out his own brains. He had gunpowder residue on his hands, and my father did not, or it was inconclusive, so I live with the image of Ward with the gun to his own head. It fits, in that it explains the shock that beset my father, that kept him there at the house. I see Norman in my mind, poor Norman, shooting at his Devil.

Sometimes I think, late at night, if Norman had not come when he did, my father would have disappeared. Nothing would ever have come to light. I pray for Sam Green at night, because he is the one true victim, but I have not the courage to redeem him or his son. I am a coward. I tell myself I would make a clean story of all of it, if it wasn't for my family.

Over that fall and into winter I also showed my father the letters I'd found, read through the haunting images of him wandering aimlessly through that war, wanting to know why he went on living. It fit so well with an image of Chester Green, with the conscience of a man with a secret. My father just nodded. I told him my confusion over the letters, over the signature *C*, meaning either Charlie or Chester, and my father said, '*C* for Cassidy, Frank,' and our eyes met, and I could see the sadness in his stare at what he'd put me through.

I told my father of that indelible memory of Sam Green coming to our house the night Chester was dying, screaming about Chester burning up, about Chester being on fire. I told my father everything, not that he didn't know already, of the tragic irony that, under hypnosis, I drew a parallel between my parents' death and Chester's death. In describing the fire, I'd mentioned Chester's name. I told him how that simple metaphor Sam Green had roared nearly ruined all of us, how Dr Brown picked up wrongly on that association and drew us all to the brink of madness, and how, if they had excavated Chester Green's grave all those years ago, Ward would surely have been found out.

Was it coincidence or retribution, the unfolding of what happened? I suppose it depends on your understanding of God and justice. We did not escape, none of us. It turned our lives sour. Ward hardened with fear and ended up blaming me. And what of my father, destined to the margin of my existence, watching his only son go mad. And what, too, of the irony of Norman finding freedom through his naive innocence. I like to think of him smashing into his personal demons on the football field, getting those sacks, just like winning the state meet that sophomore year with the weight of a child on his mind.

It took me time to sort through the flow of letters and names, the exchange of money back and forth. When I moved to Chicago, my father took an apartment near me. He said he used to shadow me around the city. He had sat beside me on buses. He had wanted so badly to tell me who he was. He had sent me the money.

My father had begun signing his correspondence with Ward simply, *Frank,* in his latter years, but he always signed the postal orders *C* since he had to use that alias when he had them filled out at the postal center.

I showed my father a postal order and one of his letters, and pointed at the signature, at the *C.* I guess I wanted to impress my own sense of fear. I wanted my father to know why I had almost murdered him, or I mean, Chester Green. Even now, I find it hard to keep it all straight inside my head.

I learned that Ward and my father had helped one another out, my father originally sending Ward money for my keep. But after my father was injured at his job he began asking Ward for loans, and these were, of course, what Martha had come across, the more recent correspondence from my father, all signed, *Frank.* Ward had already stored the old correspondence and postal order receipts in the attic.

And I finally understood why the police had not asked me about the letters signed *Frank.* The handwriting sample Baxter had given them hadn't matched. It was as simple as that.

I will tell you this much. In the cold scheme of things, my father might have gone on for a long time, but I had to intervene. I went out there one Saturday evening, when Honey was out bowling with the college team. Bob Gilmore was watching *The Love Boat.* He sang the theme all along the hallway as he walked me to the elevator.

My father was back on a ventilator. He had pneumonia. He had a mask over his face. I could tell he wanted to be elsewhere. I took away the mask, and put my lips to his forehead, and whispered an act of contrition into his ear. I put my hand over his mouth, like I was stopping him from telling a secret, and he looked at me just once, and then closed his eyes and went into the dark, into the land of the dead, where he'd been from the moment he walked away from the farm all those years ago.

When I left, Bob Gilmore was watching *Fantasy Island*. He said, 'Get this, Frank,' and he did an impression of Tattoo. He said, 'The plane, the plane!' Another planeload of people were coming to live out their fantasies. Ricardo Montalban was dressed in his white suit, like God Almighty.

My father was buried by the State. He has no headstone, save a small metal cross. His death was duly noted in the paper, but he was listed as Chester Green.

Baxter is back part-time. We drink occasionally for old time's sake, but it's not quite the same. He never did track down that kid of his over in Vietnam, and that bothers him, you can see that in his face. But one evening when we were drinking, he said to me, 'I'm glad you are staying on here, Frank, that you are giving something back.' I didn't quite understand what he meant, but I just nodded.

Baxter leaned toward me. 'They knew. Some of the old people knew, Frank.'

I felt my face flush. I said, 'I don't know what you are talking about.'

Baxter took another drink. 'In the hospital, I got speaking to some of the old people, Frank, people who remembered, remembered a lot of things, Frank, people with a memory for faces, people who remembered all that trouble there was back with Dr Brown, about his accusations.'

It was hard not to look away.

'A town like this has its secrets, secrets it doesn't give up to the outside world.' He pushed the hair back on his forehead. He hadn't shaved. He looked sort of like Jack Nicholson in *One Flew Over the Cuckoo's Nest*. I said that to him.

Baxter stuck out his tongue the way Jack Nicholson did in the movie. 'Yeah, Frank, I'm fucking crazy,' and then he spoke softly. 'But I wanted to make sure you've come out of this okay. I wanted to tell you I didn't know anything, Frank, you hear me? I didn't bust your balls for fun. I want you to know that. It was when I was getting treatment at the sanitarium that I found out.'

Baxter used his finger and made like he was zipping his lips. He half-smiled in that usual way he did when he was drunk. 'You were lucky, Frank. Sam Green was brought back here to look at the Sleeper again, but you know what?'

'What?'

'Sam Green couldn't see past his own nose. That's right, Frank. He had glaucoma bad. I guess that is what drove him over the edge, not being able to really know what had gone on, to see into the face lying before him.'

I hadn't the courage to ever admit anything.

I guess there was too much to lose in creating a spectacle, to have those old people who knew expose our own history. All we would have been was but another of those tidbits of human curiosity that passes for news these days, a town overrun with roving cameras in search of a story, something to create a pastiche of past and present, a story to hold audience attention between commercials, before TV got to do what it was intended for, to sell us things.

There is a new history unfolding in our town these days. The college is a success. There is talk of a winter resort, a convention center or retreat for game-hunting. The dean has big plans for all of us, if we will just submit to his vision.

I was taking a Political History course the spring semester I graduated, and this Richard Nixon quote struck me. When asked about his historical legacy, about his memoirs, about the boxes of material he didn't give up to prosecutors, he said, candidly, 'When I retire, I'm going to spend my evenings by the fireplace going through those boxes. There are things in there that ought to be burned,' and I think it sums up those

359

sad years of our political and personal history, the need to vanquish history, to hide from our past. It says that maybe we should not give evidence to have ourselves judged against, that the historical moment, and the crimes of which we stand charged, cannot be fully comprehended. Or maybe this is just my way of forgiving my father and my uncle and the Kens of the world. Maybe it is why the old people remained silent throughout the investigation.

Both Honey and I are college graduates now. On graduation day, as was the tradition in those parts, we graduated out on the football field, and the class threw live white mice way up into the air. I thought that was the cruelest thing you could do on what they called the greatest day of your life. By day's end the dead mice looked like a small plague of bloody tampons with those long, thin tails, and that sent a chill through me. But our bloodlust survives our education, despite our attempts at civilization. We are not so far removed from our forebears, from the fur trappers who first wandered into this wilderness we call America.